# STEPHEN J. CANNELL

# FINAL VICTIM

AVON BOOKS  NEW YORK

FOR MY BEST FRIEND.
MY FATHER,
JOSEPH K. CANNELL.

AVON BOOKS
A division of
The Hearst Corporation
1350 Avenue of the Americas
New York, New York 10019

Copyright © 1996 by Stephen J. Cannell
Excerpt from *King Con* copyright © 1997 by Stephen J. Cannell
Published by arrangement with the author
Visit our website at http://AvonBooks.com
Library of Congress Catalog Card Number: 96-16243
ISBN: 0-380-72816-8

Published in hardcover by William Morrow and Company, Inc.; for information address Permissions Department, William Morrow and Company, Inc., 1350 Avenue of the Americas, New York, New York 10019.

First Avon Books Printing: June 1997

AVON TRADEMARK REG. U.S. PAT. OFF. AND IN OTHER COUNTRIES, MARCA REGISTRADA, HECHO EN U.S.A.

Printed in the U.S.A.

WCD   10  9  8  7  6  5  4  3  2  1

# 1

## THE RAT

**H**is mother, Shirley, had transformed him into The Rat. When he was bad or woke up with an erection, she would take him into the basement and light the Trinity candles she got from church. She would hold his hand in the flame until his flesh burned. Fire would cleanse him, she said . . . and, for a while, it did. When he was The Rat, he was pitiful and ugly, but he knew everything. The smallest details were vivid and sharp. His skin never irritated him when he was The Rat, except for the last few days before he transformed, when his nipples and skin burned, but he didn't have to wear silk. When he was The Rat he never got erections.

When he was The Wind Minstrel, he was always ready to be erect. The strange thing was, those erections were pure. He would swell with penile holiness. He was glorious, but he was always in pain. He could smell his flesh burning and everything was too bright. He had to wear specially made dark glasses and rub on Vaseline. Sometimes he got a bad rash. . . . He tried not to think of it, to soar above it, but the stinging sensation on his skin always intensified through Friday, and by Saturday it burned like acid.

The Wind Minstrel was a minister of sorts . . . a God of Cleansing who synchronized the period of proclamation with the message of Revelation. He was in his time of Investigative Judgment. First with the dead and second, much later, with the living. Investigative Judgment determined who, of the multitudes, should be sleeping in the dust and who were worthy of transformation. The Wind Minstrel could always tell. He could pick them.

The Wind Minstrel lived at night because he could hide from God in the dark. He was a paradox: a God and a Devil. He was Christ and Anti-Christ. He and only he could possess. He walked on a plane of ritual dedication, and when he killed, he was emotionally naked and alone. It was only then that his skin stopped burning. It was only then that he could take off the dark glasses. For a while, perhaps only an hour or two, he would feel as he guessed other men might feel, but then he would transform into The Rat again, or sometimes he'd become Leonard and would lose all sense of physical power.

Leonard was a genius and worked in a computer store, but he was also pitiful, awkward and afraid. Leonard almost never spoke to anyone. The Wind Minstrel was god of the planet, but The Rat ruled cyberspace.

The woman The Rat was coveting worked for Cavanaugh and Cunningham in Atlanta. The firm traded on the international currency markets and she monitored foreign currencies, so she came to work at 4:30 P.M. and worked all night. The office building was deserted, except for a withered security guard who rarely got up from behind his black marble desk in the lobby. The Rat had seen pictures of her naked on his computer screen. He downloaded the file, including her application for plastic surgery, which contained her name and both her home and business addresses. He had everything, including the pictures, taped to the metal walls in the rusting, empty garbage barge where he did the human storage and reconstruction. He studied the walls with his heart pounding. Shots of her, naked, standing in profile, facing right and left, staring dully off. It was her arms that drew him. . . . Her arms were perfect, with long muscles and tight skin. The elbows were perfect. Then, as always happened, the coveting began, and The Rat started to withdraw as The Wind Minstrel emerged. During this period, The Rat would go to ComputerLand and do Leonard's job. Like Leonard, he never spoke to anyone unless it was absolutely necessary. The coveting increased over the next twenty-four hours, until The Rat couldn't resist it.

She lived in Atlanta and he knew he had to go to her, just like the others. He drove his dark blue Ford pickup there from Tampa, departing on Wednesday night, just as the aura of The Wind Minstrel began to grow. The Rat was leaving, The Wind Minstrel coming. It was always hard to drive when he was not fully transformed, but he knew it was necessary.

He arrived in Atlanta at five A.M. Thursday, and booked a room in the Marriott on Lee Street. He slept all day. He got up at four in the afternoon and went to her apartment building and parked across the street. The Rat immediately knew it would be impossible for The Wind Minstrel to possess there, because it was a huge horseshoe structure built around a pool. It was far too public and open. The Rat knew that he was ugly and would be remembered. He could not ask The Wind Minstrel to possess in such a public place. Then, while he waited, she came out, got into her car, and he followed and coveted her. She worked in a steel-and-glass building in Atlanta's Financial District. The building was called Hoyt Tower, which was something of a misnomer as it was only ten stories tall. He parked across the street and watched with his binoculars as she entered. At six P.M., he went inside the huge marble-floored lobby just before it closed, carrying a box addressed to her employer, Cavanaugh and Cunningham. He walked past the security guard, past the employees hurrying out of the building. He took the elevator up to the fourth floor and waited, holding the box, as people left for the evening.

He knew he was unusual. He was almost seven feet tall, overweight, and had absolutely no hair on his body. No whiskers, no eyebrows . . . no pubic hair. There was none on his chest or under his arms. He was smooth all over, white and shiny. His body was pear-shaped, with corpulent limbs and no muscle definition. Ever since he was ten and had gotten the sickness that made all his hair fall out, his body had disgusted him.

He sat in the lobby to disguise his height. The people leaving for the night didn't pay any attention to him. He wore a baseball cap and dark glasses, and held the box in front of him on his knees.

She passed him once, never looking, on her way to the bathroom. He could smell her perfume and shuddered with pleasure.

"The Wind Minstrel is coming, and he is God," he whispered.

Ten minutes later, she returned to her desk as the rest of the employees left for the day. Cavanaugh and Cunningham had modern offices, done in off-white. Elevator music poured out of recessed speakers—sweet atmospheric molasses. He could see her through a thick glass wall that separated the lobby from her work space. She was seated in front of a computer, looking at the infinitesimal but constant price changes of foreign currencies. She was lean and strong, with shoulder-length brown hair. He knew she was twenty-six from the Surgi-CyberNet medical records. His heart was slamming in his chest, a big, uncontrollable conga. His nipples burned like fire. Then suddenly, as if an invisible finger had tapped her on the shoulder, she glanced up through the glass wall and saw him sitting there. Her brown eyes shot him a look of disgust. A chill of sexual longing coursed through his body. His fingers convulsed, and he almost dropped the package. She got up, then moved along the glass partition toward the lobby. She had taken off her sweater, and he could see she was dressed in a sleeveless print dress. She opened the glass door and looked out at him.

"Can I help you?"

"I'm . . . I have a package for Shirley Land," he said, his voice pinched and high. It was always that way when he was coveting. He shot a sideways glance at her arms. The skin was tight around her muscles, the fibers long and firm, the elbows perfect. Only the hands were wrong. The Rat knew he couldn't use the hands.

"There's no Shirley Land in this office," she said.

"I was told to leave this for her."

"Nobody named Shirley Land works here," she said, and this time a sharpness crept into her voice.

He was staring openly at her now, especially at her arms. But The Rat was only allowed to covet. Only when he was completely transformed could he possess.

"You'll have to leave," she said, taking a hesitant step backward.

"You should cover your arms."

"I beg your pardon?"

"The true believer should recognize the body as a temple of the Holy Spirit and, therefore, should clothe the body in modest and dignified apparel." He said it sing-songy, the way he had been taught . . . the way Shirley made him say it.

"Get out of here or I'm calling Security." She moved quickly into the office, closed the heavy glass door, and bolted it. They were looking at each other now through the thick glass wall, as he got up and moved slowly into the elevator. When he stood, she could see that he was huge.

He got in and pushed the Down button. The elevator descended; after a moment, he pulled the maintenance panel open and pushed Stop, holding the car between floors. He reached for the emergency panel and removed the red telephone.

He opened the cardboard box he had brought with him and pulled out his laptop computer, connecting its modem to the elevator phone. He knew the phone was linked directly to the building security system. The elevator was stuffy from the heat of his own body. His sensitive skin stung; his nipples burned. The sweat made it worse, turning him red with an ugly rash. His cracking program began attacking the building's central computer, looking for a "hole" in the security system, firing multiple passwords he had pre-programmed into the "CrackerJack" software on his laptop. He was sure the building computer would not present much of a problem. There was nothing on that computer except programs designed to run and keep logs on the ten-story structure, so it would not be a serious security problem. Besides, The Rat was the best. Nobody could crack a computer as well as he could. At quarter past nine, his software broke through and downloaded the computer's supervisor password; then The Rat gathered all the information he would need.

By eleven o'clock, he was back in his room at the Marriott.

It took him an hour to get everything ready. He washed himself first, using a soft sponge on his sore skin. He rubbed Vaseline on until it was deep in his pores. Then, wearing a silk kimono that stuck slightly to his back, he sat on the edge of the faded bedspread. The only light was from one standing lamp, which he had draped with a bathroom towel to cut the painful glare. He put on his headset and turned on his CD player. The shrill, harsh lyrics of the Death Metal band Baby Killer wailed in his ear like the hounds of hell:

> I must breed—I have deadly needs.
> Within the corpse I plant my seed.
> Bitch, you are worthless, I feast on your snot,
> Suck your goo, smell your rot.

He began to unpack his saw. In the center of the bed, he placed the Ten Thousand Series fixed-arbor autopsy blades. First, the round 10004 blade with the crosscut teeth. Next to it, the smaller sectioned blade. They gleamed in the low light. He unpacked the stainless-steel surgical knife handles. There were seven of them. Last was the box of carbon-steel surgical blades in their individually sealed foil packets. The glistening scalpels reflected the light and shot pain into his head, but The Rat endured it because he knew it was a sign that he was almost transformed. Soon he would be The Wind Minstrel, and The Wind Minstrel was God. The last instrument he removed was the Stryker high-speed-oscillation autopsy saw. Once a blade was selected and attached, it oscillated, cutting not by rotation but by rapid forward and backward strokes. He worked diligently until all the instruments were arranged on his bed in a pattern he liked. He studied them, and his huge body shook with agony and expectation. He pulled the kimono up with his left hand, and with his right he grabbed his evil appendage. He attempted to masturbate but was unable to obtain an erection. He was not yet transformed. Tomorrow he could swell and spew his holy seed. Tomorrow his coming would be as powerful as the resurrection of the dead. It would celebrate the destruction of the self-righteous. It would establish The Wind Minstrel's everlasting glory.

# 2

## LOCKWOOD

"**Y**ou don't like being here, do you, John?" Dr. Donald Smythe said, digging with his little finger for another yellow nugget of earwax.

"I like it fine," Lockwood lied. His sinuses were killing him. He was allergic to something that was blooming in the Washington, D.C., swamp. The room was too cold; the doctor was fat. John Lockwood was being forced to submit to a second psychiatric reevaluation in a year, as part of the U.S. Customs Service's most recent Internal Affairs investigation of him, and he couldn't help himself—he resented it. Lockwood was an Assistant U.S. Customs Special Agent in Charge for the Southern District. He was also something of a legend in the Service. He made spectacular arrests which always got Federal indictments, but he had been investigated five times in the last eighteen months for various forms of improper conduct. He had yet to be found guilty of anything, but the intensity of the assault from IA was growing. Each failed attempt to discipline him had made the investigators more vindictive. They had insisted he go "stress related" until this psychological exam was complete. He suspected he might have another beef coming, because two days before, in a frustrated moment, he had slugged an Internal Affairs SAC named Victor "Brute" Kulack

8

in South Beach, Miami. It had been a stupid thing to do and Lockwood regretted it immediately, but the argument and a seething anger had escalated so fast he couldn't control it. He was becoming more and more puzzled by his own behavior. It was undermining him with his superiors. But more important, it was altering his opinion of himself. He was no longer certain of what he stood for.

"You say you don't resent these sessions, but your body language says otherwise," Dr. Smythe said, retrieving another yellow ball and rolling it between his thumb and forefinger, before ditching it surreptitiously on the carpet beneath his chair.

"If my body is talking to you, Doctor, maybe we need to change places." Lockwood smiled.

"Evasive response," Smythe said into his tape recorder. They sat in silence and regarded each other like enemy generals staring across the desolate battleground of Lockwood's career in law enforcement.

"Are you angry because you're a child of three institutions?" Smythe pushed on.

"Depends on which institutions you're talking about."

"I was referring to the Materwood Home for Boys and then the St. Charles Academy and, to a lesser degree, the Marine Corps."

"Oh . . ." Lockwood said noncommittally.

"There were others?"

"I was briefly in the institution of marriage, but I got kicked out," he said, remembering Claire with a sharp pang of anxious desperation. Claire had been his life's most damaging failure. She had been the only one to bring him softness, and he had wasted that valuable warmth, squandered it, wounding both of them with his selfishness.

"We'll get to that," Smythe said. "Could it be because you were raised by institutions, you have a latent hostility toward them, and that's what is causing this self-destructive behavior?"

Lockwood leaned back on the couch and laced his fingers behind his head.

"Well, lemme give that some thought. . . ." He closed his eyes and let some time pass. He'd learned that during an IA head test, you had to say as little as possible. Information was power. This wasn't about Lockwood's mental health; it was about getting him suspended. The less they had, the less they could use. At the same time, he had to capture Smythe and try to get him to sign the FFD slip, stipulating he was fit for duty. He listened to the desk clock ticking and kept his eyes closed. It was a humid April, Washington, D.C., day, but the building was freezing cold. An unrelenting air conditioner hissed at them. In truth, he had hated the Materwood Home for Boys. The fathers had been strict and the food stringy. He'd been small for his age and had been picked on, but he had learned to fight at Materwood—something that came in very handy at St. Charles a few years later.

"What do you remember?" Dr. Smythe prodded. "This won't work if you don't participate."

"Oh . . . Sorry, I was just going back to Materwood in my head . . . remembering the place. I guess they did all they could for us. They were underfunded. We had okay sports, but the equipment was all hand-me-down stuff from the public school system. The bats and everything were cracked, and we hadda wrap 'em tight with tape to use 'em. . . ." He was talking with his eyes closed, chewing up the hour.

"What am I supposed to do with all this bullshit, John?" Dr. Smythe finally said. "Am I supposed to just sign off on you and pass you along till you turn into someone else's field disaster? 'Cause if that's what you're planning, I can outlast you. Shit, man, I can have you lounge on that couch until your beard is gray."

John knew, eventually, he had to give this guy something. The problem was, there was some truth in what Dr. Smythe had said. Lockwood *had* been raised by institutions. The Materwood orphanage was bad, but St. Charles Academy had been a dungeon . . . a piss-hole full of social mutants. Boys with men's bodies who'd been deformed by relatives, demeaned by experience, and destroyed by their environment. He remembered the day he'd walked through the gates at St. Charles. He'd been too small and looked too easy. Fifteen years old . . . trying to saunter, trying to look tough, bouncing on his toes, rolling his shoulders. He was terrified and trying not to look it.

"Hey, tight-ass. You gonna be my weenie woman," an eighteen-year-old black inmate named Dwight Jackson yelled through the yard fence at him. Everybody at St. Charles, including the guards, called Dwight "Crazy-D." He was six-two and weighed over two hundred pounds. He had already been reprocessed by the adult criminal court and was awaiting transfer to the state pen at Joliet. He looked to John like he'd been chiseled out of purple onyx. John tried to glare fiercely at him, but Crazy-D wasn't buying.

"You my chick with a dick," Crazy-D yelled. "You're mine, sweetmeat."

The students at St. Charles slept in dormitories, and somehow it had been arranged for John to have the bunk right above Dwight Jackson. John knew that as soon as the lights were out, he would be pulled down and his head buried under a pillow. . . . His arms would be held and he would be raped by the huge inmate. This was something he was determined to prevent, even if he had to get wrecked in the process. At nine o'clock, just before the trusty pulled the power switch on Building 12, Crazy-D patted the top bunk. "Dis be de trick bunk. Jump your curvy ass up der. We gonna get to it soon as de Jelly Roll call lights-out," he said, grinning, exposing four gold teeth.

John had left his shoes on and, saying nothing, jumped up onto the top bed and pulled the covers up to his chin. Then, while Crazy-D moved around the room, laughing and high-fiving the brothers, John quietly pulled the heavy, leather-soled brogans off his feet. When the lights were turned out, he waited.

"Get your ass down here," Crazy-D whispered from the bunk below. "I got a instrument needs playing." And then he kicked the mattress above him, where John was lying.

Without saying a word, John Lockwood dropped down and, with his leather shoe in his right hand, he started to pound the larger boy in the face. He broke Dwight's nose with the first blow. The second filled his eyes with blood. Before the startled eighteen-year-old could even sit up, it was almost over. Then, with both hands laced together, John swung with all his might at Dwight's jawline. Gold teeth flew out of Crazy-D's mouth, hitting the floor and bouncing like ejected brass. In seconds, Dwight was screaming in pain. When the lights went on and guards ran in, John Lockwood was standing triumphantly over his huge opponent.

"No motherfucker in this place ever lays a hand on me!" John yelled, spewing out rage and unused adrenaline. The guards dragged him out of the dormitory. He did three weeks in isolation and three years in St. Charles, but nobody ever tried to molest him again.

One week after being released from St. Charles, John was busted in a G-ride. Rather than go to the Big House for Grand Theft Auto, he chose the Marine Corps. The Marines were his third parental substitute. He ended up, strangely enough, as an MP. He found it more than a little weird to be wearing a badge instead of looking at one, but five years later, when he mustered out, he had achieved his GED and the rank of Tech Sergeant. Some buddies had signed applications for U.S. Customs, and he had more or less gone along with them because he didn't have anything better to do. That had been ten years ago.

"You have to look at the reason all of this is happening to you, John," Smythe said, slogging on. "You pretty much do things the way you want. I think you should take a look at why that is . . . why you seem to relish breaking the rules."

Lockwood nodded. "Okay." His sinuses were beginning to ache, so he pulled out a small nasal inhaler he'd bought at the drugstore, clamped it over his nose, and inhaled the vapor, immediately clearing his sinuses. "Allergic to something," he explained.

The little alarm clock on Smythe's desk rang. The session was over.

"How about two o'clock Tuesday?" the doctor said, looking over his half-glasses at the calendar.

"Sounds good," Lockwood chirped.

He left by the side door and found himself standing in the chilly marble-floored corridor. He was cold, and it wasn't just the frigid office building. John Lockwood could hear his own blood pumping and feel his heart sinking, and he wasn't sure why.

His beeper went off. It was the DOAO's office. He found a pay phone in the lobby and called in.

Laurence Heath was one of the old breed of Customs officers, a no-nonsense commander who wanted the good guys to win. He'd worked his way up from a field office in Hays, Kansas, to become Special Agent in Charge for Arizona. Any supervisor running operations in a border state like Arizona, where the smuggling action was constant, was generally considered to be a hot shoe. The border was no place for fuck-ups. After ten years in Arizona, Heath had recently been promoted to Director of All Operations, which made him the second highest officer in the Service. He had also been John Lockwood's boss in D.C. on Operation Girlfriend.

That operation was one of the biggest drug busts in Southern Florida's history. Lockwood had been the Special Agent in Charge and had quarterbacked the case from the time an ex-baggage handler named Ray Gonzales had wandered into the Southern District office. Ray told him that he'd quit his job at Global Airlines because a lot of the baggage handlers at Miami International Airport had been opening targeted luggage from Central American flights and removing drugs or cash before they got to the Customs shed. Lockwood had convinced Gonzales to become the key informant on the bust. Drug dealers had their own universal code words when talking on open phone lines, and since airplanes were often called "girlfriends," Lockwood named his sting "Operation Girlfriend," and had proceeded to work it for almost eighteen months.

When the bust went down, Customs agents rounded up almost a hundred airport baggage handlers and skycaps, as well as two dirty Customs agents. At the last minute, Lockwood's long-awaited airport sting was kangarooed by an Internal Affairs SAC named Victor Kulack. Kulack had moved too soon and tried to arrest the two Customs agents. One of them got away and made a phone call. The bust climaxed in a deadly shoot-out. Ray Gonzales, who had become Lockwood's good friend, ended up in critical condition at Jackson Memorial Hospital in Dade County, Florida. Lockwood filed a complaint against Kulack for jumping the bust, and before they left Florida, he ran into him in a bar. When Kulack called Ray Gonzales "just another Cuban grease stain," Lockwood lost it and swung at him, knocking him out with one punch.

Now Kulack was upstairs, seething, on the Internal Affairs floor of the Washington, D.C., Customs building. Lockwood had been wondering what Kulack would do and figured the call from the Director of All Operations was the other shoe dropping.

He got off the elevator on the third floor and moved along the green-carpeted corridor. The offices were all spacious and decorated with oak furniture; very nice for civil servants. All of the men and women on this floor were in the Senior Executive Service (SES), Assistant Commissioners or above, and made their living passing paper and begging the appropriate Congressional committees to improve funding. The furniture had been purloined from a Senate office building after its renovation two years ago. As far as Lockwood could see, oak furniture and a full dental package were the best perks in SES.

Lockwood could hear Heath before he saw him.

"Where the fuck is he? I said forthwith!"

Heath's assistant, Bob Tilly, was seated at an oversized secretarial desk outside of Heath's office. He shot Lockwood a smile weak as Oriental tea and waved him in.

Laurence Heath looked like the commander of a tank division. He had a bull neck, with rolls of fat and muscle coming off the back of his shaved skull. He was popular in the Customs Service, because he was willing to downfield-block for his men. Through the large window behind him, Lockwood could see across Pennsylvania Avenue to the White House. A cloud-drenched April sun was struggling to get through. The sky looked like oatmeal.

"Are you ever gonna stop wearing your balls outside your trousers?" Heath said, without preamble. His bright-blue eyes and huge shoulders glowered.

"Larry, I don't know what Victor Kulack told you, but you can bet there's another side to it."

"He's upstairs, about to paper you for failure to correctly supervise an informant."

"That's bullshit."

"Shut up, John." Silence hung like a velvet curtain. "He says there's five thousand dollars missing from Operation Girlfriend's petty cash account." Heath held up a Customs Internal Affairs folder and waved it at Lockwood like a booking sheet. "He says you and your informant, Ray Gonzales, were dipping into that account to buy drugs, and that you put those drugs on the street to build your pedigree with the river scum down there."

"That's a lie. The money went to buy information. We were trying—"

"I said shut up. I'm not through. Stop talking for a change."

"Okay . . ."

"Then I get it in the halls that you knocked this asshole through a wall in a bar fight in South Beach before you came back up here."

"Kulack tried to steal the bust, sir. He jumped the gun. Got two guys shot."

"So you hit him?"

"Accounts vary. There was undoubtedly some kind of struggle—"

"You fuckin' amaze me."

"He tried to hijack the bust to get those two dirty counter agents. There were over a hundred baggage handlers and skycaps involved in that smuggle. Those two Customs guys were less than five percent of the bust. Internal Affairs is supposed to investigate bad police work, not cowboy investigations to get headlines. We ended up in a dick-dragging shoot-out because Kulack jumped early and the cat got loose."

"So you hit him?" Heath asked again.

Lockwood didn't answer. He could tell by the red that was working its way up from under Heath's collar onto his neck that he was probably going to come out better by holding his silence. Larry Heath leaned forward, snapping out his words. "Vic Kulack is shit on Melba toast, but he is also an Internal Affairs SAC. Internal Affairs, in case you haven't read your organization manual lately, is a couple of limbs higher on the tree than Operations. Technically, that makes Kulack your boss. Kulack says you fucked up the bust. He says five thousand dollars is missing. The hint implicit here—in case you missed it— is you and Gonzales were dealing drugs with Federal money and keeping the proceeds. I know it's bullshit, but if he files that paper and it gets into court, Operation Girlfriend develops a dose of the clap."

"Sir, if you're suggesting that I turn this over to Kulack because he filed this bullshit charge against me—"

"He hasn't technically filed it yet. He said he'd consider sitting on it to protect the integrity of the case."

"Isn't that against the law? If he's got something on me, let's do the dance."

"Shut up. . . ."

Lockwood stood in front of the desk and watched the red line finish its climb up the side of Heath's neck and begin to turn his shaved head a nice watermelon-pink.

"My job here is to manage the flow of arrests and convictions. Internal Affairs is not my favorite division, but the Customs Service has to guard against illegal action in the ranks, just like every other law enforcement agency."

"Sir . . . may I speak, sir?"

Heath didn't answer but lifted his chin slightly, indicating this better be great.

"This case was in my jacket for almost eighteen months," Lockwood began. "I developed Gonzales as an informant. I talked him into going back to Miami Airport and getting his old job back. Gonzales is a stand-up player. He risked his life for us. He solicited every one of those dirty baggage handlers without regard for his own personal safety. And then, at the last minute, Kulack moves in and jumps all over the take-down. Fucks it up. Gonzales gets a bullet in his kidney and damn near dies. He's still hung up in a Dade County hospital."

"I got all of this from the newspaper."

"Don't turn Operation Girlfriend over to Kulack."

"Why not?"

"The guy's a moron. He can't put spaghetti on a plate without a diagram. The A.A.G. is green and the case still needs a lot of evidentiary investigation. Kulack's gonna fuck it up."

"If he files this mismanagement charge against you and implies you were dealing drugs, it's gonna be in the court record and you're gonna be an anchor at the trial."

"That's blackmail."

"That's government service. He's also demanding a hearing for hitting him in Florida. It's scheduled at nine on Monday morning. The IA conference room on five. Be there. Personally, I think he's got a shot at getting you cashiered. I think I can get him to scotch the mismanagement complaint if we give him Girlfriend, but you're turning into your own worst enemy. What the hell's happened to you, John?"

Lockwood said nothing. He had no answer.

"I'll have Bob Tilly supervise Kulack and the greenie in the A.G.'s office. Tilly's got plenty of field and court experience. You can fill the prosecutor in but, as of now, you're outta Operation Girlfriend."

Lockwood stood there and felt the blood going up into his own head. But he had a thick shock of black hair and a swarthy complexion, so, unlike Heath, whose blush made him look angry, on Lockwood, it just made him look darker. Finally, he nodded and turned to leave.

"Lockwood."

He was almost out the door, but he turned and looked back at Heath. "Yes?"

"Agents like you are good for the Service, because they remind everybody else there's a creative way to do the job, a way that may not be printed in the manual. But agents like you are also an administrative nightmare, because you strain my ability to cover your ass. Whether you know it or not, son, I'm doing you a huge favor here."

"Right."

"In the meantime, I understand that Dr. Karen Dawson could use some help updating the sex offenders computer program. Since you're on desk leave, you're assigned to work with her. She's in B-16. You start down there tomorrow."

Lockwood didn't respond. He nodded his understanding and left. This run of bad luck seemed unending. He had just lost a case he had spent a year and a half working on, to a man he despised. And, if that wasn't enough, he'd been assigned to go down to the basement tomorrow morning and work on some dry-biscuit computer program with "Awesome Dawson."

# 3

## THE WIND MINSTREL

He slept all day Friday and woke up without an alarm at six, Friday evening. His skin was on fire. Glowing. He had transformed. He was The Wind Minstrel, glorious and alive. He dressed in silk pajamas, gathered his autopsy saw and scalpels. The last tool The Wind Minstrel packed in his large suitcase was The Rat's computer. He had left The Rat behind, but he was following the cunning rodent's careful plan. Every inch of his body was sore now, even the bottoms of his feet. It was as if his skin couldn't contain his glory and had been stretched, painfully, to accommodate him. He left the Marriott and approached his pickup. Earlier, he had stolen a Georgia license plate and now he attached it to the plate holder. He put on his CD headphones and played Baby Killer's new album, *Chant to the Dead*. He drove back across town toward Hoyt Tower while the music filled his head with its destructive beauty. He parked across from the building on Lee Street. Using his cellphone, attached to his laptop, he placed a call to the building security computer. On his screen, the computer answered his call:

HOYT LOGIN:

He typed "root" and pressed Enter. The system responded:

```
PASSWORD:
```

He typed in a password for root, which was GOD. The Rat had downloaded all of this from the building computer using the elevator phone the day before. Immediately he was logged in to the computer:

```
WELCOME TO HOYT TOWER.
YOU ARE LOGGED IN TO HOST HOYT AS ROOT.
GOOD EVENING, ROOT.
```

"Root" was the name a lot of computers used to identify the computer system's main user. GOD was often used as the root password because root was the "God" of the system. If you logged in and were accepted as root you could do anything you wanted. You could reprogram, delete, or change the entire system. Since the main function of the building's computer was to run the building, root controlled the brains of the building.

He accessed the building's security panel, and up on his laptop came a computer graphic of the ten-story structure. He scrolled his way down to the first-floor fire door on Center Street. Working carefully, he shut off the alarm on that door by deleting it from the program. He watched the building's "police telephone module," listed on the bottom of the screen, to see if the system sensed his tampering and if the automatic dialer would place a call to the Atlanta police. It didn't.

It was a sign. He knew that now he was completely transformed. Now he could possess.

She never saw him come through the glass door into the office. By the time she sensed his presence and began to turn, it was already too late. He grabbed her head from behind and brought a surgical knife down over her shoulder and plunged it deep into her chest. He felt the warm

blood flow over his latex-gloved hand. He held his forearm tight against her Adam's apple. He had studied anat-
omy and could feel the cricoid cartilage break, collapsing
the vocal ligament into her rima glottidis, rendering her
mute.

He held her in a strangulation embrace, with the knife
buried deep in her chest, until he felt a death shiver.
Moments later she went limp. He laid her on the floor
and moved quickly out into the hall, where he had left
his large suitcase. He felt her dead eyes watching him.
He returned with the suitcase, grabbed her sweater from
the back of her chair, and put it across her staring dead
eyes . . . eyes that mocked his ugliness.

He undressed her . . . removing her dress, her slip, bra,
and panties. His nostrils flared as he smelled her blood.
He put on his headset and punched a button on his CD
player. As the music started, he pulled down his silk pa-
jama pants and grabbed his semi-erection. Slowly, he
worked himself to climax as he swayed over her. The
music screamed in his ears:

> I slaughtered the whore,
> Skinned her alive.
> I did it for the thrill.
> It was so nice to kill.

His erection was soft, but he ejaculated onto her body.
. . . Anger flared. The bitch had scorned him with her
stare, spoiling his erection. He grabbed the scissors off
her desk and jammed them up her vagina. "Fuck, fuck,
fuck," he grunted as he plunged them in repeatedly. Then
he left them there. The song finished, and he removed
the headset. He always possessed without music so he
could hear the sounds of his work, the cutting, the rend-
ing of tissue. He picked up the saw and attached the
round 10004 blade with the crosscut teeth. It was the best
for medium and small bones.

He plugged the saw into a wall socket and tested it.
The blade oscillated and vibrated in his hand. Then he

switched it off and laid it next to the body.

"If, as you told me, fire cleanses," he said to the dead girl whose body he had just defiled, "then why does fire leave such a dirty ash?"

Using the scalpel, he started to sever the right arm, working with surgical precision. He made the incision below the shoulder, finding the brachial artery under the anterior humeral circumflex. He cut through it first. His gloved fingers pinched it off with surgical clamps; then he clamped the auxiliary artery and vein.

"If it's true that Satan is only the author of sin, then why, dear Shirley, in the fires of the last day, was he not reduced to a state of nonexistence?"

The woman, whose desk plate read CANDICE WILCOX, lay silent before him. The Wind Minstrel was lost in ritual fantasy. "You told me he would perish, but he hasn't. Would you explain that, please?" he demanded.

He turned on the saw and cut the humerus bone just below the pectoralis minor muscles on the shoulder. He worked for twenty minutes. When he was through, he carefully loaded what he had removed into garbage bags—turned the twisties and packed everything into the large suitcase he had brought with him. He arranged the body, putting some books beneath her torso so that the head was lower. This, he knew, would allow the blood to drain from the body and eliminate lividity—discoloration from the collection of blood in the lower extremities. It turned the skin a deep purple and took almost nine hours to occur. He knew the police used lividity to fix time of death.

The Wind Minstrel needed to claim the whore as his divine work. He pulled out his branding iron with the special head. He had made it from a woman's electric curling iron. He plugged it in, waited for a minute till it got hot, and pressed it to Candice Wilcox's left breast. When he could smell flesh burning, he removed it and looked at the brand:

The Wind Minstrel put his branding iron away, pulled out The Rat's notebook PC, disconnected the incoming phone line from the fax machine on Candice Wilcox's desk, and hooked it into The Rat's PC.

Once again, he typed in the system username, root, and the password, GOD. After a few seconds, the system log-on welcome message came on the screen. Then he typed in:

ENVIROLOG

The environmental log was in the building's computer under the EnviroLog program. In a few seconds, up on his screen came the building's forty zone listings. He was on the west side of the building in Zone 4-W. He had already prepared a program on his own computer and stored it for this moment. He had named the program WindLog. He uploaded the program into the building computer. WindLog would override the climate control for Zone 4-W. This new program would first drive the heat in that sector as high as it would go, approximately 110 degrees. The Wind Minstrel knew that this would keep the dead body's temperature high while he was on his way back to Tampa. Since the police also used cooling body temperature to fix time of death, the heat would throw them off. But he also knew that if he left the heat on, the police would be alert to his deception, so he had instructed WindLog to shut off the heat in 4-W at 6:30 A.M. and turn the air-conditioning on full, driving the room temperature back down to approximately 70 degrees by 7:30. Then his program would reset the environmental control to the normal temperature of 72. But The Rat was clever, and he knew that there would be a record of this wild temperature fluctuation, so he had written another program, which he had named BogusLog. It would quietly replace a section of the building's environmental log and show a normal temperature record for 4-W. As its last act, WindLog would erase itself and leave BogusLog to reflect the incorrect time and temperature information, leaving no trace of The Wind Minstrel's magic.

He waited until he felt the heat come on, then unplugged the small computer and packed it in with his other treasures. He left the office by the fire stairs, never bothering to look back at the mutilated body of Candice Wilcox.

He went down the stairs and exited through the first-floor door on Center Street, never coming close to the security guard. He was careful to leave that door slightly ajar. He walked to his truck and put the large suitcase into the front seat. He would have to drive quickly to get back to Tampa by dawn. He stopped only once in Thomasville, near the Florida border, to get gas.

It was 7:28 A.M. when he got to the computer store where he worked in Tampa. Sitting in the parking lot, he made the last call to the building's computer. Again, he used the root password, GOD. Once in, he accessed the security module of the computer. He added the Center Street door back into the system and erased his original deletion. He watched as the perimeter-breach alarm flashed on the computer graphic, indicating a break-in through the Center Street fire door. He then watched as the automatic dialer notified building security and the Atlanta PD.

The Rat knew that when the body was found by the Atlanta police, the liver temperature would still be close to its normal 102 degrees. He knew that all homicide units measure liver temperature for time-of-death estimates, because it is the hottest organ in the body. The police would find no lividity and no loss of liver temperature, even though almost nine hours had passed since the murder. The Rat knew they would place the TOD at approximately 7:30 A.M., when the alarm triggered. He had a perfect alibi: He was at work more than four hundred miles away. The Rat was cunning and shrewd. His skin didn't hurt him now. His nipples didn't ache or sting, but he was again wretched and foul. He hurried into Tampa ComputerLand, where Leonard was a part-time PC repair tech. He punched in. His time card said 7:36. All he had left to do was call and tell Satan that he had possessed the arms.

# 4

## AWESOME DAWSON

**S**he was standing naked in the cold shower, while icy water hit her face and ran like cold tentacles down her ribs, between her legs, to the tile floor. She had just come back from her morning five-mile run. Her skin vibrated with the needle-cold spray. She was beginning to suspect that her new job was another in a long line of disappointing mistakes. It always started with the decision to take up the challenge, then came the false euphoria and the fantasy expectations. But reality and boredom always followed. Despite all of her accomplishments, boredom always hovered, beating wings of emptiness and scaring her with its dark promise. Boredom was her dangerous stalker. She knew, of course, it explained a lot of things about her: the need to push herself, the life-threatening sports . . . The risks seemed to bring her alive. She had a doctorate in psychology and knew that her symptoms signaled a deep inner problem, yet she couldn't fathom why she could find nothing to hold her interest.

She reached out and took her razor, turned the water warmer, then slid down, feeling the cold tile against her back. She sat on the floor of the shower, with the spray hitting her shoulders, and stared at the razor. It had been her father's, an antique with a twist shaft that released the blade. She had inherited it from him, along with his huge, unwieldy intellect.

She opened the razor and let the water wash the blade. It danced in its open carriage as the spray hit it. She looked at the blue steel and thought how easy it would be to just let go . . . to put the boredom to rest. She closed the razor and began shaving her legs, and then, as seemed to happen more and more frequently in the morning, she started to cry. Tears racked her as she sat on the tile floor.

"Fuck!" she said out loud as she nicked herself. The blood ran down her calf and onto the tile, then circled the drain, disappearing like all her expectations. She watched it in fascination, the sobs still caught in her throat.

Ten minutes later, she was dressed in jeans, a silk blouse, and a sweater. The colors didn't match and she didn't care. She looked at herself in the hallway mirror. Auburn hair and a clean athletic frame. Men seemed to find her pretty. It baffled her. All she saw was emptiness. It was on her face like clown makeup. It was in her life like poison. And now, after hoping to add excitement with her new job in law enforcement, she had been assigned to update computer data in the basement, with an agent who was being punished because he was a notorious fuck-up. She'd accessed John Lockwood's service record by using her newly acquired interagency computer clearance. He had been under constant Internal Affairs scrutiny for misconduct, mostly rule bending and insubordination. His ID picture showed a narrow-faced, dark-complexioned man with black hair and a Roman nose. She supposed he could be called attractive, and she was sure he thought he was. To her, he only looked like trouble. There was, however, one thing in his file that intrigued her. He had been involved in apprehending the infamous Carlos "Malavida" Chacone.

She grabbed her purse and left the apartment, hurrying on shapely legs to the elevator and into the underground garage, where she got into her Honda and drove the ten

...stoms building on Constitution Av-

...heard her way before he found Room B-
1...

"...ucking piece of cyberjunk!" Her voice carried down the narrow basement hallway.

He followed its acerbic timbre until he found the open door and Karen Dawson.

"Damn. That's not the password either?" She slammed the computer console with her fist.

"Nice jab, but I've found that model PC is a sucker for lefthanded uppercuts."

She spun around and hit him with two hundred watts of amber-eyed fury.

"Hang on a minute. . . ." She turned back to the computer and punched in something. The screen said:

```
LOGIN INCORRECT
CONNECTION CLOSED BY FOREIGN HOST.
```

"Shit," she murmured under her breath, but didn't hit the terminal this time.

"So you're Karen Dawson, Ph.D., RNDNSC, CCSB . . . more letters than the Chinese alphabet."

"Chinese doesn't have letters, it has characters," she said without emphasis or a second look back at him.

She studied a manual on the table next to her, logged out, shut off the computer, turned it back on, then logged back in, and typed:

```
TELNET RING2ICE.ANON.PENNET.NO
```

They both watched as the system said:

```
TRYING 172.24.168.10 . . .
```

"Trying Norway?" he said.
"How did you know that? It's not on the screen."

"The last two letters in the Internet address, the '.no.'
That's Norway."

She hesitated and looked at him again as if seeing him
for the first time.

"Don't let it throw you. I've just worked a couple of
international computer scams. I'm John Lockwood."

"I figured. I'm Karen Dawson. Welcome to Fort Nowhere."

Lockwood had never met Awesome Dawson, but he
knew about her. She was a civilian employee who had
been at Customs only three months. Already, however,
she had created a fair-sized legend. Lockwood knew from
the gossip mill that she had an IQ that was so high it
went off the chart. It had been guessed at over 180. On
top of that, at the tender age of twenty-five, she had a
double doctorate in abnormal psychology and criminal
profiling. She was rumored to be two races away from
getting her NASCAR license and had a black belt in
some kind of Oriental kick fighting . . . all in all, a diz-
zying résumé. He'd been expecting a bull-necked, short-
haired woman with pug-nosed determination. The thing
that instantly struck him as strange was that nobody had
mentioned she was a knockout. He immediately calculated it must be a tribute to her immense skills, that
beauty was so far down her list of assets it didn't even
rate a mention.

"You're in my light," she said, pointing to a Tensor
lamp that he was standing in front of.

"You need light to swear at this stuff?"

"Hey . . . please. Okay? I know we've been assigned
to work together, but spare me the breezy bullshit."

The computer got a "timed-out" signal and she turned
to try it again.

He leaned over, picked up her crib sheet, and glanced
at it for a moment. Written on the top was "Pennet."
"What's Pennet?" he asked.

"It's a remailer computer program in Oslo, Norway.
You know what a remailer is?"

"Yeah. It's a computer that masks the identity of the

senders. You can send a message to somebody through a remailer and it will encode your name and then send it on, hiding your identity from the receiver.''

"Not exactly." Her tone seemed to say she was already tired of him.

"I thought you were supposed to be updating data for a new program for sex offenders on the VICAP computer. . . .''

"I'm caught up to everything Operations gave me. They're sending down some new packets. So until they come, VICAP can wait.''

VICAP—the Violent Criminals Apprehension Program—was a computer system originally designed by an L.A. cop named John St. John. St. John had reasoned that since serial criminals often had fractured personalities, they might also be nomads and wander. With that in mind, he had convinced police departments all over the country to put any unsolved, brutal, ritualistic sex killings into a computer data bank. The idea was that if these killers were wandering around, committing murders all across the country, then maybe the similarities in their assaults would go undetected. The computer would match them up and see a serial crime where local police might not. Because of VICAP, serial murderers like Ted Bundy and John Wayne Gacy had been discovered.

"What're ya doing, messing around with a remailer computer in Oslo?" Lockwood finally asked.

She looked at him with her jaw set and no apparent intention of answering.

"That's an official question posed by your new shit-for-brains Fort Nowhere teammate.''

She seemed to be evaluating him; then her body language changed slightly.

"Okay, look . . . I'm sorry. I'm mad, but not at you. I'm mad at the situation. They've got me updating old cases. I'm a doctor of abnormal psychology and criminal profiling. I didn't agree to a job here so I could update old computer data. I thought this remailer might be more challenging, so I'm free-lancing it. Don't burn me, okay?''

"How you doing?'' Lockwood asked, not really caring but looking for friendly ground.

"I can't get through password security. I'm trying to crack in, but they've got some kind of three-try limit on passwords. At this rate, it's gonna take me fifty years.''

Lockwood didn't know much about computers, but that wasn't something he shared with many people. In the new age of law enforcement, computers were a growing tool. Computer illiteracy all but disqualified you from the hunt. He had picked up some rudimentary stuff, but it was mostly camouflage. He was still what the chip-heads called a bagbiter—somebody who created problems on the system. So he left the hacking and cracking to other people, while he stood on the sidelines and tried to look wise. He pulled out his handbook of limited knowledge and asked a few ground-level questions.

"Are you using your own username?'' he asked.

"No . . . I'm Redwitch, but I'm not using it. For this, I'm Dark-Star—it's a name of one of our informants—and I'm using the U.S. Customs host computer.''

"What cracking program are you using?'' he added.

"I downloaded Crack off the Internet. But I'm a hacker, not a cracker, and this stuff is tougher to break through than I thought.''

"Crack is a dictionary of computer passwords or something, right?'' he asked.

"Right. The way it's supposed to work is, you dial into the computer you're trying to penetrate, and this little program starts jabbering passwords at it. You're supposed to just leave it on. I'm using a dictionary of over ten thousand common passwords. Crack runs through the whole dictionary until it hits one that the other computer accepts. It's supposed to be eighty percent reliable, but I'm S.O.L. so far.''

"What's the problem?''

"I don't know. I log in, I do the opening dance, then my Crack program shoots three passwords in, and I get this 'login incorrect' shit from Pennet in Oslo, and I'm out.''

''Lemme see . . .''

She turned, typed !! and hit Enter. The !! command told the UNIX operating system on the host computer to repeat the last command issued:

```
TELNET RING2ICE.ANON.PENNET.NO
TRYING 172.24.168.10 . . .
```

They waited. The room was very small and windowless, and he could smell her perfume. One detail intrigued him: She wasn't wearing any jewelry, not even earrings. Claire never wore jewelry, except for her wedding ring, until she threw it at him. After a second, the hookup was complete and the screen read:

```
CONNECTED TO RING2ICE.ANON.PENNET.NO
ESCAPE CHARACTER IS '∧]'
SUNOS UNIX (RING2ICE)
LOGIN:
```

She typed in ''DARKSTAR.'' They waited. After a few seconds, Pennet responded with:

```
PASSWORD:
```

She then activated Crack on her computer and it made three password attempts. After the third attempt the screen read:

```
LOGIN INCORRECT
CONNECTION CLOSED BY FOREIGN HOST.
```

Then some line noise put some garbage on the screen:

```
*!(#W&∧#%
```

''What's all that jabberwocky?'' John said, leaning in.
''It's pissed. I think it's swearing at me.''
Then the screen shouted:

```
DARKSTAR, YOU HAVE EXCESSIVE
INVALID LOGINS. YOU ARE LOCKED
OUT FOR FIFTEEN MINUTES.
NOTIFYING SYSTEMS ADMINISTRATOR.
```

And the screen went black.
''Cheese it, the cops!'' Lockwood said, grinning.
''Look, you may think this is funny. I don't. Why don't you just go get some coffee?''
''You gonna keep trying with the Systems Administrator watching?''
''What's he gonna do, jump on a plane from Oslo, come over here, and knock me in the dirt?''
''Good point.''
They waited fifteen minutes. It was a strange lull, because she seemed to have nothing to say to him and he couldn't think of anything to say to her. So they waited in silence, with their eyes on the wall clock. The basement room was cramped and underlit. The ornate Customs building had once been Washington's Department of Labor building. It was a stone-faced edifice with Corinthian columns and a brass front door. But the decorating scheme ended below the first floor. The basement would have made a good set for a Bela Lugosi film. There were exposed pipes running along hard concrete hallways.
The last minute clicked off the clock and, without saying anything to him, she telnetted to Pennet, again. They were back in the good graces of the remailer computer. The screen said amicably:

```
CONNECTED TO RING2ICE.ANON.PENNET.NO
ESCAPE CHARACTER IS '^]'
SUNOS UNIX (RING2ICE)
LOGIN:
```

She went through the same sequence and basically the same thing happened, only this time the Systems Administrator had a surprise waiting for them:

```
REDWITCH
U.S. CUSTOMS GOV. OPERATOR
YOU ARE LOCKED OUT FROM THIS HOST
FOR 90 DAYS.
ALL FUTURE PACKETS FROM YOUR SITE
*WILL*BE*REFUSED*.
```

Suddenly, she was dumped back to her own system prompt.

"Busted," Lockwood blurted.

"Shit," Awesome Dawson said.

# 5

## CELLAR DWELLERS

The Cellar was a brick-faced bar-restaurant on the first floor of an office building on Constitution Avenue. The interior was a cross between a fifteenth-century Dominican monastery and an Irish pub. Some fool had further complicated the mix by hanging a model of a Grumman Skyhawk with a ten-foot wingspan from wires in the middle of the main room. But it didn't matter, because most of the people in the Cellar were serious drinkers and seldom looked up.

It had taken Karen about four hours to decide that maybe Lockwood could be a blessing in disguise. He had invited her for an after-work cocktail, which was pretty much a Washington tradition. Most of the important business in D.C. eventually got done in bedrooms or bars. Although she was determined to stay out of his bedroom, she was hoping a few shooters would make an offbeat idea she had seem attractive to him. The Norwegian computer had caught her interest. One thing that always got Karen's motor revving was being flipped off by anybody. The Pennet Systems Administrator had dissed her, and now she was even more determined to crack the system. Lockwood might hold a key.

The Cellar was near the U.S. Customs building, so there were a lot of friendly faces as they walked in and found a booth in the bar. He ordered a Scotch shooter and a beer back. To promote bonding, she had the same, and they sat for a long moment looking at each other.

"You're very persuasive. I don't know why I came," she finally said disingenuously, wondering how to broach her question in a way that would encourage him to sign on.

"You're shooting my tender self-esteem in the heart."

"Come on, Lockwood, I've heard of you. You're a one-man Internal Affairs project," she said, choosing a direction. "How many IA investigations have you been through in the last year and a half?"

"I stopped counting."

"I heard five," she said, hitting the exact number.

The fact was, there had been three weeks last August when all he did was work with his A.G.-appointed lawyer on his growing list of Internal Affairs citations. He had offended most of the Washington, D.C., IA silks in general, and Vic Kulack in particular. Almost as this thought struck him, he saw Kulack lumber through the door, with two vertical columns of shit who also worked on the fifth floor. Kulack rolled his shoulders when he walked. It was bad John Wayne. He was big but doughy. It amazed Lockwood how anybody could make a career out of trying to destroy the careers of others. For his money, Internal Affairs was a division loaded with nosebleeds and bend-overs who had to prove that their own low agency test scores were nothing more than unfortunate accidents. Jealousy of competence was the fuel that drove them.

"I think those guys in IA suck," she said, picking up his exact thought.

"Why do you want to get into Pennet?" he finally asked, one eye still on Kulack, who went into the other room with his friends and took a table out of sight.

"The only thing that a remailer computer offers to its customers is anonymity. Pennet is a gathering place for sexual deviates. Pedophiles and necrophiliacs chat on that service regularly."

"Naaaaaw," he said, dragging it out.

"You asked me a question. I'm trying to answer you. Are you always such a wiseguy or do you ever have a serious moment?"

"I'm working off a disappointment. I got broomed off my Global Airlines case this morning," he said, wondering instantly why he'd told her that. "So, you figured to go lurking in that computer and see if you could pick off a hot one?"

"That's about the size of it. But I'm shot down. I'll never get through that blocking system. I get three chances at three passwords, then I'm locked out for ninety days. Even if I change computers, I'll be using a walker by the time I penetrate it. What I need is a *great* cracker."

"Probably right. You could use a guy who jacks these things for a living. . . . One of those cyber-thieves could probably break through that Pennet blocking device in minutes."

"Like who?" she asked, her eyes on him.

"I don't know. I'm not a subscriber to *Cyberworld*. You find somebody."

"How about Malavida Chacone . . . ?" she asked.

Instantly he looked up from his shot glass at her. "Where'd you hear about him?" he said, his guard coming up swiftly.

"Didn't you arrest him?"

"What's going on here, Karen? You trying to work me?"

"The FBI was calling him the Mac Attack when he was only seventeen. He'd been out on the electronic highway since he was twelve, driving his Macintosh war wagon, cracking into everything, buying BMWs, sending the bills out to some black hole in cyberspace. I heard you finally got him 'cause an angry girlfriend blew him in. But if it hadn't been for that, you never would've caught him."

"Actually, I try to never get out of bed when I work a case. I like to wear my silk jammies with the little pink-and-blue clowns and do it all by phone." He was choking back anger. He'd worked for six months to catch Malavida, who had been on the Customs "Ten Most Wanted" list for computer crimes that crossed the border. Lockwood had slept in his car outside Malavida's mother's apartment in Pico Rivera for four nights. He'd co-opted Malavida's girlfriend. The phone call from Tia had finally burned Chacone, but Lockwood had planted the seed.

"Don't get pissed off. I'm just saying Malavida could do it."

"He's doing a five-spot at the Federal pen at Lompoc. He'll probably do good time and be out in a year or so, but till then, he's out of service. So forget it." He didn't get any further because Vic Kulack threw his shadow across their table and conversation.

"You get the paper I sent you?" Kulack said, grinning. They both looked up at him.

"Which one? You've been papering me so much, I can't shit fast enough to use it all."

Kulack sat down uninvited, in a free chair at the end of the booth. Besides being doughy, he had hair that looked like it had been cut by a lawn mower and a big, square raptoresque jawline.

"Understand the DOAO's put you up on blocks and Girlfriend is my case after all."

"Back up, Vic. You're crowding the plate," Lockwood warned softly.

Kulack leaned over and grabbed a handful of peanuts out of the dish, then smiled at Karen. "You wanna little advice, honey? Give this Loony Tunes the gate, 'cause when I get through with him, there won't be enough left to scrape up an' flush."

"This was a private conversation. Do you mind?" she said.

"You're Karen Dawson, I heard about you. I'm Vic Kulack. My friends call me Brute, because I take guys like Lockwood here an' give 'em attitude adjustments. Since Lockwood's gonna be tied up giving IA depositions till the year 2000, why don't we get together and give lust a chance?''

Karen turned to Lockwood. ''What a specimen. Somebody should examine his relationship to the gene pool.''

''Already did. He's in the maggot family.''

''Don't maggots breed in garbage?'' she asked drolly.

''That explains the funky smell,'' Lockwood answered.

Kulack was looking from Lockwood to Karen and back. His face flushed red. ''I'm not through with you. . . . I'm gonna knock your hard-on down with a hammer, Johnny.'' He got up and lumbered off. Karen and Lockwood looked at each other in silence.

''Poetic,'' Karen finally said.

''Yeah.'' Lockwood was looking at the IA investigator, who rejoined his two buddies. Suddenly the Cellar seemed stuffy. He finished his drink and picked up his wallet.

''Wanna go?'' she said, reading his mood change again and realizing she had blown her chance to enlist him. She decided to try again later.

He nodded and they stood up. After a minute they were back out on Constitution Avenue. The gathering darkness was turning the city into a fairyland full of uplit buildings and statues. A bus lumbered past.

''For whatever it's worth, despite the mess you're in with IA, I heard you're the best,'' Karen said softly. ''Since we're assigned together, is there any way you can think of to help us get into Pennet?''

''What's with you and that Norwegian computer? It's more than just a hunch you're working, isn't it?''

''I did a field interview with a pedophile last June when I was still working on my last doctorate. Before he went to the Federal pen, he was in the D.C. lockup. He told me that the Pennet computer has code-locked 'rooms' where these sex freaks go and talk to one another. The Customs Service hired me because I have two doctorates in criminal psychology, a master's in deviant sexual behavior, and an RN in psychological addictions.''

"I got a C-plus in algebra. 'Course, I had to cheat."

"Come on. I shouldn't be updating VICAP. . . . That's for a data-entry clerk. I'm the best walking, talking criminal behaviorist in the Federal government, but they've got me picking cotton in the basement. Maybe it's because I'm not an agent, or maybe it's because I'm just a chick in this boys' club, but either way, it makes no sense. I want to use that Pennet computer and hook one of those sex criminals, but I've gotta get into the sucker first."

"Nice knowing you, Karen. See you tomorrow." And then he reached out and shook her hand in what they both knew was a ridiculous moment, so he ended it quickly and walked away. Karen watched him go . . . a thin, handsome, dark-haired man in a cheap suit.

# 6

## ROLLERBLADING

In the dream, he was on Thunder Mountain near Washington, D.C. He was trying to Rollerblade down the side of its rock-encrusted east face. His ex-wife, Claire, and his ten-year-old daughter, Heather, were watching him. The rocks were treacherous, and he was moving too fast. He kept going over one particularly steep incline and, as he did, he would look down the horrible rock-strewn face of the mountain and realize he was a goner. Then, as if by magic, he was back up on top, putting on the Rollerblades and heading off, gaining speed, out of control, just like before, the rocks making balance and purchase impossible.

The phone woke him up. He sat upright, trying to get his bearings. His bed was a mess, the sheets kicked onto the floor. He'd had better sporting experiences. It was three A.M., his sinuses were blocked again, and he had a headache. He rolled over, grabbed his pocket inhaler, and gave his sinuses a shot before he picked up the phone.

"Yeah . . . ?"

"Did I wake you?" It was Awesome Dawson.

"I was Rollerblading."

"You were what?"

"Forget it. What's up?"

"I'm back in B-16 and that Systems Administrator

41

wasn't fooling. I'm completely S.O.L. on this computer. All I'm getting is a bunch of 'Connection refused' messages when I try to log in.''

''Thanks for the update.'' He felt like hell and his mouth was dry. He guessed he'd been mouth breathing. He leaned back against the headboard and rubbed his eyes.

''I've heard the stories about you, Lockwood. They say you're a rule-breaking kamikaze. This afternoon, I was trying to con you; now I'm just going to ask you straight out—I want you to get Malavida Chacone out of jail to help us.''

''Get Malavida out of the Federal lockup? That's all you want?''

''I got his whole file here. They just sent it down from Records. He got busted the first time when he was sixteen, and get this: When his hard-nosed parole agent from the California Youth Authority started hassling him, Malavida transferred his entire bank account to Donny Osmond at the Children's Miracle Network telethon. I love that.'' She waited for some response and didn't get one, so she plunged on. ''Malavida's busted into just about every high-security computer in America, including the payroll computer at the Pentagon. I checked with a hacker friend of mine at Princeton. He said not just anybody can break into a closely guarded computer like Pennet. It's a science. Like you said, there are only a handful of crackers good enough to do it. Malavida is one of them.''

''Forget it, Karen. I'm on thin ice with the DOAO as it is. The way I'm going, my next stop in law enforcement will be riding shotgun on a Brink's truck.''

''Come on, they wouldn't do that to you. You're Customs' top gun, the old sky-guy.''

''Your doctorate is in psychology, mine's in bullshit, so knock it off. To get Malavida out of prison, I'd have to go to an Assistant U.S. Attorney in the Sixth District in California, and I'd have to get this guy to write me a prison furlough request. The PFR has to state plainly why

I need Malavida out. Illegally cracking into a computer overseas isn't gonna qualify. Even if it did, I'd have to make arrangements, in advance, to have him jailed every night in an approved lockup, and those arrangements would have to be approved by the Assistant U.S. Attorney. Then I'd have to take the furlough request to the same AUSA who put Malavida away in the first place. I'd have to get him to sign off on it. By that time, there're gonna be so many yellow lights flashing in the Federal prison system, they're gonna think there's been a nuclear war. SES is gonna find out I'm shopping this paper around, and if they don't shut me down, I'd have to get a court order written, and then, maybe, I get him out for twenty-four hours. And even if I could do all of this, it would take our clubfooted Justice Department a few years before the final paper is issued." He was wide awake now and sitting on the side of the bed. A long, thought-provoking silence from Karen greeted this diatribe.

"There's gotta be another way," she finally said, undeterred.

"There isn't. I'll see you in the morning." And he hung up.

Of course, there *was* another way, but if he tried it in his current predicament, he would be better off Rollerblading down Thunder Mountain. He suddenly wished he could talk to his daughter, Heather. He looked at his watch. It was after midnight in California. Claire would kill him if he called in the middle of the night. He looked across his neat, functional bedroom to his dresser where his ten-year-old daughter's picture was in a silver frame. It was her class picture, taken last year. Her smile was lopsided, trying to cover a missing tooth. He had joint custody but Claire had recently moved to L.A. She had been offered a vice-presidency and a big dollar promotion with the media-buying firm where she worked. He had not filed court papers to prevent the move. This act of legal generosity had cost him his weekend visits with Heather, but he didn't have the heart to deny Claire her big opportunity. He'd denied her so much while they'd been married. Sitting there at three A.M., picking at the same old emotional scab, he wondered how he had gotten so fucked up. He still loved Claire, and yet she had divorced him. He desperately missed Heather, only she was three thousand miles away. How could he have traded them away? He tried to convince himself that he'd had no choice; that events had demanded his desertion of them. Lockwood tried to believe it. He curled around that trash can fire like a beggar looking for warmth, but found none. Was that what all this crazy behavior was about? Was he so mad at himself that he was slowly causing his own destruction?

The next morning, he joined Karen in the basement in Room B-16. The VICAP packets were still hung up somewhere in Records and they still couldn't break into Pennet. The Systems Administrator had the host box saying "Connection refused" and dropping them back to their own system prompt whenever they tried. Karen was in a bad mood. Lockwood had been turning the problem over in his mind all morning. A plan was forming that, in truth, had more to do with seeing Heather and Claire than Malavida Chacone.

"Okay, look," he finally said, "there is a way I could get Malavida out. But if I screw it up, I'm gonna probably end up doing his time for him."

"We'll do it together," she said earnestly.

"That's a nice sentiment, Karen, and I don't want you to think I don't appreciate it, but the fact is, you're a civilian, and these guys can't and won't do anything to you. On the other hand, I'm dogshit on the sidewalk around here. All week, people have been stepping carefully around me. On top of that, I'm being periscoped by Kulack. So if anybody is going to get hammered, it's me."

"John, if you take the pipe, I'll take it with you."

"You really want to try this, huh?"

"Lemme hear and I'll let you know."

He told her, and when he was finished, she was smiling. "You can do that?"

"I don't know," he finally said. "I did it once before and nothing happened. But I think I got really lucky."

"Malavida's all the way out in California. How're we going to get there? We'll never get reimbursed for airfare."

"That's the easy part. We'll use the DOC's personal jet. His pilot is an old friend of mine."

"The Director of Customs?" She was shocked, but smiling. "You really do walk the edge, friend."

"Walking the edge is our basic Fort Nowhere operating philosophy," he said, and they shook hands.

Earlier that morning, he had called the DOC's pilot, Red Gustafson, in the Customs ready room at D.C.'s National Airport. Red and Lockwood had worked on a joint-op drug interdiction in Southern Florida and had become good friends. Red happened to have mentioned to him two days before that the Director's jet was due for an engine nacelle hot section sometime soon. All Customs planes were serviced at Lockheed in Burbank. Lockwood asked Red if he could make the trip that weekend, and if he and a friend could hitch a ride. Red had set it up and told Lockwood to come along.

Lockwood and Karen met Red at the Customs shed at ten o'clock Saturday morning. They walked through the humid heat to the blue-and-white Citation and got aboard. The Citation was the only jet in civil aviation that was rated to be operated with one pilot. They got in and buckled up; by 10:30 they were airborne, climbing to thirty thousand feet and heading toward California.

They settled back as Red made a banking right turn, leaving the National Airport departure pattern. The little jet hummed quietly. Lockwood could again smell Karen's perfume in the cramped cabin.

They landed seven hours later at Burbank Airport after refueling at Tucson. The L.A. time was 2:30 in the afternoon. Red said that they would have to go back to Washington Sunday night. He gave Lockwood a rough departure time of six P.M. and a beeper number, then took off across the heat-shimmering pavement, looking for the crew chief in the Lockheed hangar.

They rented a yellow LeBaron convertible and put the top down. Lockwood drove onto the freeway with his jacket off. Karen had her head back, breathing in L.A.'s funky air. Lockwood had been stationed in L.A. for two years, so he didn't need a map. He used the downtown exit from the 110 freeway, on Sixth Street.

The Federal Building was between Fourth and Olive, near the L.A. library. It was a fifteen-story brown-brick structure with no architectural significance. The top three floors were given over to Assistant U.S. Attorneys for the Sixth District. Lockwood left Dawson in the lobby coffee shop and took the elevator up.

Harvey Knox was in a cubicle on the east side of the AUSAs' division on the fifth floor, surrounded by depositions. Short and plump, Harvey had one of those haircuts that have to be carefully arranged and then patted to cover a growing shiny spot. He was ten pounds heavier than when Lockwood had last seen him, five years ago. They'd worked an international business fraud case together. One of the U.S. Customs missions was to protect business from international counterfeit merchandise, and Lockwood had been working a big ring of counterfeiters selling knock-off Louis Vuitton luggage and handbags. This kind of fraud accounted for business losses of over three billion dollars a year and occupied a good percentage of Customs resources.

Despite the size of the operation, the case had ended like the last reel of a Marx Brothers movie. The Customs agents' inside man had notified them that the main counterfeiter, a Brazilian named Raúl Ruiz, was supposedly at that moment standing in his East L.A. warehouse. Harvey and Lockwood decided to take the place down and make the arrest. They had everything they needed to take the case to trial, and the added bonus of having the Brazilian quarterback standing right in the warehouse with the offending merchandise was too good to pass up.

Lockwood and his Customs team had gone in and made the arrests while Harvey was in a plain wrapper out front, writing the paper and identifying the suspects from surveillance photographs. They swept the place and lined everybody up, but there was no Raúl Ruiz in the conga line. The warehouse was full of Mexican illegals. Lockwood had cuffed the Mexicans and was waiting for INS and an interpreter, when who should pull up in a rental car but El Jefe Grande himself with two huge Latin bodyguards. Apparently, Ruiz liked *gelato mexicano* and had gone down the street for a cone. He saw all the activity in the parking lot and hit reverse. Harvey got out of the plain wrapper and ran toward the car, his coattails and comb-over hair flapping. He tried to reach into the driver's side window and yank the keys out of the ignition, but found himself looking down the barrel of a Ruger Redhawk. The three-hundred-pound driver floored the car, but Harvey's sleeve got caught on the turn indicator, forcing him to run and hop alongside the rental, which was making a looping, tire-skidding turn out of the parking lot.

Lockwood heard the commotion and ran out just in time to take part in the Harpo Marx conclusion. He pulled his S&W long-nose and, with Harvey Knox hopping, running, and dragging ass alongside the car, Lockwood hit a Weaver shooting stance and fired one round. He'd never been a great shot. He'd been aiming at the driver, but he hit and blew the left rear tire. The car lost its rubber and skidded to a stop on the rim. The Customs team took everyone into custody. The shot had saved Harvey's life.

After he decompressed, Harvey ran around behind Lockwood like a puppy. He told Lockwood he was going to name his firstborn after him. Lockwood said, ''Not necessary.'' Then the AUSA said he was going to buy him a trip to Hawaii. Lockwood said, ''Not necessary.'' Then he said, ''What *can* I do? You saved my life. If it wasn't for you, I wouldn't be here.''

It was then that Lockwood said, ''Let me think about

that and get back to you.'' Now, five years later, in Harvey's little cubicle at the Federal Building, he was about to try and collect the debt.

"Shit, Johnny, how you doing?'' Harvey said as he clambered up from behind his depositions, briefs, and yellow pads. He pumped Lockwood's hand endlessly and Lockwood grinned, glad to see the little attorney.

Harvey was still trying to hide his bald spot under strands of wispy brown hair, but the battle lines were widening, and Harvey and his hair stylist were losing.

"How you been? Jeez, good to see you,'' Harvey said. "I got your message on my machine you were coming. But it didn't say what time. You gotta let me buy you dinner. . . . I'll call Ann.''

"I have to go up to Lompoc tonight and I'm gonna try to see Heather and Claire before I leave; then I have to get to Burbank by six tomorrow to get my ride back to D.C. So it might have to wait.''

"What's up?''

"I need a favor. . . .''

Harvey grinned at him. "I remember your style, Johnny, so I hope this favor won't cost me my career.''

"What I have in mind *is* a little slick,'' Lockwood admitted.

Harvey looked at him, shook his head. "Hey, you name it. I wouldn't even be standing here if you hadn't defrocked that Goodyear radial.''

"There's a guy up in Lompoc named Malavida Chacone, a computer cracker. He's doing a nickel. But I checked and he's getting one for three on good behavior, so he's 'short,' less than eighteen months to go. I need to get him a coffee break parole for a few days, and I don't wanna fuck around trying to get a furlough request verified.''

"You want me to write a Special Circumstances Release on a Federal prisoner?'' he said, the smile drifting sideways on his friendly face.

"You don't have to do it, Harvey, 'cause I know it's

kinda between the cracks . . . but I'm under a lot of pressure here.''

"Why? What's the reason?"

"Classified. I need him for an interview on a very important case. I'll lock him up every night. But he has information critical to my investigation.''

"Shit, John, that means I'll have to lie on the SCR, say it's life or death, or some damn thing. . . .''

"That's what it is. I shoulda mentioned that.'' Lockwood grinned.

"And you can't tell me what the case is?"

"It's a witness protection deal. I can't focus it any sharper than that. I'm really locked down tight on the talking points. But it's big. You're just gonna have to go with me or not. I can't lay it out for you, but I'll stand in front of you if there's a firing squad.''

"Where you gonna take him?"

"I won't leave the state. Hell, I won't even leave Lompoc. I'll use a motel and have my Wit flown in.''

"Chacone won't leave Lompoc and you'll have him locked up every night?'' Harvey had an eyebrow cocked. He'd been in the Justice Department for seven years, and bullshit has its own special odor.

"He won't leave the motel."

"John . . .'' It was said like a warning.

"Okay, look . . . I'll work something else out. I'll see ya, Harvey. You're looking tired. You should get some time off. Take Annie away, go drink a mai-tai under a palm tree.'' Lockwood grinned, shook Harvey's hand, and walked out of his cluttered office.

Harvey caught up to him by the elevator, grabbed his arm, and spun him around. "John, I'm not like you. You get off doing this shit.''

"It's okay—"

"No, it's not okay. You saved my life."

"Come on, Harvey, I took some target practice on a tire. The truth is, I was aiming at the palooka behind the wheel. I missed by a mile. You don't have to do it because of that. You want my opinion, you didn't even need me there. You were seconds from pulling that Brazilian sumo through the window and knocking his dick in the dirt. Least that's the way I saw it.''

Harvey stood looking at him, shifting from one flat foot to the other. ''Wait here. I gotta go upstairs and see if I can even find the forms,'' he finally said.

Lockwood knew that requests for a Special Circumstances Release from prison were like photographs of Big Foot—they were extremely rare and seldom focused. Very few got issued, because not many cases were so contingent on secrecy that the interview couldn't take place in the attorneys' rooms at the prison. The outstanding exceptions were usually witness protection cases, where the Wit's identity was secret or his life was in extreme danger.

When Lockwood left the elevator and picked up Karen in the coffee shop, he had the folded paper stuck in his pocket. Even so, he knew that unless he played it just right, the prison officials would cough up a lung laughing at him.

He had tried to call his ex-wife, Claire, twice from the Airfone and had gotten no answer. He stopped now at a pay phone in the lobby and tried again. There was still nobody answering at her rented house in Studio City. They got back into the LeBaron and headed toward Lompoc, about an hour's drive north of Santa Barbara. Lockwood found an excuse to get off the freeway in Studio City, allegedly for gas, then drove past the address on Moorpark and looked at Claire's small wood-frame house. He slowed and finally parked across the street. Karen watched, a puzzled look on her face.

''What's this?''

''I think it's my ex-wife's house,'' he said, never averting his eyes. ''I haven't been here before.''

''Claire lives here?'' Karen said, and when he glanced at her, she instantly looked away.

''You used your computer clearance to go browsing in my DOR file?'' he said, referring to his personnel folder in the Department of Records.

"Just a quick peek," she said, embarrassed, and then looked at the house, which was a duplex with blue siding and the curtains drawn. The garage was empty. He studied the house for a long time.

"I have a little girl. Ten years old, named Heather. You probably saw that in there, too. I don't get to see her much," he finally said.

"Why don't you go ring the bell?"

"I should call first," he said and accelerated away from the house. His departure had a slight flavor of escape.

Karen watched him surreptitiously. He drove stoically, but she thought she saw something glinting in the corner of his eye. . . . She wondered if it was a tear or just his reaction to the smoggy L.A. day.

# 7

## CUTTING AND PIERCING

**T**ashay Roberts had been trying to decide whether to get a nipple pierce like Satan T. Bone wanted. There was very little she wouldn't do for him, but punching holes in her titties was close to the limit. She sat on the purple shag carpet in her older sister's Tampa house in shorts and a halter, and opened the mail wearing latex gloves. Her sister had been traveling in Europe and she and Satan had the place to themselves. One thing was certain: The new Southern tour had produced results. The mail was mostly from Atlanta and Shreveport, but there was stuff from Midland, Texas, and that little town in South Carolina she could never remember the name of, because she'd been dusted the whole time they'd been there, and it was a blur. . . .

The thing about the nipple pierce that worried her was, she was afraid it would hurt. Satan had two nipple pierces and he said it didn't. . . . But it wasn't like a nose pierce or tummy button, or even the eyebrow pierce she'd had done last summer—which, by the way, hurt like a bitch, even though the hard-on who did it said she'd never feel a thing.

She suddenly realized that Baby Killer's new album, *Chant to the Dead,* was already past her favorite cut, so she got up, stretched her long tanned legs, padded across the purple shag to the CD player, and set it to replay "Redneck Burnout." She thought the *Chant to the Dead* album was a musical leap forward for Baby Killer. "Redneck Burnout" was by far the best cut on the album, the best song they'd ever done. She listened as Satan T. Bone's raspy voice screamed the almost incoherent lyrics:

"Fuck the bitch and cut off her tits," the song began. "Fill her neck with cum. . . ." Baby Killer was one of about twenty U.S. Death Metal bands. They operated on the extreme edge of rock 'n' roll. Tashay loved the lyrics. They celebrated sex with the dead, baby killing, and mutilation. The audience for this music was small but rabid, and Death Metal operated in an outer orbit of the music business.

Tashay moved back to the pile of mail and sat down. She'd been saving the interesting-looking brown-paper-wrapped shoe box with no postmark for last. She swayed with the rhythm of the song as she opened some more mail. Her job was to separate the "wet mail" from the dry. More and more, Satan had been getting blood-soaked things and he was afraid of AIDS, so she had to sit there, wearing the fucking latex gloves, and open the mail.

Satan T. Bone was tall and skinny. He had black tattoos under each eye, making him look almost like a vampire. He had stringy black hair that he never washed, and had twenty pierces. It seemed he got a new pierce every time he got really wasted. Satan's real name was Bob Shiff, but he had been so influenced by the music of Peter Van Wilkinsen, who called himself Satan Wolf, that Shiff had taken the stage name Satan T. Bone when Van Wilkinsen was arrested in Oslo, Norway, for killing that guy on stage.

She could see bloodstains through the white envelope on one of the letters and knew it should go in the wet pile. She thought it was way cool that Satan's fans sent blood-soaked letters, even though she suspected that it was just animal blood. Still, it was on there, and it was beautiful and gross. Satan T. Bone was really talking to his audience, small as it was. She decided finally, fuck it. . . . She couldn't wait to see what was in the box, so she got the sharp serrated knife and cut it open, slitting the paper along the top, then the side. She slowly pulled the top back and saw that whatever was inside had been carefully wrapped in cellophane, and then placed inside a plastic bag.

"What is this?" she said to herself, a smile on her tiny, vacant features. She pushed back her blond hair with her gloved wrist and reached for the object in the box.

"Cool," she said as she touched the object, then gently lifted it out. It was heavy, maybe almost two pounds. It was squishy yet hard at the same time. She pulled it out of the Baggie, peeled back the tape that held the cellophane, then slowly and carefully unwrapped it.

A human hand fell onto the purple shag. It had been severed at the wrist and it lay there like a small dead thing. Satan T. Bone's voice screamed through the expensive speaker system:

> It is a very strange night.
> The bitch didn't fight.

Tashay Roberts stared at the hand and then slowly picked it up with her latex-gloved fingers. She looked at it carefully. It was delicate, probably a woman's hand. She could see that the fingertips had been surgically removed.

"This is so fucking cool," she said softly, but she was also afraid. There was no postmark; the box had been hand-delivered by someone. Whoever sent it was definitely way out there . . . way, way out there. Tashay wondered if she should call Satan or Carl. She knew if she told Satan, he would want to keep the hand. He was a crazy son of a bitch. Keeping the hand could be trouble. Her first boyfriend, Carl Zeno, was a county sheriff. He was also her stepfather. He'd started fucking her brains out when she was just fifteen. He'd kept it up all the years her mother had been on the night shift at the drugstore. Occasionally, when Satan was on the road, she would still go and see him. Carl was her secret addiction. She knew the hand was very bitchin' but very dangerous. Carl would know what to do. After all, he was a cop. She looked at the hand, which was lying on the purple shag, fingers up. If Satan didn't know it had been sent to him, then he couldn't be angry at her.

She decided she'd go ahead and get the nipple pierce the way he wanted. It was a way to make up for her little deception. She moved to the phone and dialed a number.

"Carl," she said, the excitement ringing in her voice. "The coolest thing just happened."

Behind her, through the speakers, Satan T. Bone screamed his degradation.

# 8

## HANG GLIDING

After spending the night in two cheap motel rooms in Lompoc, Lockwood and Karen pulled up to the guard shack for visitors' parking at 7:30 on Sunday morning. John showed his Federal buzzer and identified both of them. He got out of the car before even being asked and handed over his gun and holster, which he had packed in his briefcase. They pulled inside the barbed-wire fence and drove to the parking lot.

They walked in under a huge stone arch where pigeons cooed down like bubbling poison. The visitors' room was ugly. Yellow linoleum, probably left over from some Federal housing project, butted up against turgid green cement walls. The sagging couches were cracked red leather. There was an interior window on one wall where a female prison guard was fielding visitors' requests. The only artwork on display was tattooed on the arms and backs of the men and women who were queued up, waiting to visit. Lockwood moved to the front of the line and shoved his badge under the glass. The stout female guard took his shield and ID, then entered his U.S. Customs badge number into her computer. After a second, Lockwood's picture and ID information came up on the screen. He motioned that Karen was with him, and the guard nodded and buzzed them through. They moved into a back room where a black prison officer sat behind a desk. A sign said this was the VISITING POLICE LOUNGE.

"John Lockwood," he said to the guard. "I need to have a chat with Malavida Chacone in a secure room. This is Dr. Karen Dawson; she's a civilian employee with U.S. Customs Service in D.C."

The guard looked at both John's and Karen's IDs, then motioned for them to be seated. "I'll have to find out where he is and get him transferred up," he said, then moved off to an enclosed phone station.

"Okay, what we're going to do is solicit this kid. We gotta get him interested. I busted him, so he'll sling a buncha barrio attitude at me, but, bottom line, he wants out of here. So after he's through dissing me, he should jump in our lap. Your job is to show him how much you care. Give him a reason to say yes. The real trick is gonna be putting a move on his counselor. We've gotta score that guy somehow. Leave that up to me."

"Counselor?"

"A young con like Malavida always has a counselor to help him through problems. It's usually just a prison guard with an unread subscription to *Psychology Today*. I'll find a way to co-opt him once I get a look at him."

"Why not just hand over the paper from Harvey Knox?"

"That paper is puppyshit. It won't smell right if anyone looks at it too long. Once we get in there, we've gotta move fast. We're either walking out of here with Malavida in an hour, or we're back in the prison Administrator's office, trying to talk our way out of an official reprimand."

She smiled at him and he looked at her sternly. "It won't be so funny if we get busted. These guys have no sense of humor. It's not like getting a late-paper markdown in college."

"I'm not worried. I don't mind risk," she said.

"You don't know what you're talking about."

"When I was twelve, I designed an airfoil. It was sort of like a hang-glider, but this was way before hang-gliders. I called it the ALFA Wing. Stood for Airfoil Light Flight Apparatus. I calculated weight and lift. I designed a rudder assembly with a ten-to-one gear ratio. I made this thing out of aluminum rods with plastic sheets and nylon line. My two brothers dared me to test it, so I took it up to the top of Eagle Rock Dam near our house. There was this three-story sheer drop. I harnessed myself in, and my brothers were now scared shitless, begging me not to do it. They released me from the dare. They promised to clean my room for a year. They were panicked I'd kill myself. But it was too late. I ran and jumped off.''

''How did it work?''

''I had rudder failure. I looped back into the concrete dam and hit about one story from the bottom. I broke both legs and had a severe concussion. I was in the hospital for two months. Moral of the story, in case you missed it, is I don't mind risk if the reward seems worthwhile.''

Lockwood didn't doubt the story was true, but he wondered what it really said about Karen Dawson. Ten minutes later, they were led by another guard with a weight lifter's body out of the police lounge and through a sally port.

They climbed some narrow wooden stairs at the end of the corridor and into the Attorneys' Wing. There were several small, windowless rooms with metal doors. In each room was a table and three or four chairs. The muscle-bound guard led them to the nearest one.

''I'll bring him up.''

He left, and Lockwood made a quick search of the room and the furniture.

''What're you doing?'' Karen asked as he was crawling under the desk.

''Hold on a minute.'' He stood and showed her a voice-activated tape recorder he'd removed from under the table. He opened the back and turned the batteries around, putting them back in backwards. ''I don't need to face this conversation we're about to have at a trial board. This way they'll just think it didn't work because they misloaded the batteries.'' He clipped the now-defunct recorder back into the bracket under the table.

"They bug these rooms?" she said, dismayed.

"J. Edgar Hoover said knowledge is power."

"No, he didn't. That was Sir Francis Bacon."

"Well, Hoover shoulda said it. . . . And, Karen, I know you can divide my IQ into yours and come out with Bill Clinton's hat size, but we'll do much better if you stop making me feel like an imbecile."

"Then stop sounding like one," she deadpanned.

He nodded and they sat down in the straight-backed wooden chairs and waited.

Malavida Chacone worked in D Block, which was the old death row. That building had one of the best air-conditioning systems in the prison, the theory being that men who were waiting to die should not be subjected to the cruel and unusual punishment of summer heat in central California. The corridors were narrow and there were no windows, but frigid air flowed through the rooms, chilling skin and nerve endings like uncut heroin. The death row inmates had been transferred to the state prison when California stopped dispensing lethal doses of Edison-Medicine and began killing its condemned with the far more humane lethal injection. Because of the air conditioners, the prison's new computers were in D Block, and because Malavida Chacone could hack into anything for anybody, he had been offered a coveted job at the computer center. He ordered food, medical supplies, tires, and shotgun shells for the prison from 7:30 till 11 in the morning. After his coffee break from 11 to 12, he opened his store for the guards and inmates, scoring everything from Nike running shoes to lifetime subscriptions to *Penthouse*. His preferred customer was any hardcase who thought it might be fun to grab him and give him a hot beef injection in the "trick bunk" located in the back of C Block. He had made himself too valuable to rape.

He'd also managed to computer-select his own cellmate. The lucky winner was a huge Native American named John HorseKiller, who had killed four Sheriff's Deputies, but no horses. The gargantuan, six-foot nine-inch Indian belonged to no gang, club, or ethnic Mafia organization. But he was fiercely loyal to Malavida because the twenty-two-year-old had arranged for Horse-Killer's dying mother to be illegally added to the CIGNA insurance group medical plan. Her chemotherapy was being paid for by thousands of unsuspecting policy owners. As compensation, HorseKiller would "run the gears" on any inmate who gave Malavida a hard time.

Malavida had it made in Lompoc. He was the Santa Claus of the joint, but he dreamed of catching tube rides at Huntington Beach on his yellow-and-orange surfboard. He missed lying on the sand, his long, black hair wet on his shoulders. He missed the girls, sunshine, and water . . . but most of all, he missed his mother.

A guard came to tell him that he had visitors in the Attorneys' Wing. Malavida shut off the computer he was working on and, without saying anything, followed the muscle-bound screw out of D Block, across the yard, and into the Administration Building. He made his mind a blank, trying not to think about who or what had just hit on his wall.

When Malavida walked into one of the attorneys' rooms and saw John Lockwood, his heart went cold. Malavida despised Lockwood. The Customs agent had done more than arrest him. . . . He had lied, but more important, he had destroyed Malavida's family and Malavida's mother had not looked at him the same way since Lockwood had arrested him. Malavida's eyes flicked over to a very pretty, slender, auburn-haired young woman, also in the room. The guard closed the door and Malavida forced his anger away. He had learned that anger rarely served a purpose. It destroyed logic and made you vulnerable. Like a well-trained fighter, Malavida was determined to meet Lockwood with cold, surgical precision.

"Make your pitch, Zanzo," Malavida said, without

emotion. "You didn't come up here to bring me cookies."

"Give it a rest, Mal. I was just doing my job."

"Who's this?" Malavida said, glancing at Karen.

"Karen Dawson. She works with me at Customs."

Karen had been looking at Malavida with open surprise. She had been expecting some nerd, an *X-over-Y* computer geek. Malavida Chacone was handsome and muscular, with long, shiny black hair and even white teeth. He was intense and beautiful and very sexy. A lone teardrop tattoo hung in ethnic anger beneath his left eye. But despite his striking appearance, his eyes were hard as black glass and revealed nothing.

"How'd you like to get out of here for a day?" Lockwood said.

"I'm doing fine. I'm keeping my house neat. I get what I need."

Lockwood looked down and saw the new Nike running shoes on his feet. "You on a track team, Mal?" Lockwood said, grinning.

"No, I ain't on a fucking track team. Why would you wanna get me out, huh? I got nothing you want."

"I gotta computer problem."

"I ain't no buster, so go get your help someplace else. 'Sides, they ain't gonna let me outta here anyway."

Lockwood pulled out the folded SCR that Harvey had made up and slid it across the table with his fingers. Malavida made no move to look at it.

"Not gonna help you, Zanzo."

"Why not?" Lockwood asked.

" 'Cause you lied in court."

"So did you."

"It's okay to lie when you're trying to stay out of prison. It's *not* okay to lie when you're a cop."

"I musta forgot that rule," Lockwood said in mock surprise. "What page is that on?"

"It ain't funny."

There was an uncomfortable silence in the room.

"We want you to help us," Karen chipped in. "I've

read your record. I think I can understand why you started doing what you did. You were trying to help your mother. We need to hack into a computer, but it's got very strict security on it. I think there are only one or two crackers in the country who could penetrate this machine.'' She watched him, hoping the flat-footed compliment would soften him. His eyes still showed nothing.

Lockwood tapped the folded paper between them.

''This is a Special Circumstances Release. What we're offering you here, Mal, is a field trip with burritos. We'll take you to Lompoc. You'll help us. Then we'll buy you some Cokes and grease. We'll let you watch the sex channel on the motel TV and we'll have you back here tonight.''

''Why would I help you, Lockwood? Gimme one reason.''

''One reason? Okay, how's this? I can't ever recall seeing an inmate wearing designer running shoes before. What would happen if I put a trace on the prison phone lines? Would I maybe find some brisk computer sales in the Nike catalog? If I shut down your deal, how long would it be till you were somebody's personal tidbit in here?''

''How the fuck do I get you outta my life?'' Malavida scowled.

''Hey, you asked for a reason. How'd I do?''

''Malavida, we need you,'' Karen pleaded. ''Please help us. It would mean so much to us. . . . Won't you do this favor, please?'' This time she was openly begging him. Lockwood thought it was arguably the worst version of good cop/bad cop he'd ever pulled.

Malavida knew he'd get no slack from Lockwood. He'd had enough exposure to the tough agent to know they were on opposite sides of the ball. But Karen Dawson looked like bait that could be stolen. He smiled at her and, after a moment, picked up the SCR form and studied it.

''How could I refuse such a pretty *chica*?'' he said insincerely, going badly over the top himself.

"Who's your counselor?" Lockwood asked.

"His name's Stan Shannahan," Malavida was now talking only to Karen. "I can get him to walk this SCR right through. All it's gonna take is maybe a pair of size ten and a half, D, Lucchese cowboy boots in black or tan ostrich. They have 'em at the Ranch Store in Santa Barbara. He's been drooling over them, but I haven't been able to score 'em for him 'cause they got no computer catalog. Throw in the boots and I guarantee he'll stamp us through."

Malavida's attitude was picking up speed as he smiled at Karen. He was definitely in a hurry to get out of Lompoc for a day. He'd already started working on a way to turn a day into a lifetime.

They met Stan Shannahan and gave him Harvey Knox's request. Stan glanced at it and took Malavida into another room. After a minute, they came back and both were smiling.

"You ain't gonna take him outta Lompoc, are ya?" Stan asked, his Texas accent twanging like a bobby pin in a Dixie cup.

"Of course not. We've got a government witness and a Federal prosecutor coming in by van. We're gonna be at the Ocean View motel back in town. We'll conduct the interview there and have him back by tonight."

"Man, these Federal witness deals are really something. What's this Cholo got you need?"

"I'm afraid that's classified, sir," Lockwood drolled, "but it's a major case. This interview was approved by the big boss, the Attorney General herself."

"Y'all gonna brung-um back chere tonight?" Stan asked, exposing both a horrible education and brown tobacco-stained teeth.

"Absolutely," Lockwood said. "Checked in before ten so we won't have to get the admittance staff back to reprocess him. No sweat, no hassle. By the way, where's that store where I get the boots? Is it off Front Street?"

"I wrote down the address. The tan ones, in ten and a half."

"Them's good-looking ones y'all got on right now," Lockwood said, putting a little twang under it for unity, while looking down in admiration at a pair of hand-stitched western boots on the fat guard's feet.

"Yep, El Dorados. Handmade. Got the bulldogger heel on 'em, too . . . great for stompin' the chit outta pissed-off little yard bunnies. Ain't that right, Cholo?"

Malavida smiled his sweet smile. "Yes, boss," he said.

"Tell you what . . . we'll bring the Luccheses when we check him back in tonight."

"Why don't y'all go get 'em now? Just fifty minutes away. An' in the meantime, I'll run this official request through the system . . . get the Assistant Warden's approval."

"Good idea. See you in a bit." Lockwood turned to go, then stopped and turned back. "By the way, Stan, we don't need anybody diming us out. The A.G. wants this kept confidential."

"I gonna be so busy lookin' at my new boots, throwin' a spit shine on 'em, I ain't gonna have no time to do nothin' else." He grinned.

They left Malavida there and drove to Santa Barbara for the boots. Karen was quiet all the way to town. "Did you really lie in court?" she finally said, as they were headed back.

"You give up a lot of yourself to do this job. You can give up your family, your life, pieces of your self-respect. You get damn little in return,'cause all the rules are written against you."

"But did you lie?" she asked again.

"Why don't you ask him if he was guilty?" Lockwood looked over and saw something in her eyes he hadn't seen before. It looked strangely like pity.

They got back to the prison an hour and a half later. Stan had Malavida waiting in the visitors' area, in handcuffs and a waist chain. He handed the keys over to

Lockwood and watched while the agent signed the release in triplicate and promised to have the prisoner back that evening. Then they all walked out to the car with Malavida where Lockwood handed Stan the boots. Stan looked at them and whistled low.

"Ain't them fuckers a sight to behold," he said.

In ten minutes, they were down the road and out of sight. Lockwood had put the fifteen-hundred-dollar Lucchese boots on his Customs Service credit card. He didn't have a clue how he'd justify the expense. But he was already hanging so far out on this deal, it probably didn't matter. In the back of his head, a question buzzed around like a fly in a bottle: He was already in deep shit with Internal Affairs, so why was he out here in California busting a Federal prisoner loose with bad paper, just so he could help Karen Dawson break into a computer he didn't really care about? It made no sense. Then a new thought hit him. Was it for his own emotional survival? Was he subconsciously trying to get himself thrown off the job before it destroyed him?

# 9

## S.O.L.I.M.F.H.O.

Malavida Chacone sat in the backseat beside Lockwood while Karen drove the yellow LeBaron. They had put the top up. Malavida was dressed in prison blue jeans and still wearing the cuffs and waist chain. They pulled into the sleepy town of Lompoc. Small, architecturally bland buildings housed 7-Elevens and chicken franchises. Malavida was straining forward, looking out the window, his senses quivering at the smell of freedom.

They rode in silence until they hit a stoplight and Lockwood said, "Whatta you need t'crack a computer?"

"A ten-dollar hammer and five swings oughta do it," Malavida said without humor.

"Don't be an asshole."

The light changed and the cars behind them started honking, so Karen accelerated.

"There's a computer store here in Lompoc," Lockwood continued. "We can pick up a laptop and whatever else you need, then we'll check into a motel and have a go at it."

"Hey, why don't you start by telling me what program you want me to crack into? It might make a difference," Malavida said.

"It's a remailer in Oslo, Norway, called Pennet,"

Karen said. "It's set up to deny access to invalid logins. I get three tries and then it locks me out."

"You using Crack?"

"Yeah, I got it off the Internet."

"Why didn't you just call the System Mangler on the phone and tell him you were trying to break into his jukebox?"

"Look, I'm not a cracker. I use *my* computer for research," she said.

"I didn't mean to upset you, Miss Dawson," he said, smiling at her pleasantly. "I was just saying that the Crack program is a primer program for newbies. If this Pennet computer is a remailer, then they got high-grade security on it. You're not gonna get in with software like Crack. They probably have the telnet daemon listening for multiple logins. And Crack is slow. It could take you six months with Crack before you randomly hit the right password. You can't use Crack on a system like that, anyway. So, what happened? The SysAdmin came on and started screaming at you, right?"

"Yeah, he locked me out for ninety days. He also knew I was working on a government computer at Customs," Karen said, surprised by the change in his language and demeanor.

"That was telnet that did that. It has to know the IP, the 'Internet Protocol' address of the packets coming in, so it can send its data back to you. It knows your host address. So, what you are is, you're basically fucked."

"You better figure out how to get us unfucked or you're basically back in jail," Lockwood said. Then Karen pulled over and parked the car in front of the computer store.

"Whatta you need?" Karen asked.

"I need my own laptop. I got a 14.4 external modem at my mom's house in East L.A."

"Nice try," Lockwood said. "But let's save that trip for Mother's Day."

"Can't we get you a laptop with a high-speed modem in there?" Karen asked, pointing at the store.

"I also need my cracking tool kit . . ." Malavida said, playing out a little more line.

"What the hell is that?" Lockwood asked.

"It's all the cracking programs I've designed. It's a buncha disks. And I need my ITL notebook."

"Your what?" Lockwood was starting to get a headache.

"ITL . . . 'Interesting Things and Locations.' It's Internet locations of stuff I might need but haven't retrieved yet." He was again ignoring Lockwood and talking only to Karen, trying to look earnest and helpful.

"So, I'll send somebody over to your mom's house and he can get this stuff and modem it up here," Lockwood said. He wondered where in town he could buy aspirin.

"*Nada.*"

"Whatta you mean, *nada*?"

"Won't work. I'm the only one who can access the disks. We need this stuff. I can't help you without it. I got a list of outdials and a copy of the C-programming language for several flavors of UNIX. I got a complete list of Internet locations and all kinds of software utilities. No offense, Miss Dawson, but you got the Pennet Systems Administrator on point with that Crack program. The way I go in, nobody sees me." He started grinning. "I'm fast and invisible. And don't think you can send some clubfoot Customs nerd over there to deuce it out and open my files, 'cause all the disks are encrypted. If anybody tries to open them, it'll automatically erase the whole kit. And then we're S.O.L.I.M.F.H.O."

"What?" Karen and Lockwood said simultaneously.

"S.O.L. means Shit Outta Luck."

"I got that much," Karen said. "What's I.M.F.H.O.?"

"In My Fucking Humble Opinion. Let's go, the Mexican ghetto's that way." He pointed. "Either that, or you should take me back to prison." He closed his eyes. "I'm just gonna bone out back here till you two geniuses make up yer minds."

Lockwood sighed and looked at Karen. "Why not?"

she finally said. "What's the difference whether we do it here or there?" He wondered whether he'd be able to steal some time to see Claire and Heather.

Karen put the car in gear and headed back onto the freeway.

"One other thing, Chacone. . . . She ain't gonna be your 'tight,' so you can stop the rubdown. I'm in charge."

Malavida nodded earnestly. "I know," he said, but he was already working on his next move. He was determined to splash on John Lockwood. Malavida hated him, and, one way or another, he would find a way to fuck him up.

# 10

## HOMECOMING

Malavida's heart started to pound in his chest as they neared his mother's apartment. Elena Chacone had raised all seven of her children by scrubbing floors and washing windows in the big houses up in La Habra Heights. She had never asked for anything in return. Malavida used to be her favorite child. Now she looked at him with sadness. He hated the thought of going home in chains.

Elena had been born in Guadalajara, Mexico, and in the evenings, she used to tell her children stories of the beautiful tree-shaded public squares in that mountaintop city. She would close her eyes and remember the colorful flowers and the children riding ponies in the park. She described the magnificent churches with their huge stained-glass windows and ornate Spanish arches. *"Dios mío, son bonitas,"* she would sigh. Her family had all worked in one of the pottery plants there, and she told her children about the blown glass and clay artifacts that had won the city international fame.

To Malavida, it seemed a crime that she had left such a beautiful place to live in a two-room apartment in graffiti-ridden Pico Rivera. She had been only sixteen when she left that Mexican paradise to come to ''El Norte'' to work on her hands and knees, scrubbing floors. In an even worse turn of fate, she had married Juan Chacone. He was also an illegal alien, but was ropy and mean. His hometown was Chubasco, which he remembered with seething hatred. Elena had seven children by Juan, and Malavida was the youngest. Juan was a brawler and a drunk, who often came home on Saturday nights and took swings at Malavida's beloved mother. Malavida hated Juan with every fiber of his existence. He prayed that his father would be hit by a car or killed in some Saturday night brawl. And then, one day, Juan had simply gone to the store and hadn't come back. Malavida prayed every night that he would never return. As the days passed, it seemed that Malavida's prayers had been answered, but his mother was paralyzed by her husband's disappearance. She had been abused by him, but couldn't seem to face the idea of living without him. His mother had been afraid to go to the police, because she was sure they would send her back to Mexico and she would be separated from her children.

When Malavida was twelve years old, he had been given a used Apple computer by one of the people whose houses his mother cleaned. He was fascinated by its bright screen and beautiful graphics. He worked at it endlessly, and in five years, at the age of seventeen, he was already so adept that he was a legend on the Internet. His username was Snoopy. Long before that, however, he realized that his computer gave him immense power over a system that had held him down and enslaved his family. One day, he decided to use this new power, and that was the day he started out on his career of crime. His initial goal had been simple. He would get enough money so that he could send his mother back to Guadalajara in style. She had finally become a U.S. citizen by virtue of the Amnesty Act of 1987, so now she could come and go across the border. He decided he would fulfill her dream of going back to the beautiful city where children played in the shaded town square and rode ponies and ate *gelato* in the huge green parks.

His first computer scam had grown out of something

very innocent. He had been up in La Habra Heights, helping his mother clean one of her houses, and saw a country-club membership book on a marble table. On impulse, he slipped it into his pocket. The book gave the addresses and occupations of the members, as well as the ages of their children. He thought such personal information surely must have some value. He turned the problem over in his mind for two days, and slowly a plan formed. He started reading *The Wall Street Journal* to pick up the terms he would need. He asked his sister's boyfriend, who was an artist, to design a letterhead. Then he wrote a letter to ten of the club members, each one selected by occupation. If the man was an insurance executive, the letter would say that an executive headhunting firm called Executive Research Foundation had been hired by an international insurance firm with headquarters in California to find a chief executive officer. This insurance company, the letter said, preferred to remain anonymous at this point, but the position it was offering paid approximately five hundred thousand dollars a year. The letter continued by telling the mark that his name now appeared on the short list of potential candidates as a result of his outstanding work at his current company. Then Malavida wrote that it was ERF's pleasure to inquire if he would be interested in taking an in-person meeting with the insurance company's Chairman when he was in town, to discuss the employment opportunity. He signed the letters "Dexter Freemantel, Vice-President of Human Resources." He sent them off and waited.

From ten letters, Malavida got four replies, all of them affirmative. Then he wrote each one back, asking the candidates for a few more details before the meeting could be arranged. He politely requested that they supply him with a Social Security number so that ERF could complete its background check, and could they also supply him with their mother's maiden name and their banking affiliation for a routine credit check? To this query, he got one reply. . . . Mr. Gregory Clayton Smith said that he was looking to make a change and enthusiastically sent back all the information requested.

Then Malavida simply sat down in front of his computer and cracked Mr. Smith's bank, which happened to be the Bank of America. He hacked into Gregory Smith's account and then requested a wire transfer of two thousand dollars to an account he had set up at a bank in Fullerton under a bogus name. He took only two thousand because that was all he needed to buy airfare to Guadalajara for both himself and his mother, with a little left over for new clothes for the trip. When the B of A computer asked for Mr. Smith's Social Security number and mother's maiden name for the wire transfer confirmation, he sent the information.

The next morning was Thursday, December 16. Malavida rode his old ten-speed bike three miles to Fullerton and checked his balance. On that day, Malavida got an early Christmas present and completed his first successful computer theft. . . . Sitting in Charles Brown's bank account was a wire transfer for two thousand dollars. He couldn't believe it had worked! With adrenaline coursing through his teenaged heart, he cashed in the account and took off. He smiled all the way back to his ramshackle apartment building in Pico Rivera, the twenty crisp hundred-dollar bills in a pocket of his school backpack. He was just thirteen years old.

He had taken his mother to Guadalajara, first class, on Aeronaves. She was wearing a brand-new peach-colored dress and shoes, and had a new leather purse and matching luggage—all of it bought at Kmart. He had told her he'd saved money from odd jobs to give her the trip. *"Dios mío,"* she had said; then she hugged him while tears streamed down both of their cheeks.

As the airliner circled for its landing at Guadalajara's airport, Malavida had been so proud he could barely contain himself. Elena had muttered quiet prayers of thanks as the plane touched down.

The trip had been a disaster. The tree-lined parks were dirty and brown. There were no ponies. Elena's family was poor; her aunt and uncle were sick, but still dragging themselves to the pottery plant, which now employed less than a third of the people it once had. There were poverty and sadness everywhere.

All Malavida had accomplished with his great gift to his mother was to steal the memories that had been sustaining her. Within days, she wanted to go home, and on the trip back to L.A. they said almost nothing.

Her life had always been a struggle, so after the disappointment of Guadalajara, Malavida determined he would use his newfound powers to make things better. He would program a new life for her. For a while, he succeeded. But then, five years later, he was arrested by John Lockwood—busted and cuffed right in his mother's living room. Malavida knew Lockwood had made the arrest there on purpose, right in front of his mother, to humiliate him. It was then that Elena realized that the gifts he had been giving her were all stolen. She gave everything back. It broke his heart that he had caused her such pain. All he had wanted to do was ease her burden. She would never again accept another gift from him.

The street in Pico Rivera where Malavida had once lived was littered with rusted-out cars, broken bottles, and smoked-out ghetto stars. There was gang graffiti all over the side of the store at the corner. The bright signs in the shop windows were red or gold, but the businesses behind them were struggling to survive. The apartment building where Elena Chacone lived was called The Ritz. It was a two-story stucco fortress with barred windows that looked as ritzy as hand-me-down clothes. Lockwood thought the neighborhood was twice as depressing as it had been when he'd camped out across from Elena's apartment for four days, waiting to arrest Malavida.

They parked in front and got out. Malavida looked down at the chains on his hands and around his waist. "I don't want her to see me like this," he said softly.

Lockwood looked at his eyes and saw a tinge of panic, so he reached out and unlocked the handcuffs and waist chain. He threw the chain into the trunk, but draped the cuffs over the steering wheel, an age-old sign to car-jackers that this was a cop's car. . . . Fuck with it at your own risk!

As all three climbed the metal staircase to the apartment, their footsteps rang in the concrete stairwell. When they got to the second floor, Malavida led them to his mother's front door and knocked.

*"Es Malavida, mamá."*

The door opened and Elena Chacone was standing there. She rushed forward and hugged her son. She was stooped over and barely five feet tall, but Karen thought there was a nobility about her. Despite her size and posture, she had the look of somebody who carried the weight of all her family's problems without complaint. But disappointments, more than years or gravity, had aged her. Her face was lined and sagging, her gray-black hair pulled into a knot at the back of her head. Karen found it hard to imagine her as a young girl.

After the embrace was finished, Malavida and his mother started to rattle at each other in Spanish. Lockwood looked over at Karen. His Spanish, like his computer skill, was rudimentary, and he could pick up only a word or two—*"Trabajo"* was one, *"Sus hijos"* another, then *"El coche no funciona bien"*—all of this from Elena. Something about a job, and the car not working. From Malavida, all he got was *"Mis amigos . . . Dónde está Ricardo? . . . Mi computer y todas las cosas . . . Teléfono."* The words hung in the air, a guttural flow of unrecognized vowels and consonants. Lockwood's cop paranoia screamed at him. He was afraid maybe Malavida was asking for help. Who was Ricardo? Would he show up with a car full of *Esses*?

"Can we do this in English?" he interrupted. "Not that I don't trust you, but I like to know what's being said."

Malavida turned and looked at Lockwood. "My mother doesn't speak much English." Then he made a very polite introduction: *"Mamá, tu recuerdas el señor Juan Lockwood, y ésta es la señorita Karen Dawson, mi madre Elena Chacone.''* They shook hands and Elena dropped her head in deference to the rich Americans. She remembered Lockwood with distress from when he had slammed her son against the wall, then thrown him on the floor and cuffed him.

"I don't want to do it here," Malavida said. "We gotta do it someplace else."

"Do what?" Lockwood replied.

"Crack the computer you're after. Let's just pick up my stuff and go."

"Where? We need a work station. All this stuff is here already. Why move it? I'll pay the phone bill if that's the problem. . . ."

"It hasn't been the same since you busted me here. Look at her. You scare her to death." Now the look in Malavida's eyes was closer to desperation. "I'm not gonna do a computer crime in front of her. That's all there is to it."

Karen thought that, despite his macho looks and size, Malavida was still just a little boy who didn't want to break his mother's heart. She grabbed Lockwood's arm, pulling him back slightly.

"Let's find someplace else," she said.

"He's conning us," Lockwood answered.

"We can rent a motel room."

"No, I got a better idea," he finally replied.

Lockwood turned to Elena and told her in his broken Spanish that he was honored to be in her home, and then asked if he could use the phone for a local call. Elena hurried into the kitchen and handed it to him. He thanked her and, after she left, dialed Claire's number again. He kept his eye on Malavida, who was in the living room talking to Karen.

"Hello," Claire said.

"Hi. It's John. . . ."

"Oh . . . Where are you? You sound close," she said guardedly.

"I am. I'm in Pico Rivera. It's a short trip. Government work, but I don't have to be back to the airport till six tonight. I thought, if it was okay, I could come over. I'd like to see Heather.''

There was a long pause on her end, then: ''Well . . . gee, I don't know. . . . We were planning something.''

''Claire, I didn't make trouble for you when your job offer came and you moved three thousand miles away. I let you come here without filing an injunction. I'm giving up my weekends with Heather. Now you're saying I can't have two hours?''

''We both know why you didn't try to stop me. What were you going to do with Heather . . . take her on stake-outs?''

The shot hit him hard because there was truth in it. His job wasn't just nine to five, Monday through Friday. Criminals didn't take the weekends off, so neither did he.

''I want to see her, okay?'' he pressed on. ''It's noon now. . . . I could be there in less than an hour.''

''I guess,'' Claire finally answered, but her voice offered no enthusiasm.

Malavida passed Lockwood as he hung up the phone. He saw a strange, sad look on the Customs agent's face. He knew he had played the Fed just right by getting Karen to convince him to keep moving. Malavida was looking for a chance to take off, but he couldn't do it here. Not in front of his mother. Malavida went into the bedroom where he and his seven brothers and sisters had all slept as children. All of them had moved out now, except for his sister Madalena, who had just broken up with her husband and was living there. Madalena's things were strewn all over the place. She had always been the messy one. It was hard living in one room with seven brothers and sisters if everybody didn't keep their belongings picked up. As a result, Malavida was scrupulously neat.

He found his computers in boxes on the top shelf of the closet, then lifted them down carefully. His prize was the now somewhat outdated Texas Instruments Travelmate 4000M notebook with 20 megs of RAM. Before his incarceration, the 4000M had been the fastest unit on the market and he ran Linux on it, a free UNIX operating system favored by many hackers. He pulled down another box containing an external 14.4 modem and his cellphone, then the plastic filecase full of his disks. This was his cracking kit. Inside, he had tools to mask and change his identity and location on the Internet, as well as many other disks that helped him penetrate a variety of systems and situations. He next pulled down his "Interesting Things and Locations" three-ring notebook, then his outdials. Last was his Sony monitor. By the time he had it all down, it made a sizable pile in the center of the room. He had stolen almost all of the hardware, buying it with jacked credit card numbers. Now he was going to use it to help the police . . . an irony that he found no humor in. The last thing he did was take his Snoopy poster off the wall. Snoopy was his icon, his good-luck charm. He rolled it up carefully.

They loaded the equipment into the trunk of the LeBaron, which was beginning to draw a crowd. The little yellow convertible stood out like a debutante among the rusted, primer-painted muscle cars. This became Lockwood's first tactical problem. They had drawn a crowd of teenaged street bravos. The G-sters were standing on the brown lawn next door, gold Turkish ropes around their necks, looking down innocently at their spit-shined Santa Rosa hightops. Their gang flags were hanging from pockets bulging with foreign automatics. They looked on hungrily as the computer equipment was loaded into the trunk, licking their lips like coyotes watching a French poodle.

Lockwood knew that if he accompanied Malavida back up into the apartment, the trunk would be pried open with a crowbar, and in ten seconds they would lose it all. He pulled Karen aside.

"I gotta stay down here and protect this stuff. You go with Mal. If he takes off, yell."

"What are you talking about? He's not gonna take off."

Malavida was just finishing packing the first load into the trunk. He turned and looked at Lockwood. "One more trip. You coming?"

"Go ahead," Karen said, catching Lockwood by surprise.

Malavida immediately turned and jogged back to the stairs. Lockwood started after him, but as he did, the street bravos surged toward the LeBaron. He had to stop or Karen would be left protecting the car alone. He knew instantly he'd made a bad field decision and had let the play get away from him.

"This is fucked. He's going to go out the window up there and across the roof. We'll never see him again."

"Nonsense, he'll be right back," she said confidently.

A minute later, Malavida came back down with the last load of computer equipment and placed it in the trunk. Then he went up and kissed his mother good-bye. Karen and Lockwood could see them on the landing. They could see Elena put her hand up to her youngest son's handsome face. They watched in silence as he hugged her . . . mother and son rocking back and forth with their arms around each other in their own special cadence. Karen could feel the love all the way from where she was standing. Her heart went out to Malavida. She began to suspect he was nothing at all like the bitter young man who was so angry at Lockwood.

"How did you know?" Lockwood finally asked as Malavida headed back toward them.

"You're a prize" was all she said.

He got behind the wheel, slightly pissed, and threw the handcuffs into the glove compartment. Malavida got into the back; Karen sat up front.

They pulled past the street gang, headed back to 605, and got on, going west. They rode in silence. Karen knew Malavida wouldn't run. She had seen it in his eyes when he pleaded with them to take off the cuffs, and again when he first hugged his mother. He would never run with Elena watching. He worshiped her. It startled Karen that John Lockwood didn't know that. And then she remembered what she'd read in Lockwood's file: He'd never known his mother. His mother had been the system. For Karen, it explained everything about him.

# 11

## CRACKING

They arrived back at the wood-frame house in Studio City at 1:30. Lockwood rang the doorbell and, after a minute, Claire opened the door. The first thing he noticed was she had cut her hair. It was in a helmet cut that would have been ugly on most women, but Claire was startlingly beautiful, and it somehow flattered her strong Scandinavian features. The short hair gave her an efficient, streamlined, no-bullshit look that he assumed was an asset in her new job at the media-buying firm of Latham, Brown, and Forbes.

They exchanged deadpan "Hi's," and then she opened the door a little further, her eyes sweeping the street where Malavida and Karen were unloading equipment from the trunk of the LeBaron. The early afternoon sun was hot and a slight breeze ruffled the maple leaves on the pretty flower-lined street. He followed her gaze.

"They're working the case with me. I was wondering if we could hook a computer to your phone. It's a long-distance call, but I'll pay time and charges—"

"I see nothing much has changed," she said.

"That's not fair, Claire. I'm out here on business. If I'd gone to the Federal Building, I wouldn't have had time to see Heather. I couldn't just drop them on a street corner." He felt himself trudging onto a familiar battlefield that, experience told him, would be won by neither of them. He knew they were only a few shots away from a series of low blows that would suck them down the drain of mutual disappointment. He tried to stop it. "Please, let's not do this. . . ."

"Okay, John, let's not." She opened the door for him. Lockwood motioned Malavida and Karen to come in. They carried the armloads of computer equipment into the house.

The house was strictly Claire. French Provincial. Oversize chintz-covered furniture stood against flowered wallpaper like overfed visitors.

He introduced her to Karen Dawson and Malavida Chacone, and thought with dread that it was a testament to the death of their relationship that Claire had not shown a single twinge of jealousy on being introduced to the beautiful criminologist. His ex-wife led them into the den. Malavida and Karen started setting up the equipment on the desk next to the phone.

"Where's Heather?" Lockwood asked.

"She's out back. I didn't tell her you were coming, because sometimes, as you recall, you didn't."

Lockwood absorbed that shot as well. He was determined not to put the gloves on with Claire. He found his way to the backyard where his daughter had set up an easel and was painting with a brush. As he got nearer, he could see she was painting a horse in remarkably accurate proportions.

"Hi, baby . . ."

She turned and, for a moment, stood frozen. He filed away a mental snapshot for the book of memories he kept in his head. She was a miniature Claire. It was as if his gene pool had not even entered the mix. She was beautiful, with her mother's blond hair and blue eyes. Then she unfroze and yelled "Daddy!" as she ran toward him. He wrapped her in his arms, holding her. He could smell her child's fragrance and was instantly aware all over again of how much he had lost. He recalled how each time he had disappointed Heather or Claire, there had seemed to be no other answer; yet when he stood back and viewed the whole ten years, he knew he had been lying to himself and to them. His job had always been the obsession he couldn't control. Whenever he was on the hunt, something he didn't understand overtook him ... a need to win, a competitiveness that couldn't be compromised. The job made horrendous demands on his life and was loaded with deadlines, court cases, depositions, stakeouts, surveillances, and drug busts. If he didn't take the junk off the streets, other men's children could die. It was a rationale that vacillated between religion and excuse. Right now, as he held his ten-year-old daughter, he knew it was also a betrayal of his parental obligation.

"Daddy, how long can you stay? Will you take me to the zoo?"

His voice was thin as he uttered the words one more time, "I can't, honey. I have a meeting tomorrow morning in Washington, so I have to leave tonight." And then he looked up and saw Claire watching through the window. Her expression told him that, without hearing, she knew what he had just said.

The den was small, but there was a nice French Provincial desk where they set up the laptop, unpacked the large monitor from its box, and connected it. Malavida attached the modem and, when Karen was not looking, he slipped a disk out of his tool kit into the laptop, and typed a quick sequence, starting a logging program which would lurk in the background and save everything that was typed in. The last thing he did was unroll his favorite poster: Snoopy, with his straight-line smile, in his trusty red biplane, scarf flying. He taped it to the desk in front of him. "Good-luck charm," he said to Karen. "We're set up now, but first we need to log into a host computer. How 'bout the one at U.S. Customs in D.C.?" he asked. "If you have a local dial-up, we won't stick Lockwood's ex with the phone bill."

"Good idea."

"You know the login password and the access codes?"

She sat in front of the terminal and then looked at him. "It's confidential. You'll have to turn your back or, better still, go stand across the room."

"Sure." He got up and moved to the far side of the room and looked out the window. " 'Cept for dream furloughs, I only got outta Lompoc once last year and that was for my appeal, which was denied. It's good to be on the outside," he said, looking out on the treeshaded street.

"Dream furloughs?" She looked at him; his back was to her.

"That's where you dream you're out of prison. . . . It's a freedom dream. It's not as good as this, but it's better than nothing." While he talked, she typed in the local phone number to access the U.S. Customs dial-up. The modem beeped out the Touch-Tones and the screen said:

```
CONNECT 57600
USCS6 LOGIN:
```

She checked to see if Malavida was still looking out the window. He seemed lost in thought. She entered her username, "REDWITCH," and password, "6793P$*M" ; then the screen said:

```
U.S. CUSTOMS COMPUTER NET, WASHINGTON, D.C.
WELCOME REDWITCH
```

"I'm in," she said.

He turned from the window and crossed to her. He didn't yet know what he would do with it, but his keyboard logging program on the diskette had secretly copied her entire login procedure. He could now access the Customs computer anytime he wanted, with her login and password. He sat down at the terminal and faced the screen.

"Okay, what's this remailer called again?" he asked.

"Pennet."

"You got the address?" He closed the keyboard log. As she retrieved the address from her purse, he popped the diskette out and slipped it into his pocket. "Okay, let's use the Customs computer as our host. . . ."

"But we've been locked out of Pennet from that computer," she reminded him.

"Won't matter. We're going to telnet to another account that I have. . . . That way, the Pennet computer will be reading an account which is not banned by their telnet. They won't see the Customs computer at all, even if they finger us."

"Okay," Karen said, and wiggled in her seat with excitement. She knew a finger program was a tracer, an identification program.

"Do we have ignition?" He grinned at her.

"We have ignition." She smiled back.

"Snoopy is cleared for takeoff," he said. He telnetted to one of his accounts:

```
TELNET REDBAR3.CC.RUTLEDGE.EDU
TRYING 192.168.43.127 . . .
```

And then:

```
CONNECTED TO REDBAR3.CC.RUTLEDGE.EDU
ESCAPE CHARACTER IS '^]'
SUNOS UNIX (REDBAR3)
LOGIN:
```

He typed "SNOOPY" and his password. When he was logged into his own account, he telnetted to Pennet at the Internet address:

```
RING2ICE.ANON.PENNET.NO
```

Then it gave its greeting, now familiar to Karen:

```
CONNECTED TO RING2ICE.ANON.PENNET.NO
ESCAPE CHARACTER IS '^]'
SUNOS UNIX (RING2ICE)
LOGIN:
```

"Instead of trying to crack it right off," he said, "let's just get on the system first and go for a low-level program like a new users' menu."

"Whatever that is . . ." she said.

"New users' menu . . . sort of lets them get to know us and vice versa. This is a secure computer whose main service is to protect the identities of senders. They'll keep us in a protective shell, so we can't crack through to the inside where the good stuff is. We've gotta penetrate that. Sometimes, it's easier from a low-level program like a new users' menu."

"Never thought of that. *Está de pelos. Andamos con más despacho, chico*," she rattled at him in Spanish, telling him, "That's cool, let's get started, buddy."

He looked over at her and they traded smiles of excitement. "You speak Spanish?" he asked, surprised.

"Spanish, French, Greek, Latin, and psychobabble. Lockwood might have been ready to let you talk to your mother in a language he didn't understand, but I checked out every word."

Malavida realized that if she had understood everything he had said to his mother without indicating anything, he would have to be more careful with her. She might not be as big a mark as he thought.

Malavida logged in as a new user. The system let him on, assigned him a new username, and made him choose a new password, then asked if he would like to see the new users' menu.

"Let's go for it." He typed *"Y"* for yes and got a menu on screen of things new users could do on the system, among them:

```
E)NTER BULLETIN BOARD SYSTEM
L)EAVE MESSAGE FOR SYSADMIN
```

"Let's try the 'Leave message for SysAdmin,' " Malavida said.

"He's a jerk. I've already had a brush with him."

" 'Cause you went right at him. I'm gonna look real harmless. The 'Leave message' option should put us into electronic mail. That's a good one for us. E-mail is an easier program to use to crack out of this protective shell. Because e-mail has to be able to write to everyone's account, it's tougher for them to protect."

He typed "L" and the top of the screen now said:

```
PICO
```

"Yessssssss," he said and pumped a fist.

"What is it?"

"We're in e-mail. PICO is a little text editor, sort of a memo writer or scaled-down word processor used on most UNIX-based systems like Pennet for typing up e-mail messages."

"What now?" Karen said.

"Now that we're in and we know exactly what editor they're using for e-mail, we can use some of its own internal commands to break out and get to the underlying UNIX system prompt where we can talk directly to the computer, using its own language. This is where it gets tricky, but with a little practice and a jacker cracker, *sus órdenes magníficos*"—he bowed slightly—"I'm gonna make this jukebox do the right thing." And as he spoke, his fingers flew across the keyboard. He typed in:

```
CTRL-X
```

That put him in at the exit options menu of PICO.

```
S)END; A)BORT; E)DIT; . . .
```

In order to keep PICO running without having the system dump him back to the users' menu, he typed:

```
CTRL-Z
```

They waited until the screen said:

```
STOPPED (SIGNAL)
```

"Win-win! We're out of the shell," he said, grinning. "Compared to the Pentagon, this is like stealing from a cart vendor."

"Are you confessing to hacking into the Pentagon computer?" She smiled.

"Aren't you supposed t'read me my rights before askin' a question like that?" Then he grinned. "Some people get high smoking crack, I get high doing a crack. Right now, this system is good as jacked."

"What's next?" she said, still looking at the screen with amazement.

"We see who else is talking to this thing. First we type in 'ps,' which stands for process or program and can show us everything running. We'll give ps three switches: an 'a,' which stands for all people using, 'u' for user info, and 'x' so ps will even show us processes which have no controlling terminal." He typed:

```
PS-AUX
```

And up on screen flashed:

```
USER  PID    %CPU %MEM ... TT STAT START TIME COMMAND

LOVER 18083 76.9 0.5  ... R5 R   23:06 0:00 PS-AUX
RAT   18077  7.7 0.3  ... PF S   23:19 0:00 /USR/UCB/BBS
BALSA 17024  0.0 0.0  ... QBIW   00:06 0:00 /USR/UCB/BBS
```

The list went on for about twenty lines.

"What's all that?" she said.

"That's who's on the remailer computer right now and what they're running. It's very thin because it's past midnight or something in Norway." He pointed to one of the symbols under the COMMAND column. "BBS stands for Bulletin Board System. Okay, since we don't have a password, let's see if we can spoof one of these users into giving us his."

"How we gonna do that?"

"We'll send one of them a message that nobody but him will see. We'll get him to log off and then log back in, but we'll be lurking here. Then we'll snarf his login with my special foo file. Okay, let's finger one of these users."

"I thought a finger was a tracking program."

"Backfinger is a sort of tracking program to see who was fingering you. Finger gets info on a user. Let's pick one of these first three guys, here. You're looking for a sex criminal. . . . How 'bout Mr. Rat? He sounds scummy." Malavida hunkered over the keyboard and typed in "FINGER-M RAT," and in response, the screen printed out:

```
LOGIN NAME: RAT              IN REAL LIFE: WINDMINSTREL
DIRECTORY: /ALUMNI3/RAT       SHELL:/BIN/CSH
ON SINCE APRIL 14 21:33:09 ON TTYR3 FROM TROPIC.SEAS.UFLA.EDU
NO UNREAD MAIL
```

"In real life, Wind Minstrel. What's that?"

"In real life his name is whatever it is, but Mr. Rat doesn't want to tell his or her real-life name. He's using a computer alias . . . Wind Minstrel. I like it. Very cool." He studied the screen. "Okay, the good news here is this tells us what host computer Wind Minstrel is using. It's a box named 'tropic' at Science and Engineering Administration Services at the University of Florida."

Malavida went into his cracking tool kit, pulled out another disk, and slid it into his PC. He typed "SZ," sending the file to his new user's account on Pennet, a file he called "FOO." It was a program he had written which would send a phony error message.

"Okay. Now, what I'm trying to do is create a phony system message on Mr. Rat's screen so he will think he has to log in again, and when he does, I'll steal his login and password," Malavida said, grinning. Then he typed:

```
FOO-TTYR3-ROOT@
```

"This program's gonna tell Mr. Rat to log in again." On his screen, Malavida showed Karen the message that was being sent to The Rat's computer:

```
MESSAGE FROM
ROOT@RING2ICE.ANON.PENNET.NO

FATAL STACK ERROR
ACCOUNT PROCESSES HALTED
PLEASE LOGIN AGAIN.

RING2ICE LOGIN:
```

"How do you know it's saying that?"

" 'Cause that's what I programmed it to say. It's total bullshit." He smiled at her.

"Cool." She smiled back, but was beginning to get lost. She had a 180 IQ, but didn't have enough ground-level information to understand all of this. She made a mental note to pick up some more books on computer hacking in the U.S. Customs crime lab and speed-read them as soon as she got back to Washington.

On the screen, The Rat logged in again with his username and password:

```
RAT
MUTIL8OR
```

"We got it. Write this down," Malavida said as Karen grabbed a pen.

"We're really in," she said.

"Now all we have to do is follow The Rat to his chat

room. That part is a snap. Then we'll just make ourselves look like him and slip in behind.''

Out in the backyard, Lockwood and Heather were talking quietly. She was telling him about her riding lessons.

"Daddy, you wouldn't believe how big he is. And I'm taking lessons twice a week. He's so beautiful. He's a Morgan gelding, but my teacher says he's sixteen hands tall. That's as big as an Arabian."

"That's great, honey. I'd love to come see when you have a dressage program."

"I'll call and tell you. This time, I promise . . . I'll give you plenty of warning." The remark stung him slightly.

Karen stuck her head out the back door. "John, you'd better get in here. You aren't going to believe this. . . ."

# 12

## CHATTING

The Rat was on the same wooden chair that Shirley always made him sit on when she found out he'd disobeyed the sanctity of the covenant or eaten chocolate or, worse still, the meat they served at the school cafeteria. He could never lie to her, because when he tried, he always lowered his head to avoid her scathing eyes. It was a reflex he couldn't control. If he got caught lying, it always ended up with the fire. . . . She would take him down to the basement and yell at him until he admitted he was foul and ugly. She would leave him there and he would sit on the straight-backed wooden chair, wondering if maybe this time she would not burn him, but she would always come back down later and light the candles.

He knew he was the anti-type of the great mosaic of her faith and that he had not yet begun his hateful journey. Shirley had told him his journey of penance would last two thousand and three hundred days, until he came to his final event, which would be the cleansing and the sanctity of his spirit. She hinted that she knew a way to avoid taking the journey, but she had not told him how or even when that six-year journey would begin. His mistake had been setting fire to the house before he knew all the answers. He had been waiting now for twelve terrible years for his journey through hell. The ax of its awful arrival hung heavy over him, its weight crushing his spirit, slowly turning him into a worthless creature who hid from God and scurried in the dark. Only when he was The Wind Minstrel did it change . . . but the change was both relief and agony.

It was almost 5:30 P.M. on Sunday afternoon as he sat in the hot enclosed space, the little generator motor purring outside. The shallow tidewater lapped at the side of the huge empty metal hull. There was no breeze and the afternoon Florida heat and humidity were oppressive in the windowless enclosure. He was deep inside an old rusted garbage barge that had once served the businesses on the Little Manatee River. He had bought it when he saw the name in faded letters on the stern.

He was wearing only his Jockey underwear, and his own foul-smelling, sour sweat was all over him. His big, corpulent thighs glistened. Slick, smooth, and white, they were like the underbellies of dead fish. His computer was on an old wooden school desk in front of him. He had a surge protector on the power line leading from the generator . . . but something must have happened, because he got the stack error message from the Systems Administrator at Pennet, then he had logged off with Satan and had just reentered the Pennet system. Once accepted, he had shot through cyberspace and returned to the locked chat room that he shared once a week with Satan. He was telnetting from his site to a second site where he had an account under a different username. Then he would telnet from there to Pennet. He had also set his client-mode to invisible, and the chat channel to private. He had created it that way for security, because he and Satan often discussed their killings.

Satan was one of his special gods. He had vision and strength and was never afraid, even now as he sat in prison on death row in Oslo, Norway. He was an unrestrained carnal visionary. The Rat had read about him in a Death Metal fan magazine. His real name was Peter Van Wilkinsen. Satan Wolf was his stage name, and he was the lead singer for the band Necrophiliac. He was on death row for killing a rival band's lead singer on stage, stabbing him twenty-three times during a battle of the bands that got out of control and turned into a riot. The Rat thought it was a glorious act that gave the singer eternal value.

Satan Wolf was the god of Death Metal. There were a few promising imitators, like Satan T. Bone, in Tampa, but they had not yet achieved the dimension of the original. Talking to Satan Wolf always made The Rat's skin begin to glow as if he were in the beginnings of a transformation. But he knew he was not. He had just coveted in Atlanta and the sensation of transforming took at least a week, sometimes two. The tingling in his nipples and on his skin was just a reminder of what was lying there, waiting to release and glorify him.

"WHERE DID YOU GO?" Satan Wolf typed onto the screen from Oslo.

"I HAD A STACK ERROR," The Rat replied.

"TELL ME MORE ABOUT ATLANTA. YOU HAVE CUT OFF THE ARMS OF THIS WHORE, THIS CUNT. YOU HAVE SEVERED HER LIMBS, WHICH ARE WORTHLESS, LUSTFUL APPENDAGES. HOW DID IT FEEL? DID YOU TASTE HER BLOOD THIS TIME? IT HAS BEEN A WEEK. HOW DID IT FEEL?"

Satan always wanted him to taste flesh or blood, but meat of any kind was forbidden and punished by fire. He didn't understand that The Rat first coveted, then The Wind Minstrel possessed. They had been corresponding for six months, always at the same time on Sunday. Sunday was a good time for The Rat because it was God's day of rest, and he felt he could better elude His watchful vengeance. It was good for Satan Wolf because the prison staff in Oslo was at half-strength on Sunday, and there was nobody watching him while he used the computer late into the night in the prison law library. He was supposed to be working on his appeal. They left him in the locked room, chained to the floor. He always took a break around midnight and met The Rat in their secret place.

"I HAVE NOT FINISHED. I HAVE ONE MORE VICTIM. . . .
MY FINAL VICTIM WILL COMPLETE THE BEAST. SHE WILL
THEN BE REBORN. THE ANSWERS WILL BE CLEAR. IT WILL
ALSO PROVE THE BITCH SHIRLEY WAS WRONG. MAN *CAN*
BE IMMORTAL. THE WICKED DO NOT SUFFER PUNISHMENT
IN ETERNAL HELL AND ARE NOT DESTROYED OR ANNIHI-
LATED IN A SPECIAL MOSAIC OF CLEANSING."

There was a short wait and then Satan replied:

"ENOUGH ABOUT THIS. I'VE TOLD YOU EACH SESSION I
CAN'T USE YOUR RELIGIOUS RANTINGS. TELL ME ABOUT
YOUR KILLS. ABOUT THE MUTILATIONS . . ."

Again there was a short lull as The Rat wondered how
somebody he held in such regard could not see the religious significance, but it was always this way. Then he
typed:

"I MUST TRANSFORM EVERY WEEK OR TWO. THE COV-
ETING BEGINS MUCH EARLIER NOW . . . SOMETIMES ON
MONDAY. I HAVE TRIED TO SLOW IT DOWN; SOMETIMES I
CAN STOP IT BY PREPARING GIFTS. TWICE I HAVE SENT
TOTEMS TO PEOPLE I ADMIRE. I HAVE SENT THINGS THAT
DON'T MATTER IN SHOE BOXES. I DIDN'T NEED THE HANDS
FROM THE ONE IN ATLANTA. . . ."

Satan replied: "YOU MUST SEND ME SOMETHING WET."

As The Rat was reading this reply, his heart froze. He
saw a small rectangle flashing in the upper right-hand
corner of his screen. A backfinger program he had running in the background had just notified him that somebody had fingered him at Pennet. Someone knew he was
there! He quickly did a names command to show him
everyone on the private channel. He saw his own alias,
WindMinstrel, listed twice. But he had logged out when
the stack error occurred and had only logged back in
once. He wondered if somebody had snarfed his password when he reentered the system and was now trying
to hide on the channel, pretending to be him. His heart
slammed in his chest, but he didn't panic. The Rat was
cunning. He didn't tell Satan of his suspicion, because it
would notify the eavesdropper that he had seen him. The
Rat started a second screen session and took a look at

the backfinger log to try to locate the intruder without alerting him. He could only do this as long as the intruder stayed online. Once the intruder's telephone connection was broken, it would be almost impossible to trace. He quietly went to work tracing the second WindMinstrel coming into the private chat channel, trying to trace it back through cyberspace to its place of origin.

In the second window, his backfinger log showed the site he had been fingered from:

```
REDBAR3.CC.RUTLEDGE.EDU
```

It was a university in the United States, although it couldn't show him who at that site had fingered him. He hacked out to a system prompt and used ps to list all processes or programs connected to Pennet. There was only one:

```
USER    PID    %CPU %MEM ... TT STAT START TIME

SNOOPY 14232 70.6  .06   ... R6  R   17:12  0:00


COMMAND
/USR/UCB/TELNET RING2ICE.ANON.PENNET.NO
```

He then fingered that account, all the while keeping up his communication with Satan, talking about things of no importance. Satan was becoming frustrated and began demanding more bloody information about his Atlanta kill. In minutes, The Rat's finger command revealed the host computer:

```
LOGIN NAME:SNOOPY          IN REAL LIFE: REDBARON
DIRECTORY:/REDBAR3/        SHELL:/BIN/CSH
SNOOPY
ON SINCE APRIL 14 17:09:23 ON TTYR6 FROM
USCS6.FEDWORLD.USTREAS.CUSTMS.GOV
```

His brilliant, twisted mind was now spinning with thoughts of survival. U.S. Customs? His fat, gluttonous body glistened with sweat. The Rat knew he couldn't safely finger a U.S. Treasury host directly and let some backfinger they had set up get a log entry on him. He'd have to go in some other way, get in and out like lightning, disconnecting from the Treasury host before someone started fingering him. His mind was racing. He knew now that he'd been followed into his invisible chat channel after the stack error. The Rat knew the sendmail program on any system always had to have high-level access rights since it had to be able to write and receive e-mail. Sendmail was notorious across the Net for security holes. CERT, the Computer Emergency Response Team, was constantly posting security hole bulletins.

As he set up a packet-sniffer on the incoming mail port, The Rat typed a message of praise to Satan. Messages telling Satan of his glory always mollified him:

"YOU ARE MORE BEAUTIFUL THAN DEATH. YOU ARE THE GOD OF FUCK AND MUTILATION," he wrote.

Then he wrote a program which would spoof sendmail at the Treasury host into executing a set of commands. He would have sendmail ''grab'' out all listings of telnet sessions to redbar3.cc.rutledge.edu. He would be waiting . . .

The instant it rolled off the top of his window, he hit <Ctrl>-<C> and killed off his connection to rutledge.

He looked through the scrollback buffer and saw:

```
LOGIN NAME: REDWITCH
IN REAL LIFE: KAREN DAWSON
DIRECTORY:/STAFF10/REDWITCH SHELL: /BIN/CSH
ON SINCE APRIL 14 17:02:51 ON TTYR6 FROM USCS-
STC5.GOV
```

It looked like this Karen Dawson person was logged via a modem from a Pacific Telephone POP (Point-of-Presence) in Studio City, California. Now, if only Karen Dawson would just stay logged on. He set his packet-sniffer on each phone connection to the POP, then set up a second window, which was the exact duplicate of the session he was having with Satan in his first window. That was the connection he would use to trace Karen Dawson.

He popped another disk into his PC from his kit. This one generated DTMF tones, "Touch-Tones" of a sort. In particular they generated an inquiry sequence similar to Caller ID. This had been designed by the phone company to allow customers to trigger an identification of any number on their system that was currently in use. It was a tracking device.

The Rat had his program send the tones. They left his computer in Florida and went through an intermediate host into the Electronic Switching System at UCLA and over to the 5-ESS switch in Studio City, California. Then the signal was traced back through The Rat's telnet connections and printed:

818/555-7693

The Rat knew he could easily get the address for this number, so he ended his conversation with Satan and shut off his equipment. Whoever had done this to him was brilliant, but The Rat now knew he was better. He had back-traced the intruder without her ever knowing. He stood up, his white body glistening in the sauna-like heat. The walls seemed to close in on him. He lumbered up the metal ladder, out onto the deck of the rusting garbage barge. The late-afternoon sun had turned the heavy cloud-strewn Florida sky orange. He didn't see its beauty. A horrifying thought had just struck him: Maybe this intrusion was the beginning of the two-thousand-three-hundred-day journey? Maybe his six years of torture had just started? He knew he could never survive it . . . but could he stop it? Could he close the door of redemptive cleansing once it had been opened? He didn't know the rules. Shirley had taken all the knowledge with her. He didn't have the answers. How could he find out?

He ran across the weeds and brambles in his bare feet and underwear, not even feeling the thorns. His run was always sort of a gallop. . . . They had teased him about it in grade school. He had looked stupid, slow, and uncoordinated on the playground, galloping as he ran. The sun was almost down when he got home. The pale moon was coming up over the swamp. He could hear the night birds flying low, hitting their wings against the swampy water. Insects keened in the humid darkness. When he got to the house, he ran downstairs and crouched in the corner of the basement, out of breath. He huddled there as the sweat cooled on his body. The Rat was vile and wretched, but his mind was clear.

"The cornered Rat will fight," he said, his voice a harsh whisper. He was already in terrible pain and he knew he couldn't stand the agony of the two thousand and three hundred days of redemptive punishment that Shirley had promised him. He knew he had to attack this clever eavesdropper. If he killed her, maybe it would close the door of his eternal cleansing.

When the screen went dark in Claire's den, it took a moment before the three of them said anything. The first to speak was Malavida: "That is one very sick puppy."

"I told you this remailer was a cesspool!" Karen said in triumph.

"It could just be a couple of white squirrels getting off, trying to horrify each other," Lockwood said, not really believing it. The ungodly nature of the messages rang true.

Karen got up from her seat and started pacing around the room. "You don't believe that and neither do I. . . . All that religious stuff, all that ersatz fire and brimstone, that's Grade A sexual repression. 'The wicked do not suffer punishment in the eternal hell and are not destroyed or annihilated in a special mosaic of cleansing.' . . . That sure ain't 'Onward Christian Soldiers.' "

Karen Dawson impressed Malavida more and more.

"Listen, guys . . . this *is* something. I know it," she

said. "The Rat sounds like a serial psychopath. According to him, he's on a two-week degenerating cycle. He said the coveting begins much earlier now, and he has to slow it down by mailing totems."

"What's a totem?" Malavida asked.

"It's a trophy," Lockwood said. "A body part . . . In this case, it sounds like he sent someone a hand."

"Get the fuck outta here," Malavida said in shock.

"Look, we've gotta go cross-check this through the FBI's VICAP serial crime computer in Washington," Karen said. "He said he killed and mutilated somebody in Atlanta. There's got to be a record of that. Let's get outta here." She moved to the desk and started to help Malavida unhook the modem from the phone and disconnect the monitor from the PC.

"We gotta get Malavida back to Lompoc," Lockwood reminded her. "I gotta drop him at the Burbank substation. I've made arrangements with the L.A. Sheriff to transport him up there tonight."

Malavida had been dreading this moment and now he made his play. "You're making a mistake, Jefe," he said. It was one of the few times he looked straight at Lockwood.

"I'm sure I am, but it happens all the time, so I don't let it bother me."

Malavida finished unhooking the computer and they moved the stuff into the living room, where Claire was standing with Heather.

"This guy constructed an invisible chat channel on the Internet," Malavida continued. "You know how hard that is to do? Forget for a moment that he's going around killing people. This guy is a real ace computer hacker. Nobody but me would have ever found that room, let alone gotten in there. He may even know we cracked in." That thought had been bothering Malavida. In his haste, he had not bothered to mask their location. "If he does know we were lurking, he'll be even tougher to find. If you ever want to catch him, you're gonna need me. Nobody else could do it. Certainly not that bunch of middle-lane road dogs you got working for you in Customs. I'll shoot this puke down. . . . You got the Snoopy double-your-money-back guarantee.''

"That's great, but I still have to get you back to the Federal pen or take a pile of heat, and I still have to catch the six o'clock flight out of Burbank to make my Internal Affairs hearing Monday morning.''

"Take me with you, Karen," Malavida said, his eyes turning soft as a puppy in the pound. "I can help you. Honest, I can. What good am I gonna do you in prison? You'll be wasting a generic resource.''

"Wasting a generic resource?" Lockwood said, amazed.

Then Karen nodded her head. "You should've seen him. He went through that computer's security like he had Nintendo magic mushrooms. I can't do what he can. Our only other choice is to just walk away from this, and I think this Wind Minstrel guy, or Rat or whoever he is, is white-hot. He's degenerating. If he's for real, he could kill again in two weeks or less.''

"Okay," Lockwood said after almost no thought. "I'm probably gonna get benched by IA tomorrow anyway. I might as well go ahead and clobber my pension while I'm at it.''

They loaded the stuff in the trunk of the LeBaron, and Lockwood went back to say good-bye to Heather. Claire was standing by the door with her hands on her hips and watched while he hugged and kissed his daughter. Then he faced Claire. She was so beautiful he was momentarily stopped. The afternoon light played on her face and made his heart ache. . . . How could he have let this divorce happen? He could find no words, so he walked back across the street, but she dogged him. When he turned and faced her, he was looking into ice-cold Nordic blue eyes.

"Thanks for bringing a convict over to meet our daughter, John.''

"Claire, he's just a computer hacker. He wouldn't hurt anybody.''

''One of these days, you're gonna get a sobering experience. I just hope it grows you up before somebody else gets hurt.'' Then she turned and walked back across the street and into the house. She never looked back.

# 13

## BACKTRACK

At seven o'clock Sunday evening, the blue-and-white Citation jet climbed out of a dingy brown smogbank that was choking L.A. and headed east across the San Gabriel Mountains.

Before it was seized by the U.S. Customs, the plane had belonged to a Colombian drug dealer who had outfitted it with a TV, videos, and electronic games. Malavida had found some Nintendo software and hooked it up. He had his feet up on the couch, halfheartedly playing Donkey Kong, gonzoing dinosaurs and collecting massive bunches of electronic bananas, while Karen began to construct a criminal profile of the man they had found on Pennet. She took out a yellow legal pad. Under "The Rat," she wrote: "a.k.a. 'Wind Minstrel'—male, probably Caucasian. Twenty-five to thirty-five, organized, compulsive, bad self-image . . . nocturnal?"

Across the aisle, Lockwood was on the Airfone trying to hose down an angry Harvey Knox.

"Look, Harvey, I know what you're saying and, believe me, if I could have gotten him back there by tonight, I would have. But this thing just started growing on me. I can't let him go back for a couple more days. You gotta call the prison for me, give 'em the big okey-dokey from DOJ."

"John, you kill me. I told you this was in the margin to begin with." Harvey's voice squeaked over the Airfone.

"Yeah, I know, but he's in custody, cuffed to a bed. Wanna talk to him?" He didn't wait for an answer. He put his hand over the receiver. "Hey, Malavida, pause that thing. This is Mr. Harvey Knox. . . . He's your stay-out-of-jail card, so be nice. The answer to any question he asks is: 'Mr. Lockwood told me I can't say anything about that.' "

Malavida paused the Donkey Kong and moved back and took the phone. "This is Malavida Chacone. It's a pleasure to talk to you, Mr. Knox," he said in perfect, unaccented English.

"Where are you guys? You in Lompoc?" Harvey asked.

"Well, sir, Mr. Lockwood said I can't say anything about that." He looked over at Lockwood who raised his eyebrow and nodded approval. "But, sir . . . I'm being very well guarded, and I promise there will be no problem, and I think I'm really helping the U.S. Prosecutor with this case."

"Who's prosecuting? Who you working with?"

"Mr. Lockwood said I can't say anything about that." Chacone repeated the sentence again as Lockwood smiled, put his feet up on the facing chair, and picked up a newspaper.

"Mr. Chacone, would you be kind enough to put that son-of-a-bitch Lockwood back on?"

"Yes, sir. And it was a pleasure making your acquaintance."

Malavida handed the phone to Lockwood and went back to Donkey Kong.

It took Lockwood another five minutes to strike the right note with Harvey, who reluctantly agreed to make the call to the prison. The phone connection started to get weak as they passed out of California.

"Where're you calling from? This line sounds funny.

You in the air? You're in the air, aren't you, you son-of-a-bitch!''

"I'm on a scrambled line at a protected location, Harvey. You know better than to ask me where I'm interviewing a Federal witness in the protection program. I'm surprised at you. I gotta run. Make that call or we're both toast." And he was off the phone as the static started to sound like bacon frying at a Boy Scout cook-out.

Lockwood knew that the small Citation jet didn't have the fuel capacity to fly all the way back to Washington. They would have to make a gas stop somewhere along the way. He felt the plane make a banking turn and glanced up at the "air show" in the cabin that depicted their location. According to the electronic video map, they had just passed over the California/Arizona border. "I'd like to get him to set down in Atlanta . . ." Lockwood said to Karen, who was still scribbling notes followed by question marks on her yellow pad. "If The Rat killed a girl in Atlanta, it'd be nice to talk to the homicide dicks . . . maybe take a look at the crime scene."

"Atlanta is a little out of the way, isn't it?"

"Not really," he said earnestly. "Instead of taking the boring, obvious route over Missouri and Kentucky, we'll take the more cultural southern route through the glorious picturesque Panhandle." He realized, as he looked at the video map, that this route would add hundreds of miles to the journey.

"Red will never go for it," Karen said. "We kept him waiting in Burbank as it was."

Lockwood took a deep breath and lunged out of his chair. "We'll never know if I don't try," he said as he moved up to see his old buddy.

In the cockpit, Lockwood settled into the seat beside Red and looked out the windshield at the clear night and the twinkling lights below. "You ever had Georgia cray-fish in Cajun gumbo?" he said, knowing Red's weakness for food. "They've got the best Cajun food in the entire South in downtown Atlanta. . . . Joint's called Little

Beauregard's. It's even better than New Orleans Cajun.''

"I'm not refueling in Atlanta, John. 'Sides, there's a weather front down there.'' That was where they started. It took Lockwood almost forty minutes, and the Dallas game off his Redskins season tickets, to talk Red into the course correction.

They made their approach to DeKalb Peachtree Airport in Atlanta at two A.M., Monday morning. A thunderstorm was throwing big chunks of lightning around in thick, ominous cumulonimbus clouds. They got bounced around badly on the approach, before Red finally got the wheels down and rolled out on the rain-washed tarmac. He taxied to a stop in front of the Executive Air Terminal. Red got out and ran through the downpour to the private executive lounge to try to find the gas truck driver.

Lockwood, Karen, and Malavida stood in the jet's door for a moment and watched the pelting rain. Lockwood had put the cuffs back on Malavida. They turned up their collars and made a run for it through the wet night into the terminal.

Ten minutes later a taxi arrived, and they promised Red they'd be back in three hours. He had decided to sleep on the sofa in the terminal till they returned. He told them if they didn't get back by six A.M., he was taking off without them.

The Atlanta Police Department was housed in a huge building on Ponce de Leon Drive. It was extremely busy at three A.M. There were more cops standing around than Lockwood guessed would be normal for the graveyard shift. He'd been in enough cop shops over the years to spot an angry vibe. The blues stood in clusters, wearing crisp uniforms and slack expressions. Lockwood knew something must have just happened. They found the Chief of Detectives for the watch. He was a rumpled twenty-year veteran named Bryce Oakland. Sometime during his twenty, he'd taken a knife or a bullet in his vocal cords. The scar ran down his neck, into his day-old white shirt collar. When he spoke, his voice sounded like sandpaper on steel. His unpleasant attitude said he didn't have much time for them as he settled into his squeaking wooden swivel chair in the command cubicle. Glass walls looked in both directions at the littered homicide squad room. He glared at them over a walnut desk that had been scarred by the rings of insolent killers. . . . FUCK YOU appeared in three languages.

"This is Karen Dawson," Lockwood began. "She's a U.S. Customs psychologist and criminal profiler. And this is Mr. Chacone. He's a Federal informant."

"Looks like a Federal convict to me," Bryce Oakland said as he glanced at the handcuffs.

"Just think of those as funky New Wave jewelry."

"You're a funny guy, Agent Lockwood, but I'm having a horrible night. I had a patrolman pull over a hot roller 'bout two hours ago. One a'them boys in the stolen car opened up on my man, who's in Atlanta General breathing through a tube and, according to the docs, ain't never gonna wake up. Right now, half my department is up outta bed. They got their noses wide and their shotguns cocked. If they find those hucklebucks, I'm gonna have a hollow-point street dance on my hands, but in my spare time, what can I do to serve my Federal government?"

Karen leaned forward. "Hey, Captain Oakland, we didn't come here to get in your way. We're working a degenerating, homicidal-sexual psychopath, and we think our perp may have killed here. Maybe he even lives here. Now, if that's too much trouble for you, could you please turn us over to somebody who can give up a few minutes without pissing all over us?"

Lockwood was taken aback by Karen's approach. He'd never seen her like this. Then she softened slightly. "I'm sorry about your patrolman," she added and reached into her purse, took out some bills, and put them on his desk. "I'm sure there's a fund that's been started for the patrolman's family. There's fifty you can add to it. But a killing is a killing, and it shouldn't be more important because the victim's a police officer."

Bryce Oakland leaned back. The chair squeaked in the suddenly too-quiet room. Finally, he nodded his head. "Point taken. Go on."

"Did you have a killing here, a murder of a woman, probably happened a few days ago . . . ?" Lockwood asked.

"This is a big ol' place I'm policing. I got a population a'five million. I got twenty-five hundred square miles. I got hooker murders every night or so in them skin shops down on the Chattahoochee River. Maybe you could be a little more specific."

"This one you wouldn't miss," Karen said. "It was probably a hard kill with peri-mortem mutilation. . . . The UnSub probably also had peri-mortem sexual paraphernalia."

". . . the fuck you talkin' about?" he rasped. "Speak English. The what?"

"UnSub," Lockwood said. "It stands for unknown subject. We use that term to avoid saying 'him' and subconsciously attaching a gender specification."

"The body was sexually attacked, ferociously . . . probably mutilated at the time of death," she added, finishing the translation.

"That sounds like that Financial District killing. Happened Saturday morning, woman in her thirties. Perp killed her, hacked her arms off. Name was Candice Wilcox."

"Can we see the homicide folder?" Lockwood asked as Bryce leaned forward, put his meaty arms on the desk, and glared at them. "We'd also like to go see where it happened, if that can be arranged," Lockwood said, pushing his luck.

"Okay, I'll give you a couple'a them trigger-happy troopers out there. Anything to keep 'em from sitting around, rubbin' Hoppe's Number Nine on their sidearms. The detective on that case is off duty. I'll have to call and wake the poor bastard and ask him if he don't mind if ya see his notes."

"If it's not too much trouble," Lockwood said, as

Bryce got up and moved out of the cubicle. When he was gone, Lockwood turned to Karen. ''You don't pull any punches, do you?''

''Just a little psychology. He was angry about his police officer. That cop means a lot to him, so he put him first, our dead woman second. I caught him leaning the wrong way, and to make up for it, he's now over-compensating.''

Lockwood nodded. He had been worried about getting cooperation when they first walked in and felt the intensity in the place. Karen had quickly turned that to their advantage.

The two police officers who drove them to the Atlanta Financial District were both lost in thoughts of their fallen comrade. When they arrived, there was a young man with curly hair and a thick moustache waiting for them at the door of a ten-story building named Hoyt Tower. He was holding a case file and looked about twenty-five. He introduced himself as Detective Bill Stiner and said he was the primary on the Wilcox homicide. The rain had stopped, but thunder and sheet lightning still rumbled on the Atlanta horizon like Sherman's artillery. The security guard let them into the lobby and they went up to the fourth floor to the offices of Cavanaugh and Cunningham. The crime scene had been totally destroyed since the murder. The floors had been scrubbed of Candice's blood, but tomorrow, Lockwood suspected, the people who worked here would come to work and subconsciously walk around the offending spot where her body had been found.

Lockwood and Karen both read the crime scene and lab reports. Then they looked at the victim's desk and watched while Stiner showed them the location where the body had been found. Lockwood opened Stiner's folder and laid out several gruesome crime scene photographs. Malavida flinched, then moved over to the windows and stood there with his back to them, rattling his handcuffs. Lockwood studied the photographs—the clean surgical cuts, the identical incisions on both shoulders. The killer had placed Candice Wilcox's sweater over her face. The scissors from her desk set had been shoved into her vagina. The UnSub had branded her on the left breast. Lockwood studied the brand:

R. 13–15

Something started tugging at his thoughts. He passed the pictures to Karen.

"The burglar alarm went off at seven-thirty A.M.," Stiner said. "When we got here, at about seven-forty-five, we found the body. She monitored foreign money exchanges for this firm at night and was alone on the floor. The coroner measured her liver temperature at eight o'clock and it indicated that she had just died. So we figure that the killer set off the silent alarm when he entered by the Center Street door at seven-thirty A.M. We also figure that while the security guard was checking the building, the perp came up here and killed her . . . did the mutilations. We musta just missed him."

Karen sat down at Candice Wilcox's desk and looked carefully at the crime scene photographs. Then she reached into her purse and took out her yellow pad. She began to add to the list she had started on the plane. The scissors that were stuck into the vagina were a sexual substitute, so she wrote down: "Sexually immature, inadequate individual."

"I think it's possible he may have stood here and masturbated," Karen said. "Did you check her body for semen?"

"I don't think so, not yet," Stiner said. "The autopsy won't be till nine this morning."

"Check. If he's a secretor, we could get a blood type from the semen," Lockwood said.

Karen looked at the pictures again. The sweater was carefully placed across Candice Wilcox's face. . . . She felt this could mean one of two things. The killer could have felt bad about the crime after committing it and covered her face as some show of respect. . . . Karen tried to think like this monster. The scissors connoted anger, sexual frustration. The mutilations had been precise and surgical. The post-mortem behavior had been methodical. The killer had stayed with her for a long time, working to remove the arms. . . . Karen didn't think he had respect for Candice Wilcox. After she was dead he had butchered her, harvesting body parts. She decided the sweater had not been placed there because he felt bad about the crime. . . . On her yellow pad she wrote: "Possibly very ugly, even disfigured." She thought it was possible the UnSub had covered Candice's face so her lifeless eyes would not stare at him. She studied the brand. It looked like an S inside a C . . . It could mean anything. It looked partially like the Chinese yin-and-yang symbol, but not exactly. She sketched it and copied the symbol along with the "R. 13–15" that appeared underneath. She wondered if it was some kind of computer symbol. She would study it in detail later.

Karen then turned the page and started a file on Candice Wilcox. Under her name, she wrote: "Victimology." She knew that profiling the victim was as important as profiling the UnSub. On this page she wrote: "Blond, thirty, Caucasian." She was almost certain that the UnSub was also white. . . . Ritual or serial killers almost never kill outside of their own racial group. She thought it was probable that Candice had been a victim of choice. She had been selected by the UnSub for murder. There had to be some specific reason why she had been targeted for death. What did she represent to the killer? How had he selected her? What were the things about Candice that had led her to this terrible end? Candice did not seem to have led a life that would make her an easy target. She wasn't a prostitute or a small child who could easily be lured into a stranger's car; she had been working in a secure building, with a guard at the door. It was a high-risk crime committed against a low-risk victim—a difficult crime to pull off. Karen flipped the page back to her criminal profile. Under "UnSub," she added, "Possibly very smart, cautious.'' Her primary list of profile characteristics was beginning to grow.

She continued to study the photographs of the crime scene. She saw that the head was lower than the torso and that there was a large pool of blood around the body. Then she noticed the books propped under Candice.

''I wonder why he had these books under her like this?'' she said.

''We don't know,'' Stiner replied.

''Sometimes a psychopathic killer will arrange a body in a special way,'' she said.

''You mean posing the corpse?'' Stiner asked.

''Well, I'm not sure,'' Karen said, chewing on the tip of her pen. ''There's a difference between posing and staging. I'm not sure yet which this is. Posing is something the killer can't control, it's part of his ritual. . . . He has to degrade the body for psychological reasons, dealing with a whole range of emotions—anger, hatred of women or his mother, sexual fantasy. Staging, on the other hand, is a post-mortem behavior aimed at throwing the police off.''

Stiner looked at her for a long moment. ''No kidding?'' She nodded and looked again at the pictures. ''So which is this?'' he continued.

''I don't know for sure. . . . Let me take a guess.'' She looked at the spot on the floor where Candice had died . . . then back up at Stiner and Lockwood. Malavida was still at the window, but he had turned slightly to listen to her.

''This crime scene was organized,'' she said, studying the pictures. ''That means the guy we're dealing with is slightly older than the mean age of sex killers, which is twenty-five. He's more sophisticated, less frenzied. He cleaned up after himself. Probably used garbage bags to carry the limbs out, because there's no blood trail I can see from the crime scene pictures of the hall or the staircase.''

''That's what we figured,'' Detective Stiner said.

''My guess is that since he cleaned up after himself,

this thing with the books probably isn't ritual. He was trying to throw the police off somehow. I think it's staging.''

''How would that do anything?'' Stiner asked, puzzled.

Lockwood moved away from them and stood looking out the window. He could see down into the still-wet street and he wondered if the killer had watched her from there. Her desk was near the window. After a minute, Karen moved over to where he was standing and noticed a frown on his face. ''What is it?'' she asked.

''Karen, did you ever take any pre-med when you were getting your doctorates?''

Malavida was standing next to them, listening.

''They aren't that kind of doctorates.''

''Well, I've been to maybe a hundred autopsies,'' he continued, still looking down into the street. ''You have any idea how hard it is to sever somebody's arms like that? How long it takes? You need bone saws and clamps, extremely sharp instruments. Those photographs show clean incisions. Clean bone cuts. This guy didn't do this in a frenzy. This was methodical. I just . . .''

They stood in silence and waited for him to finish his thought.

''. . . Okay, so he comes in, sets off the alarm at seven-thirty. He kills her, surgically removes both arms, brands her, then arranges the body with books . . . then bags all this up, cleans up the site, and leaves. All of this in fifteen minutes?'' He turned now to face them. ''That sound right to you?''

''Liver temperature is just approximate. It could be longer,'' Karen said.

''You know why he might have arranged the body like that? With the books under it?'' Lockwood said, looking at the place on the floor where her body was found.

''No, why?''

''This is just a guess, but maybe he was trying to drain it so it wouldn't register lividity.''

''Lividity?'' Karen said. ''If I remember correctly, lividity doesn't take place for eight or nine hours. So why would he worry about lividity? When the police arrived, her liver temp was still one hundred and one degrees. The liver is a chemical factory, the hottest organ in the body. In a normal human, it is one hundred and two degrees, and cools at one point five degrees per hour. That means the police found her body less than an hour after he killed her.''

Malavida was again very impressed. Karen Dawson really knew her stuff.

''If he couldn't have done these amputations in fifteen minutes, then maybe the whole timetable is off,'' Lockwood continued.

''How could it be off? The burglar alarm marks the entry,'' Karen replied.

''I don't know. . . . Maybe he changed the timetable somehow.''

Malavida sat down at one of the desks, took the plastic cover off the computer, and turned it on. . . . The PC booted up and the screen said:

```
HOYT LOGIN:
```

He typed in:

```
ROOT
```

And the computer said:

```
PASSWORD:
```

He typed the most common supervisor password, which was:

```
GOD
```

And the computer responded:

```
WELCOME TO HOYT TOWER
YOU ARE LOGGED IN TO HOST HOYT AS ROOT.
GOOD EVENING, ROOT.
```

Malavida smiled, then scanned the directories on the host computer. He saw one called /urs/bin/building and moved into that directory. There he saw a program, EnviroLog, which he knew contained all of the major systems in the building including phone, security, fire, etc. He typed:

```
ENVIROLOG
```

And in a few seconds the system said:

```
ENVIROLOG VERSION 3.1.2
ENTER YOUR PASSWORD:
```

"I could get into the guts of this thing if I had my tool kit," he said, "but I left it on the plane. . . ."

"What are you looking for?" Karen asked.

"I won't know till I see it. But we already know this guy is a master hacker, and all these new buildings are run by computers. I was thinking, what if he gronked that alarm, triggered it somehow, then bogused the time when it started ringing . . . ? That wouldn't be hard to do. He could set a different time of death by accessing the security program for the building. I can crack in here by random trial and error, but it could take hours. The other way is, we get the building supervisor outta the sack and try to get him to do it, but he won't probably get here for an hour. Then he's gonna wanna get permission from the building's owner, who won't get in till noon. So why don't we save all the hassle and get my metal suitcase full of cracker-jacks."

Lockwood looked at his watch and then at one of the patrolmen who was standing near the elevator, staring at his shoes. It was already 4:30 in the morning. Lockwood was supposed to be in the D.C. fifth-floor conference room at 9:00 A.M. to face his IA trial board. If he missed that, he'd be dust. He wondered why he didn't give a damn. "Could one of your guys run Miss Dawson out to the airport and back?" he finally asked a patrolman, who glanced at Stiner. Stiner nodded his approval and Karen left with him.

Forty minutes later, she was back with Malavida's metal suitcase. The Chicano cracker opened it up and started selecting disks. The sun was just coming up on the cloudy horizon as he started, hunched over his keyboard. He was still in handcuffs. Malavida knew he needed to get them off if he was going to get loose from Lockwood. He looked over at the Customs agent. "Can't we lose the jewelry, Hoss?" He said, smiling. "I'm not going nowhere."

Lockwood hesitated.

"For God's sake," Karen said sharply. "What are you worried about? You've got a gun. Where's he gonna go?"

Malavida held up his manacled hands, and finally Lockwood unhooked the handcuffs from the waist chain to give him more mobility, but he didn't take them off.

"You're very careful, Zanzo," Malavida said as he turned back to the computer and Karen glowered at Lockwood.

Malavida had tried the system supervisor password, GOD, but the EnviroLog program's password was different and would have to be obtained from scratch. He worked patiently as time clicked silently off everybody's wristwatch.

At 5:50, Lockwood picked up the phone, dialed the Executive Air Terminal, and got Red on the line. When Karen had returned to get Malavida's suitcase, she'd seen him sleeping there on the sofa and decided not to wake him.

"Look, this is taking a bit longer than I thought," he told the pilot.

"I gotta go at six-thirty, John. I got the D.O.C. coming back to Washington. I'm on standby for him. If I'm not in the Ready Room when he calls to use his bird, my ass gets transferred back out in the field, and I'll be taking nut-pucker rides on Doper Cessnas again. This is the best job I've had in this outfit and I'm not gonna lose it.''

''Six-forty-five,'' Lockwood pleaded.

''I'm wheels-up at six-thirty, with or without ya.''

At six-thirty, just as Red roared down the Atlanta runway in the empty Citation and lifted off for Washington, D.C., Malavida finally got into the building computer and began surfing around in the security system, while Lockwood and Karen and Detective Stiner all watched over his shoulder. He accessed the records for Saturday morning, April 13, the day the police thought Candice had been killed. The security profile for that morning showed that the Center Street fire door alarm had gone off at 7:30 A.M., just as the police said. Malavida moved on. When he finally got to the environmental log, he wasn't paying too much attention so he almost missed it. He had already scrolled that log off the screen when his mind caught up with his vision. Had he seen a slight jitter on one of the log files? He opened it again and began to study the information more carefully. He saw that the building environment was broken up into forty different zones. The one that said 4-W had a slight quiver when he scrolled by it. He leaned in and looked at it more carefully. Then he backed the log up to April 12 and looked at 4-W.

''What is it?'' Karen asked.

''I don't know. There's a phase jitter on this EnviroLog data. On 4-W, for April thirteenth . . . but not on the twelfth. Snoopy smells dogshit.''

''What's 4-W?'' Lockwood asked.

''Not sure, think it's the west side of the building, fourth floor,'' Malavida said.

''That's this office. We're on the west side,'' Stiner said.

''No shit.'' Malavida grinned. ''So what do we have here, Curado?'' he said to the screen. Then he started to bring up other file information . . . under Power Monitor: no surges, no sags, nothing . . . Phone Usage: nothing . . .

Then he opened the time and temperature log again and paged down. He leaned closer, scrolling the log quickly up and down. . . . He saw something. There was a minute difference in how one of the columns of data lined up on one part of the temperature log.

"Something isn't right about the temp log," he said, looking at the time and temperature readings for April 12–13, from 10:30 P.M. Friday night to 7:30 A.M. Saturday morning.

"What?" Karen asked, leaning in.

"I think there's some kinda bogus log that's been substituted for the actual log, giving out its own information. Just a minute . . ." He typed:

```
RESTORE-I
ADD ENVIROLOG.LOG/APRIL 12–13, 22:30–07:30
EXTRACT
```

And like magic, the bogus log that The Wind Minstrel had laid down in place of the temperature log disappeared.

"*Hola,*" he said. And they all leaned in.

"It went up to a hundred and six degrees in here," Karen said.

"My man changed the temperature." Malavida grinned. "He cranked it up to a hundred six; then, look here . . . at six-thirty it starts going down again. At seven-thirty, it was back to seventy-two degrees."

"How'd he do that?" Lockwood asked.

"Crafted some program to overwrite the files," Malavida said.

"Can you get that program? Download it?" Lockwood asked.

"It's probably not here," Malavida said as he looked around for the bogus EnviroLog. "But that's not surprising. If I was going to do this, I'd put in some kinda odor eater to erase the thing after it's done its work. He couldn't erase the temperature listing, so he just stuck a bogus log in front of it for camouflage. Unless a very clever *vato* was sniffin', you'd never see it,'' Malavida said, exposing some ego.

A minute went by as Lockwood stood, thinking. ''Okay, so when did he kill her? He obviously was trying to alter the time frame to give himself an alibi.''

''The temperature started changing at ten-thirty Friday evening. That's gotta be the new time of death,'' Karen said, looking in at the screen.

''Shit . . . wait a minute, I got an idea,'' Malavida said, and he surfed back into the security log and searched until he found the exact time the alarm was set off . . . 7:31:07.

Malavida accessed the Southern Bell accounts log. He was looking for a long-distance call to the building phone number that came in at exactly 7:31:07 Saturday morning. It took him only ten more minutes to find it. The call was made from a cellphone, so he could only trace it to its general area code; half an hour later he determined that the call had been made from Tampa, Florida.

# 14

## LEONARD

Leonard Land had awakened in the basement of his house. He didn't know why he was there, but he knew he had to hurry. It was 4:30 on Sunday afternoon. He grabbed a suitcase and drove his dark blue pickup straight to the Tampa Airport. He bought a ticket in coach on the American Airlines 5:30 flight to Los Angeles.

His row was halfway back in the L-1011. He had the aisle seat, but his huge body overflowed it; twice the flight attendants tripped over his legs as they rushed back and forth on their important pre-flight tasks. Manufactured air came out of the nozzle above his head and spilled down on him like the cold breath of redemption. He looked at his green corduroy pants, stretched tight over his huge, corpulent thighs. He was wearing a Disney World ballcap to hide his shiny naked head, but no matter how hard he tried to camouflage his grotesqueness, people still stared at him.

Leonard tried not to exist. In the back room of the computer store, sometimes he could concentrate so hard on a program, it was almost as if he ceased to be. Leonard could be free of himself in cyberspace. When boxes of new components arrived at ComputerLand from IBM or Texas Instruments, it was always Leonard whom Mr. Cathcart asked to assemble them. When he was working with new equipment, he could disappear, completely transported by the challenge . . . but afterward, inevitably, he would return. He would go to lunch and people pointed at him and whispered behind their hands. Leonard was forced to wear his awkward ugliness like a sandwich-board.

He missed his mother. He'd read in an old newspaper that she had burned to death in a fire. He couldn't remember the day it happened. Sometimes the anguish of missing her was so great, he lay in his bed and cried. . . . Tears would roll down his hairless cheeks onto his sheets. Leonard was very alone, always frightened and confused. He couldn't remember long periods of time; sometimes whole weeks would disappear from his memory like misplaced keys. Like waking up in his basement with a mission to go to L.A. and not knowing why. He had become terrified of these huge blacknesses . . . these holes in his existence. He wondered where he had been. His time cards at ComputerLand said he had been at work, but he couldn't remember any of it. Once he had found dried blood all over his torso and legs. He didn't know why or where it had come from.

He wasn't sure why he had to go to Los Angeles, but he knew his very survival was at stake. He had an address and a message written in his spiral notebook. . . . It was in his own handwriting but, try as he would, he was unable to remember writing it.

The seat-belt sign was turned off and he struggled up out of his seat. He took his small notebook and lumbered to the lavatory. He went inside and locked the door. The fluorescent lights shone down on him, finding only ugliness on his huge, fat face . . . his sagging eyelids, his horrible burned and scarred ears. He sat on the lavatory seat and opened the notebook:

GO TO 1265 MOORPARK STREET, STUDIO CITY.
CLOSE THE DOOR OF REDEMPTION.

He looked at the note again, reading it over yet one more time. *What door of redemption?* he wondered. *What does it mean?*

Leonard found the small wood-frame house on Moorpark, then parked the rental car across the street. He didn't know why he was there. He looked at his watch. It was 12:30 A.M. in Tampa, but only 9:30 P.M. here in Los Angeles. He reset his watch. Was that important? Was the door of redemption in the house across the street? He was frightened, confused, and alone.

He put his head back and touched his nipples. They were stinging slightly against the fabric of his shirt. He watched as a tall, beautiful blond woman with very short hair drove her blue Volvo into the garage, got out with some groceries, and walked toward the house. She entered and closed the door. He put his head back on the headrest and, in minutes, went to sleep.

The Rat woke up at ten and moved across the street, clutching his case. His eardrums pumped the rhythm of his heartbeat. He knew where he was and what he'd come to do. He moved in darkness around the small house, looking in the windows. The Rat had never killed. He had coveted but never possessed. He was frightened of his mission. He knew The Wind Minstrel was three or four days from coming, but he couldn't wait. He had to close the door of redemption. He walked to the back of the house. A child's easel was set up there. He looked at it and wondered where the child was. Then he saw, through the window, that a blond woman was preparing food in the kitchen. He moved to the back porch and stood, listening. The eavesdropper had been calling from this address. Could the tall, beautiful woman in the kitchen be Karen Dawson, who had been lurking in his chat room?

As always, The Rat had taken his sneaky precautions. After he had found the eavesdropper, he had made his plan. He had tracked the LAPD number long distance from Tampa and begun cracking into the police computer, while frantically packing The Wind Minstrel's tools for Leonard to take. He had finally broken through the LAPD's computer security and had saved the entire dialup and login sequence to the Police Mobile Digital Terminal system for Studio City. He stored it in a fully automated script on his PC which he could recall at any time.

He now put his fat, hairless hand on the back doorknob of the house in Studio City and tried it. It was open. The Rat took out his gloves and put them on. He set the suitcase down on the dewy, wet grass and popped it open. He removed the shiny scalpels that The Wind Minstrel used to possess. They seemed awkward and heavy in his hand. He closed the suitcase and carried it with him as he moved to the back door. Could this tall, beautiful woman work for U.S. Customs? he wondered. Could she possibly be clever enough to penetrate the mysteries of his secret room? Had Shirley sent this bitch to open the door to his two-thousand-three-hundred-day Journey of Redemption?

He opened the back door and silently entered the sun-room. He set down the suitcase and moved toward the kitchen. Finally, he pushed open the swinging door. He carried only the long scalpel with the number 10006 blade. He put the surgical instrument between his teeth. He was not coveting. He was not possessing. The Rat was fighting to protect his immortal soul. Before he killed her, he had to ask her questions. He needed to know the answers.

She had her back to him when he entered the kitchen, but she heard footsteps.

''Heather, how was the movie? I didn't hear Mrs. Klein's car pull up.'' She was turning, smiling when he attacked her. He grabbed her and clapped his big, meaty hand over her mouth, cutting off her scream. Then he hit her hard with his fist. She sagged in his arms but did not go down. She fought him savagely as he tried to control her, slashing wildly in fear with his knife.

The Rat dragged her into the bedroom, tipping over a

bedside table, breaking a lamp. He threw her on the bed and hit her again, knocking her unconscious. He pulled down all the blinds and stood in front of her, whimpering. He didn't know how to wake her. He needed to know the answers. Then he placed his hand over her mouth and held her nose. She choked, coughed, and opened her eyes.

"Why were you in my secret room?" he asked.

"What . . . ? Who . . . ?" Claire was struggling to get her mind to focus. She was looking up at a huge man she had never seen before. She fought to control her spiraling emotions. Panic would only make things worse.

He leaned down close to her; his breath was sour. "I see only what he lets me see. The final vision is hidden. I don't understand the cleansing, but I will not suffer," he told her. "I will not suffer or be tortured for six years. So, you answer me," he said in a deadly whisper.

Claire had seen him too late to defend herself in the kitchen, but now, lying on the bed, she started to take stock of her situation. He was huge but slow, and obviously deranged. She was strong and quick, with good upper-body strength. She hoped she could mollify him until she got her senses back in order. He had hit her hard and she was still fighting to clear her mind.

"I have the mark of the Beast on me," The Rat told her. "The mark of the Beast is for unclean sinners. It cannot be refuted or changed. But I will not be tortured for crimes I was told to commit," he said, as if that would explain the scalpel and his presence in her bedroom.

"I understand."

"Were you the one who eavesdropped?"

She didn't know what to tell him. She didn't know what he was talking about.

"You will answer."

"I don't . . . I—"

And he swung the scalpel, slicing her right arm open. She screamed in terror and pain as he hit her again with a short, chopping blow. It knocked her back into the headboard. And then he heard a high scream behind him. He turned and, standing in the bedroom doorway, there was a beautiful blond girl, about ten. He lumbered up to grab her, but the woman on the bed kneed him in the groin, grabbed him, and, with a strength he would never have thought she possessed, pulled him back on top of her. Her blood-soaked right arm found her left wrist behind his huge back. She clung to him.

"Leggo . . . leggo me," he gasped in panic. The Rat had no experience. He had never killed. The girl had seen him. The Wind Minstrel would never have made such a mistake.

"Heather, run! Call the police!" the woman screamed. The Rat pulled half-free, enough so he could grab the scalpel on the bedspread where it had fallen. The little girl ran. He knew he had to move fast to catch the child, but the woman was struggling to keep him from following. She held him with the strength of a demon. He lifted the scalpel high over his head.

Claire saw his hand come down, but barely felt the scalpel as it plunged into her chest. She was holding on, gouging with her nails. She knew if she could only hold him for a few more seconds, Heather would have time to get away. She heard her daughter screaming for help in the front yard. Claire desperately held on. She felt the pain when the scalpel was pulled from her chest, and then she saw it coming down again. This time, her heart exploded when it plunged into her. She felt a terrible agony shooting in all directions . . . through her chest, her arms and legs, out to the tips of her fingers. She felt a convulsion rack her. Then, as if somebody had pulled a curtain on her life, she saw black and let go of the man attacking her. Her last hope was that she had saved her daughter's life.

The Rat was soaked with her blood. He started to whimper in fear. He grabbed his computer and sat at the table in the den. He was shaking uncontrollably, dripping her blood on the keys. He didn't know how much time had passed, but then he heard a distant siren and it snapped him alert. . . . *Be cunning, be shrewd. You are the planner and the schemer*, his mind lectured him. He hooked up the modem to the phone and turned on the power.

Then he hit a key and started the automated script which accessed the dialup and login sequence he had cracked earlier. Within a minute he was into the LAPD computer dispatch system. Suddenly, the LAPD Mobile Digital Terminal dispatch popped up on his screen:

```
LOS ANGELES POLICE DEPARTMENT
MOBILE DIGITAL TERMINAL
DISPATCH SYSTEM
```

He chose the option:

```
REVIEW ACTIVE CALLS
```

And scrolled it to the last computer call:

```
INCIDENT#6108002340 UNIT 15A56 HANDLE CODE 3
ADW SUSPECT THERE NOW                3245X
1265 MOORPARK STREET
MORE ADDITIONAL
```

He scrolled down and saw a unit confirmation:

```
15A56 WILL BUT THAT CALL
WILL HANDLE CODE 3
```

He could hear the siren in the distance getting nearer. He typed a new address into the computer, reversing only the first two digits, hoping this would look to the police later on like a simple transposition mistake.

He sent the new message:

```
INCIDENT #6108002340 UNIT 15A56        3245X
RESPONDENT REPORTS *INCORRECT* *ADDRESS*
```

```
GO TO
2165 MOORPARK STREET
```

He hit the "SEND" option and waited, his heart pounding. The siren was getting closer: on this very block, approaching the house. Then it stopped and seemed to turn around. He could hear the police car siren speed away, the piercing sound diminishing. He grabbed his laptop and his suitcase, packed everything up, and ran through the mess he had made, out of the house through the front door. He was frightened and galloped as he ran. He got into the rental car and pulled out and down the street, going fast.

From the house next door, Heather watched him go. She was crying. "Why did the police go away?" she asked the next-door neighbors. The man and woman shook their heads, bewildered.

It was twenty minutes before the police returned. By then, Heather had already found her dead mother's body and was sitting on the floor in a corner of the bedroom, her mother's blood all over. The police tried to question her, but Heather Lockwood was deep in shock.

# 15

## FREEDOM AND REGRET

**M**alavida saw his opening when he first scanned the building graphics on the Hoyt Tower computer, but he wasn't quite sure how to use it. He knew Lockwood was sharp and had a tender ear for bullshit. Malavida figured this was going to be his only chance to escape, but he had a few problems to solve: First, he had to get the handcuff key out of Lockwood's pocket and into a place where he could get at it; second, he had to lure Lockwood, Karen, and the two Atlanta patrol officers into the file room he'd spotted on the sixth floor. Fortunately, Detective Stiner had been forced to leave on another call. The question was how best to do it. He had been turning over the problem in his mind for almost an hour while he'd worked with Lockwood and Karen, uncovering potential clues the killer had left in the Atlanta building's computer. He knew he could send the security system a time-delayed command, but once he set events in motion, the timetable would be critical and there would be no turning back. Half an hour ago, he'd started to write a pirate program that would accomplish his plan. It was now almost complete, but time was short. He could see that Lockwood was getting ready to pull out. In the last hour, the Customs agent had become restless. That could work to Malavida's advantage. He knew that once they were on a plane headed to Washington, his chances of escape would diminish drastically. All of these things were playing in his mind when God stepped in and changed the flight schedule.

The electrical storm which had been hovering at the edge of the horizon all night finally rolled back in and pelted the eight o'clock traffic with BB-sized hailstones. A thick cold front moved in behind the storm and buried Atlanta in a blanket of fog. Lockwood called the airport, but it was closed. The agent was staring morosely out the window at the gray soup, unable to even see the drug-store across the street. His body language indicated that he was in a different place. Jumpiness had been replaced with an uninterested calm. Malavida knew now was the best time to try his escape. He hit Enter on his computer, then surreptitiously uploaded his pirate program into the building's host computer.

"Gotta go to the bathroom, Jefe," he said softly.

Lockwood continued staring out the window at the thick fogbank. "One of the patrolmen will take you," he said, not turning from the window.

"You gotta uncuff me."

That got Lockwood's attention. The Fed turned from the window and looked at Malavida.

"Not very damn likely," he said, his voice flat as an Iowa landscape.

Malavida leaned forward. "Gotta shit, man. How'm I supposed to do that with these on, huh? Dumb and Dumber over there can cover me while I take care a'business," he said, indicating the two Atlanta cops.

Lockwood was not paying very close attention to Malavida's request. His mind was replaying the dark fugue of self-destruction he had orchestrated for himself.

"Come on, man. . . . What's with you?"

"One of you guys go with him," Lockwood finally said to the two Atlanta cops as he pulled the handcuff key out of his pocket and moved over and unlocked the bracelets.

Malavida got up and stretched elaborately. He had deliberately left his computer on. The screen showed a computer graphic of the sixth floor, which included the windowless steel-doored file room he had found. He assumed it was part of the building's management complex. His pirate program had now pre-set his commands into the Hoyt Tower security computer. He had given it a fifteen-second delay from the time the computer in the file room was accessed. He hoped that would be enough time. Now all he had to do was lure all of them up there and activate the plan. That was going to be the tricky part.

The taller of the two Atlanta patrolmen got to his feet and accompanied Malavida as he went into the lobby in search of the men's room. It was ten to nine on Monday morning and the building was now filling with employees of Cavanaugh and Cunningham. They got off the elevator like reluctant children, talking in low, tense voices as they moved to their desks and set down briefcases and purses. Candice's murder had been on all the weekend TV newscasts. The employees looked around, their eyes darting over Lockwood, Karen, and the one remaining Atlanta cop. Then, with hooded glances, they looked for the spot on the floor where Candice Wilcox had made her last stand.

The men's room on the fourth floor was a white tile rectangle, over-lit with bright fluorescents. The police officer watched, demanding Malavida leave the stall door open as he dropped his pants and sat on the toilet.

"Can I take your order, please?" Malavida smiled at the cop, who stared back at him as if he'd not spoken.

After he'd finished and washed his hands, they headed back to Cavanaugh and Cunningham. The short patrolman told Lockwood they had to get moving, and Lockwood nodded. He turned to put the cuffs back on. Malavida tried to avoid him, suddenly leaning forward with feigned interest, staring at his computer screen. "Son of a *bitch*," he said, convincingly.

"Put your hands out," Lockwood barked, grabbing his wrist and cuffing him.

"Look't this. . . . How could I've missed this?" Malavida went on undeterred. He was eyeballing the computer graphic on the screen.

"What is it?" Karen asked as she moved across the room through the gawking employees of Cavanaugh and Cunningham, who were still looking on in dismay and sorrow.

"What is it?" Lockwood asked, staring at the graphic on the screen, the handcuff key, forgotten for the moment, in his hand.

"This guy went into the file room. See this here. . . ." Malavida pointed at the security entry/exit logs for the file room that were displayed on the screen. "This room on six was opened around ten-thirty that same night. That would have been just around the time of the murder."

They leaned in and looked at the columns of time logs on the screen. Malavida had accessed the daytime logs on the file room for the previous Thursday. He had found a 10:30 A.M. entry and was pointing at it, hoping desperately that they would not look at the top of the screen, where the wrong date and daytime listings appeared.

### THURSDAY, APRIL 11, A.M. PERSONNEL TRAFFIC LOG

It was the only listing he could find for a 10:30 entry into the file room.

"Maybe this guy wasn't wearing gloves when he went in there," Malavida volunteered.

"Why would he go into this file room?" Lockwood pondered.

"Why? Is that the question, Zanzo?" Malavida shook his head in disbelief. "We ain't exactly dealing with a normal wiring diagram. This guy's got his clock wound backwards. He kills these women and then joints 'em, remember?"

He was trying to keep Lockwood distracted, hoping he wouldn't discover the deception. The Customs agent was staring at the screen.

"Let's go take a look," Karen finally said. "If he's right, there might be some trace evidence in there."

Lockwood hunched forward, looking at the computer,

his brow furrowed. "It's a file room," he said slowly.
"What could be in there that he'd want?"

"Names of other victims, employee records?" Karen
suggested.

"You sure he was in there?" Lockwood looked at Malavida.

"Not positive. Maybe it was the security guard went
in. But somebody was in there just before the murder."

"Let's look," Karen repeated. "We can't get out of
this town anyway. Airport's closed."

The file room on the sixth floor was salvaged space
that had been gleaned from the interior wall configura-
tion. It was a long, narrow room that got wider as it went
toward the back wall. There was a gray metal desk at the
front of the room with a computer on it to access files.
The walls of the room housed file cabinets for computer
disks and metal racks that were being used for stationery
storage. Malavida knew from the two hours that he'd
already spent working on the host computer that the file
room terminal was hooked into the building's network.
He reached out his manacled hands and turned on the
computer. His plan was now only seconds from going
into action. His pirate program had left a command with
the host computer, which had already accepted him as its
root. It had reprogrammed everything he asked. His program also told the host to activate the security locks on
the sixth-floor file room fifteen seconds after the computer was logged on. He had also instructed the host computer to lock out the file room terminal from access to
the building's computer net for the next hour. That would
keep Karen Dawson, with her limited hacking skill, from
getting the door unlocked. He had also instructed the host
to turn off the phone, keeping his prisoners incommuni-
cado.

He had the computer booted up and, while Karen and
Lockwood were walking the room looking for evidence,
and while the two Atlanta cops standing behind him were
looking at their watches, Malavida logged in to the host,
triggering his pirate program. His escape plan was now

fifteen seconds from activation. He had no wristwatch to
keep track of the seconds, so slowly he began to count
them, being careful not to let his adrenaline speed him
up. If he went early, it could end in disaster. *One thousand one, one thousand two*, he counted in his head.

"We gotta get outta here. We're gonna miss EOW,"
the tall cop said, referring to his shift's end-of-watch. "Is
this gonna take much longer?"

"I'll be damned. Look't *this*, I found something," Malavida said to the two patrolmen, who, after a second,
moved forward sluggishly and looked at the screen without interest.

"What?" they said simultaneously, both staring
blankly at a monitor crowded full of time logs.

*One thousand seven, one thousand eight, one thousand
nine* . . .

The cops were on both sides of him now, looking at
the gibberish on the screen. Lockwood and Karen were
walking back toward him, only fifteen feet away. *One
thousand ten, one thousand eleven*, and Malavida suddenly lunged to his right, hitting the tall cop with his
shoulder, shoving him into a file cabinet. Then he lunged
left, knocking the other startled policeman off balance.
He turned and bolted for the door. *One thousand twelve.*
Out of the corner of his eye, he could see Lockwood
going for his gun, but Malavida already knew he was a
free man. *One thousand thirteen.* Once out of the file
room, he grabbed the metal door. *One thousand fourteen.*
He slammed it shut. "One thousand fifteen!" he shouted
and he heard the electronic security locks buzz shut. Then
Lockwood was pounding on the door. "Get fucked, asshole," Malavida shouted through the thick metal; then
he moved quickly to the elevator. He went back down to
four, into Cavanaugh and Cunningham, and over to
Candice's computer. While the startled employees looked
on in disbelief, with cuffed hands he picked up Karen
Dawson's purse, pulled out her wallet, and removed several hundred dollars in cash plus one credit card. Then
he looked at the roomful of openmouthed employees.

"I'm sorry about your friend," he announced. "Somebody will catch the animal who killed her.''

They murmured back at him in stunned agreement; then he leaned down and typed a message on the screen, sent it into the building's computer net, shut off the computer, picked up his cracking kit, and left.

In the file room, Lockwood had given up on the door and turned back to the computer. Karen slammed down the phone in disgust. ''Phone's off,'' she growled.

''That son of a bitch lured us up here and set those locks to go off. Damn,'' Lockwood said. But for some reason, he felt no anger. He knew that his career at U.S. Customs was over. He had missed his IA review and now, more importantly, he had lost a prisoner whom he'd released illegally. It was a simmering pork stew, and he had the apple in his mouth. From now on, it would turn into a familiar feast where his bones would be picked clean, like carrion. Internal Affairs Inspectors would all march solemnly to his final trial board. Waiting at the end of this sit-down dinner would be certain dismissal and disgrace. Old friends would stare expressionless, while the music of defeat played.

Lockwood could not manage to feel anything. Was this what he'd been hoping for?

Then the computer gave off a series of beeps. On the screen, in irritating bold caps, came Malavida's message:

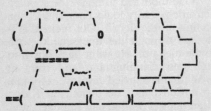

LOCKWOOD:

YOU SHOULD NEVER

HAVE ARRESTED

ME IN FRONT OF

MY MOTHER . . .

NOW WE'RE EVEN.

SNOOPY

Lockwood looked up. ''Cute kid,'' he said to nobody.

# 16

## DESTRUCTIVE NEWS

It took exactly one hour before the phone in the file room was turned back on and Karen dialed out. Minutes later, a sixty-year-old building security cop let them out. Lockwood felt lower than whaleshit and, looking back, it still turned out to be the high point of his day. He called Harvey Knox to tell him Malavida was in the wind.

"This is a joke?" the little Assistant U.S. Attorney asked, his voice in a strange no-man's-land between humor and consternation. "I've been working all night. . . . You're joking, right?"

"I wish I was," Lockwood said apologetically.

"So he's running around in Lompoc. Did you tell the sheriff up there?"

"No."

"*NO?*" Harvey shouted the word through the receiver. "Why the hell not? Listen, John, that Special Circumstances Release I wrote is vacuum bag dirt. We both know it won't hold up. I'll have to eat it page by fucking page. My bosses up at DOJ are gonna pound on my nuts for this."

"I know, Harvey. I'll take the hit. . . . I'll tell 'em it was my idea."

"You gotta get him back in custody, John. Call the sheriff in Lompoc. Get a dragnet out."

"It wouldn't snag him."

"Why not?"

" 'Cause he's not in Lompoc." Lockwood sighed.

"He's not in Lompoc," Harvey repeated, deadpan.

"Right, he's not in Lompoc."

"Where is he? Santa Barbara?"

"Atlanta."

*"Atlanta?"* Harvey's voice said he could barely comprehend it. "You took this guy to Atlanta?"

Lockwood said nothing. The silence on the line was long and meaningful and crackled with Harvey's disbelief. "There's no witness protection case, of course. We both knew that was bullshit from the beginning. Right, John?"

"Right. Look, Harvey, I'm gonna get slaughtered for this anyway . . . so I'm gonna tell 'em I forged your signature. Okay? You just say I came by asking for the SCR and you threw me out. Okay? There's no need for us to go into this coffin together."

Another long silence.

"Atlanta?" Harvey said in disbelief. "Why the fuck is he in Atlanta?"

"Harvey, hold your dirt on this. I'll take the torpedo. Just don't go soft and admit to anything. You threw me out. . . . You're pissed I stole the forms. I'll back your story." There was a long, empty, friendship-ending pause from the attorney. "I'm sorry," Lockwood said and hung up. Karen had been strangely silent, watching him while he talked.

"I was actually beginning to like him," she finally said. "He used me, didn't he?"

"Yep," Lockwood said, "but I'm the dummy who let him get away. . . ."

They headed back to Washington on the three P.M. Delta flight. People chattered and sawed on cardboard steaks. Lockwood called his boss, Laurence Heath, on the Airfone and was greeted by long, awkward pauses.

Heath finally cleared his throat. "John, I'm going to have a car meet you at Dulles."

From Heath's voice he could sense foreboding.

"Look, Larry, I'm sorry I missed the IA hearing. I got grounded by fog in Atlanta and I—"

"I'll see you when you get here, John," he said and hung up.

Lockwood looked back at Karen, who was sitting in coach still poring over copies she had made of the Atlanta crime scene report. He moved back down the aisle and sat next to her.

"How'd it go?' she said.

"Not good. I'm staring at a hanging. If you want a good seat, show up early. It's gonna be crowded."

"It can't be that bad," she said, looking up from the report. "You're one of their best agents."

"That's a nice confidence boost, but I've got way too many 'silent beefs' in my packet."

"Silent whats?"

"When you're the subject of an internal investigation and there isn't enough evidence to take action and the investigation gets dropped, it doesn't exactly go completely away. It's what they call a 'silent beef.' It's not on paper, but the people involved remember. I've got hundreds of those in my record. Lotsa brass in the agency have been shining up their swords, waiting for this day. But it's okay. . . . I think maybe I've been trying to make this happen, anyway. The IA shrink who's doing my head-pressure test says I've been courting this disaster for years . . . that I wanted this to happen. And I think maybe he's right. . . ."

"You want a second opinion from a more friendly doctor?" she said, putting the police report down on her lap.

"Anything friendly would be welcome right now," he said, thinking that she was way too young and way too pretty to be dealing with head cases like him and the psychopathic nut who had killed Candice Wilcox. Karen should be out dancing in the sunlight, interacting with people who didn't have emotional problems, or the stink of this job clinging to them.

He didn't know about the demons stalking Karen Dawson.

"We are a species of hunters and gatherers," she began. "Society's rules have attempted to regulate our behavior, but primal urges and genetic behavior codes determine our natural law and are much more defining than any human laws. You break the rules because your sense of the hunt is more important than your sense of self-preservation. In Greek mythology it would be a heroic trait. In the Customs Service it causes problems."

"It's caused problems in my life, in my marriage. I've been cruel to people I love."

"You're wrong," she said softly. "Cruelty and sentimentality can sometimes be companion traits . . . but never cruelty and love." She touched his arm. "Don't be so hard on yourself, John. You know something . . . ?"

He looked at her in a different way . . . seeing different qualities.

"If you let it happen, you might actually turn out to like who you are," she said.

There were four men whom Lockwood had never met before waiting for the Delta flight at Dulles Gate 12. They introduced themselves as members of Laurence Heath's administrative staff and then walked without speaking, next to Karen and Lockwood, out into a surprisingly cool April day. A wet, gusting wind was scattering the brown and gold leaves of spring, occasionally lifting them in eddies of air, swirling them around in tiny, twisting tornadoes. Lockwood watched a one-foot-high twister whirl across the parking lot and spill into a Chevy hubcap . . . mindless motion followed by an abrupt collapse. The perfect metaphor for his career.

They got into two cars. Karen sat beside him on the backseat as they pulled out of the huge Dulles Airport and took the forty-minute trip through Virginia's countryside into Washington, D.C.

Lockwood had been expecting to be taken to the IA floor on five, but instead they went to SES on three. He was led into Laurence Heath's office. Bob Tilly avoided his eyes when he looked at him. *Oh boy*, Lockwood thought, *they're not even gonna give me a blindfold this time*.

Laurence Heath was standing with his back to the door, looking out the picture window at ominous clouds and the White House administration annex. His hands were clasped behind him and the Teutonic wrinkles in the back of his head bristled from a recent haircut. When he turned, Lockwood saw a different expression from the one he had been expecting. Heath had sad compassion pasted on his rough tank-commander's face. His blue eyes seemed watery and distant. "Sit down, John."

He didn't sit. He wasn't going to take this on his ass. "Do I get a last meal and a cigarette?" Lockwood said, trying to find the right tone for the final note of his career.

"John . . . I have bad news . . ." Heath started slowly. "There's been a tragic circumstance. There's no easy way to get to this, so I'll just say it straight out. Claire has been murdered."

Lockwood stared at Heath. . . . The words failed to penetrate his brain. "What?" he said, even though he'd heard Heath clearly.

"She's been murdered. A man broke into the house in Studio City and killed her. It happened Sunday night. It's been kept off the news until you and her family could be notified."

"Heather . . . Is Heather okay?" he said. His mind was reeling now; his body starting to sweat uncontrollably. It was a cold sweat that turned his stomach sour. "Is she . . . is she . . . ?" He couldn't finish the sentence.

"She's okay. Well, not exactly okay . . . She apparently walked in while the man was . . . while it was happening. She wasn't attacked but she's in traumatic shock.

She's at Children's Hospital in Hollywood . . . under sedation.''

There was a long silence. John's thoughts swirled like leaves in the wind. His emotions were at war with this devastating news. He looked at his boss, who was shaking his head sadly.

"Heather . . . Heather is . . . in a hospital?'' Lockwood finally managed.

"Yes. In a hospital . . . Children's Hospital. The body, Claire's body, is with the L.A. Coroner. She was killed with a narrow blade of some kind. At least that's the Coroner's initial description of the wound. He believes she died quickly.''

"A scalpel,'' Lockwood said dully. He felt himself begin to sag. He caught the arm of the sofa and sat down on it heavily. One thought kept trying to penetrate his churning emotions. Claire was gone. She was really gone. He would never see her again . . . not in love or in anger. He would never see those Nordic blue eyes; eyes that could smile without her lips moving. He would never again hear the husky rasp in her breathing when she made love. He had lost her forever. He had left her in his own selfish wake, and now there was nothing he could do but hate himself for his senseless behavior.

"I want to go see Heather. I want to go now,'' he said softly.

"I've arranged for a plane. It's standing by at National.''

Lockwood tried to stand but his legs wouldn't hold him. Larry Heath moved to him and helped him to his feet.

"Bob, get in here!'' he yelled.

Tilly arrived on the run and, with the two of them holding on, they walked Lockwood down the hall.

"She's okay,'' Heath said. "Your daughter's okay. She's just in emotional shock. The doctors know how to deal with it. We'll get the man who did this. I promise you, John, we'll find him.''

"I know where he is," John Lockwood said. "I'll get him myself. . . ."

"You know . . . ? How do you know? Who is it?"

"I don't know . . . not really. I just . . . Look, Larry, just let me go, will you?"

They moved down to the elevator and Heath pressed the button. The four men in suits who had met Lockwood at the airport were waiting on benches nearby. They stood immediately to go with him.

"John, you can't get involved in this investigation. If you know anything, tell me now."

"Just get me out to L.A., Larry, okay? Don't tell me what I can't do."

"It's policy, man. You can't work on a case involving a loved one."

"Fuck policy!"

"You've been suspended, John. I wasn't going to tell you that until later, but IA suspended you when you failed to show up this morning. Kulack had the hearing without you."

The elevator door opened and one of the gray suits caught it. They all stood there, not knowing what to say . . . frozen in a tableau of embarrassed silence.

"When I first saw Claire, we were at the park," Lockwood finally said. "It was a summer day and I was there with some guys and we were drinking beer and looking for girls. I saw her and I thought, that is the most beautiful woman I have ever seen—"

"She was beautiful," Heath interrupted.

"Listen to me," Lockwood said sharply. "I don't know if I can say this so you'll understand, so *I'll* understand. I saw her there, backlit, wearing a white sundress, and with those blue eyes . . . and I said, 'God, if you'll let me have this woman, I won't ever ask you for anything else again.' And I guess God was listening, because it happened. He gave me Claire. I . . . I loved her, but I didn't deserve her, Larry, because everything in my life was always so hard and cynical . . . from the institutions that raised me to this job. I never let her have the good parts of me because I was always playing defense, trying not to get hit. That's the way I was taught to survive. And now, for the last few months, I've been seeing how unfair I was to her and to Heather and hating myself for it. I gave her my promise of love, but I never shared myself with her. And now, when I want to . . . when I've been dreaming about finding a way back to her . . . it . . . it's too late.''

There was a long silence. The four gray suits shifted their weight.

''There's only one thing I can do for her now, Larry. Only one thing. It's too late and too little, but I'm gonna do it, nonetheless . . . and not you or Customs or anybody else on this planet is going to stop me.'' He reached into his pocket and handed Larry Heath his badge and his plastic ID. He pulled his government-issue S&W .38 out of its holster and handed it to the DOAO. Then he turned and walked on rubber legs into the elevator. The four men trailed in behind him, and in seconds the door closed and John Lockwood was gone.

Malavida was in a truck-stop motel in Macon, Georgia, when he saw the story on TV. The lacquer-haired commentator said that the release of the woman's name and picture had been withheld until the family could be notified. Then, up on the screen came Claire Lockwood's beautiful face.

''The L.A. Coroner estimates that Claire Lockwood was killed at approximately ten o'clock last evening. She was stabbed in her bedroom several times and was pronounced dead at St. Joseph's Hospital in Burbank at eleven-fifteen P.M., Sunday. Her ten-year-old daughter may have witnessed the crime but is in traumatic shock at Children's Hospital in Hollywood.''

''Motherfucker,'' Malavida said out loud, his heart sinking.

The news anchor continued: ''The L.A. Coroner says that the penetration and track of the wound indicates a very narrow blade, perhaps a fruit knife.''

"Scalpel," Malavida said under his breath.

". . . Mrs. Lockwood was recently divorced from her husband, John Lockwood, a Customs agent who, police say, was in an airplane with other Customs employees when the murder took place and is not a suspect."

When the story was over, Malavida turned off the TV and sat in the dark. He didn't move for almost an hour. He thought back to Sunday afternoon, working his cracking program from Claire's French Provincial desk in her sunny study. He'd had a feeling even then that it had been a mistake not to put a masking program on his UNIX host's address, but he'd been in a hurry and had wanted to impress Karen. He was being Snoopy, wirewalking in cyberspace, performing his amazing magic, working carelessly without a net.

Now he sat in the dark motel room in Macon. Over and over, he replayed the events in his mind, looking for another explanation. But there was no denying it. He punished himself with one thought: It was his fault that Claire Lockwood had been murdered.

# 17

## DEALS

**"I**t's a small world after all . . ." leaked musically out of recessed speakers. The song was stepped on by occasional doctor pages coming through the same sound system. A few children on crutches or in wheelchairs moved down the brightly colored hall to the skylighted playroom at the end of the floor. The area managed to be both cheerful and sad at the same time.

Lockwood moved out of the elevator with a young, earnest woman named Beth something-or-other. She was a volunteer who said she was getting her master's in child psychology.

"She's in emotional traumatic shock and she's blocking the whole event. Dr. Levitt says the best thing is to just let her come out of it naturally. Right now, when she gets agitated, we medicate her slightly."

Lockwood heard almost none of it as he plowed on blindly, looking for his daughter's room.

"It's in here," Beth said, taking his arm and turning him as he moved aimlessly up the hallway.

He entered a small room with two beds and a window that overlooked a concrete courtyard. The room had wallpaper with lots of little multi-colored balloons on it. An artist had painted animals everywhere. A large hot-air balloon dominated the far wall. Purple hippos with wide eyes looked over the side of the honey-gold basket. Heather was lying in the far bed, staring up at the animals on the ceiling.

"Daddy," she said, turning her head to him as he entered the room. "Daddy, it's all over and I didn't feel a thing . . . well, not really, but almost. I don't have a sore throat or anything. . . ."

He moved to her and gathered her up in his arms and hugged her. He clung to her desperately. Heather struggled slightly to be free. She pulled back and looked at him with stern wisdom.

"I thought it was going to hurt because of what Lenore said when she had it done, but I woke up and it was almost like nothing happened. I tried to call Mommy but I guess she's at work. . . ."

He sat on the bed, held her hand, and looked down at her. She seemed excited and happy, but there was a tightness around her eyes that betrayed everything; a shrillness in her voice that he had never heard before.

"So anyway," she continued, "they wake you up and make you take icky, syrupy medicine that's supposed to taste like cherry but doesn't . . . but they also wake you up all the time and feed you ice cream . . . and there was this girl, Sara, that was my roommate, who fell off her bike and hurt her head. But she went home yesterday. . . ."

Then it dawned on him what she was talking about. She was back almost a year when she'd had her tonsils out. It had been at this very hospital. She was pretending desperately that it was a year ago, that the operation was over, and that explained why she was there. He looked into her pale-blue eyes, Claire's eyes, and felt tears come into his own.

"You wouldn't believe this neat doctor I got. His name is Dr. Dumbbell. . . . That's what he told me and Mommy his name was . . ."

Lockwood knew she was talking about Dr. Dumbolten, who had performed the tonsillectomy last year.

"Isn't that a stupid name, Dr. Dumbbell? I think it's

very stupid, but he's a good doctor anyway, because I don't even have a sore throat. I called Mommy and I tried to tell her, but I can't find her anywhere. She's not at home or at the office. I talked to Mrs. Watkins, that's her new secretary, and she kept crying and wouldn't say where Mommy is. And I'm ready to go home. . . . Where is Mommy . . . ?''

Lockwood looked at his daughter, then at Beth, who shook her head in a gesture that said, *Don't tell her*. He didn't. They talked about her year-old operation and they talked about her cat, Fluffy, which had been run over by a car last summer but which was now still very much alive in Heather's mind. Then she said something that almost doubled him over with anguish.

"Daddy, do you ever talk to God?'' she said, looking at him earnestly and holding his hand.

"Sometimes I do, yes . . .''

"Well, see . . . I talk to him all the time. I think God knows best . . . and God would never let anything happen to hurt me because He loves me . . . just like He loves you and Mommy.''

"I know He does. . . .''

"When I talk to Him, you know what I ask for?''

"What?''

"I ask for you and Mommy to get back together . . . for you to fall in love again. I ask God in my prayers. I've been doing it every night for a year. I don't want to bug Him, but it's very important, and guess what?''

"What?'' Lockwood said.

"God answered my prayers.''

"Good . . .'' Lockwood's mouth was dry. His heart was skipping beats. He could feel it pounding in his throat.

"See . . . 'cause last Sunday, after you came, I asked Mommy if she still loved you like before . . . if we could ever be a family again. And you know what she said?''

"No, honey, what did she say?''

"She said she always loved you . . . that she never stopped and that she always would. Then she said that it was up to you. She said, 'When Daddy wants it, it will happen.' That's what she said. So now I'm asking God to make you love her back.''

Lockwood had lost so much. His timing had been simply terrible. He had realized the enormity of his mistake just as Claire was snatched from him. He held Heather's hand and smiled at her through his tears. ''I'll make you a deal, Pumpkin,'' he said, using the childhood nickname he had for her. ''When we go home to Mommy's house, I'll come home and I'll live with you. I'll take care of you.''

''But Mommy does that, and you have all your important work in Washington. How can you, Daddy?''

''I'll get some other kind of work. I'll get a job that will give us lots of time together.''

''Can we go riding?'' she said, smiling.

''Anytime you want.''

''Can we paint pictures?''

''You bet. And you wanna know something else? I won't ever break this promise to you. It's a promise on a promise.''

She smiled at him and squeezed his hand. ''See, when you ask God for stuff, He listens,'' she told him sagely.

''I know. . . .''

He reached down and hugged her again, and this time she didn't squirm. But after a moment he felt her stiffen slightly, so he pulled away and looked at her. Her eyes were clouded with concern.

''Daddy, I wonder where Mommy is. . . . She's never late. You don't think something could have happened to her . . . ?''

Lockwood didn't trust his voice to answer.

Malavida couldn't bring Claire Lockwood back, but he made a deal with himself. He decided he would find out where the crazy son of a bitch who killed her was hiding. He had the number of the cell pod in Tampa, where the call to Hoyt Tower had come from. He had his computer and he had Karen Dawson's credit card.

He would try to set up a triangulation. He had bought some surplus clothes with Karen's money at a second-hand store and hitchhiked to Macon, where he'd stolen a car from a supermarket parking lot. He had loaded his meager belongings into the trunk and driven from Macon due south into Florida. It was ten P.M., Tuesday night, when he pulled into a Best Western motel off Interstate Highway 75 and parked his stolen car in the back where the plates wouldn't be seen by a passing patrol car.

He set up his computer in the single room he'd rented on the second floor of the large Colonial structure. He could hear trucks on the Interstate growling like Rottweilers. He plugged his computer into the wall and went to work, trying to get a list of calls from the cellphone site that had relayed The Rat's call to Atlanta. He was focusing on time charges for April 12-13, the night of Candice Wilcox's murder, hoping The Rat hadn't bothered to hide his billing address for the call.

The Rat was worried. The barge where he had been doing the reconstruction and storage was buried deep in the Tampa swamp, but he felt exposed like never before. He hoped he had closed the door of redemption by killing the woman in Studio City, but he couldn't be sure. Only time could answer it. So The Rat waited and worried. He knew he had to reconstruct the answers that Shirley had taken to her grave. Her grave was actually empty. Her remains had perished in the fire, but her empty grave beckoned him. He had been there often. He would go after dark and roll in the dirt, trying to relive the wonderful, terrifying memory of her death. But finally he got no pleasure from going. Her grave held no wisdom. . . . It was a place without meaning that was filled with the darkness of oblivion.

Shirley had told him he had the mark of the Beast on him and was destined to go to the grave-like pit of darkness. To avoid this, he had burned the house where he lived, killing Shirley. He'd hoped the Deity would be fooled and think he had perished with her. From that point, The Rat had become a vile creature, scurrying in the darkness, hiding from God. But he was always afraid God would spot him and punish him for his deeds.

It was this fear that made him finally decide to move the barge. He made a deal with himself. Despite the huge effort involved, he would find a better place—at least until the Second Resurrection, which The Wind Minstrel said was coming soon. It was not the resurrection of the Holy Spirit, as lied about in the New Testament. It was, instead, the resurrection of the unrighteous. When that glorious day arrived, The Rat could destroy the forces of Christ and his armies. He could stand in the sunshine. He could finally breathe the clean air. He could finally spit into the face of God.

Karen had watched Lockwood's plane take off, heading back to California. She felt lost and abandoned. The tragic, strained look in Lockwood's eyes had shown her the depth of his grief.

She had cabbed back to the Customs Building and ended up at the little office in B-16. She sat in front of the computer, looking vacantly at the starburst on the cobalt-blue screen. . . . A stack of new VICAP folders was sitting on her desk and she thumbed through them listlessly. . . . Her mind went back to her father, Robert Dawson, Ph.D., DNSC, BSEE. More letters than the Chinese alphabet. She smiled, remembering Lockwood's remark. She always remembered her father with both love and regret. He had wanted so much for her. . . . His dying wish had defined her, but it had altered her life.

Her father had always been preoccupied. His high-horsepower thoughts had consumed him, and it was this trait that finally claimed him. He had stepped out between two cars at the university and been hit by a van driven by a student. He hovered between life and death for weeks. Karen and her mother stayed awake nights and prayed that God would bring him back. . . . While they prayed, the vacuum pumps hissed, the catheters dripped, and the monitors beeped. It was an ugly concert of fluids and electrodes that played to a frightened audience of two.

Then, one afternoon, he regained consciousness and asked for her. Karen was in school. Her mother came and got her and brought her to his bedside. He looked up and told Karen that the best of him was in her, that he had given her his greatest gift . . . his unrelenting mind. And it was true. She was a brilliant student and had been advanced beyond her grade three times. She was only twelve years old and in the eleventh grade. He had insisted she take her practice college boards and she scored a perfect 1,600. As he lay in his hospital bed, he made her promise that she would go to college immediately. That she wouldn't waste any more of her valuable learning time in high school. She said yes because she didn't want to say anything that would upset him. He looked so weak and frail . . . She knew once he was better, she could talk him out of the promise.

Two days later, Robert Dawson died of pneumonia. He slipped into a coma, leaving them as quietly as a drifting cloud. He had been the main force of her life. She felt his dying wish could not be broken. She entered the University of Michigan four days after her thirteenth birthday. She lived with her widowed aunt in Flint, just up the road. Every afternoon she sat alone in the main quad outside the student center and ate her lunch while she watched the other students talking and laughing. She graduated three years later and did her postgraduate work at Princeton. She had been given great gifts. She knew it must be true, because her father had told her so. She had the gifts of health and looks and her wonderful analytical mind . . . but despite it all, she was always lonely. It was shortly after graduation that she began to battle boredom.

By Tuesday afternoon the room in the basement was getting unbearably stuffy. She had caught up with all the updates that Operations had sent. She looked at the computer and the completed stack of VICAP folders, then she reached into her briefcase and again pulled out the

Rat's profile. "The Rat," she had noted, "is a nocturnal rodent." She turned on the computer and accessed VI-CAP. She inputted all the information on Candice Wilcox's death: the surgical data on the removal of her arms, the fact that her face was covered by her sweater, the peri-mortem masturbation, the sexual substitution with the desk scissors, and the overpowering blitz attack, including the wound made by a narrow blade or scalpel. She entered it and waited. . . . After less than a minute she got a hit. Up on the screen flashed a case code:

H.F. DT.MI. 67-94 108.01

She knew that stood for "Homicide, Female. Detroit, Michigan." The sixty-seventh killing in that city in 1994. The 108.01 was a Uniform Crime Report number. All crimes were categorized by number, starting with criminal enterprise homicides at 100 and going all the way to group excitement homicides at 143. The decimal points were for sub-headings. The 108.01 stood for indiscriminate felony murder, which meant that the police in Michigan felt that it was a homicide planned in advance without a specific victim in mind.

Karen asked the computer for the case file . . . and in seconds she was looking at the face of a woman named Leslie Bowers, age thirty-five. She had been murdered in her house late at night. Leslie's house was at the end of a cul-de-sac. She had a similar narrow-blade knife wound in her chest. The angle and depth of the track indicated she had been grabbed from behind. The crime scene photos, and police and autopsy reports, showed that her legs had been amputated surgically, her face covered by a tablecloth. When they found her, she had been masturbated on. The perp was a secretor, and from his sperm they determined he had AB blood. A candlestick from a nine-foot-high dormer shelf had been jammed inside her vagina.

This, in Karen's opinion, was not an indiscriminate felony murder. The Michigan police had mislabeled it.

She thought it was more likely a personal cause homicide. Karen also knew instantly that it was the work of the same killer when she saw the identical brand on Leslie Bowers's left breast.

The National Crime Institute said any series of more than three murders—that included a cooling-off period between crimes—represented serial murder. Karen was now sure The Rat was a serial killer. God knew how many others he had murdered and mutilated. For a case to be in the VICAP system, the local police department had to take the time to enter it. Often they didn't go to the trouble; that was the system's tragic flaw.

She picked up the phone and called Detective Stiner at home in Atlanta. She finally tracked him down at his house, where he was having dinner. He told Karen that the autopsy had proven that the cause of death had been the initial strike to Candice's chest with the narrow blade. And all of the mutilations had been post-mortem. He also confirmed what she had already suspected: When the coroner took swabs off Candice's body, he had found traces of semen.

"Was he a secretor?" Karen asked.

"Sure was."

"Was it AB blood?"

"How'd you know that?" he asked.

"There was another murder in Michigan, same kind of wound, same kind of surgical amputations, only he took her legs below the knees. Her name was Leslie Bowers. It happened in November of '94. She had semen on her and it was from AB blood."

"You know, you're pretty good at this, Miss Dawson," Stiner drawled. "I ever need any help on something, you mind if I send you some crime scene pictures and forensic printouts?"

"Anytime . . . Listen, Detective, this guy, I think he may be very, very big. . . ."

"Where'd that come from?" Stiner said, his wife now glaring at him from the dining room table.

"The sexual substitute in this Michigan murder was a

candlestick. . . . The mate to it was on a nine-foot-high shelf. . . . I doubt the UnSub would climb up to get it. It was a random choice; I think he just reached up and pulled it down.''

''Nine-foot shelf? He'd have to be at least seven feet tall.''

''I know. It's just a guess, but anybody that big might have been noticed. . . . You should ask around. This UnSub spent a lot of time setting up Candice. That means he probably went up and checked the office, maybe pretending to be a deliveryman . . . or a messenger, or something. He'd want to get the lay of the land. You might ask if anybody saw a very tall man, perhaps disfigured. Maybe we can get an eyewitness description.''

''Okay,'' Stiner said, and, seeing his wife's rising anger, he got off the phone.

Karen was alone in the basement, looking at the computer. The silence and her loneliness began to get to her. After a minute she downloaded the Leslie Bowers information, including all of the police reports and autopsy photos, then left the room.

It was nine o'clock when she got back to her Washington apartment. She sat at her desk and read the rest of the Bowers file; it was full of unanswered questions. She finally pushed it aside and looked at her watch. She knew that Lockwood was in California by now and she found herself thinking of him. Three or four times she reached for the phone to call, but she didn't have anything except his beeper number and she wasn't even sure he had it with him. She promised herself she would do something to help Lockwood escape his pain. She would use her profiling skills to find this animal who had killed his wife. Maybe that would help mend him. It seemed like a project worthy of her huge intellect. She had somehow become attached to him in a very short time. It didn't feel like just sexual attraction; this was something else as well. John Lockwood presented a different equation. She had tried to understand it, but the more she analyzed it, the more it mystified her. It was emotional and chemical and very unsettling. She knew it might hurt or disappoint her, or even destroy guarded parts of her, but maybe it wouldn't bore her. She also knew she had a delicately balanced emotional and mental mechanism. It was all she could do to keep the twelve-cylinder monster in her head from attacking her.

The phone on her bedside table rang. She reached over and picked it up. ''Hello . . .'' she said hesitantly.

''If I asked for your help, would you give it to me or get me busted?'' the voice on the other end of the line asked.

''Malavida?'' She was surprised to hear from him.

''I fucked up, Miss Dawson . . . fucked up big. I got that lady killed.''

''I know,'' she said softly.

''I wanna run a campaign on the buster who did it. I think I can find out where he is. But it needs two people. . . .''

''You still using my credit card?'' she said, '' 'Cause I canceled it yesterday.''

''I maxed it out yesterday.''

''Where are you?''

''You blow me in and I'm gonna go back to the joint for twice the time,'' he said. ''Can I trust you?''

''You're too much. You called *me*,'' she said.

''I need to hear it, *chica*. Can I trust you? Tell me.''

''Yes, despite the fact you played me like a mark,'' she said hotly.

''I had to. I apologize. I couldn't go back.''

''Where are you?'' she asked.

''You got a cellphone?''

''Yeah . . .''

''Gimme the number. . . .''

She gave it to him, and, while he was writing it down, she asked again, ''Where are you, Mal? You're in Tampa, aren't you?''

''Yep. I'm gonna use the Snoopy Home Shopping Network to pick up what we need. Get on a plane and get down here. I'll call you at noon tomorrow and give you an address where we can meet.''

She was silent. She wasn't sure what she was getting herself into.

''Have we got a deal?'' he asked.

''Deal,'' she finally answered.

# 18

## THE KILL/DIE RATIO

He never left her room. All night, Lockwood slept on the short, hard leather couch under the basket of colorful, wide-eyed hippos.

When Heather was awake, he held her hand and talked to her about horses and her painting, her school and friends. He let her know that her grandparents were coming to visit. Heather's concern about her mother's disappearance was growing hourly. She was increasingly agitated, her eyes darting wildly around. Any noise in the hall brought her to an upright position. "What's that? Is that Mommy?" she would demand.

It finally happened when she was sound asleep. At three A.M., Lockwood was awakened by a mournful cry. He sat up, not sure for a moment where it was coming from. He looked over and saw that Heather was tossing in a desperate tangle of bed sheets and blankets. . . . The horrible sound coming out of her seemed manufactured in some primal cavern deep in her soul. He moved quickly to the bed and grabbed her shoulders.

"Honey . . . honey, wake up," he said, and her eyes snapped open as she let out a frightening scream. The sound startled him and carried out into the corridor. He tried to calm her but she wouldn't stop struggling. He reached out and grabbed her, pulling her to him, but it did no good.

In seconds, two nurses ran into the room and over to Heather. "Get a trank," the senior nurse said. And then the doctor came in. He was young, in his late twenties, and Lockwood hadn't met him before. He moved to Heather and pried her gently out of Lockwood's arms. She had stopped screaming now, but was whimpering. Her eyes didn't seem to focus on anything.

"Mommy! He killed my mommy!" she said over and over.

The nurse came back in with a hypodermic, but the doctor waved it off.

"Let it come out. Let it come out, honey. Say it . . . say it . . ."

"He killed my mommy. He killed her. He killed her. . . ."

Her eyes were now as big and round as the hippos on the wall. Then she looked directly at Lockwood.

"DAAAAAADYYY!" she wailed, drawing it out. But it was a cry of desperation and longing for her mother. He reached out and took her into his arms. "Oh, Daddy . . . Daddy . . . He killed her. He killed her with a knife. I saw it happen. Oh, Daddy . . . Mommy's dead. . . ."

He rocked her in his arms. He could think of nothing to say that would ease the memory, no words that would comfort her, so he just held her.

She was clutching him tightly, her fingernails digging into the flesh on the back of his neck and shoulders. He ignored the pain and held her. After a while, she began sobbing, and Lockwood could feel her tears on the side of his face. They ran down his neck and onto his shirt collar. He embraced her, squeezing her, wanting to give her something to comfort her and knowing he had nothing to give.

"Daddy . . . oh, Daddy . . ." she finally choked. "Daddy . . . don't leave me, Daddy. . . ."

"I'm here, Pumpkin. . . . I'm here," he said softly.

Marge and Gunnar Neilsen arrived from Minnesota at 9:30 in the morning. They were tense and agitated. Gunnar was in his late sixties, the American-born only son of Norwegian immigrants. Since childhood, everyone had called him Rocky. His wife, Marge, was thin and weathered and was holding Rocky's hand as they looked at Lockwood through bloodshot eyes.

They had raised Claire like a hothouse flower. Nothing was spared, nothing too expensive. They had run a ma-and-pa grocery store in Midland, Minnesota, called Rocky's Green Market. It had been a constant struggle to survive, but the market managed to support them and allowed them to provide for their daughter. When she was twelve, they had paid for her braces and the tap dance lessons by working extra hours. When she was sixteen, they had stayed open Sundays to pay for her cheerleading uniform and singing lessons. Fifteen years ago, when Claire was nineteen, they had sold the grocery store to an Armenian named Androsian to pay her tuition at the University of Minnesota. Rocky still worked behind the meat counter at Rocky's Green Market, which was now called Androsian's Food Center. They had come to Los Angeles, a town with violent graffiti and menacing headlines, to pick up Claire's body. They were about to spend their last dollar on her, for interment and shipping expenses home for her funeral.

Lockwood and the Neilsens had maintained a ten-year no-fire zone, but it had taken a monumental effort on both sides. Rocky never liked the fact that Lockwood had been in reform school; he never liked it that his high-school diploma came from the Marines and that he had not gone to college, except for night school and correspondence courses; and he never liked it that Lockwood made his living chasing monsters. In short, Rocky Neilsen had tolerated John Lockwood with that stoic reserve common to men who live in infuriating climates. He had weathered Lockwood like a bad winter.

Marge Neilsen had seen the better side of her son-in-law, but she found it difficult to discuss it with her husband. She had heard the "girl talk" from her daughter and she knew that there had once been a beautiful tenderness between Claire and John. A tenderness that she envied and had never found in her own marriage. She thought the divorce had been a shame for everyone. She had agonized through it with Claire. But nothing had prepared her for the utter helplessness she felt now that Claire was dead. She was swamped by an emotional tidal wave that washed over her, drowning her spirit and turning her vision black. Marge stumbled along beside her husband in catatonic darkness.

She looked at Lockwood and could see that same desperation in his eyes, and her heart went out to him.

"Heather . . . She walked in on the guy . . . and she's got very bad memories," Lockwood said.

The Neilsens nodded. Marge reached out and took Lockwood's hand. Rocky glowered at the gesture. "Let's go see her," he said gruffly, pulling Marge out of the handclasp and up the corridor.

Lockwood let them have time alone with Heather, knowing Rocky didn't want him imposing on their visit. They stayed with Heather for an hour; then Lockwood suggested lunch in the hospital cafeteria.

After selecting their food, they stopped at the cashier with their trays. Rocky refused to let Lockwood pay. It was a small gesture but it accurately communicated the disdain he felt for his son-in-law. They moved to an empty table and sat down.

"The police are sending a sketch artist to work with her," Lockwood began. "I'm not sure it's a good idea until she's stronger; but the Homicide dicks want to get something on the wire. . . ."

Rocky grunted and poked at the soggy, unappetizing, gravy-soaked wedge of meat loaf in front of him.

"Rocky . . . Marge," Lockwood said, looking at them, "I've got to admit something to you both. It's something you have to know. . . ." They listened as he hesitated before going on. "The guy who killed Claire . . . was after me. . . ."

He waited for it to settle in. Rocky Neilsen set down his fork and put both of his hands on his thighs and looked down at the floor between his knees. When he looked up, his face showed the struggle going on inside him, but his voice was under control.

"So you're responsible for her being dead then," he said.

"I was trying to get a line on a killer. I used a computer at Claire's house and somehow he back-tracked my program through the phone lines and got her address."

"So like I said, it's your fault she's dead." He looked at Lockwood with contempt.

"Okay, Rock, it's my fault she's dead. Does that make you feel better?" He could feel the heat coming into his face and he knew he was seconds away from losing it. Not that he could blame Rocky . . . It *was* his fault. But he hadn't seen it coming. He hadn't understood the danger! Shouldn't that count for something? Or was he just trying to get it to come out that way in his mind, so he could say it had been one of those things that happen that you can't control. . . . Was he somehow engaged in some classic face-saving exercise? "I need for you to take care of Heather until this guy is off the road."

Rocky said nothing. He looked off across the hospital cafeteria at doctors and nurses in green disposable shoes and surgical smocks. They glided around silently like paper angels. "Why don't we just keep her for good and save you the bother?" he finally said, turning his gaze back at Lockwood.

"I've quit law enforcement, Rocky. I handed back my badge. But I've got to finish one thing and then I'm outta that life. I'm going to take care of my daughter full-time, the way Claire would want."

"You were never there for either of them before."

"I know, but that's gonna change."

"This thing you gotta take care of . . . is it the guy who killed my baby?"

Lockwood nodded, then continued, "Until it's finished, I can't take the risk of being with Heather. This

guy is after me. If I don't bring it to an end, it could go
on for years. I need you to keep Heather out of the way,
take care of her till I can get it done.''

''And what if this guy gets you instead?''

''Then you raise her. If she comes out like Claire, I'll
have nothing to complain about.''

Rocky was looking at Lockwood, a strange expression
on his face. ''Y'know, all my life I tried to make things
come out right by sheer force of will. I figured if I work
hard enough, play by the rules, I can make the ball fall
into the hole. And most of the time I done okay. Then
you came along and you play by rules I don't know
about. You say you'll love Claire, you stand up in church
and promise, in front of God, that it's forever, then you
get yourself divorced. You say you quit your job, handed
back your badge, but you're going after this guy anyway.
Now you say you're gonna be there for Heather 'less this
guy kills you, and then it's up to us. I never understood
you, John. I never could understand what made you do
this work.''

Lockwood looked at him for a long time, not sure how
to respond. He felt, for the first time ever, that Rocky
actually wanted to understand. ''I don't think this time I
have any choice, Rock,'' he replied. ''This killer is going
to deal the play. I don't want Heather to get caught in
the crossfire like Claire did. I can't change what happened and I'll live with the guilt the rest of my life. But
once this is over, I'm retired. I'll do everything in my
power to do right by Heather. I don't know how else to
say it.''

''Your family, Heather and Claire, didn't never matter
that much before,'' Rocky said softly.

''They always mattered to me, Rock, but I was focused
on something else. . . . It was a mistake. I admit it.''

''Just what was so important you didn't have time for
your family?'' Rocky said, remembering the years he had
put in as a provider for Claire and Marge.

''Something is wrong out there and it's going to destroy us if we don't destroy it first,'' Lockwood an-

swered. "If we don't, then we're just contributing to the problem by running from something that will end up devouring everything we care about." Rocky and Marge were watching and listening intently. "Seems to me there's way too many people on earth right now who are willing to kill for things they're not willing to die for," Lockwood continued. "You've got gang kids on street corners willing to machine-gun other kids for wearing the wrong-color bandanas, but if you ask 'em, 'Would you be willing to die for that?' they say, 'Hell, no.' Same with this guy who killed Claire. He's killing to relive some sick fantasy that he certainly wouldn't want to die for. Vietnam screwed up the kill/die ratio. We were killing people over there for reasons we didn't give a damn about, and after the war, we brought that sickness home."

There was a long silence. "I thought somebody had to do something about it," he continued. "Every time I saw a needless death, I put Heather or Claire into the equation and I thought . . . What would I do if it was them? I felt I had to get rid of this sickness before it could touch them. And now it has. I know you're right, Rock. I was focused on the wrong things. I should have been there for them. The hours, the days lost I can never get back."

Rocky finally nodded. "In World War II, I was in at sixteen 'cause we were fighting for a country we loved and would die for. The cause was just, so we never felt bad about what we were doing."

Lockwood concurred and then he leaned in. "I'm willing to die to get this animal off the street, so I guess that gives me the license to kill him . . . or at least to try. If I succeed, I'll come back and get Heather, and I'll be there for her from then on. If I fail, I want you to take care of my little girl for me, 'cause I know with you she'll have a great home."

Marge reached out and took Lockwood's hand. Rocky looked at the gesture, and this time, he didn't seem annoyed by it.

Lockwood had finally connected with them. But, like everything else, it happened too late.

# 19

## TRIANGLES

She waited, standing in the tropical sun next to her rental car, which was parked outside the Foley D. Knight International Airport in Tampa. Malavida's call came at exactly twelve noon, as promised. Her cellphone rang once and she flipped it open.

"Yeah?"

"It's me." His voice sounded pinched and thin.

"I'm here. Where the hell are you?"

"Listen, Karen—"

"Miss Dawson," she corrected him.

"Miss Dawson. I'm a Federal fugitive. I'm in no hurry to go back to Lompoc. I don't completely trust you. You could be transforming on me right now, so cut the shit. Okay?"

"Okay."

There was a long silence and then he said, "I'm in the phone booth across from the Hertz counter. I can see you from where I am. Pull out and drive slowly toward the gate. I'll come to you. Leave this phone connection open so I know you ain't dimin' me out 'fore you get here."

"Okay." She got in, put the cellphone down on the seat, then drove the blue LeBaron slowly toward the Hertz return. She saw Malavida sprinting across the pavement—a tall, handsome young man who suddenly looked

163

much different, dressed in khaki pants and a white shirt. He moved quickly in front of the car and jumped in. He picked her cellphone up off the seat, checked it, then switched it off.

"Let's go," he said, and she drove out of the airport.

They rode in silence while she concentrated on getting onto the right interstate. Once she picked up Highway 42 across the Charles Owen Expressway, heading toward downtown Tampa, she looked over at him. "Why?" she said.

"Why what?"

"You bullshitted us. You got away. You were free. Why call me?"

He looked out at the flat landscape rushing past the window. "I told you. . . . It was my fault Lockwood's old lady got put down. I never was directly responsible for somebody being dead before. It feels horrible. I can't just let it be." There was heavy self-disgust in his voice. "I was showing off. I was trying to make you think I was hot shit. I didn't bother to consider that the guy we were cracking could be as good as me. I didn't figure on him using a backfinger, getting the address. I gotta put that right 'fore I move on."

She thought he somehow looked older. She could sense him beside her. He seemed different, more assured, more in control . . . sadder. She stole a glance at him. In that moment he looked almost god-like, his square jaw jutting, his glossy black hair and penetrating eyes flashing in the sunlight. But she was still angry at him for playing her like a mark.

He gave her directions and they arrived at his motel, which was near Tampa Bay, just off the Courtney Campbell Causeway. He had her park in the back.

"Where's your car?" she asked. "Or don't you have one?"

"I had one. It was a G-ride. I left it in the airport parking lot this morning. If the hubcap cops don't find it, it'll be a duck in two days."

She thought he was saying that if the cops working

auto theft at the airport didn't find the car, it would get stripped. But she didn't want to give him the satisfaction of asking.

They climbed the exterior stairs to his motel room on the second floor of the colonial building. He unlocked the door and she walked into a cluttered room that looked like the repair center at Radio Shack. There were directional loop antennas, resistors, capacitors, and wires everywhere. Open on the bed was a suitcase with an assortment of wire clippers and needle-nose pliers, along with digital volt-ohm meters and screwdrivers. Two radios, stripped of their casings, were on the bed, center stage.

"What's all this?" she asked, looking around.

"It's how we catch this buster," Malavida said. "It's all stuff from Rat Shack. This zoot is using Pennet to make his calls. Unless he changes locations or computers, I think I have a pretty good chance of finding him by triangulating on his cellphone." He was looking down at the radios on the bed. "This stuff is just high-frequency receivers with direction loop antennas I made from HF wire. I'm pretty sure he'll stick with the name Rat or Wind Minstrel, and that's gonna help us."

"Why would he?" she interrupted.

"Two reasons. Because it's already in Pennet that way and it would be a hassle to change, and because hackers get attached to their usernames. I've been Snoopy for almost ten years. But you can bet he'll be more careful about his security next time he's on-line. The one part of the link he can't protect is from his cellphone to the pod that puts him into the phone line. He's vulnerable there and that's how I'll get him."

"How do you know he'll use a cellphone?"

"Anybody wanting to protect their POO usually uses a cellphone."

"Their what?"

"Point-of-origin. Sorry." He smiled at her, and she couldn't help noticing that the smile was dazzling and lit his handsome features. "Cellphones are better, because with no hard wire, they're harder to trace.'' He continued, ''All you can do is get to the local cell pod, like we did. We know its origin is here in Tampa. He knows that's a huge area. Now we've gotta narrow it down.''

''Go on.'' She took a sheet of writing paper out of the desk and began to make notes.

''We ain't gonna be having no test here, Miss Dawson, and I don't need all this down on paper if I get busted.''

''I wanna know what you're doing. Since I'm certain we're breaking half a dozen FCC regs and a couple of dozen State and Federal statutes, I wanna have a list so I'll know how many years I'm gonna serve.''

He looked at her and put his hands into his back pockets. ''Why are you willing to stick your nose out, anyway? It wasn't your fault Lockwood's ex got killed, unless you got a thing for him.''

''It was my idea that got her killed,'' she said, feeling her face redden.

He cocked his head and raised one eyebrow in disbelief.

''Come on . . . let's give each other's personal motives a rest,'' she said, back-pedaling. ''You wouldn't be my first guess to be helping Lockwood either. I'm willing to buy your reason. Why don't you just buy mine and tell me how all this works?''

''Okay. You're gonna take one of these units and go check into a hotel in St. Pete, across the bay. I'm gonna be right here with the other unit. We're gonna wait for this guy to make his call. When his cellphone opens up, we'll grab the signal and triangulate on it, then get an approximate location.''

He opened a map that he had taken from her rental car's glove compartment and laid it on the motel's cigarette-scarred desk. It showed the Tampa Bay/St. Petersburg area.

''How will we know his signal? There's gotta be thousands of cell calls to this pod.''

He turned around and tapped a key on his computer, which was near him on the bedside table. It had been on, silently firing screen-saving electronic starbursts onto its cobalt-blue screen. As soon as he hit the button, twelve tones sounded through the computer's speakers.

"What's that?" she asked.

"Those twelve tones are the sound he's gonna make when he punches in the twelve letters of 'WindMinstrel.' I also have a six-tone sequence for 'The Rat.' My computer will be scanning Pennet for those exact tones. As soon as it hears them, we know this guy is hot. I'll double-check Pennet for his username and once I see it we'll know he's out on the Net, using his modem via the cellphone. Then, I'll scan the cell frequencies he could be using. When I hear a modem hiss, I'll feed it to my computer and see if it's The Rat. That'll get his frequency and I'll give it to you. Then you and I have to locate the signal by triangulating on him from two separate locations before he stops transmitting."

"With this stuff?" She was looking at the equipment on the bed.

"Yeah." He picked up one of the smaller radios and turned it on. It wasn't much bigger than a cellphone. He had a homemade loop antenna on the top. "He's using a cellphone operating in the eight-hundred-megahertz band. This is a Uniden BearCat 200XLT hand-held scanner," he explained. "It's one of the few radio scanners that can be modified to scan the eight-hundred-meg frequencies his cellphone uses. They quit making this unit when the FCC made it illegal to listen to cell calls. There are scanners you can buy at Rat Shack, but they are real expensive and automatically lock out the cell frequencies we want. So we pick up this guy's signal, on whatever frequency it goes out on. Then we'll look for the 'null point' in the signal."

"The null point," she said, writing that down.

"Yeah. You got any idea what you're even writing?"

"Don't be an asshole. Just tell me."

"The null point is the weak spot in the signal. Every transmission has a strong point and a weak point. The null point is the spot where the signal disappears when you make the three-sixty spin of the antenna.''

"Don't we want the strongest point? Isn't that the transmission point?''

"Theoretically, yes, but the weak spot is in the exact opposite direction and it's easier to locate. The absolute absence of sound is much easier to find than an abstract guess at where sound is loudest in the spectrum.''

"Got it,'' she said.

"Once we find the null point, we line it up with this Boy Scout compass.'' He held it next to the loop antenna, reading the direction of the plane of the loop. "For instance, if my antenna is pointing like this, it would be exactly two hundred sixteen degrees.'' Malavida set the compass on the road map and turned it until he found 216 degrees. "My motel is here, so we draw a line through my motel out at two hundred sixteen degrees.'' Using a book as a straightedge, he drew a light line on the map. "Now say you're over here in St. Petersburg,'' he said, pointing to another spot on the map. "It doesn't matter how far away, as long as it's far enough to get a baseline on the triangle. You're doing the same thing as me, and let's say you get eighty degrees on your radio, then I plot it in like this. . . .'' He turned the compass till he found 80 degrees, then drew a straight line through her hotel on that heading. The two lines converged and intersected. "Where the lines cross, that's where he is, give or take a square mile or so.''

"A *what*?''

"You gotta figure we're gonna be off a few degrees. This isn't a satellite fix. That few degrees off from several miles away could give us an area as much as a square mile.''

"Shit,'' she said, disappointed. "One square mile in a huge city . . . ? It might as well be a hundred.''

"Look, right now, all we got is metropolitan Tampa. I'm trying to narrow it down. If he's not using tempest shielding, which he's probably not, then there's ways to get closer. Just do what I ask.''

She looked at him and saw that she had hurt his feelings. The dynamics between them had changed. There was something about his energy and bearing that made her see him differently. He no longer seemed like the convict they had picked up in Lompoc. He seemed older and sexier—a thought that struck her as strangely inappropriate. She was having trouble reading her feelings of late. She had made several mistakes in recent years, when she had confused the transitory absence of loneliness with sexual attraction. Her emotional survival alarm went off and she pulled back. "You're right," she said softly. "This is better than where we were. Good going."

"And I don't need a Vaseline rub either," he said sharply.

She reached out and picked up the compass and looked at it for a long moment. "But could you use a hamburger?" she asked recklessly.

# 20

## TRICKY LANDING

They went to Crawdaddy's, which was located at the end of the Courtney Campbell Causeway near St. Petersburg. There were no hamburgers on the menu, but the sign advertised SOUTH FLORIDA CUISINE, and the place was packed.

A calypso steel-drum band was pumping up the atmosphere. Karen and Malavida sat in the rustic bar and waited for a table. Malavida seemed absorbed in thought. Finally he looked up at her and she saw pain in his dark eyes.

"What's wrong?" she asked.

"Claire Lockwood." He pronounced her name slowly, tasting the syllables. A bitter expression drifted across his face. "I just keep thinking . . . what was she doing when The Rat got her? Did she die in pain? Did she die slowly? Did she even know she was dying when it was happening?" He looked down at the Scotch-rocks in front of him and stirred the ice with his finger.

"You didn't kill her, Mal. You were just doing what you were told."

"Yeah." He looked up at her but refused to elaborate.

"You're not at all what you try to look like," she finally said.

"And what do I try to look like?"

"I don't know. I'm not sure yet . . . but it's not what you make people think."

"Nobody is," he said, "you included."

"Especially me." She took a long swallow of her margarita and set it down.

Malavida looked away as he spoke. "You can't show who you are in there. You let 'em see what's really inside, they take it from you the hard way."

"In prison?" she asked. But he didn't answer.

"The only place I ever saw weakness on the inside was Z Block. I used to score medicine on my computer for the queens on that tier. You'd go over there and you could feel the humanity, but the place was like something outta a bad sci-fi movie."

"Z Block . . . ?"

"It was a place where they put all the cons who were infected with AIDS. It was nothing but a coroner's waiting room. The state didn't have the cash to treat those guys, so I tried to score AZT from the pharmaceutical companies on my computer. When I'd get the drugs, I'd take the shipments over. The place was horrible. The smells would gag you . . . decaying flesh, open sores . . . the sounds of men dying. Vomit ran like rainwater down the drains. They had a stroll up there, on the top of the block. It's like a place you can walk all the way around. There were guys on Z who I'd known before they got the virus . . . cons who I thought were violent and unredeemable. One day I saw a guy they called the Maytag Man. He was a prison mechanic, a hit man. He used to take cigarette contracts on other cons. He'd wash you out for two cartons of Camels. He ended up with the virus. One day, I looked up and saw this hardcase helping a dying con walk the stroll, half carrying this skeleton around the tier so he'd get some exercise. Z Block was the only place in the joint I ever saw weakness, the only place where you could give a shit without looking like a target . . . and it was the most unrelenting, horrible place I've ever been."

She looked up at him and saw he was deep in the memory.

"It's why I took off," he continued, "why I ran in Atlanta. Once I was out, I couldn't go back. The place was changing me. There is no friendship in prison, only arrangements to survive. There's no seasons, only time. . . . Your release date and your death certificate are the only two things that change anything."

The maître d' came to show them to their table. They moved across the crowded restaurant as the calypso band played "Yellow Bird" on the steel drums. The people in the restaurant clapped in rhythm to the music. Malavida and Karen sat near the window and she could see the moonlit water in the distance.

She had also been sent away when she was in her teens, to a different kind of prison, being punished for her huge intellect. Her greatest asset, like Malavida's, had ended up costing her her childhood and her freedom.

She looked across the table at him. Again she was startled by the transformation in her attitude toward him. He had opened up to her, shared some feelings. It was as if by shedding the prison dungarees he had altered his whole persona. She knew that if she stopped to examine her feelings using her Ph.D., she would warn herself to be careful. The differences between them far outweighed what they had in common, and she knew opposites attract only in science class. But something deeper drew her to him. In this tall, handsome Chicano, she was seeing long-lost parts of herself. She had read his yellow sheet and knew that his early crimes had been committed to give gifts to his mother, whom he worshiped. He had tried to please her just as Karen had tried to please her father . . . but his sentence had been more severe.

At dinner they talked about things that didn't matter. Malavida continued to come alive, revealing a droll sense of humor. She had two more margaritas. She was beginning to feel fuzzy and warm. She knew she had hit her limit.

The calypso band was replaced by a jazz combo at ten,

and they danced on the small dance floor. She could feel his strong, hard body against hers, and she gripped him tightly, laying her head against his chest. She warned herself again, briefly, then clutched him and forgot the warning.

"Are you okay?" he finally asked.

She smiled up at him. "I think so . . ." she said, but she wasn't at all sure. Several times while she danced, she found her mind drifting to thoughts of Lockwood. She knew Lockwood was a mistake for her. He couldn't nourish her. He was focused on other things, lost in guilt over Claire and remorse over Heather. Karen knew she was just furniture in Lockwood's life. She was resigned to being alone. She couldn't invest herself in another failed relationship. She was too fragile to withstand another loss. Malavida had ulterior motives, but at least she understood them. She clutched him tighter and swayed with the margaritas and the music.

They left the restaurant a little past midnight and walked slowly into the parking lot. Karen took his hand and led him past the car to a small wharf near the restaurant. They sat on a small iron bench on the pier, and she looked out at the shimmering, moonlit water.

"It was nice that you sent away for the medicine."

"It was computer theft . . . Class A felony."

"So why did you do it?" she asked, looking up at him curiously.

He smiled, his white teeth shining in the moonlight. "I don't know, Karen. It's hard to tell with me sometimes. . . ."

"Because you wanted to help them?" she volunteered.

"I'm not that noble. Maybe ten percent . . . but mostly it was like everything else, I just wanted to see if I could do it."

Karen had lived her life on the edge of that temptation. The trouble was, once you strapped yourself into an ALFA Wing and jumped, there was no turning back. You had to live with the outcome.

She reached out and touched his face.

"Karen . . . you're very beautiful and I desperately want to make love to you," he said slowly. "But I owe something to Claire Lockwood. I won't feel right until I pay the debt. . . ."

She knew he was right, but she had already strapped on the ALFA Wing, already started her run. She needed desperately to be close to someone. She was so damn lonely. She kissed him just as he finished the sentence. He put both of his arms around her. She could feel an exchange of chemical electricity. The kiss lasted for almost a minute and then it was followed by another. She wasn't sure what she was doing, or why this was happening. But she knew she needed human warmth, just like the cons on Z Block. She couldn't function in The Rat's depraved world of mutilation and death without some compassion and humanity.

Back at the room they shed their clothes quickly, and, in the dark, they tumbled onto the bed. He was a good lover who took his time. His body was hard and ridged with muscles. The lone teardrop tattoo hung under his eye like a beacon symbolizing their differences. But having already run toward the edge, she now jumped, sailing out into space, falling free, her rudder assembly barely intact. She circled blindly in the dark. He entered her. She found immediate direction in the pleasure. The lovemaking was slow and rhythmic and they both reached orgasm together. They held each other afterward in the dark. She felt his heart beating, his breath on her shoulder. She was lost in the moment. They were sailing together. He had said that only a release date or death certificate changed anything. But what about this? she wondered. Then her practical mind overtook her fantasy. She lay on the bed with his weight on top of her and knew that this would probably be one of her trickiest landings.

# 21

## SATAN'S MESSAGE

The Rat had found a new place for the barge. It was miles farther down the Little Manatee River in the heart of the wetlands. He'd gone searching in his air-boat and he was sure it was deep enough for the heavy metal garbage barge, but he had not yet moved it. He sat in his underwear in the hull, enduring the intense late-afternoon heat. Deep in thought, he looked at the rusting walls. He had been waiting for the coveting to begin, for the sensation of need that filled him like electricity, making his skin burn, turning his mind taut and his emotions quick with longing. He sat in the stifling heat, wondering if he dared turn on the computer again. He knew he was engaged in a vicious, deadly, apocalyptic struggle with the Deity. He knew the answers he needed were more important than the risks; that the Beast must be constructed and given life so the answers could be told to him. He reached out and turned on his computer. He dialed into his account at the University of Florida on his cellphone, which was connected to his modem. He had decided not to use a hardwire phone hookup to reduce his risk of discovery. He would continue to use Pennet as his host computer because he generally trusted the high-tech security on that system, despite what had happened last

Sunday. He decided it was his own carelessness that had caused that disaster.

All week he had worked to make a new program that would be even more secure. It would protect him by using a leapfrog Internet address which was designed to work as an electronic trap. Anybody backfingering to that address would be busted by his alarm program and he would be alerted before they could get to him, allowing him to disconnect from Pennet and vanish into cyberspace.

The Rat knew it was time for a new coveting to begin. He would go back into the SurgiCyberNet, which was where he made all his parts selections for the Beast. It was where he had been given the message almost two years ago that told him how to proceed. He logged on and typed in the name of his electronic trap:

```
LOGFINGER
```

He then telnetted to Pennet at:

```
RING2ICE.ANON.PENNET.NO
```

And his screen said:

```
CONNECTED TO RING2ICE.ANON.PENNET.NO
ESCAPE CHARACTER IS '^]'
SUNOS UNIX (RING2ICE)
LOGIN:
```

He typed in:

```
RAT
```

And the password:

```
MUTIL8OR
```

And was quickly accepted into Pennet:

WELCOME TO PENNET, RAT

He checked the private chat channel to see if Satan might be there, typing:

BBS/NICK WINDMINSTREL

And was greeted by:

WELCOME TO PENNET CHAT, WINDMINSTREL

When he saw Satan wasn't there, he left chat and shot through Pennet and out into cyberspace, then cracked the SurgiCyberNet system with a username/password he had already stolen months ago. SurgiCyberNet was a network for plastic surgeons, who left "before" and "after" pictures of patients and procedures so that they could share new techniques. The Rat had found the SurgiCyberNet chat line two years ago and had begun scrolling avidly through pictures of naked women. Its symbol on the Internet was $\mathbb{S}$. The symbol had fascinated him. The $S$ inside the $C$ seemed to beckon him. $S$ was Shirley's initial; $C$ and $S$ stood for cyberspace, which was his most powerful universe. Could this be a sign? As he looked at the pictures of naked women, his mind was still on the symbol. Then, by accident, he came across a picture of a woman who had unshaven legs and stocky, Shirley-like ankles. Shirley had never shaved her legs, because she said shaving one's appendages to attract sexual favors offended God. The Rat looked at the picture of the woman with Shirley's ankles for hours. Her name was Leslie Bowers and she was scheduled for liposuction on her thighs. It was almost as if Shirley's lower legs were there on the screen. His heart pounded and he wondered how two people could have identical calves and ankles. Had God also told this woman not to shave her legs? Then a mind-numbing thought hit him: Unless Shirley and the woman had a genuine correlation in the universe, unless they were part of the exact same eternal mosaic, how could they have calves and ankles that looked exactly the same? He knew that no two faces or fingerprints were identical. With legs, of course, there were far fewer identifiers, but still the thought intrigued him. It buzzed in his head like a broken speaker for days. It plagued him at night and kept him awake.

He had returned to the SurgiCyberNet chat line every evening. Each time, he would find Leslie Bowers's picture and surgical data. Then one night, he saw the message! Under the picture of Leslie Bowers, it said:

SURGERY DATE 1/13/94

And below that:

R. 13-15

Had the surgery date been revised from the thirteenth to the fifteenth? He wondered if it could mean something else. Could it be a clever message? The Rat had learned that numerals were often disguised messages. And then the true meaning screamed at him. . . . How could he have missed it? He ran upstairs and found Shirley's Bible. His hands shook as he looked up chapter 13 of Revelation and read verses 13 and 14:

*And he doeth great wonders . . . And deceiveth them that dwell on the earth, by the means of those miracles which he had power to do in the sight of the beast; saying to them that dwell on the earth, that they should make an image to the beast, which had the wound by a sword, and did live.*

He read on to verse 15, his throat dry, his mouth open:

*And he had power to give life unto the image of the beast, that the image of the beast should both*

*speak, and cause that as many as would not wor-
ship the image of the beast should be killed.*

It had taken a great deal of effort not to shout his joy.
He had found the answer. He should make the image of
a Beast. . . . He had long known that he had the mark of
the Beast on him. Shirley had told him, when he got the
sickness and all of his hair fell out, that he had been
marked by the devil. Revelation 13:15 said that he had
the power to give the miracle of life unto the image of
the Beast, that the image of the Beast should speak, and
that all who would not worship the image would be
killed. . . . He knew this message was from the Anti-
Christ, and the clever devil had used the Lord's own
testament to send it, using a woman who had Shirley's
unshaven legs as the messenger.

From then on, his mission had been clear. He would
construct the Beast. Shirley had all the answers and so it
was Shirley to whom he had to give life. That prophecy
in Revelation had been made clear to him two years ago.
It had been the beginning of the reconstruction and resurrection. The Rat had learned to covet and The Wind
Minstrel had come forward in all his glory to swing the
sword of reckoning. The first victim had been Leslie
Bowers. She lived in Detroit. Her fat calves and ankles
were in a freezer not ten feet from where he now sat in
the rusting garbage barge. There had been five others
who had contributed to the Beast; everything was there
but the head. But the head was a special problem. It had
to look exactly like Shirley. The head would be his final
victim.

Malavida had driven Karen across to St. Petersburg
early the next morning. She had checked into the Comfort Inn, which was well positioned, right on the bay.
They had stood in the parking lot, holding hands in silence. "I better get back," he'd finally said. They both
felt awkward, wondering if they had true affection for

each other or had just taken care of long-overdue emotional and biological needs.

"I'll call you. Get all that stuff set up on the balcony," he'd said, then gotten into his rental van and driven back to Tampa. That had been four hours ago.

In his motel room, Malavida's computer picked up the tones of The Rat's login and rang an alarm, bringing him in from the balcony where he'd been setting up his direction finder. He grabbed his phone and dialed Karen Dawson's cellular. Karen picked up on the second ring.

"Hello?"

"He's hot." Malavida looked at his computer screen, which had captured the exact frequency of The Rat's cellphone:

876.000 MHZ

"See if you've got anything on eight-seventy-six megahertz," Malavida said, and both of them were silent as they carefully twisted their antennas. He could now hear the sound of electronic static, indicating that on 876 megahertz he had a cellphone in use with a modem somewhere on the Tampa pod. "I got it!" he said.

"Me too," she answered.

"Find the null point and gimme the degrees," he commanded.

Karen had her radio unit and loop antenna out on the tenth-floor balcony of the Comfort Inn, overlooking the windswept bay. She twisted the antenna loop until she could no longer hear the transmission static, quickly finding the null point. She laid the Boy Scout compass that Malavida had given her on the table and rotated it to line up with the loop antenna.

"One hundred and sixty-four degrees," she said into the telephone.

Malavida, with his phone cocked under his ear, also found the null point. His compass said 193 degrees.

"Hold on a second," he told her and ran inside. He laid his compass on the map. He found Karen's coordinates first. He had marked her hotel's location at the end of the Howard Frankland Bridge on Highway 275 with a big *X*. He marked a course 164 degrees from that location and drew a line with a pencil and ruler. Then, from his own location, he found 193 degrees and drew another line.

The lines intersected in the wetlands south of Tampa, about a mile and a half up the Little Manatee River.

''Gotcha, you cocksucker,'' he said under his breath.

# 22

## RUSH TO THE APOCALYPSE

"**Y**eah?" Lockwood said into the telephone.

"How you doing?" Karen's voice came back softly.

"Not good," he sighed. He was standing at the hospital nurses' station. It was nine P.M. and, after almost four hours of tossing and turning, Heather was finally asleep in her room down the corridor.

"I'm really so sorry, John," she said, and when he didn't answer, she went on. "How's Heather?"

"You tell me. She saw this guy kill her mother. She's just coming out of traumatic shock."

"That's horrible," she said, stating the obvious and feeling dumb because of it.

Karen was calling from Malavida's motel room in Tampa. Malavida had made her promise that she wouldn't tell Lockwood he was there. He was afraid Lockwood would run a team in and bust him.

"Did Heather get a good look at who did it?" Karen finally asked.

"Yeah. She said he was huge, fat, and bald. She said he was killing her mommy with a knife and that he didn't have any eyebrows. I'm not sure it's a good description. A lot of it may be mixed up with the shock."

"John, I'm in Tampa. I'm working with a friend of

182

mine from the University of Miami. He's an ace computer cracker. We did a triangulation program down here, looking for the guy Malavida found on Pennet. We think we picked up his cellphone location. My friend tells me it's accurate within a square mile or so. . . .''

Lockwood straightened up and looked at the nurse who was preparing a tray of night medicine a few feet away. "You're doing *what*?"

"It's a long story, but we've got the location of his cellphone site pinned down to about a square mile. Unfortunately, it's in a huge swampland that's fed by a Tampa Bay river. It's gonna be hard to find him in there because it's marshy and pretty dense, but my friend says there's a way to narrow the location down further. It might go faster if we had a helicopter and some boats. I thought you could arrange that through Customs—"

"Let me get this straight. You're in Florida? You went to Tampa? You looked up an old friend from the University and you're working this headcase on your own?"

There was a long pause. "Not smart, I bet, huh?"

"It's way south of not smart, Karen."

"Well, John, it's done, and we got the fix without leaving our hotel rooms. So we weren't in much danger. If we narrow it down, I thought you'd want to be in on it," she said, knowing he wouldn't refuse.

After he hung up with Karen, he booked the 11:30 red-eye to Tampa. Then he went back into Heather's room. She was awake, looking at the door as he moved through it.

"Daddy," she said softly.

He gently sat on the bed and took her hand.

"I'm scared, Daddy. What if he comes?"

"I won't let that happen, honey."

"How do you know he won't?"

" 'Cause I'm gonna go find him and catch him and put him away where he won't be able to ever hurt anyone again."

"Daddy . . . I don't want him to hurt you," she said suddenly.

"He won't hurt me. He can't . . . not ever."

"Why not?"

"Because I have your love to protect me." He leaned down and hugged her. Her face felt warm against his. He sat back and looked at her; he saw in her Claire's cobalt-blue eyes. Their legacy haunted him. "And then we'll go away and live happily ever after," he said, smiling. "Maybe on a farm. Just you and me, a few horses, some chickens and ducks . . ."

"And a hippopotamus." She was looking at the colorful painting on the wall.

The airplane took off on schedule, and he tried to sleep but his mind raced. He had not told Karen that he'd lost his badge, that he was now just John Lockwood, unemployed private citizen. But he was still one of the best pound-for-pound bullshitters on the planet, and, even without his badge, he would find a way to even out the terrain. He leaned back and tried to get some sleep as the jet engines hummed, but his eyes kept popping open. He felt strange, as if he'd lost something he couldn't fully calculate. It was tied to Claire's death, of course, but it was also more than that. . . . It was as if everything was flat, with no depth or substance. It was as if he'd somehow lost a full dimension. He was afraid, unable to control his course. . . . Like the purple hippo on Heather's wall, he felt like he was looking down with wide eyes, riding powerless under a brightly painted gas balloon.

Karen Dawson got to the airport early, had a Coke, and watched an old Roy Rogers movie on the TV over the bar in the passenger lounge.

It was 7:30 A.M. when Lockwood's plane landed and Karen met him coming off the American flight. They moved quickly out into the humid Florida morning. She led him across the street to her blue LeBaron and filled him in on how they'd triangulated on The Rat's cell-phone signal, explaining the 800-megahertz band and all about null points. He listened and settled in next to her in the passenger seat while she put the car in motion.

"Okay, where to next?" he asked.

"My friend has a lot of stuff in a motel room. He says the next part of this operation is to get into that swamp and start scanning for the computer The Rat's using—"

"And how do we do that?" Lockwood said, looking at her.

"Well, my friend says that every radio, as well as every TV and computer console, acts like a transmitter as well as a receiver. . . . He says electrical equipment in use always transmits radio frequency signals. He also thinks our killer is using top-of-the-line stuff—"

"Really?" Lockwood interrupted.

"My friend says that crackers are all equipment freaks; they need to have the latest stuff. A generation in computer technology is six months or less. If this guy's current, he'll have a TI or Toshiba Pentium 166-megahertz notebook with 128 megs of RAM, or some equivalent. Like I just told you, all electrically powered units transmit radio frequency signatures while they're on. He says there's a thing called TEMPEST; it means Transient Electromagnetic Pulse Emanation Standard and it's the maximum amount of electromagnetic radiation the Federal government will allow high-security devices to emit.

"Even the best-shielded system still leaks. It's unlikely the killer has lined his computer and keyboard with lead foil to decrease its TEMPEST emissions, because my friend says nobody but spies and cold-war spooks ever did that."

"Who is this guy? What's your friend's name?"

Karen, who did not have a degree in bullshit, threw out the first name that jumped into her head. "Dale Evans," she said. Immediately her face turned red.

"Dale *Evans*? Like in Roy Rogers?"

"Yeah. In college we called him Trigger. Pretty funny what some parents will name their kids, huh?" She felt moronic, but Lockwood turned away, looking out the window.

He always thought that Florida was beautiful, even

though it was flat as a table. He marveled at the white, puffy clouds that hovered over Tampa Bay, throwing dark shadows across the aqua-green water.

They arrived at the motel. Karen unlocked Malavida's room and they entered. Lockwood looked down at the electronic equipment scattered on the bed. Then the bathroom door opened and Malavida stepped into the room.

"How you doin', Zanzo?" the tall Mexican said.

"Well, whatta we got here? . . . Is this good ol' Mr. Trigger?" Lockwood said, his face going cold.

"That's him," Karen said, hoping the whole plan wasn't about to go ballistic.

"You're under arrest, Chacone. Turn around, put your hands on the wall."

Of course, Lockwood didn't have a gun, badge, or cuffs, but he went through the pat-down anyway. Then he spun Malavida around, shoved him against the wall, and glared at him.

"Are you through with this chickenshit performance?" Malavida said, his back to the wall.

"Karen, if you came down here with this guy, you're an accessory-after-the-fact in a Class A felony."

"Actually he called me and invited me down."

"Hey, Lockwood, instead of fronting me off and getting your balls all puckered, why don't you calm down and listen for a minute?"

"I'm not gonna calm down. I'm gonna drag your ass right down to the Federal lockup."

"You and me got something in common."

"Yeah? What's that?"

"You made a mistake taking me to your wife's house to do that crack, and I made a mistake by being careless and not using a masking program. Between the two of us, she got dead."

"And you give a shit about that?"

"Yeah, I do. I never helped someone get dead before. I can't stop thinking about it. But I know how to get this guy, Lockwood. I'm better than him and I can do it. I can find him . . . but you gotta help."

"I do, huh?" Lockwood glowered. "And then what?"

"I help you get this asshole. Once we get him, you close your eyes and count to a hundred. After that, you can do whatever you want. You can go get a drink and toast my escape, or you can load up a posse and come after me. I just want a running head start."

Lockwood stood looking at him for a long time. He could see in Malavida's young face both a resolve and a sadness that matched his own.

"You really think you can find him? He already burned us once."

"Hey, Lockwood, I'm the best there is. The best cracker-jack in the world. Nobody's ever been born was better, and that includes this scalpel-wielding, zooted-up dickhead. I made one careless mistake, but it won't happen again. I'll get him, but you gotta give me some slack and a little equipment."

There was a long silence while Lockwood considered it. He knew Malavida was probably the best chance he had.

"Okay, Mal . . . you got my help and the head start, if and when we find him."

"We need a helicopter and some airboats," the Chicano said, still leaning against the wall.

"That's gonna be tough."

"Call Customs. Tell 'em you need 'em."

"Wouldn't help. I handed back my badge. . . . I was about to get suspended anyway."

"You mean now you're not even a cop?"

"Oh, I'm a cop. That doesn't ever go away. I just don't have any jurisdiction or authority. The good news is, I'm not stuck fighting a bunch of regulations anymore. From now on, far as I'm concerned, Miranda is just a lady who danced with fruit in her hat."

# 23

## THE PLAN

They spread the map out in the motel room, which suddenly seemed too small and too hot for the three of them. Lockwood was good at reading unspoken language between people, and he could see that there had been a shift in the dynamic between Karen and Malavida. She occasionally looked at the young Chicano with something other than clinical interest. She wrote down a lot of what he said and rushed to help him with small tasks. Malavida seemed to smile with his eyes when he talked to her.

Lockwood hated himself. It was just days after Claire's murder and he shouldn't give a damn about what happened between them, but he couldn't help it. He did. Not that he had a romantic interest in Karen Dawson . . . Maybe under different circumstances he could have, but under these, it was impossible. Nonetheless, he didn't want to see her with Malavida Chacone. This was made doubly difficult by the fact that he had to relinquish control of this part of the operation to a long-haired Chicano convict. Lockwood was lost in his cybernetic world. Malavida had written down all the information about the radio wave emanations he could dig out from the owner's manuals. He felt The Rat might have the latest and greatest TI and Toshiba Pentium notebooks, plus large-format monitors from Hitachi, Sony, or NEC. Malavida was packing his two radio receivers into a suitcase while Lockwood was studying a map of the Little Manatee River that he had picked up from the Tampa Tourist Bureau.

"This place is crisscrossed with shell roads. Some may have been washed out by summer rains, some might have been taken by high tides. The whole area is marshy and unstable," he said.

Karen moved over to look at the map.

"We've gotta split up," Malavida said. "Karen and I will take a boat. You take the car. Try to get in there close enough to receive his computer transmission. It should be detectable from a mile or so; then we'll see if we can walk each other in."

Lockwood noted that "Miss Dawson" had now become "Karen," but decided to wait until they were alone before saying anything to Malavida.

"We need walkie-talkies," Lockwood said, looking at Karen. "You'll have to go. My Customs credit cards are stopped. Find a radio store, get the Sony 1600s with extra battery packs and charging units."

Something told Karen not to leave them alone.

"We'll be okay." Malavida grinned. "If he gets bored, he can just pat me down again."

"I'll be right back," she finally said and reluctantly left the room.

Lockwood waited till the sound of her footsteps disappeared; then he turned to Malavida, who was still packing the suitcase.

"Let's me and you get something straight. . . ."

"What's that, Zanzo?" His back was to Lockwood.

"You wanna help. Okay, I'm gonna take you up on it 'cause, frankly, I'm outta options. You want a running head start when this is over. . . . Okay, I hate it, but that's the price of the ticket. But you better stop giving Karen back rubs. She needs a massage, I'll find a tall Swedish guy."

Malavida stopped packing and Lockwood continued:

''She's in over her head. She hasn't got a clue what she's signed on for. You an' me, we've spent time around sprung motherfuckers like The Rat, but this is just a field trip for her. He could kill her without raising his heartbeat. She needs all her senses focused on the game.''

Malavida turned now, and Lockwood saw he was smiling.

''Something I said was funny?''

''You fuckin' amaze me, John. You left your badge upside down in a bucket of shit, so let's you an' *me* get something straight. I don't have to listen to your bullshit. I'm a wanted man, but you're harboring a fugitive. You're also fucked up and operating illegally. The reason I'm doing this isn't so I can bump Karen Dawson. I'm doing it 'cause I wanna make up for getting your ex-wife killed. You, I could give less of a shit about. You got some limited law enforcement skills and they might come in handy, but dating advice you can stick up your ass. Back off or I'm shutting my end down, and without me, you won't get him.''

They stood glowering at one another. The silence grew heavier in the room, but neither had anything else to say. Lockwood hadn't slept in more than twenty-four hours and his eyes were grainy. He moved to the window and looked out at the Florida interstate.

''How's your little girl?'' Malavida asked, his tone softer.

''She wants her mommy. So do I . . .''

''We'll get this guy. Let's just not forget what's going down between us. Things have changed.''

Lockwood realized he was right. He looked at the young Chicano and believed he had come down here for the right reasons.

''Are you strapped?'' Malavida broke through his thoughts.

''No, they took my gun in D.C. I need to pick something up. I've got a friend down here, Ray Gonzales. He's in Jackson Memorial Hospital with a leaky kidney, but I think he's got family in St. Pete. I'll make a call, see if I can line something up.''

"Get one for me.''

Lockwood smiled. ''That's just what this caper needs . . . another unlicensed shooter.''

Lockwood got in touch with Ray Gonzales in the renal ward at Jackson Memorial in Miami. Ray told him that his nephew would deliver something. Lockwood gave him a list of favorite handguns, starting with a nine-millimeter Beretta and working down to an S&W Chief with a two-inch barrel. It was the same piece Customs had issued to him, and although he'd never been able to hit anything with it, at least the short muzzle didn't poke him when he sat.

"How you feeling, Ray?'' Lockwood asked his friend at the end of the call.

"I'm hoping I can get out of here in a month. Then I gotta take it easy for a while. I only got one kidney now, and it ain't looking so hot.''

"That means you're gonna have to stop drinking all that cheap Cuban rum, amigo.''

"I'd rather float face-down in the bay.'' Gonzales's voice grinned at him over the line.

Ray's nephew, Enrique, showed up in the motel parking lot two hours later. He turned out to be a sixteen-year-old hardcase with a bad complexion and a surly attitude. He handed Lockwood a box wrapped in brown paper.

"Ray, he say you some big-time coco-cop. You the one gonzoed them meltdowns at Miami Airport, shoot up the place, go crazy, fucking cowboys an' Indians. *Mi tío* works with cops, whatta fuckin' nut.''

"Your uncle's diamond-hard. He's a man. You should try and be like him,'' Lockwood volunteered lamely.

"You think?'' the boy said sullenly. "I think he's a buster.'' Then he moved off, bobbing his head slightly, his long black hair bouncing. He got into a primer-patched car with two other Cuban boys and they roared off, leaving a trail of blue exhaust on the asphalt.

Lockwood opened the box in the parking lot. The gun was a twenty-year-old army-issue .45 with a weak clip spring. There was half a box of ammo. Somebody had started cutting dumdum crosses in the soft lead noses of the slugs. "Great," he said to himself in disgust.

He climbed the stairs and reentered the motel room. Karen showed up twenty minutes later with the walkie-talkies. All they needed to do was rent an outboard tomorrow, get into the Little Manatee River, and wait. It was already Friday afternoon. It seemed hard for Lockwood to realize that all of this had happened in less than a week.

That night, Karen was sitting on the bed, looking at Malavida and Lockwood.

"I know you guys are sort of humoring me," she started, "and that the only reason I'm still here is because we have a severe lack of manpower."

Lockwood forced a tight smile; Malavida remained expressionless. She picked up her yellow pad, which now had pages of annotations and profiling information.

"I thought before we go get this guy, we should try to understand a little about him. I already told you I got Leslie Bowers out of the VICAP computer. Using her murder and Candice's and Claire's, I've got a beginning read on this guy, plus a couple of pretty good hunches. . . . Wanna hear 'em?"

Both Lockwood and Malavida nodded.

"Okay. To begin with, aside from being big and ugly, I think The Rat could also be a multiple."

"Multiple personalities? Where'd that come from?" Lockwood asked.

"It's a little oblique, but follow me on this." They both waited. "We have two killings that fit one pattern, and one killing that fits a completely different pattern. All of them, we're reasonably sure, were done by one man. Candice Wilcox and Leslie Bowers were killed by a very sophisticated, very organized, highly intelligent perp. This guy used his computer to set the stage and change the time frame. He used trash bags; he used a blitz attack, taking the first two victims quickly and killing them instantly with one stroke from behind, using a narrow blade which we know, or suspect, is one of his scalpels.''

''So?'' Lockwood said.

''Pre-, peri-, and post-offense behavior was exact and planned in detail . . . very obsessive. The UnSub who killed Candice and Leslie is manipulative, compulsive, and dominant. In short, a control freak. Claire's murder, on the other hand, was sloppy: He walked in the back door, neighbors say he left his car parked in plain sight across the street. He probably didn't case the crime scene. . . . He failed on his opening blitz attack, which looks like it happened in the kitchen and ended up with her still alive and fighting in the bedroom. He hacked and slashed at her in a frenzy. It was a mess. Then, to top it off, he got walked in on by Heather. There's no post-mortem mutilation, there's no masturbation, no sexual substitutes.''

''That doesn't mean anything,'' Lockwood said. His heart was skipping beats as they talked about Claire's murder. He was determined not to let his voice or face betray the frightening loss he was feeling. ''If Heather walked in, the UnSub wouldn't have time. He killed Claire for lurking in his computer chat room. He was trying to eliminate an eavesdropper. . . . That's why there's no ritual.''

''I understand,'' she said, ''and I agree, but the guy who did the first two murders, in my opinion, wouldn't have done the third. The first guy would still have tried to control the scene. He gets nothing for doing a hasty, sloppy job—he put himself at risk.''

''So you think he's got two personalities?'' Lockwood said slowly.

''Or more,'' she said. ''We know he's on a week or ten-day cycle and he's degenerating. Maybe he's different people at different times in the cycle. When he sees us in the chat room, he's the wrong guy. But he has to move, he's panicked. So he comes out to L.A. and does his thing, but it's not with the same control or preparation. . . . It's spur of the moment, amateurish. Off the cuff and sloppy. But we know the murderer is the same physical being, because he used the same weapon all three times.''

"That's pretty farfetched," Malavida said. "What if it's two guys?"

"I don't think so," she said. "My gut tells me this guy's a loner."

"I think she's got something," Lockwood said, giving it careful thought. "I mean, maybe it's not exactly right, but it fits the crime scene information. Psychiatrists always start with a personality and infer behavior, but you can make mistakes that way. The way she's doing it is better. You start with the behavior, what he actually did, and infer personality from his acts.''

"Another thing," she said. "He kills quickly. One strike to the chest, attacking from behind; they're dead in seconds. If he's seven feet tall and as big as Heather says, he could easily control his victims. Why the blitz attacks?"

"I give up, why?" Malavida asked.

"I think he's afraid of women—not in a physical sense, but in an emotional one. He's been hurt, possibly terrorized, by a woman as a child. He's afraid of emotional or mental contact. If he was abused by a mother or older female adult when he was young, that could fit in with the split in his personality. He becomes a multiple, splits into a separate new personality, so he doesn't have to deal with the pain of the abuse against him by the adult female.''

"Why do we need to know all of this?" Malavida said. "We just go out there and level the bastard."

"Because this is not somebody who will act or react the way you think he will. We have to study The Rat, learn who he is, to be able to anticipate him." She said, "Look, this is my field, I've spent years learning this. It's all in *DSM* if you wanna plow through it."

"What's *DSM?*" Malavida asked.

"*Diagnostic and Statistical Manual of Mental Disorders,*" Lockwood explained. "And I'm listening. As a matter of fact, I'm impressed. You got anything else?"

She looked down at her yellow pad.

"He'll probably drive a dark blue or black van or truck."

"Oh, come on," Malavida said.

"He's orderly and compulsive. Orderly and compulsive people like dark cars . . . ask any car salesman. Repeat killers tend to prefer windowless vans or trucks; it gives them a work space and room for the body if they need to move it. That, by the way, is a computer-generated fact."

Malavida leaned back on the bed and smiled at her as she went on.

"The last thing you need to know is he's got what we call, in the language of mental disorders, an assassin's personality. He's a loner, nocturnal, extremely compulsive, and is probably an incessant journal writer. He's probably got books full of his ideas and rantings. If we find them, his handwriting will be cramped and tiny. When cornered he will be ferocious beyond description, vicious beyond belief. He has no empathy for anything. He lives in a world he's created. He's shut out most human contact." She turned the pad over on the bed and looked at them for a moment. "I've got some other things here, but they're still too farfetched to really talk about, till I get more."

"That's a hell of a start, Karen," Lockwood said.

"Here's a problem you can work on." Malavida moved from the bed over to the direction finder on the table. "We can only home in on this guy while he's using his computer. . . . We could be drifting around out in the swamps forever, waiting for him to get hot, which is the only time we can read the electrical leakage from his equipment. I'd sure like to narrow the time frame, or we're gonna be using a hell of a lot of bug repellent."

"I think we should be out there at about the same time

we first intercepted him," she finally said. "That will be day after tomorrow, say four-thirty in the afternoon."

"Why?" Lockwood asked.

"There was something about that call that seemed like it was scheduled," she continued.

"What it seemed like to me was a lotta sick, rambling bullshit," Lockwood corrected her.

"Satan in Oslo said, 'You have severed her limbs, which are worthless, lustful appendages. How did it feel? Did you taste her blood this time? It has been a week. How did it feel?' A week. Maybe he's saying it's been a week since they last talked."

Again, Malavida and Lockwood were both impressed by Karen's total recall of Satan's message on the monitor. It was becoming obvious that she had a photographic memory.

Lockwood stretched out on the adjoining bed and laced his fingers behind his neck. "He could have been talking about a week since The Rat's last kill, not since his last call."

"Yeah, I thought of that too. But after The Rat unrolled all that religious gobbledygook about the wicked not suffering punishment in eternal hell, Satan said, 'Enough about this. I've told you each session I can't use your religious rantings.' Each *session* ... A session is generally by appointment. I was wondering, what if these two freaks have a weekly date to talk on the Internet?"

"This guy is in Oslo, Norway. Why wouldn't he just send e-mail to talk to The Rat? Why would it have to be by weekly appointment?"

"I think he's in prison," Malavida volunteered.

"He's where?"

"In prison. I did a UNIX 'who is?' on Pennet. I found he was on from the Inselbrook State Penitentiary in Oslo. The number he was calling from is in the law library. They wouldn't tell me who was there last Sunday at midnight."

"If he's got a prearranged time," she said, "we could just show up out in the wetlands when they're chatting on the Net. We'd have a much better chance of catching The Rat if we knew the exact time."

Lockwood knew Karen was right. He sat up on the bed.

"How come you didn't come up with this?" Malavida said.

"Cut me some slack. I'm just here with my limited law enforcement skills," Lockwood said, and then suddenly all of them were smiling.

Lockwood slept all day Saturday and into Sunday. He woke up a few times and saw that Karen was watching television while Malavida was working on his equipment. At noon Sunday, he called Heather in the hospital in Hollywood, but was told by the nurse that she was sleeping.

At two P.M. they drove south, toward the Little Manatee River, on Interstate 75. A few miles north of Sun City, they saw a wooden pier with a small shack that advertised boat rentals, and pulled into the gravel parking lot. They went inside the shack and rented a fifteen-foot aluminum boat with two wooden benches and a fuel-stained twenty-horsepower Evinrude outboard. The man who rented it to them was as stringy as alligator bait, with the name "Gilbert" stitched on his greasy shirt. Lockwood asked him about the roads in the wetlands and if there was a map.

"Ain't no road map. Them roads change ever' season. Y'all try an' take that blue LeBaron in there, y'gonna be buyin' it from Mr. Hertz straight off."

The man took forty dollars cash and Karen's driver's license as a deposit, and told them that the Little Manatee River was about a mile farther down the bay. After warning them to stay out of the marshlands, and that if he had to come pull them out it was an extra hundred, he gave them a quick instruction course on how to operate the tired motor, and then he wandered back up the pier to his shack.

They needed to change the plan. Since the roads

weren't marked and Lockwood would be at a distinct disadvantage in the car, they decided to go together in the boat.

They loaded in the equipment. Lockwood hit the starter button and the Evinrude coughed to life. Malavida untied them, jumped aboard, and pushed off. Lockwood had little experience with boats and was delighted to find that Karen Dawson came from a family of recreational fishermen; he readily handed over the helm.

A mile down the bay they found the mouth of the Little Manatee and glided into its reeded silence. Karen idled the engine down and they slid along the placid waterway. The dense reeds on both sides lined the channel like slats on a picket fence. It was as if they had moved back in time. The muted colors were washed and cooked pale from the Florida sun. Once they saw a gator slide off the bank and submerge itself in the pale-brown water by the edge of the river. Blue herons sat on dead logs and watched with curious, frightened eyes, their long necks stretched forward like old men in church. Water bugs slithered across the surface, their large, winged bodies making the feat seem impossible. The ever-present keening of insects was overpowering.

Lockwood was trying to keep his senses alert, although the placid scenery had a dulling effect. . . . The marshy wetlands were desolate and beautiful in their peaceful isolation. Occasional deciduous trees hung out over the river, gnarled stick figures pointing the way.

At ten past four, Malavida, who was in the bow, held up his hand. "Hold it. Got something." He was looking at a volt-ohm meter attached to the radio receiver. "Turn right," he commanded and Karen swung the boat right. "Hold it, hold it!" he shouted. "Shut off the engine."

She did, and then they were drifting. Lockwood grabbed the paddle in the boat and put it into the water to stop their turn.

"Back to the center," Malavida said, and he waited while Lockwood made the correction.

"See this?" He pointed at the little digital display on

the meter attached to the radio receiver. ''That's a very weak, fluctuating electrical signal. It's consistent with the kind of TEMPEST output we should get from a new TI or Toshiba notebook. It's coming from that direction. . . .'' He pointed at a wall of reeds on the side of the river.

''We're gonna need a dozer to get through there,'' Lockwood said.

''Maybe there's a tributary farther up that heads back around,'' Karen ventured.

''Okay, let's look,'' Lockwood said.

She hit the starter and the engine coughed and turned over, running roughly, choking on unused gas and oil. She smoothed it out and they continued on up the river, which was now beginning to snake back and forth as it transected the watery swamp.

Lockwood opened the box and checked the clip on his .45. He had loaded the dumdum bullets in so they would be fired last, just in case the first several shots failed to do the job. The saying in law enforcement is ''If you don't get 'em with one, you'll be carried by six.'' But Lockwood was such a bad shot, he liked a full clip.

Karen was right. They found the tributary about a quarter mile farther up on the left. She turned into it and they headed back in the direction they had just come from.

The channel was twisting and blocked in narrow spots by fallen trees. A few times Lockwood and Malavida had to get out of the aluminum boat and pull branches out of the stream. It was slow going, but Malavida said the computer signal was getting stronger.

''This guy is up here somewhere,'' Malavida said.

At 4:15, the signal abruptly stopped and the needle gauge went to zero. They were moving slowly up the river. ''Cut the engine,'' Malavida said, and Karen shut off the outboard. They were drifting silently, the river narrowing and getting shallow. They listened to the keening insects, their ears desperately trying to peel some other sound out of the wall of noise.

"Keep going," Malavida finally said. "Use the paddle."

Lockwood put the paddle into the water and pulled them along. The late-afternoon sun glistened on the rippling water. The desolate beauty somehow managed to steal from their sense of danger. Karen found herself watching wild flowers and brightly colored swamp birds hopping from limb to limb, flying low among the river foliage.

They rounded a corner and almost ran smack into it. Tied to a tree with a rusting chain and two ropes, it loomed in ghastly decaying ugliness. It was some sort of old metal garbage barge. Lockwood estimated it was about two stories high and maybe thirty feet wide. Painted on the stern, in faded chipped letters, was WIND MINSTREL.

Lockwood pointed at the name, and Karen and Malavida nodded, their lips tight.

"Okay," Lockwood whispered, "let's beach it over there."

He paddled the aluminum boat silently toward the wall of reeds and the bottom slid up on the marshy, shell-encrusted ground, making a slurpy, scratching sound as it stopped. They got out, ruining their shoes with river mud.

Lockwood motioned with the gun, and they pulled the boat up out of sight and then silently moved away from it toward the barge. Lockwood wanted a visual reconnaissance before he moved in. They crouched in the reeds and looked at the barge in the gathering twilight. From the side, it appeared much larger than he had originally anticipated. It was at least a hundred feet long.

"Okay, I'm going in. You stay out here and make sure I don't get surprised. . . ."

"You any good with that thing?" Malavida asked, pointing at the .45.

"Not much," Lockwood admitted.

"I'm going with you. I'm not gonna do you any good out here. At least I can throw a punch."

Lockwood nodded. "But Karen, you gotta stay here and watch the back door. If this guy's aboard, that's one thing. If he's not, I don't want him coming in behind us." He handed her one walkie-talkie, which was set on Channel 72. He kept the other unit himself. "It's on. If you need help, trigger it twice. Two static bursts and we're back out here. If anybody's coming up behind us, give us one."

"Okay." Her voice was tight and she looked scared, but he knew she wouldn't bolt or go soft in the clinch. He motioned to Malavida. "Okay, Ladrón, it's you and me."

"Let's go, Zanzo."

They moved around to the right, looking for hard ground, which they found a few yards upriver. Moving in a crouch, they headed toward the small ramp that led from the ground to a door cut halfway up in the vertical face of the hull. It appeared to be a hatch that had been used to off-load garbage from amidships.

Lockwood went first, with the gun at port arms. He moved up the ramp with Malavida on his heels. Lockwood pushed the door gently, but the rusting hinges squealed loudly. Lockwood froze and listened for movement. There was nothing, so he pushed it farther open, ducked quickly through the hatch opening, and pressed himself flat against the interior wall. Malavida came in behind him.

It was humid and dank inside. The walls reeked with the smell of old refuse. Lockwood's stomach leapt up in his throat. His eyes adjusted to the darkness and he moved along a narrow gangplank to a descending ladderway. He glanced back at Malavida, whose face was tight and eyes large. "Here," Lockwood said, handing him the .45. "Cover me. I'm going down the ladder."

Malavida took the gun as Lockwood turned and climbed down the metal ladder. His back was to the huge open hold. He was an easy target as he climbed down. His neck hairs and shoulder muscles tingled as he risked exposure. Malavida watched the dark companionway, staring out at the blackness, his mouth open so he wouldn't have to breathe the stench through his nose.

Lockwood reached the bottom of the ladder. "Throw it down," he whispered. "Put the safety on first."

Malavida pushed the safety on and dropped the gun down to Lockwood, who caught it; then Malavida climbed down the ladder while Lockwood covered him. . . .

Karen was in the weeds and brambles, holding the walkie-talkie. She moved slowly to her right so that she could get a better view of the barge. The dense brush and thorns ripped at her ankles. Then she saw something out of the corner of her eye. She turned and glimpsed a shape moving some distance away through the reeds. She didn't know if it was a man or an animal, but it was large. She turned and edged in the direction of the moving form, which had now disappeared. Her problem-solving mind instantly calculated that there must be a path over there, because she had heard no reeds or underbrush snapping as the figure passed. She moved slowly in that direction, her hand on the button of the walkie-talkie.

She came out of the dense brush and saw there was a one-lane dirt road cut through the foliage that was wide enough to accommodate a car. She edged out onto the road and looked in the direction the shape had been moving. Off in the distance, through the dense reeds, she could barely make out something that was painted a pale shade of blue. She moved toward it, hugging the overgrown dense brush at the side of the road. Then she saw the pale-blue house. . . .

It was about twenty yards away. The yard was cut from the thick surrounding underbrush; the roof was pitched and the entire structure made of wood. A well-maintained porch fronted the house and in the yard were several old cars, a bicycle, and a swing. It was picturesque . . . a peaceful house deep in the middle of a lush watery swamp.

\* \* \*

Lockwood and Malavida opened the large hull door and found themselves in the center hold of the barge. This was the main area where the garbage was once carried. The metal hatch overhead was rusting, and when Lockwood and Malavida looked up, they could see only a few pinholes of sunlight leaking through. Malavida found a light switch and turned it on.

It was hard to believe what they saw. The computers were all brand-new warp-speed, superhighway monsters from Toshiba. There were three of them, all placed neatly on a wooden desk pushed against the rusting hull. Also on the desk was an external 28.8 modem with a line-conditioner. There were hundreds of utility disks in disk holders on a free-standing wooden bookshelf. Malavida moved to them and started rummaging through the index tabs.

"He's got it all . . . various flavors of UNIX, crackers for UNIX, VMS, Novell, 'elite' addresses on the Internet, CERT security advisories . . . He's fully locked and loaded.'' Malavida glanced at Lockwood, who was moving toward a coffin-sized freezer. He tried to open it, but it was locked. Over the freezer, taped to the wall, was a large blowup of an old photograph.

"The fuck is this?'' Lockwood said. It was a picture of a woman with dishwater-blond hair. She was in a bathing suit, standing next to a tree. There was a portable pool out of focus behind her. The woman was holding a cat and smiling into the camera lens. Her body was muscular but trim; she had even rows of teeth and iridescent eyes. But her smile was mean, mixed with a defiant glare. The thing that was strange about the photograph was that certain parts of her body had been transected with a dark Magic Marker. The legs and arms were numbered and dated; so were both feet and the torso. Lockwood took a mental picture of the photograph.

Then the walkie-talkie erupted with two frantic blasts of static and went dead.

Lockwood looked at Malavida and they took off,

climbing quickly up the stairs, running along the interior gangway, and exploding out of the barge into the evening darkness. The sound of night birds greeted them as they ran down the ramp. Malavida looked where they had left Karen, but she was gone. Then they heard her scream.

Lockwood and Malavida bolted in that direction. They were moving through a wall of heavy brush, crashing through thickets, tearing their skin on brambles and thorns. They plunged on blindly, Lockwood leading the way . . . until the ripping thorns became too painful . . . then Malavida pushed past him and took the lead.

Finally, they broke out into a clearing and saw a blue house some distance away. Lockwood, gun in hand, moved in a low crouch toward the house, Malavida right beside him.

The sun was down but the horizon was a soft pink, lit from the afterglow in the western sky. They got to the front door. Lockwood found it ajar, kicked it wide, and ducked inside.

A huge man lumbered out of the kitchen. He was dressed only in baggy shorts. His pale white body had no definition. He had a cellphone in a holster on his belt. His bald head gleamed in the pink light coming through the living room window. Lockwood guessed he was almost seven feet tall. Heather had been right—he had no eyebrows, no hair on him at all.

"Get out of my house," he said, his voice was tight and high.

"Where is she?"

"Get out . . ." he repeated.

Lockwood brought the gun up. "I'm John Lockwood, U.S. Customs. Put your hands up and get on your knees, facing the wall. Do it now, you cocksucker, or I'll blow you to fucking pieces!" It was all Lockwood could do to keep from shooting the man who had mutilated Claire.

Then the huge man bolted out a back door. Lockwood pulled the trigger and the gun jumped in his hand. A piece of the doorway splintered. The shot missed and the man was gone . . . out into the backyard.

"Find Karen, I'll go after him!" Lockwood commanded and took off after the seven-foot apparition.

When he got outside, Lockwood could barely see him. Then his eyes finally picked him out in the dim light. He appeared to be galloping, favoring his right side, running for all he was worth through the weeds. Lockwood covered the ground more easily and athletically, but the man was now out of sight in the reeds at the water's edge. Then Lockwood heard an engine start. He saw the path the man had taken and ran down it. When he came out at the water's edge, he saw the second tributary. An airboat was skimming across the marshy lowland, cutting down swampy undergrowth as it went, moving like the wind, the doughy seven-foot bald psychopath at the helm. Lockwood crouched and fired twice but the airboat was picking up speed. He knew the old army .45 automatic was barely accurate at ten yards, let alone a hundred. The shots crashed out into the dense foliage, snapping leaves and branches, before whistling away uselessly into the night.

The Rat was flying, the air drying his teeth. He grabbed the cellphone on his belt. Holding the wheel of the speeding boat with one hand, he dialed a number. Deep in the basement of the house he had just left, a phone rang. . . .

Malavida had found Karen in the kitchen. She was dazed and almost unconscious. He picked her up and carried her out of the house. When he laid her on the grass, her eyes opened.

"Thanks," she finally said.

Then Malavida heard the distant sound of the phone ringing. He looked down at her. "It's him," he said. "I wanna talk to him." He started back into the house.

"No . . . don't . . ." Karen said. Malavida hesitated for a moment, unsure; the phone kept ringing; then he bolted for it, running up the steps and into the house.

He didn't get far. He was two steps inside the living room when the explosion took him. It started in the basement and erupted up through the floorboards of the old house, throwing concrete and plaster into the air like papier-mâché.

The concussion rocked Lockwood, who was forty yards away, and caused him to go down on one knee.

Malavida Chacone was blown backward out the front door. He landed ten feet from Karen, his body broken and bleeding. Karen screamed in terror as she looked over at him . . . while the remnants of the house rained down around them.

# 24

## THE BURDEN

After the deafening sound of the explosion, the swamp went dead silent. Thousands of keening insects paused to listen as pieces of Leonard Land's house rained down on the wet ground or splashed into the swamp water hundreds of yards from where the house had been.

Lockwood was already back up and moving before the last pieces hit the ground. He could see Karen and Malavida not far away and he ran toward them. A huge piece of tin roof fell not three feet from him and stuck, edge down, into the wet ground, quivering like a thrown knife. The air was pungent with the smell of dust and cordite. By the time he got to them he could see that Malavida Chacone was critically, if not fatally, injured. He was bleeding from half a dozen serious wounds, but the thing that worried Lockwood most was the weirdly unnatural position of his broken body. Wide-eyed, Karen was staring down at Malavida when Lockwood arrived. Her eyes had the glassy look of desperation. "Oh, my God . . . I think he's dead," she said, her voice eerie as it pierced the unnatural silence.

"Go see if that truck over there has a key in it," he commanded. "If not, check under the bumpers for a hide-a-key box." He knew he could hot-wire it if necessary, but he wanted to get her in motion. If there was a chance to save Malavida, he'd need her help.

"We can't move him," she said, her voice shrill. "He could have spinal injuries. . . . He could have internal bleeding. It could kill him."

"He's gonna be dead if we don't." He took a breath and talked to her in a calm voice. "There's nothing here we can use to help him. He's gonna pump himself dry if we don't move him. Do what I said. The truck will get us to a hospital faster than that boat. We move him or lose him."

She hesitated for a moment and then got up off her hands and knees and ran, stumbling toward the vehicle that was parked in the yard. The pickup was sprinkled with dirt and small chunks of the house. She opened the door and looked in at the ignition. There were no keys. Then, as Lockwood had instructed, she climbed under the bumper. Sliding on her back she felt around, looking for a hide-a-key box . . . and under the back bumper, she found one. Karen squirmed out with the box in hand, removed the ignition key, and started the engine.

Lockwood pulled Malavida's light windbreaker off to get a better look at his wounds. He was having trouble finding Malavida's pulse. He put his fingers on the carotid artery in his neck but could feel nothing. Lockwood's hands were shaking so he couldn't be absolutely sure.

He put his ear to Malavida's chest. He thought he could hear a heartbeat, faint and thready. Then he felt light, raspy breathing on the side of his face. He looked up as Karen pulled the old pickup in beside them. "Be tough," he said softly to Malavida. Then he scooped his arms under the Chicano cracker and, using all of his strength, he struggled to his knees, then finally stood and moved on unsteady legs to the truck. He knew that if there was a serious spinal injury he could be dooming Malavida to a life of paralysis, but he had done a few field triages at accident scenes, both in the Marines and early in his government career when he was in uniform and working Customs sheds at the border. He had pried people off their steering columns and out from under dashboards. He knew that Chacone was in the red zone where survival odds were meaningless. His will to live was the only cord that held him.

As Lockwood lifted him onto the truck bed, he heard something in Malavida's body snap. Lockwood cursed under his breath, then jumped in and pulled Malavida by his shoulders toward the front so his feet were clear. Then he scrambled back and pulled up the tailgate. He saw Karen staring back through the window of the cab, a bloodless look on her face. He grabbed a broken brick which had fallen into the bed of the truck. "Watch out," he yelled. "Turn around and cover your eyes."

She did, and he slammed the brick into the rear glass window of the cab. It shattered, spilling shards onto the seat, but clearing the opening so he could talk to her.

"Let's go. Get moving. I'll stay back here with him."

"How're we gonna find Tampa? That road could lead anywhere."

"I don't know," he said. "Let's go, we'll do the best we can."

Karen Dawson had driven in two NASCAR stock car races. She was a natural hot shoe with a God-given gift for driving. She slammed her foot down. Mud shot into the air. The truck leaped toward the shell road at the low end of the yard. By the time she got to it she was totally focused, her hands on the wheel at ten past ten. Her vision was searching the road just beyond the headlights, where she could occasionally see the startled eyes of swamp creatures reflected in the yellow light, just before they scurried away to escape the churning tires.

In the back of the truck, Lockwood hung on desperately, trying to support Malavida while they jounced along the uneven road. He managed to remove his jacket and put it under Malavida's head.

They had traveled half a mile when Karen hit the first deep and unavoidable pothole. In the back of the truck, Malavida and Lockwood bounced hard. When he landed,

Malavida groaned, opened his eyes, and looked up at Lockwood. He said nothing, but his dark eyes pleaded. Lockwood reached over, found his hand, and grasped it. Malavida held on to it in desperation as the truck rattled and banged down the rain-rutted road.

Karen knew she had to keep the truck from bouncing. A short distance in front of her, the headlights were swallowed by the swamp's hollow darkness. She was trying to spot the potholes in the shell road before she hit them, maneuvering and down-shifting to get around them without losing time. After ten minutes, she came to the first fork in the road. She wasn't sure where she was or even what direction she was heading. She slowed and stopped. "Go right," Lockwood said. But Karen ignored him and jumped out of the cab to look up at the stars. "What're you doing?" he yelled as she scanned the starlit horizon. It was a clear night, and the starscape glittered like pinholes shot through black velvet.

"Goddamn it, he's dying! Let's go, whatta you doing?" Lockwood shouted.

"Looking for the Orion constellation."

"Get the fuck out of here," he said, amazed. "This isn't a Girl Scout camping trip. Get in! Go right!"

Karen spun on him and glowered. "You heard that guy back at the dock. These shell roads could go anywhere. This one's been wandering right and left. I don't even know which way I'm going. I want to go west, that's where Tampa is. Orion is at nearly zero declination. It rises to the southeast. The coordinates on the celestial sphere are analogous to latitude and longitude on the earth." He was looking at her with flat-faced wonder, but she missed the expression because she was again looking up at the sky. "I'll find it for you, and you keep pointing me in the right direction. I won't be able to see it from the cab, it'll be too high overhead." Then she pointed up in the sky. "Okay, see that line of stars? Right there," she continued, "those three little stars? They're called Orion's Belt. The nebula is below them. The kinda reddish one, not as bright, it's called the Jewel of the Sword. You see it?''

He looked up at the sky, trying to find the stars she was pointing at, feeling utterly ridiculous.

"I . . . I'm not . . .''

"Find the North Star. It's at the end of the handle of the Little Dipper. You know that one? Go forty-five degrees right and across, the first one you come to.''

"Okay . . . yeah, I guess . . .''

"That's the Jewel. It's due west. Keep pointing me that way.''

She jumped back into the cab and turned left on the shell road, heading in the general direction of the nebula.

"Celestial navigation,'' Lockwood muttered under his breath. "Gimme a fucking break.''

Each time they came to a fork in the road, he looked for the constellation, tried to spot the tiny star in Orion's Sword, and then yelled to her which way to go. At least, he finally admitted to himself, it was giving them a consistent course. He hoped they didn't end up in the middle of a Florida swamp. Fifteen minutes later, they hit a paved road with a sign that said TAMPA.

Karen found Interstate 75 and headed north. The first hospital sign they saw was for the University Community Hospital, on South Hillsborough Road.

Karen pulled the truck up to the emergency entrance and Lockwood leapt out of the back. He banged through the double doors and grabbed a trauma nurse in the ER. "I've got a Code Blue out here!'' he said, pulling the startled woman toward the truck.

Lockwood and two ER nurses loaded Malavida onto a gurney. There was a moment before they wheeled him inside when Lockwood was looking down at the badly wounded Chicano . . . then Malavida opened his eyes. "It's on you now, Hoss,'' Lockwood said softly. "We got you here, now paddle. Catch a ride, we'll be on the beach waiting.'' Karen moved up and looked down at Malavida. Their eyes held each other. She was still looking at him when they wheeled Malavida inside.

Karen had removed the vehicle registration from the glove compartment. She handed it to Lockwood and he pulled the registration slip out of its yellow, faded plastic holder.

"Leonard Land, Twenty-two Hundred Little Manatee Road, near Tampa," he read. "This guy is going down," he promised softly.

Tampa Detective Grady Raynor had a complexion like lunar lava. His pockmarked face and close-set, steel-gray eyes accurately forecast a cold, uneven personality. He entered the hospital cafeteria with Dr. Susan McCaffrey from the trauma ward. She pointed out Karen Dawson and John Lockwood to him. They were just throwing away coffee cups and moving toward the door. Grady blocked their exit and held up his badge in its leather case.

"Grady Raynor, detective, Tampa Major Crimes. You brought in the Mexican kid who got caught in the explosion?"

"He's not a kid," Karen said.

Lockwood caught her protective tone, but went on, "We called you an hour and a half ago . . . where you been?"

"You ain't the only clambake on the beach, Buckwheat. Let's go somewhere a little more private."

He led them out into the corridor. . . . Dr. McCaffrey took them down to the Doctors' Lounge and opened the door, but remained outside as they entered.

"Okay, let's have a little ID, folks," Raynor said as soon as they were in the colorless lounge. Karen pulled out her Customs ID and handed it to him.

"Doctor of Criminal Profiling, U.S. Customs. What's that mean, exactly?" he said, his gray eyes crawling over her like sewer bugs.

"What it means, Detective, is I do criminal profiles for U.S. Customs . . . just like it says."

"And you, Mr. Lockwood . . . whatta you do?"

"I'm the food critic for the *Tampa News.*"

"This kid you brought in is critical. Somebody blew him open like a can a'corn. Now, you can stand there and crack wise with me, or you can come to the dance. I don't fuckin' care. Get cute and I'm gonna hang you by your thumbs until you start makin' kissin' sounds. Now this kid has prison art on him. He's done time in somebody's brickhouse. So either I print all a you an' waste a few hours of everybody's time, or you can bring me up to date now, an' save us all a lotta grief an' pain."

"His name is Carlos 'Malavida' Chacone. He's a Federal convict who was released from Lompoc prison to work a case," Lockwood said.

"Yeah? How does that work?"

"I'm a SAC with U.S. Customs, retired. It's my case. He was released to my custody."

"Retired? You got a badge? Got any prison paperwork on this kid?"

"Left it in the boat out in the swamp."

"You wanna show me where that is?"

Lockwood had seen his share of Grady Raynors. They muscled their way through police work, passing out negative attitude like Halloween candy. They were dick-measurers. Police power was their job perk. Lockwood wanted to go back out to the house in the swamp alone and set up his own crime scene investigation, maybe call in a few Miami lab techs he was friendly with to see what they could pull out of the ashes. The truck might still have trace evidence, but he knew they'd contaminated it by using it to bring Malavida here. The main target, however, was the rusting barge: It was the heart of his investigation. He wanted to do a vacuum-bag and forensic sweep of the inside. He had a hunch that locked freezer wasn't going to be full of TV dinners. The computers in the rusting barge needed to be downloaded. If he got lucky, the whole case could be in there.

Lockwood also knew that he was running out of time. Detective Raynor was two phone calls away from finding out that Malavida was an escaped fugitive with a fresh arrest warrant, and that Lockwood was suspended and working off his badge on a homicide he'd been directly ordered to stay away from. Once Customs was alerted, he'd be swept up like broken glass and that would be it. He didn't want a bunch of local smokies wandering through his crime scene, tracking mud and dropping cigarette butts, but he didn't seem to have much choice. His best bet was to try to co-opt the dial-tone standing in front of him . . . try to control the investigative fallout as best he could.

"Okay, Detective, I think we should go out there together. I think we should also take a crime team with us."

"Yeah? Why is that?"

"That house was rigged to explode by a man we think might be a serial killer . . . a man who's committed at least three murders we know of and probably more. His name is Leonard Land. I ran him ten minutes ago and came up with nothing, but he lives in the wetlands off the Little Manatee River. There's a garbage barge out there that needs to be gone through by Forensics. There's a freezer in the barge that is locked. I'd like to get a warrant to open it."

"You got a lotta stuff you want. Why don't we just go out there and look 'fore we rile up the whole department?"

"This could be a national murder case and you could be standing on page one with it."

"Would that be page one of the Food Section?" He smirked.

It took them almost an hour to get back out to the house. Karen was in the back of Detective Raynor's car while Lockwood sat up front giving directions.

Raynor got a radio call from Tampa communications. They all listened in stony silence as the dispatcher informed them that Malavida had been medevacked by helicopter to a hospital in Miami where they had a state-of-the-art trauma surgery unit.

They pulled back into the clearing a little past midnight. The headlights illuminated the spot where the blue house had once been. Now all that was left was the foundation and the railingless front porch. Smoke still curled up from hot spots in the rubble-filled basement.

Lockwood got out of the sedan and looked toward the house. Malavida's jacket was gone.

"He's been back here," he said softly. Then he took off, running in the direction of the barge. Karen jumped out and ran after him. They pushed through the brambles at the foot of the property with Raynor a good distance behind.

"Where the hell you goin'?" he shouted. "Come back here!" But they moved on. The weeds and thorns tore at them, but Lockwood was moving more carefully than last time, and used his hands to keep the sticker bushes away from both of them.

They finally got to the dock where the huge barge had been tied, but the barge was nowhere in sight. The chains and ropes hung loosely from the pilings, dangling into the water. The ramp that had once led to the high double doors amidships was floating upside down in the brackish water.

Karen was breathing heavily beside him. "He came back and got it," she finally said. "I didn't think it was floating . . . I thought it was parked on the bottom."

Lockwood nodded but said nothing. He had his hand in his pocket, rubbing the plastic-covered truck registration. His thumb went back and forth over the plastic cover like a scanner looking for clues, as if there was still something more it could tell him.

He thought of Claire, now in her grave. He had missed her funeral in his rush to seek vengeance for her death. He thought of Malavida, fighting for his life in one hospital, Heather in another three thousand miles away. So much human wreckage caused to fulfill one man's twisted fantasy. Never had Lockwood dreamed an investigation could enter his life and cause such darkness. He had told Heather he would catch this monster. But, even with that thought still in his head, the promise felt empty. He could never restore things to the way they were. He remembered a time long ago when he had been just nine or ten years old, and Father McKnight at Materwood Home for Boys had caught him stealing food from the kitchen. "You can't unring a bell, John," the old priest had lectured him. "Once something's done, it's part of your history, and it becomes a burden you must always carry with you." Lockwood stood on the wharf and looked at the spot where the barge had once been. He wondered if he was strong enough to carry this burden.

# 25

## THE HALL OF SLEEPING SPIDERS

The Rat suspected that he had started the journey. There was no other explanation. He sat on the floor of the garbage barge, rocking slightly back and forth. His mind flitted across the pitted landscape of his problem.

It seemed big and unfixable. He wondered, if he sacrificed himself, would he change the timetable or just make everything happen sooner? He wondered if there was still time to build the Beast and get the answers he had been looking for. He wondered why he was always so frightened and alone . . . why, in his whole life, nobody had ever tried to comfort him. And then he got angry. They would pay. He would be taken on this Journey of Redemption clawing and biting. He would not walk obediently into the Hall of Sleeping Spiders.

He had seen them leave in his pickup truck, from a hiding place downriver. He had sneaked back and found the Mexican's windbreaker. In the pocket was a receipt from the Radio Shack. The credit card belonged to Karen Dawson, the woman at U.S. Customs who had invaded his chat room. *Was it possible that she was still alive?* The signature on the receipt read Malavida Chacone. He thought he knew that name from somewhere. He ran back, untied the barge, tied his air-boat to it, and climbed aboard. The barge started to drift slowly downriver, riding on the current. He stood on the deck and steered with the big hand rudder. Twice the barge almost got stuck in the shallows, but miraculously he managed to keep it from going aground. He finally arrived at the hiding spot he had found before. It was a place deep in the wetlands of the Little Manatee River, almost four miles from his house. The barge was now tied under a dense growth of mangroves and weeds. It would not be visible even from the air.

He wondered if he dared go back to Shirley's house. He had burned it down twelve years before, then had run away and lived in the park. The property had been sold to a retired plumber who had rebuilt it. Five years later the plumber had died of a stroke. Because of its remote location, nobody had bought it. The Rat knew it was currently boarded up and empty; he had gone there once and looked at it from the road. It didn't look like Shirley's house anymore. This new place the plumber had built was stucco, with no porch and a low, sloping roof. Still, it was where his home had once been. He had lived there till he was fifteen. More important, it was a shrine of sorts, because it was the place where he'd first met The Wind Minstrel.

He had been just fourteen when that happened, and very sick with a high fever. His ears had become infected because of the burns. Shirley would not let a doctor come. She said Leonard was weak, and that if God decided to take him for his weakness, then she would bear that consequence. The Rat had already learned to control Leonard. He hid inside him like an evil shadow and listened to Shirley's shrill condemnations.

That night his fever grew. He slipped into a delirious sleep and had a frightening, life-changing nightmare. In the dream, he was both The Rat and Leonard, walking in a hall of huge sleeping spiders. Leonard was so scared he could barely breathe. He whimpered constantly, but The Rat was cunning, moving silently between the spiders' hairy legs. Their eyes were closed, their huge mandibles dripping moisture at his feet. The Rat knew that if he woke them, they would tear him apart, chew him slowly, and eat him alive. Somehow he also knew that the Hall of Sleeping Spiders was at the beginning of the Journey of Redemption.

Then, as if by magic, he was somewhere else, strapped on a plank before an altar, while God screeched at him through huge speakers in a voice that growled and barked. God threatened him with more fire and scorned his weakness. The Almighty cursed his impotent wretchedness. Leonard shuddered and cried in fear. The Rat calculated his odds and schemed and lied, telling God he worshiped Christ and the Apostles. It was then that The Wind Minstrel appeared before them. God stopped screaming. Suddenly it was very quiet. Leonard was still strapped down before the altar, unable to move. He whimpered and The Rat looked over Leonard's bloated stomach at the apparition. . . . Physically, The Wind Minstrel was exactly like Leonard, only somehow he was also very different. He had beauty and authority. He could get erections. The Rat instantly worshiped him.

The Wind Minstrel told The Rat that Leonard would always be a supplicant, always be afraid, because he believed in Christ and the Apostles. Doctrine, The Wind Minstrel explained, was inflexible. Inflexible things were brittle and could be broken. You only had to see the way. And while he slept and dreamed, The Wind Minstrel let him see. In the dream, The Wind Minstrel entered him. The Rat knew it was sexual, but it was also spiritual. While he slept, for the last time in his life, Leonard became erect, but The Rat saw true everlasting glory. He saw the way it could be. He knew God would no longer control him. From now on he would break God's doctrines. He would fight against Christ and the Apostles. Leonard never dreamed about The Rat or The Wind Minstrel again. He never remembered what they did, although they shared his body.

After the dream The Rat had a direction. . . . That night he decided he would set fire to the house and kill Shirley.

The Tampa police set up a crime-scene perimeter around the remains of the house and started to sort through the evidence. By ten A.M. Monday morning there were twenty reporters and three TV news crews. Nobody respected the police crime-scene tape.

Lockwood and Karen tried to supervise the Tampa police, but Detective Grady Raynor pulled them off the scene and made them sit in the back of his car, under threat of arrest. They watched helplessly while news crews trampled through the smoking rubble and did stand-ups in front of the missing house. Karen's mind was far away. She was thinking of Malavida. He had looked so vulnerable on the gurney. She was still having trouble sorting out the way she felt about him. Was it something to preserve, or was she again just tempting fate?

"If there's any evidence here at all, it's been contaminated by this circus," Lockwood said, interrupting her thoughts.

Karen nodded. "Maybe we oughta run some of this new stuff through VICAP," she said, bringing herself out of it. She forced herself to focus on the problem. "We've got some pretty good partial data on Leonard Land. A computer hacker, mutilations, maybe he's got a record somewhere. Maybe we even have enough to get a match on some more killings."

"Good idea, if we can get away from Barney Fife over there," he said, nodding toward Grady Raynor, who was doing a stand-up interview for a local news station.

"Lemme give that problem a little attention," she said, and got out of the car, heading over to where Grady was blowing hot air at a black field reporter named Trisha Rains.

"Right now," Raynor was saying to the camera, "we know that this property was rented by a man named Leonard Land. We're checking for State Tax Board employment records. No charges have yet been filed against Mr. Land, but this explosion was caused by unnatural products. A well-known computer criminal named Carlos

'Malavida' Chacone was also involved and is critically injured. . . .''

"Can you tell us a little more about Malavida Chacone's condition?" Trisha Rains asked, her straightened black hair bobbing and beginning to lose its tight set in the oppressive morning heat.

"He was a fugitive from justice and is now back in the hospital being closely guarded. If he survives his injuries, he will be transported back to Lompoc, California, where he was doing time before he was released by a Customs agent named John Lockwood. We're still trying to get to the bottom of that." He paused, wondering if he'd said too much. "That's about all I can say for now," he concluded.

The camera crew shut off their lights and Trisha Rains put a hand on the back of her neck, holding her hair away to cool herself.

"I need a reverse. We can shoot it over by the house. Get the smoking remains over my shoulder," she said to her crew, and they moved off, leaving Grady Raynor smiling. He then saw Karen as she held up her cellphone.

"Just got a call from my SAC in D.C. and my District Supervisor down here. They want me and Lockwood back, at the Federal Building in Tampa, forthwith."

"In the words of that great American sports legend George Steinbrenner, 'Fuck 'em.' "

"Hey, Detective, I'm just a bystander here, but your best bet of holding on to this case, which is about two hours away from going national, is to set up a joint-op with Customs. If you don't, they're gonna go over your head to the Governor and you're gonna be up in the bleachers with Steinbrenner eating a foot-long."

He looked at her for a puzzling moment while his walnut-sized brain calculated the truth in her remark.

"You do this for me, and I'll do a Grady Raynor commercial at Justice," she added. Then another news crew moved in, looking for a statement. They turned on their lights. Raynor's eyes darted over to them, anxious to get at it.

"Okay. You gimme a number where I can reach you."

"We're at the Best Western in Tampa, the one by the water."

"Roommates?" he said, a leer creeping up on his disorganized, pockmarked face.

"Grow up, Detective," she said softly.

"Lou," he yelled at a police lieutenant in a brown uniform, "take these two back to Tampa an' drop 'em at the Federal Building. Stay with 'em."

The lieutenant handled the first part of the order, not the second.

They called a cab from the lobby of the Federal Building and slipped away from their police guard through a side door. They picked up Karen's car at the boat rental, drove over and got Leonard Land's dark blue truck at the Tampa hospital, then headed back to the Best Western, packed everything, and checked out. It was noon by the time they stood in the dense heat in the parking lot, trying to decide where to go.

"Let's get a place in St. Pete or in Clearwater," Lockwood said. "We get out of this dickhead's jurisdiction, maybe get a little breathing room."

"I drove through Clearwater Beach yesterday. There's an Econo-Lodge near the water, with special rates," she volunteered.

He nodded and they drove out of the parking lot. Lockwood, in Leonard's truck, followed Karen's rental car. They crossed Tampa Bay on the Courtney Campbell Causeway, drove through Clearwater, then took the smaller Garden Memorial Causeway over to Clearwater Beach.

They rented two rooms at the Econo-Lodge. The accommodations were clean, bland, and decorated in pastels. Both had windows that overlooked the Gulf of Mexico across a wide, sandy beach. It was almost three in the afternoon by the time they had all of this accomplished.

"I'm going to run this reg slip with DMV and load this new stuff into VICAP," she said. "I can use the modem on my laptop, then go right into the system from here.''

''Okay. While you're doing that, I'll go through the truck, see if anything lives there we can use.'' She nodded and went inside.

He looked down and saw some of Malavida's dried blood in the truck bed. He wondered how Mal was doing. He and Karen had discussed going down to Miami and sitting there until Malavida was out of danger. After a spirited argument, he had convinced her to discard the idea as sentimentally worthwhile, but operationally stupid. He knew it would be a game-ending move for him. He was a loose cannon by anybody's calculation. Going to Miami was an invitation to an arrest. He knew, so far, he was good for at least one count of obstructing justice; probably also good for felonious malfeasance of duty, and aiding and abetting a prisoner during an escape. That charge was probably beatable, but not the reckless endangerment of a prisoner, impersonating an officer, withholding evidence . . . The list was endless. Lockwood and Karen had decided to keep track of Malavida's progress by phone, maybe risk a visit once he was conscious. Karen had called the Miami hospital just before they checked out of the Best Western. She'd gotten almost nothing from the floor nurse, who had told her Malavida was out of surgery and listed as critical. ''How critical?'' Karen had asked.

''*Critical* critical.''

Lockwood had been surprised by the depth of Karen's concern. He was now sure that, during the short amount of time he had been in California, something had started up between them. It annoyed him. Had he been harboring a secret fantasy about Karen? In the wake of Claire's murder, had he been secretly hoping for a shot at Awesome Dawson? He hoped he wasn't that shallow, but he had been surprising himself a lot lately.

Inside the motel room, Karen hooked her modem to the computer and started to check out Leonard Land. There was no criminal record on him in the Federal computer. She cross-referenced with NCIC, the National Crime Information Center. Nothing there either. She punched the name into the Florida Department of Motor Vehicles, including the truck registration number, and up on her screen popped a driver's license picture. Leonard looked slightly different from when he had attacked her. In the picture he seemed wistful, almost pathetic. He was smiling earnestly, his bald head and missing eyebrows not as menacing as in the awful moment when he'd grabbed her outside the house in the wetlands. The address they already had: 2200 Little Manatee Road. The license said he was twenty-seven years old, six feet eleven inches tall, and 367 pounds. No hair, brown eyes. That was it. She downloaded the information and picture, then stored them in her hard drive. She wished Malavida were with them; his dark eyes and dry humor hung with her like a lingering fragrance. She prayed quietly for him. "Please, God, don't let him die," she heard herself whisper.

She turned her mind back to the target. She was pretty sure that Leonard wouldn't go back to his job even if he had one. He was in the wind, hiding someplace, ready to strike from the darkness. Something else was moving restlessly in the back of her mind . . . a thought or feeling that she couldn't quite capture. Finally she slapped it down. It was a feeling she'd gotten when Leonard grabbed her out in the yard and dragged her into his kitchen. He had held her down on the table, breathing through his mouth. She was looking up into his crazed eyes, and before he hit her with his fist, in that instant she knew that this was about more than just ritualistic homicides. It was about survival. She didn't know how she knew that, but somehow she read it on him or in his eyes.

Karen sat thinking for a minute, then turned back to her computer. She needed to see if she could throw a wider net and get a better VICAP sample with the new specifics she had. She always learned a lot about a killer from studying the victim. Something had drawn Leonard

Land to Candice Wilcox and Leslie Bowers. . . . And then she remembered the strange picture that Lockwood had told her about, the one that was in the rusting garbage barge. He had said that the woman's body had been divided into parts with Magic Marker and that each section had been dated. She wondered if Leonard was constructing a woman out of harvested body parts.

She reviewed again what she knew, trying to arrange the facts differently to get a new pattern. Leonard Land was twenty-seven, and thus fit perfectly the mean age for serial murderers who left behind "organized" crime scenes. She knew from her research that most serial criminals began to realize the scope of their hopelessness in their early twenties, and it was at this time that fantasies about striking back began to grow. Around age twenty-five, the anger and depression would get to the point where they could no longer relieve the pressure by the torture or killing of animals. They would then begin to kill people. An organized crime scene indicated a slightly older killer. And two years were usually added to the mean age. Traditionally, a serial murderer killed to relive some specific sick fantasy. The act was often ritualistic in nature. Karen knew that the ritual surrounding the murder rarely changed because it was the ritual that was the real reason for the crime. The ritual drove the act thus creating a pattern that could be used to match other murders. After a serial killing, there was a cooling-off period, which could be anything from less than a week to several years. Then, inevitably, the subject killed again to relieve the pressure, and the whole cycle started over. If the time period between murders shortened, the subject was said to be degenerating, becoming potentially more destructive and more violent, as well as more careless.

Karen sat in the room in Clearwater Beach, listening to the distant surf. Leonard had told his pen pal in the Oslo prison that he mailed totems. She wondered if he used everything that he harvested at the crime scene. He had taken both of Candice Wilcox's arms, both of Leslie Bowers's legs. She wondered if he had discarded anything. She leaned over her keyboard and began to construct a new query. She asked VICAP to list any record of body parts being sent through the mail. She narrowed the request to within a week or two of the dates of Candice's and Leslie's murders. She entered the data, then sat back and waited. Just as she was about to lose hope, she got one bounceback.

The computer showed that a Florida Sheriff named Carl Zeno had taken into evidence a severed female hand with the fingertips removed. The hand was at the Tampa Coroner's Office. It had been delivered to a woman on April 13, one day after the murder of Candice Wilcox. The name of the woman who had received the hand was Tashay Roberts, 901 Court Road, Tampa, Florida.

"John," Karen called excitedly, "I got something!"

# 26

## FIVE O'CLOCK NEWS

**S**heriff Carl Zeno leaned back in his metal chair and put a dusty boot up on the corner of his desk. He sucked loudly on a toothpick and spun his wide-brimmed Smokey hat insolently on his index finger as he looked at them.

"Tashay, she gets herself in with some pretty strange people," he said, dropping the hat on the desk. "I'm her stepdaddy and that gives me some rights, I spose, but you know how that is. . . . I ain't blood, so I do what I can t'help her mom, Cherise, with her . . . but it don't always go down the way I want."

They were in the Sheriff's sub-station in Fort Myers, Florida. Karen had shown Zeno her Customs ID and introduced Lockwood as a Customs Inspector. Zeno had written down their names but had not asked to see Lockwood's badge. The office was a five-man cop-shop in a one-story brick building. Yellow linoleum floors, metal desks, and the smells of disinfectant and tobacco smoke completed the ambience.

Carl Zeno was blond, with a rock-hard handshake and a Sam Brown gun harness stretched tight over a potbelly. He had good-ol'-boy charm that barely hid a nasty disposition.

Karen thought she'd hate to be pulled over by this guy

on an empty highway and say the wrong thing.

" 'Course she's got this Bobby Shiff guy she lives with now," he said sneering. "Hosed off and naked, that freak don't weigh a hundred pounds. Tashay, she's real easy on the eyes, but you oughta see Shiff . . . looks like an extra in a vampire movie. He sings in a Death Metal band called Baby Killer . . . calls himself Satan T. Bone. Don't y'love that?"

Karen looked over and caught Lockwood's eyes.

Zeno caught the glance. His gaze was lazy and insolent, and there was a small smile playing at the side of his mouth.

"What'd you say your name was again, sugar?"

"You wrote it down. It's right in front of you."

He smiled at her. "We don't get good-lookin' lady cops in this unit. All we got is bats with hats. Got one patrol woman on this shift, looks like Mike Ditka."

"That's real helpful," Lockwood said, smiling. "But we'd like to get in touch with Tashay Roberts. We checked the address on Court Road in Tampa; nobody answers the door."

"She and Shiff are down in Miami. He's got a gig down there. Left last night. She dropped by an' gimme two tickets . . . like I'm gonna go down there an' listen to that stringbean holler into a twenty-dollar sound system. I can hear better music sitting right here, listening to drunks fart."

"If you're not using the tickets, we'll take 'em," Lockwood said.

"Let's see here . . ." He reached into his pocket slowly; then, not finding them, into his desk drawer. He finally extracted two tickets and held them up. "Twenty dollars gets you into seats C-16 and 17, front an' center. Ear and nose plugs are extra."

Lockwood pulled out his wallet and dropped the twenty on the desk. "That hand she got sent, is it still in the Tampa morgue?" he asked as Zeno handed him the tickets.

"Far as I know. But it ain't got no fingertips so y'can't print it. . . ."

"I wanna get a blood type and tissue match. I think it came off a dead woman in Atlanta."

"You go on up there an' talk to Deke Sanders. Dr. Death . . . dead bodies, bad jokes, and Muzak. Runs that icebox like it was the fuckin' *Tonight Show*. You laugh at his jokes, he'll give you anything you want."

Lockwood looked at Karen. "Anything more you wanna ask him?"

"Down here," Zeno said, "the men do the investigatin' an' the ladies string the yellow tape an' chalk up the sidewalk." He turned and smiled at Karen. "But go on an' ask anyway, Honey."

"You ever sleep with your stepdaughter?" Karen deadpanned.

Zeno sat up straight in the chair. It was as if she'd lit him up with a thousand volts. Then he started to flush and stammer. "Uh . . . I . . . What you talkin' 'bout? What the hell kinda dumb-ass question is that? 'Course not. Why don't you two get outta here? I got a heapa things to attend to."

Karen got up; as they left, a light sheen of sweat had already started to form on Carl Zeno's forehead.

Outside the sub-station, Lockwood stopped her before they got into the car. "Bull's-eye, but where did that come from?"

"Guy was pissing me off."

"How did you know?" He grinned at her.

"Picture of his family behind the desk. I figured the sexy one was Tashay. He was holding her closer than his wife. And that story about her dropping off the tickets . . . She drives all the way down here to give that slimeball two tickets instead of mailing 'em? And the way he said she was easy on the eyes. I don't know, it just hit me as possible."

Lockwood smiled as he got into the car. The best cops always had that instinct: the ability to play streaky hunches that sometimes defied logic but hit the 10 ring.

Often that ability could make a case. You couldn't teach it; it didn't come with a uniform or badge, or in the long, tedious classes at Quantico. You got issued that instinct by a higher power.

He'd once been trying to arrest a child pornographer in a small Georgia town. The investigation had led him to a psychologist who treated disturbed children. He'd been there just to get background information, but he'd looked at the photographs of children on the wall and knew instinctively that he was talking to the perp. . . . It was such a long shot, it was off the boards. But he *knew* the child psychologist was molesting the children. There was something strangely sexual about the innocent pictures. Lockwood couldn't describe it or say how he knew, but he did. He set up a stakeout and busted the doctor two nights later.

The five o'clock news had the whole story. The Rat watched it on the television in the darkened hull of the rusting barge. The generator hummed outside, causing a pleasant vibration in the hull. He saw what was left of his house on the newscast . . . scattered debris, the smoking ruins. He saw the picture of Malavida Chacone with his prison number across his chest. The field correspondent, Trisha Rains, said Chacone was a famous computer criminal. And then The Rat knew where he'd heard the name. The black eyes of the Mexican convict stared straight at him from the TV and bored holes of pain through The Rat's head. Malavida was a famous cracker, some said the best ever. He'd read about the "Mac Attack" in computer journals. The Rat now knew it was Chacone who had penetrated his secret chat room on the Internet. Killing the woman in Studio City had solved nothing. It had only made things worse, because now there was this other man, this Customs agent whom the newscasts had mentioned.

The Rat had been clever and lucky. The bomb in his basement had gotten Chacone. The newscast said that he was hanging between life and death in a Miami hospital.

The Rat wondered if he could use his computer to find a way to cut the cord. Then the story switched to John Lockwood. It showed a picture of a handsome, dark-haired man standing at the crime scene. Next to him was a woman. Her back was to the camera. She was identified as Dr. Karen Dawson. The Rat moved closer to the TV screen and leaned in, looking intently at the woman. Then she turned and he could see her more clearly. It was the woman he had caught snooping at his house. He was troubled and frightened. The newscast ended, but The Rat remained unusually agitated for a long time.

Malavida Chacone, John Lockwood, Karen Dawson . . . What was the significance? Was it a sign? What should he do?

"When cornered, The Rat fights." His voice echoed in the hollow barge. Then he turned to his shelf of cracking tools. He selected his best UNIX cracking kit. He booted up his Toshiba notebook. When it was up, he slipped the program into the machine. He would start with John Lockwood and the Government computer at U.S. Customs. He hunched over his keyboard, his body damp with sweat. His fingers danced on the plastic stage before him. . . .

The Loomis Theater was on Fourth Street and Miami Avenue, a half block from the downtown bus terminal. It was in a bad neighborhood. Taggers had scrawled bizarre artwork everywhere. The old theater had been shut down for almost two years, giving up its audience to the busy mall Cineplex Theaters. The Loomis had three hundred seats and a steeple tower that rose two stories above the marquee. Pasted onto the billboard was a sign scrawled in Magic Marker on butcher paper:

BABY KILLER
FEATURING SATAN T. BONE
TONIGHT 8:30 P.M.

The doors opened at eight and approximately a hundred lost souls wandered into the theater, high-fiving each other and laughing too loud. Outrageous colored hair was hiked and spiked. The audience wore leather, see-through tops, tattoos, punk rock jewelry, and pimples. The concert started, as promised, at eight-thirty.

The sound was discordant and horrible. Lockwood and Karen pulled up and parked across the street, then moved toward the Loomis. Even outside they could hear Satan's horrible, raspy voice. There seemed to be almost no melody to the music. Percussion, bass guitars, and a hammering keyboard competed viciously with each other. Satan screamed out the lyrics like an umpire calling out a slide at home plate.

> Cut off their tits while they sit on your dicks.
> It's a burnout, brother, burnout.
> Make 'em be *brava* while they suck-a your flava.
> It's a burnout . . . baby, burnout.
> Righteous and rich, bloody the bitch.
> It's a redneck burnout, yeah.

There was nobody to take the tickets at the door, so they just went inside and stood near the back. The theater was musty and underlit. Faded red-velvet curtains lined both walls. To both Lockwood and Karen, the spectacle was close to indescribable. Satan T. Bone strutted on the stage like a wild animal. His long, stringy black hair and the tattoos under his eyes made him ghoulish. He was, as Zeno had said, only about a hundred pounds, and was stripped to the waist, wearing leather pants. His nipple jewelry swung against his hairless, skinny, sweat-soaked chest. He harangued the audience, screaming and growling into the mike. Behind him, on the small stage, the other members of Baby Killer were beating on their instruments as if they hated them. Lockwood thought they didn't even seem to be playing the same song.

After each ghastly number, the audience would go wild, trying to rip out the seats and throw them, swinging each other around, leaping on the backs of the chairs.

Satan raised his arms like a drug-crazed Anti-Christ and drank in their adulation, screaming insults at them through the mike. ''Eat shit, pus heads!'' he screamed. ''Swallow my cum!'' Then he'd launch into another braying, discordant song, which seemed even more horrible than the last. All the lyrics were about death and dismemberment. Huge pictures of Charles Manson, John Wayne Gacy, and Jeffrey Dahmer hung from ropes in the center of the stage.

''They don't mean it, they're just kids having fun,'' Lockwood said sarcastically between numbers. They were looking for Tashay Roberts and hoped they could recognize the pretty blonde from her photograph in Zeno's office. At one point, two teenaged boys with spiked hair, tattoos, and pierces everywhere moved up to Lockwood and Karen.

''Twist a braid, dude,'' the larger one said.

''Whatever the hell that means.'' Lockwood smiled.

''It means get outta here, you don't belong. Get sideways, fuck-face.''

''What're you guys supposed to be, comedy relief?'' Lockwood kept smiling.

''Event Security,'' the bigger one said. ''Go before you get wrecked.'' When Lockwood didn't move, he took a swing without warning. It was maybe the worst right cross Lockwood had ever seen. It was wide and so slow, he ducked under it by just bending his knees. Then he hit the boy with a vicious uppercut. He didn't need a follow-up punch; the boy woofed out stale air and sat down right where he was standing. The other bouncer looked at Lockwood.

''I suppose you want some of this too?'' Lockwood said.

Satan had begun the next song; the noise level rose. The smaller boy held both palms up, moved backward, and disappeared out the front of the theater.

''I think we should wait at the stage door. I've seen enough of this to last me forever,'' Karen said.

"You'd think guys who looked this grungy could fight a little better," he said, as they moved through the lobby to the door.

"Eat me, fuckers . . ." Satan T. Bone screamed at his cheering audience, but by then Lockwood and Karen were back in the street.

Parked in the alley near the backstage door of the theater was a brown primer-patched VW van.

"Looks like ye old band bus to me," Lockwood said and circled it, checking the doors.

"Don't you need a warrant or something to look in there?"

"Yeah, probably . . . but I'm not a cop anymore, so this is just gonna be a straight felony B and E." He pulled out a pocketknife. Using the short blade, he pried up the rubberized strip on the door and pushed his finger through the opening, popping the lock and opening the van. "Didn't it bother you at all that John Wayne Gacy, Jeffrey Dahmer, and Uncle Charlie's pictures are hanging up in there?" Lockwood said disgustedly.

"You mean instead of Abraham, Martin, and John?"

"Here we are working a possible serial killer, and three maniacs turn out to be the mascots for this band of jerk-offs."

Lockwood started looking around in the van. He pulled the registration slip out of the holder on the visor. "Bob Shiff. Same Court Road address." He returned it and started looking under the seats. He worked his way around until he got back to the front seat on the passenger side. It was a hot night and his shirt was beginning to stick to his back. He found what he was looking for in the glove compartment.

The three brightly colored balloons were knotted at the neck. He pulled them out and poked the knife blade through one of the balloons. He poured white powder into his hand. He smelled it, then tasted it. "Heroin. But it's flea powder, been cut way down." He put the balloons back inside the glove compartment, rummaged around in there some more, and this time pulled out a syringe. He laid it on the seat in plain view, closed the door, and relocked it, putting the strip back on.

"Y'know, John, if this is the way you did the job, no wonder IA was all over you."

"We're not gonna arrest anybody. We're just looking for information. You always do better if you get them playing defense."

He moved to the chain-link gate and closed it, blocking the alley from the front of the theater. He found an open padlock hanging on the fence, slipped it through the gate, and snapped it shut.

Two hours later the stage door opened. Bob Shiff and Tashay Roberts came out. Tashay was wearing a lace see-through top and denim shorts cut so that there was almost no back on them. She was holding on to Bob Shiff's skinny arm. Behind them were the other members of Baby Killer, all of them lugging their instruments. Some of their fans were now moving around to the back and hanging on the fence Lockwood had padlocked shut.

"Hey, man, open the gate," they shouted.

"Who locked the gate?" Shiff asked, looking at Tashay.

Lockwood stepped out from behind the van.

"Who the fuck're you?" Shiff said.

"Space Patrol . . . You guys look like intergalactic travelers. Wanna roll up your sleeves, show me your arms?"

"You got a warrant?" Shiff said.

"Don't need one. Got probable cause for a search. You left your pump on the seat there." He pointed through the window at the hypodermic. "Gimme the key to the van or I'm gonna knock out more than your window," Lockwood said.

After a slight hesitation Shiff handed the key to Lockwood. "Those aren't my works, man. I never saw that before."

Lockwood opened the van and started to look under the seat, working his way up to the glove compartment. He opened it and pulled out the three brightly colored balloons. "Somebody having a birthday party?" he drawled, then took the balloon he had already slit open and poured some of the heroin into his hand. "Looks like Mexican marching powder."

"That's not mine," Shiff whined.

Lockwood spun and grabbed his wrist, turning it palm up so he could see the vein in his skinny arm. There were track marks all over it.

"Bullshit, Bob. 'Less you're a diabetic, you been slammin'. I think if we went down to the station you'd 'Jones' in two hours. . . ."

By this time there were thirty hopped-up kids rattling the chain-link fence. Shiff looked over at them, a gleam in his eye. "Hey," he yelled, "come get this guy off me. . . ."

The crowd of fans yelled out and surged at the fence. Two of them started to climb over; two more were climbing around the sidepole. Lockwood pulled the old .45 out of the back of his belt and fired one shot at the wall of the theater. The report of the gun was deafening in the concrete-and-brick-enclosed alley. All motion stopped. The kids on the fence froze. Lockwood turned to Shiff. "Why don't we have this discussion somewhere else?"

Lockwood parked the band bus in Bayfront Park. The moon was full and shimmered across the water on Biscayne Bay. A light sea breeze vibrated a palm frond next to the van. He turned around in the driver's seat so he could see Bob Shiff and Tashay.

"Nice concert," he said, looking at them carefully. "If you don't mind pukey lyrics and a fistfight with a downbeat."

"You a music critic?" Bob Shiff protested. "I thought you were a cop."

Karen reached into her purse and pulled out her ID, flashed it at him, then returned it before he could see that it was a civilian ID.

"We're working a murder case. . . . I understand you

got sent a woman's hand,'' Karen said, looking at Tashay.

''What the fuck you talkin' about? What hand?'' Shiff said.

Lockwood leaned toward him. ''Carl Zeno said Tashay gave it to him. It's been booked as a partial Jane Doe in the Tampa Coroner's Office.''

''Tash, you got a fuckin' hand sent to us and you didn't tell me?'' An amazed look spread across his narrow face.

''Hey, Bobby, we're getting a lotta wet packages. It's very cool an' everything, but I was afraid that whoever sent it was over the edge . . . y'know? So I called Carl. He made me give it to him.''

They sat looking at one another for a long time. The silence became overpowering.

''We think the killer we're after may be the fan who sent you the hand. Maybe he came to one of your concerts?'' Karen said.

''Lotta people come to our concerts,'' Shiff said insolently.

''This guy you wouldn't miss,'' Karen said. ''He's almost seven feet tall, weighs three hundred seventy pounds.'' She reached into her purse, pulled out the printout of Leonard Land's DL picture, and handed it to them.

''Ever see him?'' Lockwood asked.

Shiff studied the picture. ''Ugly son of a bitch,'' he said, without interest.

Then Lockwood handed it to Tashay, who looked at it for a long time, her features furrowed in thought. ''I don't think I seen this guy. You seen him, Bobby?''

Shiff looked at the picture again. ''No, I'd remember. Can we go home?''

Lockwood took the picture back. ''How 'bout the mail? You say you get wet packages. If he delivered this hand to you, maybe he sent you something else before this. You keep the mail?''

Tashay looked over at Shiff and he shook his head.

"No, we throw it away," Shiff mumbled.

They sat there for a long moment in a dark no-man's-land. . . . A full moon lit the horizon to the east; the illuminated buildings of Miami framed the city behind them. A boat without running lights whined at high rpms somewhere out on Biscayne Bay.

"If you see this guy at one of your concerts, get in touch with us. This is my beeper number." Lockwood handed one of his cards to Tashay and then one to Shiff.

"Look man, it's real late. I need t'get home. Have we done this or are you gonna bust me?"

Without answering, Lockwood put the VW van in gear and drove out of the park and back along Miami Boulevard, past the graffiti-lined buildings, to the Loomis Theater. He knew they were probably lying. They were out on the edge, where bizarre behavior blends with anarchy. He was a cop and the enemy.

Lockwood set the hand brake and moved around the van as Shiff got behind the wheel. Lockwood slid the door open and Karen jumped out. Before he could close the door, Tashay Roberts stuck his business card back into his hand. She closed the door and Bob Shiff, a.k.a. Satan T. Bone, pulled the van out, squealing the tires slightly for effect. Lockwood looked down at the card. . . . Tashay had written something in cramped handwriting on the back. He held it up in the dim light of the street lamp. "Call me, 555–6245. I know something," he read.

He spun back just in time to see the van speed around the corner and out of sight.

# 27

## PROFILE

The barge rocked softly on a wind tide.

The Rat leaned over and got his CD headset. He put the earphones on and hit Play. . . . Satan T. Bone's raspy voice filled his head with glorious hatred:

Hit on the girl, screw her at last,
Cut off her arms, plug up her ass.
The screaming will end when the body goes soft.
The fucking will start when her head is cut off.

He swayed to the music in the cooling air as he worked. He had saved the head for last. The Rat knew there were more than one hundred identification points on the face and neck. For the Beast to come to life, it had to look like Shirley. So far, all of his searching had found nobody who answered his need. He had always known the head would be the hardest. The head would be his final victim. He was being pursued now, so he had to turn away from this difficult selection and deal with his enemies.

Using his modem and cracking kit, it had taken The Rat almost two hours to penetrate security blocking codes in the computer at the U.S. Customs Service. As was always the case, he had searched for a hole in the system, and had finally broken through. Lockwood's picture and file were now in front of him on the screen. He read it quickly, his eyes scanning the information. The sweltering afternoon heat in the wetlands around the Little Manatee River had lessened with the evening breeze and he had left the hatch open to catch its wispy coolness. Sweat was drying on his slick, shiny skin. He could feel the beginning of the stinging sensation which indicated that The Wind Minstrel was starting to emerge. In two or three days, he would claim The Rat's body. He knew when that happened, The Wind Minstrel would be enraged. The Rat had made no selections for him. He was not ready to give The Wind Minstrel the final victim to possess.

John Lockwood's file gave The Rat a quick but thorough look at this enemy: unorthodox, talented, frequently reprimanded but usually successful. There were pages of Internal Affairs complaints against Lockwood, and yet there were pages of official commendations for excellence. It was a confusing picture of success amid failure.

The Rat realized, after reading the file carefully, that Lockwood was an awesome threat that would not go away. The picture of the handsome agent stared accusingly out of the computer screen at him. The Rat hated him on sight. Lockwood had been given a gift of physical attractiveness, while The Rat had been forced to live in Leonard Land's fat, ugly body . . . always hiding, always being laughed at and despised.

A plan formed in The Rat's clever brain. He felt he could attack and kill Lockwood without ever leaving the rusting barge. It required very little beyond his genius and a little luck to accomplish the feat. He needed to download Lockwood's Customs picture and prints . . . and he had to alter them slightly and add a few manufactured details. Then he had to crack into one more "secure" computer. After he had accomplished that, he would simply wait for the right moment to spring his trap. In the meantime, he would take care of a much easier problem. He would reach out and end the life of Malavida Chacone.

The gas station was at the north end of Miami. Karen was filling the tank while Lockwood stood at the pay phone near the corner, gripping the receiver too tightly. He had tried to call Tashay Roberts but had gotten her answering machine. Then he dialed Children's Hospital in California.

Heather's voice sounded frail and uncertain, coming across three thousand miles of telephone cable. "I'm okay," she said bravely. "When will you come home, Daddy? I'm worried for you."

"I promise nothing will happen to me, but I have to finish this. . . . It's very important. I'll be careful. Don't worry about me."

There was a long, awkward silence on the phone and then, "Daddy . . . I want us to live on a farm, like you said. I've been thinking about that. I want to leave Los Angeles. Can we really do that?"

"It's a promise."

"A promise on a promise?" she said, her voice small.

"A promise on a promise."

"I love you, Daddy. I've asked God to look after you. Mommy's with Him, and they're both looking down. I'll pray to them not to let anything bad happen."

"I'll pray too."

"Here's Grandad," she said. "Bye."

Then Rocky was on the line.

"She sounds better," Lockwood said.

"Think?" the voice was gruff and distant. "She cries in her sleep and don't talk much . . . lookin' out the window most'a the time. . . . If that's better, then she's better."

Lockwood winced at the remark but kept going.

"When will she be getting out of the hospital?"

"Couple a'days. Then we're gonna take her back to Minnesota, whether you agree or not."

"Maybe that's best. It's familiar surroundings. I can meet you there when this is over."

"I'm sure you'll do whatever it is you want," his father-in-law said without emotion. "But this little girl can't take no more, John."

And then, without saying good-bye, Rocky hung up and left Lockwood with the phone pressed hard against his ear. He replaced the receiver and looked over to Karen, who had finished gassing the car and was wiping the windshield. He moved to her slowly.

"How is she?" Karen asked.

"She's . . ." He stopped, not sure how to put it. "Hurting," he finally finished, deciding to leave it at that.

He got into the passenger seat, and Karen pulled out of the gas station. The silence in the car was nerve-racking. Lockwood looked over at Karen; her brow was furrowed and she was deep in thought.

"You're worried about Malavida?" Lockwood said, and she looked over. "I'm sorry about not going down there, it's just I know what would happen."

"It's okay," she said. "It just seemed like we owed him some support. Not that he'd even know we were there."

The silence brimmed around them. Lockwood speared it again. "What happened between you two while I was gone?" he finally asked, and she turned her gaze quickly out the front window in a reflex action that Lockwood didn't need twenty years in police work to read. She focused her gaze on the flying night bugs lit by their headlights: specks of light that vectored and occasionally wiped out on the windshield.

"Whatta you mean, what happened?" she said, so softly he had to strain to hear it.

"Y'know, Karen, it's not a good idea to get romantically involved with people you're working a case with. Especially people like Malavida, who see life from a completely different angle."

"Why are we having this conversation?" she finally asked, still not looking at him.

"I have a distinct feeling that something changed while I was gone. I'm just telling you that we're up against a monster here. We can't have our personal feelings changing the perspective on our judgment."

"It sounded for a minute like you had something else you were trying to say." She now turned and looked at him.

He felt his heart beating in his throat; he shifted in his seat under her gaze. His face reddened slightly. "Whatta *you* mean?" he finally asked lamely.

"It sounded like you were staking out some sort of claim yourself, to use at a more convenient time."

Again they fell into an awkward silence. Lockwood felt himself choosing his words carefully. "I like you, Karen. I didn't think that was going to be the case when we first met in Washington, but you turned out to be a very pleasant surprise." He stopped because he was sure he was moving in the wrong direction. He didn't want to declare any intentions. . . . He was too mixed up.

"But . . ." she prodded.

"But, my life is in turmoil. Claire is dead. And I'm responsible. I'm not dealing with that well. I have Heather to think about . . . and I want to catch this son of a bitch who killed her, or I won't be able to sleep."

"You're not saying anything that I don't already know."

"Malavida's not for you," he blurted. "I know guys like this, he's on the con. He sees people as targets, he'll work you like a mark to get what he wants."

"I see. And what do you want . . . ?"

Lockwood fell silent. Finally, he looked over at her. . . . "I'm not sure how good a friend I can be to you or anybody right now. I know I want to be, but—"

"You're right, John. Something happened between us, and I'm not sure right now how I feel about it. But Malavida is in the hospital, he may be dying. If he lives, he may never be the same, and I'm worried about him. I think you should be too. It bothers me that you aren't.'' Lockwood looked over at her; she was very beautiful in the reflected dash lights. He hated hearing her admit that she had started something up with Malavida. Was she right? Was he staking out some claim to pursue when the timing was more acceptable? He had come to the point where he didn't trust his ability to evaluate himself anymore. He had been doing things for all the wrong reasons lately.

''I can't trust Malavida because I know how he thinks,'' he started by saying. ''I'm sorry we got him hurt, but I'll never be able to trust him. I know you probably think that's cold, but he and I come from the same place. He and I were both disenfranchised by the system and then incarcerated by it. I've been behind bars. I know how that changes you. He sees everything and everybody as a player. He calculates everything by how it affects him, or how he can use it. I know because it's still how I think. I'm not sure you should take a chance with either of us.''

''You know what I like best about you?'' she finally said. ''You never try and lie to yourself or about yourself. You wound yourself with honesty. It's noble, but hard to witness.''

Lockwood knew she was close. He had come to believe that in most people, their strongest link was directly hooked to their weakest link. He thought his strongest link had always been his ability to level frank appraisals. He cut himself no slack. It was also this quality that was now destroying him. ''Why don't we get something to eat?'' he finally said, desperate to change their conversation.

They stopped at an all-night fish house called The Blue Fin, at Miami Beach Marina. They got a table out on a deck that overlooked the water. A fleet of commercial and private fishing boats was slipped there. A light breeze swayed the boats' outriggers. Water lapped up against the concrete pilings under the deck. The waitress had a name tag that said she was Claudine. She wiped a shiny varnished table next to the rail before they sat down.

"Cocktail?" she asked.

"What's it gonna be, Lockwood?" Karen said. "Another Scotch with a beer back?"

"That was Washington. Up there in the spring I drink Scotch to forget my sinuses. I'm allergic to something blooming in that damn swamp. Down here I'll just have a Heineken in a bottle."

"Two," she said. And Claudine moved away on shapely legs.

Lockwood surveyed the fishing fleet. His brow furrowed while Karen looked at him. The residue of the conversation in the car was still on them, and they were both unsure about it, trying to put it behind them.

"John," she finally said, a bit too brightly, "I know if we get The Rat, we go a long way toward making things better. So let's get started." She pulled a yellow legal pad out of her purse.

He looked down at it, nodded without speaking, then reached over and turned the pad so he could read it. He glanced at the columns of behavioral traits she had listed, and then turned the pad back.

"A real psychotic?"

"Far from it," she said. "A psychotic is someone who's lost touch with reality. Psychotics are easy to catch. They don't usually have a plan. The Rat has a strong reality. He knows what he's doing. He's organized, methodical, and very smart."

"So what is he?" Lockwood asked.

"He's a psychopath," she replied. "Psychopaths are much more dangerous."

"I stand corrected," he sighed, "but you know what I meant."

"Right. Sorry. In my field of study I tend to be a little anal." She smiled. "I've been trying to predict his behavior," she continued, "because all of this is useless unless we can figure him out and get a step or two ahead of him."

"Right."

She paused as Claudine brought back the beers and waited while they glanced at the menu. Both of them ordered stone crabs and key lime pie.

After Claudine had gone, Karen went on. "I think his post-offense behavior is very significant. I've been focusing on that. He does his mutilations after death. That probably means he's not a sexual sadist. He's not killing for sexual gratification. Even though he masturbates at the scene of the crime, it isn't, in my opinion, the main reason for the killings. I've been trying to categorize these murders. I think they belong under the general classification of personal cause homicides."

Lockwood's career in law enforcement had concentrated on drug and gun smuggling and money laundries. Psych murders were a category he had never focused on.

"They are acts resulting from interpersonal aggression," Karen explained. "The victim in a personal cause killing might not know the killer, and the homicide is not generally motivated by material gain or sex. Emotional conflict usually drives the act."

"Oh," Lockwood said, not much closer to understanding.

"To further tighten the classification, he shows some signs common to two sub-categories: One is Erotomania, which is fantasy killing stemming from the UnSub's fusion of identities. The other category is Extremist Homicides, which are characterized by an overwhelming political or religious belief. I also think he may be a Collector. He's collecting body parts. . . ."

Lockwood winced. "Neat hobby, but why?"

"There's no way we're gonna figure that out until we catch him. The reasoning with these UnSubs is always very twisted. There was a guy in California who was killing women and eating their reproductive organs, because he believed that his skin was dying and that the reproductive organs would reproduce new flesh and keep him alive. Doesn't make sense, but the guy in California killed ten women as a result."

Lockwood lost his appetite for a moment, then nodded. "Go on," he said.

"So his post-mortem behavior is methodical. He surgically removes parts, he burns his brand on their left breast. By the way, that may indicate that he's right-handed, if he faces them, stands over them when he does it. Then he cleans up his crime scene and leaves. He cools off for a while, a week or two. During this period, he could contact people, become slightly more normal. If he's a multiple, as I suspect, he might even return to his core personality, Leonard Land. This phase is probably short-lived, and then his cycle begins again."

She flipped two pages back on the pad and glanced at what she had written. "I think the choice of the name 'Rat' is significant. I've done a profile on that animal's real and perceived characteristics—"

"Come on, Karen. You're profiling rodents?"

"John, everything this guy does in connection with these crimes is significant. If he'd called himself The Shepherd I'd be looking at sheep. There's something in that name . . . a reason he chose it. Hang with me, it comes out with a conclusion."

"Go."

"Under factual information, the word *rat* comes from the Latin *rodere*, meaning to gnaw. There are two kinds of rats that make up the majority of the American rat population, brown ones and black ones. In general, black rats live aboveground, brown rats live in walls and dark spaces and underground. I'm going to concentrate on the brown rat because he seems to fit better. . . . He lives and feeds frequently on garbage. . . . I think it's more than mildly significant that our boy works in an abandoned garbage barge. Rats are known to be extremely wary and cautious creatures that quickly detect approaching danger. They usually feed at night and are classified as nocturnal." She looked up at Lockwood. "So far, our Rat is a night killer. Rats tend to live in small concise areas, usually not more than one hundred fifty feet in diameter, but if food is scarce, they can travel long distances to forage. I'm not sure how appropriate that characteristic is and I don't want to beat this analogy to death, but from what we know, our Rat seems to move around when he kills. Maybe that's because he can't find the 'food' he needs near home.''

"Okay, or maybe his selection process isn't based on geography, maybe it's based on something else.''

"Exactly . . . According to scientists, rats are generally considered to be the most dangerous animals to people on the face of the planet.''

"Come on, really?''

She nodded. "In terms of sheer body count, it's true. They attack infants, often killing them. They frequently cause apartment fires by chewing through wires. And then, of course, there's disease, plague, rabies, you name it.'' She looked up. "Okay, that concludes the factual data.

"Now we go to folklore . . . what people believe about rats. We have assigned them a very low place on the personality scale. They are considered to be mean, vicious, and disloyal. Rats are also thought to be sneaky. I think these are traits that Leonard believes he has. They're ugly and dirty. I think our Rat hates the way he looks. Rats are shrewd. He might think of himself as cunning and shrewd. I'll tell you this. . . . He's no dummy. That trick with the heat and air-conditioning in Atlanta was very inventive and difficult to achieve . . . close to brilliant. Without Malavida, we never would've come upon it.''

"Okay, so he's smart, cunning, ugly, vicious, disloyal, and nocturnal . . . what else?''

"Rats are ferocious. When cornered, rats will attack viciously with little regard for their safety . . . and this is a point I'm most interested in. I think our going to his place could represent, in his mind, an attack on him. It caused him to blow up his own house, move his barge. I think he may feel cornered.''

"You saying he's going to attack us?''

"I think we have to consider the possibility.''

"How's he gonna attack us? He doesn't even know where we are."

"I don't know. It's just something to be alert to."

Lockwood looked out at the boats tied up at the dock. He listened to the rigging rattling against the aluminum masts. His mind skipped across what she had said and a thought hit him. He turned and looked at her, realization in his eyes.

"If he's been watching the news, he knows where Malavida is," Lockwood said.

"You're right, he does. But Malavida's under guard. Hard to attack when there're cops outside his door."

They sat in silence for a minute, and then the stone crabs came. They cracked them open, pulled out the meat, and ate, both of them deep in thought.

"Look, let's say I wanted to get to Malavida," Lockwood ventured. "This guy hacked into one computer very efficiently. How hard would it be to hack into the computer network at Jackson Memorial Hospital?"

Karen looked at him, realization dawning. "Shit," she finally said, as they both scrambled to their feet. . . .

The Jackson Memorial Hospital records were on The Rat's screen. He was looking for Malavida's blood products sheet. He quickly found it. Malavida had type O-negative blood. The Rat knew that if he could change the negative to positive, once the foreign blood went into his body it would stop Malavida's heart within minutes. The Rat had cracked into the computer and could now easily change the records. The Rat knew he had to take care of two things: He couldn't just change Malavida's blood type; he also had to tinker with the cross-matching safeguards the hospital maintained.

The Rat checked the orders for Malavida. He scrolled down through pending orders for other patients until he found a patient with blood type O-positive. He knew from the one time he'd been in the hospital for surgery that the technician drawing the blood would check Malavida's wristband, then hand-write the patient number on the blood tube after drawing the blood. When it reached the lab, a generated label keyed to that number and printed with the patient's name, would be stuck on the tube. The Rat looked and saw the labels were already in the computer, waiting to be printed. He scrolled down to the one for the patient with O-positive blood, deleted that patient's name, and replaced it with Malavida's.

Now, if he could change the blood designation in the blood bank before the new shift came on and hung another unit of blood, the new nurses would, unknowingly, be ordering up the wrong blood. Malavida would be dead by 12:30. The Rat switched to the patient records section in the blood bank and searched for Malavida's record. When he found it, he leaned over the keyboard and positioned his cursor in the "O-NEGATIVE." He pushed Delete four times and his cursor ate the "NEGA" letters. Then he typed in "POSI" and looked at his magic up on the screen.

He wanted to watch Malavida die. He went back to "Log Listings." He found "Video Security" and punched it up on the screen. His console now showed that there were twenty different camera positions in the hospital, mostly hallways and nurses' stations, and a few operating theaters. The hospital also used video-conferencing technology to send doctors radiology images. He knew from the records that Malavida was on the fifth floor. He found that designation and punched it up. On his computer, he was now looking at the fifth-floor sub-acute nurses' station. Three nurses were working at the desk. Off to the right of his screen, up the hall, a uniformed policeman was sitting on a metal chair outside a door. The Rat guessed this was Malavida's room.

"When he's cornered, The Rat will fight," he said, then sat back and watched the black-and-white security picture in fascination. His gaze was focused on the door, behind which he knew his mortal enemy, Malavida Chacone, was close to death.

The nurses on the evening shift moved onto the floor a little before midnight and quickly began to make their rounds. They glided silently on crepe-soled shoes, taking pulses, blood pressures, and temperatures, entering the data into the hospital's on-line CardEx system via the PC work stations outside the rooms. At 12:15, nurse Eleanor Fleetwood noticed that the whole-blood bag on Malavida's I.V. stand was low. She checked the orders at her work station and saw the doctor had okayed an order for another unit, as needed. Malavida's pressure was still low so he needed the extra blood volume. She switched to the appropriate screen and placed the order for a unit of blood to the hospital blood bank via the computer system. A unit of O-positive blood was delivered to Malavida's room at 12:20 and was attached to his stand at 12:25.

Lockwood and Karen had tried to finish mapping out The Rat's logic as they raced the rental car toward Jackson Memorial Hospital. Lockwood was at the wheel and he had his foot to the floor. They could have called ahead but nobody would have believed them. Rather than argue about it, they just made a run for it. They were only ten minutes away. "If this guy gets into the computer," he said as he ran a red light on U.S. 1, "then he could change medication, create an overdose, anything . . ."

They screeched into the hospital parking lot at 12:30 and ran through the huge double doors. They were slowed for a few minutes, trying to obtain directions to Malavida's room. The hospital was fifteen stories high and included several annexes which were sprawled across four acres. They found themselves running down polished linoleum corridors, dodging gurneys and wheelchairs, looking for the sub-acute unit.

The nurse in Malavida's room opened the valve and let the O-positive blood drip into Malavida's vein. He was unconscious, pale, and broken, lying in the bed in a single-patient room. The explosion had torn through his body, embedding chunks of plaster and wood in his abdominal cavity, one piece barely missing his fifth lumbar nerve. Had that nerve been severed, he would have lost the use of his right leg. His entire abdomen was badly perforated. The surgeons had sewn up what they could save and removed what they couldn't. The medial umbilical ligament was a mess, and they had almost lost him because his superior mesenteric artery was pierced and pumping blood into his abdominal cavity, causing a life-threatening drop in blood pressure. They had managed to clamp it off just in time and repair it. That had been eight hours ago. Now, the barely functioning remains of Malavida Chacone were strapped to a bed next to a metal I.V. stand, which, aside from whole blood, was feeding him saline fluids and strong antibiotics. Because his GI tract had been so badly ruptured, there was a fear that he might develop peritonitis. Only time would tell if he would survive his injuries.

The Rat watched his computer screen and saw Lockwood and Karen rush onto the hospital floor. Nervous sweat dripped from under his arms as they ran to the nurses' station. He watched in horror. ''The wicked raised in the Second Resurrection will go up on the breadth of the earth with Satan at their head,'' he said in a monotone, rocking back and forth on his wooden chair. On the closed-circuit TV, Lockwood appeared to be shouting at the frightened nurse. Then he broke away and ran up the hall toward Malavida's room. The cop who had been sitting on the chair exploded up and grabbed Lockwood. The Rat cursed and leaned close to his screen as the two men wrestled in the narrow doorway—the way the shot was framed, The Rat could barely see them.

Then The Rat screamed in protest as Lockwood pinned the cop against the far wall. . . .

In the hospital, Karen saw Lockwood struggling with the Dade County policeman. She ran to help him. Nurse Fleetwood came out from behind the station after her.

Lockwood could see Karen coming. He had the cop pinned against the wall. He timed it perfectly and threw his first punch as Karen got there. The cop went down, clawing for his holster. Lockwood stepped on his hand as Karen rushed into the room.

She could see Malavida taped up and unconscious in the bed. She ran to him and frantically started pulling I.V.'s out of his arm. Then she looked up at the blood bag.

"What the hell're you doing?" Nurse Fleetwood yelled as she ran through the door a few seconds later. Karen had now unhooked Malavida from all of his I.V. drips and was removing the whole-blood bag from the stand. She was reading the label as Nurse Fleetwood grabbed it away from her.

"What's his blood type?" Karen demanded.

In the hall outside, Lockwood stepped away from the cop, who pulled his gun and aimed it at him with the hammer back. "You done, greaseball?" The cop's voice was shaking with anger, and Lockwood put his hands in the air.

"I'm done," he said softly.

The cop grabbed him and spun him around, then he muscled Lockwood into the wall so hard that pieces of bad hospital art fell and shattered on the floor. The cop slammed handcuffs on him, ratcheting them tight.

Karen grabbed the clipboard from the foot of the bed and looked at it. She saw the blood delivery slip clipped on the top: "O-positive." Then she flipped back one page and looked at the earlier slip that had been clipped to the board in post-op. The first slip said "O-negative."

"Let go of that!" Nurse Fleetwood yelled, as she snatched the clipboard away from Karen. Now there were frantic footsteps in the corridor and the room filled with white coats. One was the surgical resident for the wing.

"Which is it?" Karen shouted at the nurse. "O-negative blood, like it says on the page from this morning, or O-positive, which you're putting into him now?"

The young resident grabbed the clipboard and looked at it. "What the fuck is going on, Eleanor?" he said, anger beginning to swell. "You're giving this guy O-positive? He's O-negative. I typed him myself. How much went in there?''

Nurse Fleetwood was now in full retreat. ''I don't know, Doctor. We just hooked him up. The slip said O-positive.''

The resident turned to the cop. ''Let's go! I need help getting this guy back up to ICU.''

The two of them yanked the bed away from the wall, spun it, and pushed it out into the hall. Lockwood and Karen trailed behind. They shoved the bed into the express elevator and went to ICU, a floor above. The resident and two ICU interns grabbed the bed and pushed it quickly down the hall, leaving Lockwood and Karen standing with the startled policeman they had fought with seconds before. It was an awkward moment.

''Maybe you could unhook these cuffs?'' Lockwood finally suggested. The cop reluctantly took out the keys and released him.

The Rat climbed up the steps in panic and stumbled out onto the deck of the barge. The swamp was pale in the three-quarter moon that lit the dense undergrowth of the Manatee wetlands. He filled his lungs with its heavy, moist air and let out a scream of fear and anger. His screech carried across the murky wasteland like the scream of a dying animal. Night birds broke for the sky in a flurry of beating wings. He was in agony. God had finally focused on him.

''When cornered, The Rat will fight,'' he cried at the moonlit night.

# 28

## SWAT

**T**he moon lit the scattered clouds over Miami Harbor, looking to Lockwood like beautifully spun piles of silver-white cotton. They stood by the rental car in the hospital parking lot while a warm night wind flapped flags a few yards away. They had been told fifteen minutes ago that Malavida was out of danger. Karen put out her hand. "Good going," she said. "I think we finally got one step ahead."

"Who woulda thought you could do that by profiling a brown rat?" He grinned and shook her hand.

"I think I got lucky," she said. Although they had saved Malavida's life, they knew they had to stay close to him or this could easily happen again. For that reason, they decided to take a couple of rooms at a Ramada Inn close to the hospital. They got into their car and pulled away from Jackson Memorial Hospital.

The Rat watched them go from the dark blue Ford he had rented. He had driven fast to get there from deep in the Little Manatee wetlands. It had taken just under three hours, and he had been in the hospital parking lot for only five minutes when he saw them exit. He followed them at a safe distance. Two blocks later he watched as they pulled into the Ramada Inn. He was wearing the baseball cap that he always wore to hide his ugliness. He watched as they registered, and as they walked along the outdoor passageway on the second floor and stopped at separate doors. The Rat used his binoculars to read the room numbers: Lockwood went into Room 37: the woman was three doors down in Room 40. He put the car in gear and drove out of the parking lot. He found a secluded pay phone two blocks from the Ramada Inn.

"Dade County Sheriff's Office," a female voice answered after two rings. The Rat could hear the beeps on the line that indicated the call was being recorded.

"I know where there's somebody you want. I need to talk to SWAT," he said, disguising his voice, trying to make it sound lower. Then he told SWAT a story. . . .

The SWAT room sprang to life. Six cops grabbed Second Chance Kevlar vests and laced them on. They grabbed Heckler and Koch MP5s with full-load banana clips off the weapons rack. Tear gas, launchers, and shotguns were in the truck. They were rolling in thirty seconds.

SWAT Leader Lieutenant MacLamore showed the Ramada Inn night clerk the picture of Lockwood he'd taken from the NCIC "Wanted" computer.

"This guy's a cop killer?" the desk manager said, astonished.

"Is he here?"

"Yeah. Checked him and a real pretty girl in about an hour and a half ago. He's in Thirty-seven, she's in Room Forty."

MacLamore looked at his watch. It was almost five A.M. He knew time was an important part of the equation. In an hour, the streets would begin filling. . . . The more looky-loos, the more confusion. He wanted his to be a quick surgical extraction. Tactically, he had two ways to go: One was to evacuate all the rooms to avoid any possible collateral damage. But he was afraid a full evacuation would make too much noise and alert the perp. The other option was to do a hard entry—swarm both rooms simultaneously and light up the perp at close range if he got frisky.

Lieutenant MacLamore decided on a compromise. He evacuated the rooms on both sides of 37 and 40 to avoid the chance that a stray round might go through a wall and hit someone.

The residents of those rooms now stood across the street, talking in hushed tones, not ten yards from where The Rat was parked, watching.

An ambulance called by MacLamore pulled in silently, and the paramedics walked to the SWAT truck and checked in. MacLamore did the pre-op briefing by the back of the black SWAT step-van.

"Okay, according to the NCIC computer, this guy killed two cops in Illinois," MacLamore said. "We got an anonymous tip and the desk clerk confirms his picture ID. This is a redball, so don't hesitate to light him up. I'll take Room Thirty-seven, along with Delgado and Smith. Procopio, Nash, and Washington—you guys take Forty. Remember, he could be in there fucking his bitch. So just 'cause you got the girl's room, don't cut them any slack. Go in hard. If he twitches, use him up fast, everybody get some. We go on my signal. I'm Blue, Procopio's Red."

They nodded solemnly.

"Standard-pattern entry—wide deployment, forty-five-degree cover fire. Questions?" Nobody spoke. "Let's do it."

They moved away from the SWAT van, slamming banana clips into the HK-MP5s and chambering rounds in their automatics. They were all pumping adrenaline as they climbed the interior stairwell to the outdoor corridor on the second floor. They began edging down the wall quietly on rubber-soled combat boots. When they got to Room 37, MacLamore and his two-man Blue Team deployed there, as Procopio and his Red Team went on to Karen's door. Once they were positioned, MacLamore and Procopio motioned each other and took out room keys. Simultaneously, they slid them slowly and silently into both locks.

Inside his room, Lockwood had been unable to go to sleep. He was lost in a jumble of thoughts about Claire, Heather, and his bumble-fucked career. His mind turned to his confused feelings about Karen. He had always had problems, with the new academics that were showing up by the busload at Customs. Brainiacs with no field experience, who felt their degrees gave them sway over any situation. But Karen had proved very different. She had, in a short time, managed to penetrate his defenses. Maybe it was that daredevil streak or her gentle smile. He had finally begun to sort out his feelings about her. He knew now that what bothered him about her relationship with Malavida was his own desire to explore his feelings for her. But he had promised his daughter that he would raise her, and he was determined to keep that promise. He didn't think there was any way that these desires could coexist. Besides that, he had other problems: If he was fired from Customs for malfeasance, his pension would be dust and he'd have no job. He couldn't figure out where the money to buy a farm was going to come from, but one way or another, he would make it happen.

Then he heard a metallic click in his door. It sounded like a tumbler in his lock being turned over. Lockwood quickly rolled, and his hand went for the .45, which he had put on the bedside table. He just got the gun in his hand when the door was kicked open, and three men in black jumpsuits were instantly in the room.

"You're dead, motherfucker!" MacLamore yelled, aiming his weapon.

Lockwood was already squeezing off a shot. The .45 bucked in his hand as he rolled backwards. His shot hit one of the three SWAT team members. The man screamed and went down. Lockwood completed his somersault and landed on the far side of the bed as two 9-millimeter rounds thunked into the mattress where he'd been. A third round went whizzing over his head.

"Police! Drop it, police!" MacLamore found cover as he yelled at Lockwood, curled low behind the bed.

"Prove it," Lockwood yelled back.

MacLamore threw his badge case over the bed. It landed next to Lockwood. He looked at it. "I'm coming up. Nobody shoot. Here's the gun."

He flipped the .45 onto the mattress and started to rise. He got halfway up when he was high-lowed. His chin took a flying head butt from Lieutenant MacLamore; Smith hit him with a shoulder tackle from the far side. They drove him backwards into the wall. The three of them went to the floor in a tangle. Then MacLamore and Smith pinned him. They slammed Lockwood's head into the floor several times to get rid of unburned adrenaline. They put handcuffs on, ratcheting them as tight as possible, cutting off his circulation, then yanked him to his feet. MacLamore checked Delgado, who was bleeding from a through-hole in his hip, then triggered his walkie-talkie. "Blue Team. We're clear in Thirty-seven. One down. Delgado needs a dust-off. It's through and through, but he's spilling blood like a son of a bitch."

Procopio's voice answered immediately. "Red Team is also secure," he said. "No injuries. I'll notify the parameds."

They sent Delgado off in a wailing ambulance. Lockwood and Karen were isolated in separate rooms as MacLamore began a preliminary interrogation.

"Shut the fuck up," MacLamore yelled when Lockwood started to say something.

"I'm a Customs officer on leave of duty."

"You're wanted for a double police murder in Illinois and you put a round in one of my men."

"You came through the door waving a machine gun. You never identified yourself as a cop! Who taught you your hard-entry tactics? You fucked up!" Lockwood shouted back.

Both of them were still yelling as the Watch Commander hit the scene. He was a bull-necked sixty-year-old captain named Fred T. Fredrickson. In Miami police

circles, he was known as Fred T. Fred. He had thirty
years on the force, a command persona, and a no-
nonsense, take-charge presence in a crisis. The minute he
arrived, everybody settled down.

As the sun came up over Miami, Lockwood and Karen
were transported to the Dade County Sheriff's Office in
the backs of two separate squad cars. They drove past
The Rat, who watched from his rental car across the
street. He had heard the gunfire and been sure they would
be killed. His nipples were on fire. They had been burning all afternoon; his skin was tender and growing red.
A sign that The Wind Minstrel was coming. As he
watched Lockwood and Dawson being taken away, he
wondered if they were archangels, sent from heaven.
*How else could they have managed to survive?*

# 29

## DISGRACE

Vic Kulack arrived in Miami with Lockwood's Federal arrest warrant in his pocket. The last time Kulack had been in South Florida had been a disaster for him. He had left in defeat with an official reprimand because of the cluster-fuck during the take-down on Operation Girlfriend. All of his troubles after that had been courtesy of John Lockwood. It was one thing to have Lockwood go stress-related and have him run through a head check in Washington . . . but this was too good to be true. This was the all-time, outta-the-park, bounce-it-in-the-parking-lot home run.

He was picked up by an IA-ASAC from the Miami office named "Pecos Bill" Broder. Broder had been raised in Texas and had an accent you could hang a Stetson on. He had been Kulack's second-in-command on the IA investigation on Operation Girlfriend and shared Kulack's hearty dislike for Lockwood. As they rode across town to the Dade County Sheriff's Office, Broder filled Kulack in.

"They got our boy strung up t'the barn door," Broder drawled. "The list a'shit he's pulled this time is impressive, even by his standards. In descending order: He put a hole in a SWAT commando, hit a cop at Jackson Memorial, and ditched a police escort at a crime scene. He also moved evidence, the suspect's truck, I think. Dade Sheriff's recovered it last night, but as evidence, it's vomit. Got Malavida's blood and everybody's prints, including Karen Dawson's, all over it.''

''Ah, yes,'' Kulack growled, ''Awesome Dawson . . .'' Kulack knew that since she was a civilian, there wasn't much he could get her for. Aiding and abetting, or maybe some after-the-fact bullshit. He'd elected to leave her off the warrant because she had juice at DOJ.

They arrived at the Dade County Sheriff's Office, and, once Kulack had checked in with the Extradite Transfer Office, he left Broder downstairs and was taken to a tobacco-colored room on the third floor. The Sheriff's main building was in downtown Miami, and Kulack thought the place looked like it had been designed by Plains Indians. It was a bunch of big, square structures with flat roofs that looked like a series of huge shoe boxes, which were called annexes because they'd been added over the years as the department grew to accommodate the ever-increasing need for South Florida law enforcement.

Kulack sat impatiently in a wood-backed chair in the windowless, badly ventilated interrogation room and waited.

His prisoner was finally led in by a detective. Kulack noted with displeasure that Lockwood wasn't in restraints, even though he had been arrested for a handful of Class A felonies.

''Shouldn't this piece of shit be handcuffed?'' he said without waiting for an introduction.

The last to enter the room was the Watch Commander, Fredrickson. He closed the door behind him.

''I'm Captain Fred T. Fredrickson,'' he said, extending his hand. Kulack made no move to accept it.

''This douchebag walked a Federal convict out of Lompoc Prison using bad paper,'' Kulack said. ''Then he gets him critically injured. He's not an active Customs Officer anymore, but he's down here pretending he's on the job, which is a violation of Title Eighteen of the U.S. Penal Code, Section Nine-Twelve: Impersonation of a

Federal Officer. That's before he even gets around to plugging one of your guys and swinging on some poor schmuck working a folding chair at the hospital.''

"Why don't you slow down," Fred T. Fred said as he found an empty seat and plopped down in it. "You're filling this little room up with exhaust.''

"I got the paperwork here. I wanna get moving. I got a plane t'catch." Kulack pulled the warrant out of his pocket and smiled over at Lockwood. "If you're hoping that the DOAO is gonna pull your flaming gonads outta the campfire again, you're in for a big shock.''

Lockwood let it all fly past. He saw no need to start up with Kulack. The game was over.

"You're a little rigid, friend," Fred T. Fred said, looking with disgust at Kulack's bulging, throbbing neck veins. "What happened down here was a mistake. Our SWAT team had bad information. Looks like this Leonard Land character hacked into the Customs computer, stole Lockwood's picture and prints, then put it all in the NCIC database, along with a phony Illinois police report saying he killed two cops. . . . Didn't happen. I think we should—''

"Not to be rude or undiplomatic," Kulack broke in, "but I really don't give a flying fuck what you think. This turkey is stuffed and already cooking. I wanna get him outta here.''

"I think," Fred T. Fred said slowly, "we may have a serial killer operating in Southern Florida. I think this guy wants Lockwood, and John's agreed to be the bait.''

"Unless you wanna file some paper with the A.G.'s office, it'll have to wait. I'm taking him with me now.''

Kulack stood, pulled out his cuffs. "Turn around," he barked and, when Lockwood did, he slammed the bracelets down on his wrist. Lockwood hadn't been in cuffs since he'd been caught stealing cars as a juvenile. Yet this was the third set of bracelets he'd had slammed on him in less than twenty-four hours.

Kulack yanked him around and pushed him toward the door.

"You have to pick him up at the prisoners' exit. That's where the paperwork gets signed," Fred T. Fred told Kulack, who grunted and left them all standing there.

Lockwood rode down in an old, slow Otis four-man elevator with Captain Fredrickson. "Listen, Captain, you seem like a pretty okay guy. . . . I'm worried about Karen Dawson. . . ."

"She's still upstairs. She'll be fine. She's about to get released."

"I know . . . but this guy who came after me, he probably was coming after both of us. She's a civilian. If I'm not here, she'll be walking around unprotected."

"Why don't you ask Kulack to take her back to Washington as a material witness?"

"He won't do it."

"Whatta you want me to do?"

"You've gotta put somebody on her . . . somebody who won't get faked out. The Rat is smart and he's dangerous. That computer of his is lethal. It's an offensive weapon. He can strike from long range through the phone lines. He almost got Malavida and he almost got me. We're only alive 'cause we got lucky."

The elevator door opened and Fred T. Fred looked at Lockwood. "I'm short-handed. I'd like to help, but I can't supply bodyguards to everyone who might get attacked. You should convince her to go back to Washington."

"I tried," Lockwood said. "She won't go."

"Then there's nothing I can do."

Kulack signed the papers and took custody of Lockwood minutes later. He shoved him out the door into the bright Florida sunshine.

Karen had been naked and sound asleep when the door to her room in the Ramada Inn had been kicked open. She caught a glimpse of three men in black rushing at her, but before she could sit up, they landed hard on top of her and pinned her to the bed. Then they dragged her up, naked, and cuffed her. She hadn't been patted down.

Without any clothes on, she clearly wasn't armed. She'd been Mirandized, and for the next hour she'd been forced to sit in the backseat of a Miami Sheriff's car in a Ramada Inn terry-cloth robe and answer questions about the murder of some cops in Illinois. They had quizzed her repeatedly about her relationship to John Lockwood. She had endured it till sunup, when she'd been officially arrested and taken to the Sheriff's Office, where the interrogations began all over again. After a while, she guessed she was not going to be formally charged. She waived her right to an attorney to help calm things down, and eventually things seemed to get straightened out. She was told around ten that they had been arrested because Lockwood's picture had been placed in the computer at the National Crime Information Center, along with an APB for his arrest for a double police homicide. Miami's SWAT team had received an anonymous tip. The minute they said the word *computer*, she knew it was the work of The Rat.

She was finally released at 11:30 and the fatherly Watch Commander, Captain Fredrickson, offered to take her to her car, which was still in the parking lot of the Ramada Inn. When she asked to see Lockwood, he told her that Lockwood had been taken back to Washington under guard.

The drive back to the Ramada Inn was strained. Fredrickson was trying to be a good guy, but Karen was in a foul mood. She'd had less than two hours' sleep, and her unscheduled wake-up call had been unusually aggressive.

"Look," she finally said to him, "Malavida's life is in extreme danger. I don't think you quite get the gravity of that."

"There's a man outside his door at the hospital," he said.

"This killer isn't going to come within a mile of the hospital. He'll do something long distance with his computer," she said, a little too hotly. "Malavida is going to be murdered in there unless you people wake the fuck up!"

"Miss Dawson, I'm sorry for the inconvenience we've caused you, and I am very aware of the menace that Leonard Land might present to Mr. Chacone. However, so far we can't directly link Land to anything. I don't have enough evidence to even issue an arrest warrant for the crimes you're talking about. We have no physical evidence that he killed Candice Wilcox in Atlanta, or Leslie Bowers in Michigan. And as far as Lockwood's wife . . . I guess his little girl could potentially pick the guy out of a lineup, but that hasn't happened yet. Furthermore, all of this is out of my jurisdiction. It's Tampa's case. Best chance I have here is, if I get my hands on him, I can voice-print him and maybe get a match with that recording of the phony tip he called in. Maybe then I can get the DA to file on him for attempted murder. But even that is a long shot."

"What about his rigging that booby trap and blowing up Malavida?"

"Tampa PD would have to file that charge, but the way I hear it, technically you were trespassing without a badge or a warrant. I guess maybe they could file on him for arson or endangering or hazardous behavior or some damn thing. But he'd make bail in about an hour."

"You're telling me to go away and shut up?"

"No. I'm telling you I think you're right, despite the lack of evidence." Fredrickson's voice was soft and his eyes seemed concerned. "I agree this guy's probably a full-on maniac. But even if I knew where he was, I can't arrest him until he does something I can prove. I've done a lousy job of protecting Chacone, I admit it. I don't want the same thing to happen to you, so I'd feel a lot better if you'd get on a plane and go back to Washington."

There was definitely something fatherly about Fred T. Fred. Karen finally nodded her head. "Maybe that's a good idea," she said.

They were parked in the Ramada parking lot, next to her car. Fred T. reached across her and opened the door. "I'll work it as hard as I can. If this guy goes hot, at least this time we'll know who we're looking for."

"Thanks for the ride," she said. "I hope you don't mind if I call you from time to time, for an update . . . ?"

"You'll be calling from Washington?"

"From Washington," she lied.

After he drove off, Karen got into her blue LeBaron and put the top down. It was noon, and the Florida sun was oppressively hot. She drove back to the Jackson Memorial Hospital. Ten minutes later, she was on the sixth floor checking on Malavida.

A new nurse told her he was still resting. She nodded and peeked into his room. The Miami cop was gone. He'd been replaced by a Federal agent in a suit. He watched her without interest as she showed her Customs ID and entered. Malavida looked very small in the hospital bed. She couldn't see the dressings because he had the covers up under his chin, but she knew he was wrapped in tape. As he lay in bed, his eyes closed, she could see what he must have been like as a little boy. There was an innocence about him. She moved closer to the bed and looked down. The lone teardrop tattoo hung under his right eye, a dangerous exclamation mark. She wondered if Lockwood had been right about him. She had made love to this person. She had found warmth in his tenderness. She wanted to believe that she had given that gift in honesty, but the events of the last two weeks had moved with frightening speed. Maybe she had been swept along by the current. She looked again at the tattoo. The teardrop was a symbol of distress. She had been told once that Mexican gang kids got teardrop tattoos when a good friend died from a street action. It represented the cultural ocean that separated them. Although Malavida's need for freedom had caused him to run away from them in Atlanta, his conscience had brought him back. He had tried to help them. She was supposed to be able to profile behavior, to predict what an UnSub would do . . . but she was badly confused by Malavida Chacone.

Then Malavida opened his eyes and looked up at her. They locked gazes for a long time.

"Hi," she said to him softly.

"Hi," he said back, his voice just a whisper.

She was about to say more when he closed his eyes. She thought he would open them again, but in seconds he was back asleep. She stood there for several more moments, trying to decide what to do.

Karen was suddenly bone-weary. She had eaten nothing since yesterday but two bites of stone crab. She knew that with Lockwood gone it was up to her to protect Malavida. She also knew that would be next to impossible in the hospital. There were too many systems The Rat could penetrate. Too many people, too many ways he could slip through electronic defenses and attack. She had to get Malavida healthy enough to move him. She had to find a way to sneak him past the Federal agent who, she suspected, was not there to protect his life so much as to keep him from escaping. She had walked right in, flashing civilian ID, while he read the paper. She had been giving the problem some thought and had the beginnings of an idea, but her head was so thick from lack of sleep, she needed to get a few hours to clear the cobwebs. She moved away from Malavida and back out into the hall . . .

Karen slept for four hours on the hard vinyl sofa in the visitors' area.

She opened her eyes when she heard Lockwood's voice. She looked around and finally saw him on the TV screen over the nurses' station. It was the five o'clock news. They were running file footage taken three months ago after the shootout on Operation Girlfriend.

The shot then switched to Trisha Rains in front of the Dade County Sheriff's Office: "That footage, many of you will remember, was taken last January when U.S. Customs Agent Lockwood was involved in a shootout at Miami International Airport. . . . Agent Lockwood was arrested today by members of his own Internal Affairs Division. The arresting agent was Victor Kulack, also a participant in last January's gunfight. Apparently, Lockwood had been suspended a few days ago and was in Miami working on a murder case after having illegally freed a Federal prisoner named Malavida Chacone. As reported earlier, Chacone is now in critical condition at Jackson Memorial Hospital.''

Karen sat up, went to the ladies' room, washed her face, and put on fresh makeup. She combed out her auburn hair and straightened her clothing.

Malavida was still sleeping, so she went searching in the huge hospital for Lockwood's old friend Ray Gonzales.

She found Gonzales in the Renal Care facility. He looked terrible. His skin was papery and so thin that the bones in his shoulder seemed to protrude sharply. He was in a hospital bed, hooked up to a dialysis machine and reading a Cuban tract called *La Revolución*, when Karen walked in.

*"Señor Gonzales?"* she asked.

*"Sí."*

*"Soy una amiga de Juan Lockwood."*

"Then you don't have the sense God gave a goose," he said without an accent as he smiled at her.

"Probably not." She smiled back.

"How's my Anglo brother?"

"He's under arrest and on his way back to Washington, so I guess you could say he's pretty shitty."

"I know. He was by here yesterday. He looked tired and confused. Claire's death hit him hard. But he didn't say nothing about that killer, or busting Chacone outta Federal prison. I got that offa TV this evening."

"Vic Kulack from Internal Affairs came down with a warrant for pursuing an investigation against orders."

Gonzales laid down the magazine, and his face formed into a scowl. "Kulack is a low-life. He's the reason I'm hooked up to this damn machine. Kulack's been working overtime on Johnny. He doesn't like the fact that Lockwood gets results, that he gets newspaper ink, that the agency brass loves him. All these years Lockwood gets invited to the ball and gets to eat off lace doilies. Kulack gets invited to the outhouse, eats off toilet seat covers. Now, I guess he figures he's even.''

A nurse came in to check the levels on the dialysis machine. After a minute, she left. Ray Gonzales studied Karen openly. "It was too bad about Claire," he said. "John was still carrying a big torch for her. Don't often see a man pining over his ex-wife with that much sincere energy. All through Operation Girlfriend he was talking about getting together with her again."

Karen nodded. Her eyes showed him nothing, but she felt a tinge of sadness at that remark.

"You didn't come down here 'cause you wanted to watch my blood get cleaned," Gonzales said, bringing her back, "or because you wanted to catch up on John Lockwood's past. You got another reason?"

"You're pretty perceptive, Ray," she said.

"Cut the bullshit . . . let's hear what's really on your mind."

So she sat in the chair facing the bed and told him her plan.

# 30

## THE WIND MINSTREL IS COMING AND HE IS GOD

**H**is nipples were on fire. He faced the computer in his barge and endured his stinging flesh. The TV news said that Lockwood had been transported to Washington for a Friday morning nine-o'clock hearing at the Department of Justice. The Rat had cracked the DOJ computer and obtained a valid username/password by fone-phreaking a DOJ agent's modem call into work. He brought the DOJ Administration Building's menu of Building Services up on the screen:

```
2300 CONSTITUTION AVENUE
WASHINGTON, D.C.
CENTRAL COMPUTER MENU
```

H)VAC
  HEATING
  VENTILATION
  AIR CONDITIONING
  ENERGY STAR

P)HYSICAL PLANT, MISC
  DWP
  GAS
  ENERGY MGMT.
  SYSTEMS
  MAINTENANCE SCHED.

S)ECURITY
  ACCESS CONTROL &
  ACCOUNTING
  VIDCAM MONITORING
  LOCKDOWN
  ALARMS

B)UILDING SERVICES
  PA/MUSIC
  ELEVATOR SCHED/
  CONTROL
  COMMON AREA
  LIGHTING
  ENERGY STAR

C)OMMUNICATIONS
  PHONE
  DATA
  RADIO
  PAGING

E)MERGENCY SERVICES
  PUBLIC SAFETY
  AUTOALERT
  HELIPAD
  POWER BACKUP

He selected the "SECURITY" sub-menu. The DOJ in Washington was housed in a "smart" building, and everybody in the Justice Department had a "smart card" which they inserted in a slot when they entered. He chose "ACCESS CONTROL & ACCOUNTING," which showed the names and times of everyone entering and exiting the building, as well as certain high-security areas. Lockwood had entered the building at eight A.M. It was now quarter to nine. The Rat exited the security access log and chose "EMERGENCY SERVICES" from the main menu. A sub-menu appeared, and he chose "PUBLIC SAFETY." Up onto the screen came a list of sub-headings:

P)OLICE
F)IRE
M)EDICAL
S)EISMIC

He selected the "FIRE" option, then scanned the map of the fire suppression systems of the DOJ Building on Constitution Avenue. Most of the old buildings had $CO_2$ or water sprinkler fire systems, but The Rat had found something interesting when he'd gone hunting in the system yesterday. On the bottom floor of the building, he had discovered a room labeled "Paper Files." It took up half the sub-basement, and it was where correspondence and memos that had not been transferred onto diskettes were stored. The room had become the center of his plan.

The hearing was in a small conference room on the ninth floor of the Department of Justice Administration Building. It was beautifully decorated: deep-green carpet, silk wallpaper, hunting prints in lacquered frames. The nine o'clock hearing started ten minutes late.

Laurence Heath had walked over from Customs two blocks away, and now sat at the oak conference table next to Bob Tilly and across from Vic Kulack. They were all waiting for the U.S. Prosecutor, a narrow-shouldered man named Carter Van Lendt.

"This guy really dropped the basket," Kulack said to fill the empty air as Heath's gaze fell on him. "He thinks he can just do whatever he pleases. I've got a file on him two inches thick. Damn thing looks like the Georgetown phonebook."

"Why don't we wait for Van Lendt?" Heath said without emotion.

Then the door opened and DOJ Prosecutor Carter Van Lendt entered the room, carrying some brown manila files. "Hi. Sorry I'm late. Had to clean up a mess on a case in pre-trial." He sat down and dropped his armload of folders on the conference table. He hunted for the one that said "Lockwood" on the tab. Then he looked up and smiled thinly. "Lockwood and Alex Hixon are in the next room. Wanna bring 'em in and get started?" Van Lendt said, as he put a tape recorder in the center of the conference table.

"I've got something I wanna say first," Kulack said, and they all turned to him.

"Is this for the record, Vic?" Van Lendt asked, reaching to turn on the tape recorder.

"No, hang on a minute, not yet. Before we start, I just want you to know where I'm coming from." He looked at them for a theatrical moment. "It's no secret I want this guy cashiered, and it's no secret I want him to do some hard time. John Lockwood operates outside the purview of this agency. He treats the agency guidelines like they're shit—"

"Okay, I think we got the gist of it, Vic," Heath said, agitated. "This is supposed to be a hearing where both sides are present. Let's stop loading the deck and get Lockwood in and do it for real."

Kulack plowed ahead. "I'm just saying, you let a guy like this break rules, run roughshod over agency policy, and then call him a hero, you can't expect the new guys coming up to think we stand for anything. Lockwood is supposed to be some kinda Customs legend. But I think he's a fucking disaster. I just want you to know I'm looking to max him out."

"Are you through now?" Heath growled. "Can we get Lockwood in and do this for the record?"

"Sure."

The Rat selected the "VIDCAM MONITORING" option from the "SECURITY" menu. The selection of cameras was now on the lower left quadrant of the screen. This was one of the new breed of buildings which routed video images around its network for video-conferencing. The security system used the network too for monitoring all the security cameras. The system had cameras everywhere, even in the elevators. The Rat punched them up, one at a time, scanning shot after shot of corridors full of agents carrying armloads of folders here and there. He watched elevators crammed with people coming to work. He wasn't sure where Lockwood was, so he kept surfing the sixty or so shots, looking.

For his plan to work, he needed to know exactly where Lockwood was. He hunkered over his screen, sweat dripping off his rib cage and between his feet. Then he punched up the ninth-floor hall. A door opened. Lockwood and another man stepped out. He watched in fascination as the two men walked down the hall. . . .

The conference room door opened and Lockwood stepped into the room with his Federal Law Enforcement Attorney, Alex Hixon. Hixon was a precise man of forty with short, rapidly receding brown hair and wire-rimmed glasses. He moved to the head of the table and sat, Lockwood taking the chair beside him. They all exchanged looks and nods, but no salutations.

"Okay," Heath finally said, "this is a Justice Department internal review. Your agency, John, gives you the benefit of this preliminary hearing before any charges are brought against you. It's your chance to give your side of it with the U.S. Prosecutor present. In the event that the A.G.'s office, after this hearing, decides to pursue an indictment, then the rest of your IA hearing will be suspended and the tape of this meeting sealed and held as confidential agency material. It can't be subpoenaed. The criminal proceeding then takes precedence. The reason we do it this way is so that the results of this hearing, which are not conducted in accordance with your Constitutional rights, cannot be used against you in court." He finished, took a deep breath. "You all know this, but I'm required to say it for the record."

"Fine with me," Lockwood said.

Kulack leaned forward in his chair. "The list of charges against you is extensive," he said. "I'm going to take them chronologically and not in order of their magnitude: First, it is our contention that you and Harvey Knox in the Los Angeles DOJ office conspired to go outside Federal guidelines to write a fraudulent Special Circumstances Release for the purpose of getting Malavida Chacone out of the Federal penitentiary in Lompoc."

They all turned from Kulack to Lockwood.

"Harvey Knox was not in any way involved. I dropped by his office on Saturday afternoon, April thirteenth. I went through his desk while he was downstairs. I got one of those SCR forms out and forged his name to it. So I don't want him taking the heat for it. That was me."

"So you're admitting you're guilty of illegally releasing a prisoner without proper authorization?" Heath said, his eyebrows climbing his forehead.

"Yes, sir. I thought he could help me with a case. I crossed the line. I'm sorry."

"May I ask, why the fuck . . . ?" Heath growled, his disappointment filling the room.

"Because, sir, I was trying to penetrate a remailer computer in Oslo, Norway, which I believed was a chat line for sexual psychopaths."

Kulack cut in, "Okay, so we've established that you illegally released Chacone from prison and took him to Florida, where he became critically injured due to your actions." The IA silk was grinning slightly.

"Actually, Vic old buddy, I took him to my wife's house in Studio City, California. He used her phone, at my direction, to penetrate the Pennet computer in Oslo. I fucked up because the UnSub back-tracked the line, and my wife, Claire, was murdered as a result." The bitterness in Lockwood's voice was tangible. The room grew still.

"Go on," Heath said. "Take us through it chronologically."

And Lockwood did. He told it all, not leaving out any detail: He told them about the chat room, Candice Wilcox's murder and mutilation in Atlanta, The Rat's clever use of the computer to change the timetable of the murder, Malavida's escape, Lockwood's return to Washington and handing his badge in, Karen Dawson's discovery of Leslie Bowers's murder and mutilation, finding Leonard Land's house, the explosion and the cybernetic attack on Malavida in the hospital, Lockwood's assault on the

Miami cop so Karen could pull the tubes out of Malavida's arm, and the shootout with Dade County SWAT at the Ramada Inn. Each incident by itself was arguably defensible. But when they were all strung together in one telling, even Lockwood had to concede, it seemed like reckless behavior at best. In his memory, he heard DOJ psychiatrist Dr. Smythe: "John, are you acting in this destructive manner because you want to punish yourself for your thoughtless actions against your loved ones?" It was hard to believe that he had to come this far to finally begin to buy into that idea.

"I think we should suspend this hearing," Kulack said, the grin growing. "I think Mr. Van Lendt will want to ask the Federal Grand Jury for an indictment."

Van Lendt closed his notebook. "Seal the recording and save it until I see if the A.G. wants to seek an indictment for Felonious Malfeasance of Duty."

"You guys don't have all that much, the way I see it," Alex Hixon finally said. He had said nothing till now, but he had been making notes through the entire meeting. Now he looked at them. "According to everybody, John gave Director Heath his badge back in the hall at Customs a week ago, making the charge of Malfeasance of Duty a complete 'so what.' "

"He was suspended, not fired," Kulack said, "then he went all over the place saying he was on the job . . . calling himself a Customs agent . . ."

"We can all go get depositions from the people you say he said that to, and argue semantics forever. Way I see it, he canceled his employment with U.S. Customs by verbal agreement when he handed back his badge, making all of the Customs Service rule-book violations beyond the scope. As a private citizen he doesn't have to report to his supervisor, doesn't have to take orders from Director Heath regarding what to do. As an American citizen, he could certainly ask a few questions after his wife was murdered. I believe there were four other agents standing at the elevator when Lockwood resigned and handed back his badge.'' He turned to Heath. ''Is that right, Larry?''

Heath nodded his head.

''So I'd urge you guys to leave that one in your brief-case,'' Hixon said. ''As far as getting Malavida out of jail is concerned, it is, at worst, a Class B felony. The way I see it, we cop to that and get some kind of sus-pended sentence. The other stuff is just ratshit, and you all know it. This looks to me like a personal vendetta by an IA investigator who's made more bogus charges than a credit card thief, and I intend to put that fact in evi-dence.''

There was a deafening silence which lasted for almost thirty seconds. Kulack finally broke it. ''I'm not with-drawing the complaint. In the meantime, he spends the night in jail.''

The meeting ended and they all stood.

On his way out, Laurence Heath approached Lock-wood. ''If it means anything, John, I'm sorry. You were one of the best. You had good stuff.''

They all left the room together and moved to the ele-vators. Bob Tilly went up the hall to the bathroom while Kulack pushed the Down button and they waited.

The Rat had shut off the five other elevators in the DOJ Administration Building. Once he had figured out the system, it had been amazingly simple. Under "EMER-GENCY SERVICES," he had accessed "PUBLIC SAFETY." Contained in its sub-menu was a seismic activity sensor which shut down the elevators during any seismic event. Once the main computer received a seismic alarm, it au-tomatically told the elevators to perform their pre-set emergency duties, which were to return to the lobby, their ''Emergency Home Floor,'' and shut down.

The Rat had first put the sixth elevator on ''Mainte-nance Setting.'' This effectively cut elevator six out of the system so it would continue to operate, but strictly by its own call buttons, at least for the time being. Then he had sent the system a phony seismic alarm which had deactivated five of the six elevators. The sixth elevator opened on nine and took in Lockwood, Laurence Heath, Vic Kulak, Carter Van Lendt, and Alex Hixon.

The Rat watched on his high-resolution monitor as elevator six passed the lobby level. Heath started to pound on the lobby button, but The Rat had reset the elevator's "Emergency Home Floor" from "Lobby Level" to "Sub-basement," then brought it back on-line. The seismic alarm, overriding the button system, caused it to go directly to the sub-basement. As soon as the door opened, The Rat shut the elevator off, leaving it stuck there and locked open. Then he shut down the ventilation system in the sub-basement. The five men walked into the file room that The Rat had selected the day before.

"The Wind Minstrel is coming," The Rat whispered in awe.

In the file room, Laurence Heath moved around looking for a fire door. He found one, but it had an electric lock and wouldn't open. He looked for a phone. There wasn't one.

"I've never been down here. Gotta be a way out," he said.

Lockwood picked up the emergency phone in the elevator and tried to dial out. He couldn't get a dial tone. "Is all this stuff on one central computer?" Lockwood asked, his heart rate beginning to climb.

"Yeah, this is a 'smart' building. They retooled it a few years ago. Systems are all on the main computer on the first floor," Carter Van Lendt said.

"Shit." Lockwood had already begun to suspect the worst. He looked up, saw a security camera, and wondered if The Rat was watching them. "Anybody got a cellphone?"

"Why?" Kulack said. "Let's just go find the fire stairs on the other side."

"They're gonna be locked. Gimme a cell."

Hixon popped open his briefcase and handed his to

Lockwood. Lockwood dialed the DOJ building's switchboard.

"Department of Justice, one moment please," the operator said and immediately put him on hold. His heart was racing and he made a conscious effort to calm down. There was not much down here. How could The Rat attack them with a room full of files? *Take it easy*, he told himself.

"Whatta you doing? This is nuts," Kulack said, reaching for the phone.

Lockwood yanked the phone out of his reach. "What's down here?" he asked Van Lendt.

"Files."

"Not the files. What kinda systems?"

And then they heard a Klaxon horn from above and all of them looked up. Immediately a siren started to sound from the other end of the sub-basement.

"What the fuck is that?" Lockwood asked.

"I think it's the halon system. All the paper file rooms got 'em last year," Van Lendt answered.

"Halon? Doesn't that shit eat oxygen?" Lockwood said, as the switchboard finally took him off hold.

Then over the screaming Klaxon they heard vibrating coming from the vents above them. They looked up. A white gas was flowing from vents in the ceiling and cascading down off the file cabinets like dry ice vapor. It started to swirl and pool on the floor.

"Department of Justice," the operator chirped in his ear.

"This is a medical emergency. I'm with Customs DOAO Laurence Heath. We're trapped in the basement of this building. The door's jammed! He's had a heart attack! Get down here fast! Break the door and bring oxygen!"

"I'm sorry, sir . . . what?"

"Do what I said. Now! He's dying."

Lockwood had instantly decided not to try to explain to her what was really happening. He had read only one report on halon gas and it had stuck in his mind. A system in Denver had accidentally gone off and killed several people in less than three minutes. If the heavy foglike substance continued to pour into the room, within minutes there would be no breathable air left in the sub-basement. Already Lockwood felt a shortness of breath . . . a ringing in his ears.

"Hold your breath," he said, "don't breathe this shit. If it gets in you, you're gonna lose oxygen."

They were all backing away from the halon, which was rolling toward them, flowing freely from the ceiling. The cloud of gas was expanding as it flowed into the elevator, where they had retreated. It began to fill the box. Even the air above them was dissipating. It began to climb rapidly in the enclosed space.

On the monitor The Rat watched the suffocation of Lockwood and the four strangers with rapt interest. He was rocking back and forth, his huge body causing the wooden chair to creak loudly.

He watched as the first death occurred. The narrow-shouldered man dropped his armload of folders and fell to his knees. He reached up and grabbed at his shirt collar, ripping at his tie. His mouth was open, his teeth protruding. The Rat remembered the cats he had strangled as a boy. . . . They also died with their mouths wide open, their tongues curled and out. Then the narrow-shouldered man was clawing at his neck. Lockwood reached out to pull him up, but before he could get to him, the man fell sideways into the white fog. The Rat could barely see him in the mist. The man bucked once in a final convulsion, swirling the cloud of gas, then fell beneath its deadly blanket.

In the elevator, Lockwood was holding his breath. His lungs were aching, his nose and throat burning. The halon was now all around them. He tried to reach up and punch the top out of the elevator ceiling but, when he hit it, it rang solidly, sending a bolt of pain down his arm.

Heath was beginning to gag and foam at the mouth.

"Can't breathe," he gasped. Then his barrel chest heaved five times as he sucked in huge lungfuls of nothing. He grabbed at his chest and, with his mouth wide open, fell forward on his face.

Kulack went down seconds later. Both of them disappeared under the heavy blanket of white gas. Lockwood and his lawyer, Alex, were the last ones standing. Both holding their breath, looking across and through the sea of halon with bulging eyes. Finally, Alex couldn't hold his breath any longer and took one gulp of the deadly lifeless atmosphere. He looked at Lockwood for a moment and then, in panic, took another gulp, and another. He convulsed while still standing. His wire glasses fell off his face. His brain was dying. He started to lose consciousness . . . falling slowly to one knee. He reached out to Lockwood, who grabbed his wrist to hold him upright. The gas was now chin high and the oxygen around them was dissipating. Then Hixon fell backwards, slipping from Lockwood's grasp, dropping from sight.

Lockwood could hear pounding somewhere in the basement. He slowly let out all of his breath. His lungs were empty. His reflexes were screaming at him to breathe, while his iron will was forcing him not to. He couldn't hold his breath any longer. He was seconds from death when his hand brushed against his side coat pocket and he felt something. His allergy inhaler! He yanked it out and jammed it against his nose, then took one life-sustaining inhalation, sucking the little plastic vaporizer empty. He almost choked on its pungent fragrance, but he had quarter-filled his lungs with the aerosol mist. Then, seconds later, he began to lose consciousness. Falling forward, he grabbed the elevator rail, his chin just above the deadly fog.

As Lockwood floated into the tunnel of death, he thought he saw the fire door at the far end of the building fly open. He thought he saw Heather rushing toward him, carrying an oxygen bottle, but she was too far away to save him. "Daddy, Daddy, don't leave me," she cried, but it was too late.

Lockwood fell forward into the deadly mist.

The Rat shut off his computer and went up on the deck of the barge. He climbed down the ladder into the water. He rolled in the shallows next to the rustling hull, to cool his blazing skin. The salt water stung him, bringing tears to his eyes. He could bear the pain no longer. Finally, he rolled up on his knees. He raised his hands over his head.

"The Wind Minstrel is coming," he screamed at the heavens, "and *He* is God!"

A flock of herons broke from the treetops and wheeled in crazy circles above him.

# 31

## MOVING DAY

**K**aren had visited Malavida for an hour on Thursday night. He was conscious but very weak. The Federal agent sat outside the door with one ear cocked, but they were talking so softly that he finally gave up and went back to the book he was reading.

Karen filled Malavida in on the close call he'd had with his blood type, and the one she and Lockwood had had at the Ramada Inn.

"Where's Lockwood now?" he said, his voice raspy from the anesthetic tube he'd had down his throat for ten hours yesterday.

"He got arrested," she said softly. "They took him back to Washington Tuesday. He's having a hearing tomorrow at nine, for a bunch'a stuff they say he did. . . . It's all bullshit. In the meantime, I'm going to get you out of here."

Malavida lay there looking at the ceiling for a minute. She watched him and, when he didn't comment, she went on. "Look, I think if you stay here with all the shit they're pumping into you, you're taking a big chance. The Rat will out-think this bunch'a white coats. You'll be getting battery acid in your coffee or some damn thing."

"You're gonna move me? I feel like hell. I can't even sit up."

"I got chummy with the surgical nurse. She said the surgery was a success. They have you scheduled for X-rays tomorrow at ten to check their work. The big danger for you now is peritonitis,'cause your intestine got ruptured. They've been pumping you full of vancomycin. But they're slacking off now. If you start running a fever, I'll bring you back. Another thing . . . that Fed out there isn't gonna let you get your hands on a computer, and I need you to help me get The Rat."

"Am I the Lone Ranger or Tonto?" he said softly.

"You're Snoopy, remember?" She smiled at him and took his hand. "They say they're gonna keep you in here for another three days. According to the nurse, all they're gonna do is watch you, take your temperature. I can do that . . . and remember, Mal, in three days, you're on your way back to Lompoc." She knew he would do anything to avoid that.

"I'm a Federal prisoner," he said softly. "You bust me outta here and you're gonna be guilty of conspiracy, and aiding and abetting. Both felonies. You could get five years yourself."

"I don't want to go to jail . . . but in case you haven't noticed, I can handle risks. And I've developed an affection for you, so shut up." He smiled at her, and she reddened slightly and rushed on: "I also think The Rat is about to go hot again. It's been two weeks since Candice Wilcox died. I don't want another woman killed and mutilated. We said we were gonna get him for what he did to Claire. I haven't changed my mind; I hope you haven't."

Malavida finally nodded. "Okay, you're on."

"I've been working at the library all afternoon. I found some pretty interesting stuff in the newspaper morgue."

"Like what?"

"The woman you saw in the barge, the blowup taped on the wall with the markings and dates on it . . . ?"

"Yeah?"

Karen dug into her purse and pulled out a Xerox of an old *Tampa Tribune* newspaper article she had found at the Miami Public Library that afternoon. "Was this her?" she asked and held up the picture.

Malavida was looking at a shot of the same woman he'd seen on the wall of the barge. "It's her. . . . Who is she?" Malavida finally said.

"Meet Shirley Land, Leonard's foster mother. That's the obit photo. She died in a fire twelve years ago. Shirley had quite a history. She was a seventies hippie who turned away from sex and drugs, and found religion. According to this, she was a Seventh Day Adventist, but the church in Water Valley, Mississippi, where she lived, threw her out for bizarre behavior. Apparently she was religiously obsessed. She had a foster child in 1980 named Robbie Land. I checked with Social Services in Water Valley, and their records said they'd been out there a bunch of times 'cause Robbie's grade-school teachers said he looked beaten up. One time, when he was twelve, his hair got set on fire. Shirley said he'd done it himself, playing with matches. Social Services was getting set to take him back when Robbie ran away, never to be seen again. Shirley took off and left the state. My guess is Robbie is dead, buried in a shallow grave somewhere. Shirley moved to Florida and applied for and got another foster child. That was Leonard Land. Nobody checked with Mississippi, 'cause she never told 'em she was from there. She bought a house out in the boonies not too far from the Everglades. There were no Social Services complaints on Leonard's condition. Then, twelve years ago, her house caught fire and she died. Leonard disappeared, end of report," she said. "Not too hard to read between the lines, is it?"

"That's pretty good." He smiled weakly.

"It all fits the profile of a killer dominated by a violent female adult. The blitz attacks are because he's afraid of women, he needs to kill them before they have a chance to dominate him. His 'relationships' are all post-mortem.

He probably feels he can only interact with women once they're dead.''

"Did you call Lockwood with this?"

"I'm gonna get in touch after his hearing tomorrow," she told him.

"You didn't call him because he'll put the kibosh on this nutty idea of breaking me out of here, right?"

She started to smile and he smiled back.

"How you gonna do it?"

She sat next to his bed and filled him in.

At 8:30 that night, Karen pulled off her first computer crime. She was sitting on the bed at the Ramada Inn, talking with Malavida in the hospital on her cellphone. With the hard line from the Ramada phone, she had hooked up Malavida's computer and modem. Malavida talked her through a computer crack into Jackson Memorial Hospital. It was harder than they had anticipated because the hospital administrator had already started to upgrade his security. Malavida finally found a hole in the system, going in through the Payless drugstore in the hospital lobby. The drugstore had a link that interfaced with the hospital billing records. He used that to move into the Jackson Memorial computer network and, before long, he talked Karen right into the Patient Records Log. She found Ray Gonzales's ID number and deleted it, then put Malavida's ID number in its place. She found Malavida's account, deleted his number, and supplanted it with Ray's, completing the switch. She then found Ray Gonzales's medical record. . . . It was extensive. She scanned it, feeling guilty as she snooped. Ray's prognosis wasn't good. He was going to need a kidney transplant soon. Then she skipped to the bottom of Ray's records and started typing. She scheduled him for an X-ray at ten the next morning.

Karen was dressed and checked out of the Ramada Inn by 6:30 A.M. She had rented a Ryder van and was now driving around looking for a motel room that would work. The early morning traffic was surprisingly light. Beautiful white clouds drifted like whipped cream across the blue Miami sky.

She finally found a place that looked good. It was called The Swallow Inn and was on the Miami River, off Fourth Street, two blocks from Highway 9. She drove around it once, looking it over. It was an old wood-frame bungalow-style motel. The bungalows were private, set away from one another. She needed privacy. She decided the best unit for her needs was Bungalow 7. It was well away from the others and close to the service road, which would give her a back way in and out. She parked the step van on the shell drive and walked across the crunchy surface to the office.

A room cost nineteen dollars a day. She asked for Number 7 and got it. She registered under an assumed name, Karen Styles, and paid cash. She took her key, stepped back outside, and looked around.

She knew from the map that the Miami River went inland for about three miles, then became so narrow and marshy it was more of a swamp than a river. The wide mouth of the river was in Biscayne Bay. The river was like no place else in Miami. It could have been in a third-world country. She glanced at two Haitian freighters that were tied to wharves across the river. They were big, ugly, rusting hulks piled high with junk that would eventually be bound for Haiti. A favorite item seemed to be plastic Clorox bottles. They were strung by the hundreds on ropes and draped along every convenient rail. She couldn't imagine what they would be used for. To carry water maybe? The freighters were also stacked high with old mattresses, broken furniture, and stolen bicycles.

She could smell the thick, pungent odor of moss and drying seaweed. Still, this was not a place where neighbors talked to the cops, or where she thought anybody was going to look for Malavida.

She went to Bungalow 7. It had once been bright blue, but now the paint was faded and eaten by the sun. She opened the door and went inside. The two small rooms were clean but musty. She opened a window to air it out, then checked the TV to make sure it worked. She picked up the telephone and found that it was a direct line out. Then she locked up and left. She had one more stop to make at the hospital. She had volunteered to be a candy-striper and needed to pick up her uniform.

Malavida was transferred to a gurney and rolled down to X-ray at quarter to ten. Ray Gonzales was lifted onto a gurney for the same destination at about the same time. They were both wheeled down to the X-ray room and arrived five minutes apart. Both were parked in the anteroom adjoining the X-ray machine. Ray had been thoroughly briefed by Karen and was conscious, but pretended to be asleep. Malavida was sleeping off and on, due to the heavy medication he'd been given. The agent assigned to accompany Malavida was different from the night before, and sat on a chair out in the hall as Malavida was wheeled into the X-ray room. At quarter past ten, a technician put the lead vest over his chest to protect his heart and lungs, then moved the nozzle of the X-ray machine down and began taking pictures of Malavida's abdomen.

After the X-rays, the technician parked both beds in the anteroom. As both patients appeared to sleep, he read their wristbands, then checked the computer for their IDs and destinations. The computer identified Malavida as Ray Gonzales. So the technician pushed Malavida's gurney out the east door, into the main lobby. He told the waiting attendant to take the patient back up to the Renal Care ward. The Federal agent who was supposed to guard Malavida was still sitting in the main corridor outside the X-ray department, reading the sports page. Five minutes later, they sent Ray Gonzales out to him.

"Here's your boy," the X-ray technician said. The agent slowly got to his feet. He walked around to confirm that the man on the bed was Malavida. It was only then that he realized they had returned the wrong man to him.

Karen Dawson, in her fresh, new candy-striper's uniform, took Malavida's gurney from the attendant as he wheeled it off the elevator on the third floor, near the Renal Care ward.

"Got it. Thanks," she said as she pulled it out of the elevator. After the attendant left, she pushed the elevator button and got the next car down.

Once downstairs, she pushed the gurney right out the front of the hospital. To her surprise, nobody said a word. She wheeled Malavida around the side of the hospital and finally arrived at the rented van. She opened the back doors, then pushed the gurney up hard against the back bumper. The gurney bed overhung the legs by almost three feet and extended into the vehicle. She then collapsed the front legs so that the gurney's skids were resting on the bed of the van. This accomplished, she jumped in and pulled with all her strength. . . . The gurney slid into the van on the metal rails under it. She looked around to see if anybody had witnessed the operation.

Her heart was pounding. She was having a ball. She knelt down and put her hand on Malavida's forehead.

"I'm awake," he grimaced. "That was the worst ride I ever took, even worse than the shore break at Huntington."

"Sorry." She smiled. "We're a little shorthanded this morning."

He looked up at her and saw her grinning. "What the hell's so funny, Karen?"

"Nothing. Sorry, I get off on strange stuff."

In twenty minutes, she had Malavida back at The Swallow Inn and propped up in bed. The room seemed suddenly small, as both of them communicated silently . . . each remembering another motel room where they had clung to each other in ecstasy and then awkwardness. Karen moved quickly across the room and turned on the TV. She finally found an all-news station. She set the volume and went back out to unload some hospital supplies she'd filched. Ten minutes later there was an update on a story in Washington, D.C. Neither of them was paying much attention until they heard Lockwood's name.

Karen quickly turned up the volume.

". . . at D.C. General Hospital. Agent Lockwood is in a coma," the gray-haired news anchor said.

"What . . . ?" Karen almost shouted at the screen.

"As we reported earlier, the Director of All Operations of U.S. Customs, Laurence Heath, died in the mishap when halon gas accidentally escaped in the locked file room in the basement of the Department of Justice. Heath was the second-highest-ranking officer in the service. Along with him, and also dead on arrival, were Agent Victor Kulack and two attorneys: Carter Van Lendt, with the Justice Department, and Alex Hixon, who was representing Agent Lockwood at his Internal Affairs hearing. Government engineers are still studying the mishap to determine why the elevators in the building locked and the halon system malfunctioned. That report is due shortly. In the meantime the lone survivor, Agent John Lockwood, barely hangs on to life at D.C. General."

They called the hospital, but there was a stop on Lockwood's phone; Karen's call was transferred to a man who sounded like a cop. She quickly realized that he was not going to give out any additional information. She hung up and cursed under her breath. Karen looked at Malavida, who was now propped up in the bed.

"Did that news guy say 'mishap'?" Malavida finally asked, his voice still whispery.

"That's what he said." She was consumed with fear for Lockwood.

"Bullshit. The Rat set that system off," he said.

Karen's emotions were rolling. She had come to rely on John Lockwood. He had been their leader. She was devastated by the news. She could not believe the depth of her feelings. She had always seen herself as a rational and deductive person, despite her love of death-defying risks. Yet here she was, between two men, both of whom she had strong feelings for. Was it just another game of chicken? Had she fallen into bed with Malavida to preclude a relationship with Lockwood, because she wasn't able to commit to anybody fully? As these thoughts tumbled in her mind, she looked at Malavida. They held each other's gaze. They both knew they were thinking the same thing. . . .

The Rat had cut them down, one at a time. Only Karen remained standing.

''I'm going to get this motherfucker,'' she finally said.

Malavida had never heard a woman sound so dangerous.

# 32

## SAND

In the dream, he was at the bottom of a sand dune, struggling to climb to the top ... but the harder he tried, the more sand came down on him. It carried him back to the bottom of the pit, where again he would claw his way up toward the top ... only to have it happen again. It was a struggle he knew he must win. If he could climb to the top, he would wake; if not, he would be doomed. Over and over he would almost get to the lip of the sand dune ... barely seeing the light before slipping back down again.

Finally, at about nine on Saturday night, he made it. Victorious, he opened his eyes and looked at the white acoustic tiles of the hospital ceiling. He had been unconscious for thirty-five hours. A nurse who had been taking his blood pressure ran to get a doctor. Lockwood tried to move. Something was wrong. His coordination was off. He couldn't control his muscles. Then a doctor came into his line of sight.

"Welcome back," he said.

Lockwood tried to nod. He didn't think he could speak. He tried to clear his throat.

"You've had a severe loss of oxygen and you were unconscious for about a day and a half," the doctor said, "and that is going to affect you for a while. Do you remember your name?"

Lockwood lay in the bed. His name . . . his name . . . He knew his name. He struggled for it. It was there, just out of reach, just on the edge of his memory. His name was . . . it was . . . ?

"It's okay. It's gonna come," the doctor said. "Time for a Paul Revere. Hold tight, I'm gonna run tell a few people you're back."

Lockwood watched as the doctor moved out of his sight.

"Paul Revere," he said softly. His voice was strange in his ears. The name was familiar but he didn't think he was Paul Revere.

As time passed, things came further back into focus. He was still unable to move freely. His arms and legs didn't seem to obey his mental commands. His thoughts were jumbled and confused. When he finally came up with his name, he told a nurse that he was Lockwood, John W., Sergeant, 3769007656—his name, Marine rank, and serial number. They took him carefully from the bed and gave him an MRI scan. They explained to him what had happened in the Justice Department file room, but he had trouble remembering any of it. His short-term memory was a mess. He remembered parts of what had happened in Florida. He remembered chasing a huge, bald man and firing two shots from an old .45 at a fleeing airboat. It was like a five-second movie loop in his head. He could replay it but not see around either side of it.

"In a while we're going to take you down for some physical therapy," the doctor said. "What has happened is that when you were unconscious, your brain was deprived of oxygen and parts of it died. Unfortunately, brain matter doesn't regenerate. Your vital signs are fine but you're going to have trouble with some things for a while, until other parts of your brain can take over those functions. We might as well get started and find out how much stuff got shorted out. You get what I'm telling you?"

"Yes. Do I sure," he said, realizing that it didn't sound quite right. "Sure do I," he corrected himself. Still wrong. *Fuck it*, he thought.

"Trust us, John, we'll get your engine up and running again."

They helped him out of bed. He had almost no control of his body. He wobbled horribly the first time he tried to walk. He fell after one step. They were there to catch him before he hit the ground.

"Bitch of a . . ." he said angrily as they helped him back up.

He looked at the door, which seemed to be miles away. There was something wrong with his depth perception. It was as if he were looking down the wrong end of a pair of binoculars. Everything seemed remote, as if he were watching it through a strange lens and was not a part of it. "Can't see right," he said, rubbing his eyes.

"The part of your brain that controls your sight and speech was affected. Another few minutes and you'd have been a vegetable. Fortunately, John, this is a partial paralysis. It should all come back, but you've gotta keep working. I won't BS you, it could take months, even years."

They helped him walk down the corridor of the hospital, one attendant holding each arm. He could see where he wanted to go, even though his depth perception was altered, but as he tried to get there he would veer and stumble. Often his legs buckled under him without warning.

They got him down to therapy in a wheelchair. A very strong, thirty-five-year-old, muscular blond woman, with a friendly smile and a face like a torn softball, helped him up out of the wheelchair. She almost lifted his 190-pound frame singlehandedly. She joked with him as she pushed and punished him for an hour without much result.

He was back in bed when Bob Tilly from Laurence Heath's office came in to see him. "You don't have to talk, John," he said.

"S'okay," he slurred. "Heath, sorry Larry." He paused. "Larry Heath I'm sorry about," he said, getting closer.

"Not your fault."

Lockwood was struggling to recover something. It had to do with the large bald man in the air-boat. "Leonard Land," he finally said. "Leonard Land did something," Lockwood said. "This did he with . . ." His mind reeled, looking for the answer.

Tilly couldn't make out what Lockwood was saying, so he went on. "It was some kind of computer fuck-up, John. The whole building went goofy. The system that runs things just went psycho . . . sent an earthquake message to the elevators, which locked them and set off the halon extinguishers."

Lockwood was struggling with it. He was very, very close. He had to tell them something . . . warn them. "I know it what is. I happening is . . ." He stopped. "Fuck!" he shouted in a burst of anger. "I know what happened," he finally said. "Reprogrammed computer . . . from Florida."

"Who?"

"Land Leonard."

Bob Tilly looked at him for a long beat. "The serial killer you were working on in Miami reprogrammed the computer? Made all this shit happen?" he said.

"Yes. Leonard Heath killed Larry Land," he said, and then he lay back, exhausted. "Fuck . . . You know what I mean, Bob."

Bob Tilly looked down at Lockwood. He was sure that his old friend was still delirious. How on earth could some guy in Tampa, Florida, lock the elevators in a Washington building, close down the ventilation, then set off the halon fire extinguishers? It had to be a computer malfunction. Lockwood just wasn't making any sense at all.

# 33

## THE KILL ZONE

At five P.M. on Saturday, Karen went to the store to get food and medical supplies for Malavida. After she loaded her purchases into the van, she stood outside the run-down, graffiti-damaged market in a litter-strewn parking lot and made a second call to Trisha Rains on her cellphone. She had been told when she called earlier that the TV reporter was in the field doing a remote and wouldn't be back till five. Karen had timed her trip to the market to coincide with Trisha's planned return to the news room.

"Trisha Rains," the TV reporter said as she finally came on the line.

"This is Karen Dawson. I saw you out at Leonard Land's house."

"The mystery woman the cops wouldn't let me talk to. Nice to finally hear from you." Her voice was aggressively friendly and Karen winced slightly. "Do you have any idea where Carlos Chacone is hiding?" Trisha asked without any warm-up or chitchat.

"Before we get into that, I need to know a few things. I'm taking a lotta chances right now. I'm legally and physically at risk. I need to know if you and I can have the right kind of relationship."

"I'm not going to commit a crime to do my job, Doctor."

"You know I'm a doctor?"

"I have your whole résumé right here. 'Awesome Dawson,' the 'Michigan Miracle.' Since the cops wouldn't let me interview you, I ran a background check. A Ph.D. in psychology before you were twenty. I'm glad you weren't busting the curve in any of my college courses."

Karen let that one go and pushed on. "I don't want you to break any laws, Trisha, but I need to know that you and I are going to have a First Amendment relationship . . . that you're going to protect me as a confidential source and not divulge anything until I give you permission."

"That goes without saying."

"Yeah, but let's hear you say it anyway."

"As long as you don't bullshit me, girlfriend, I'll protect you as a source."

"I think I might know how to lure Leonard Land out into the open, but I need your help."

Trisha Rains was skeptical at first, but when she heard Karen's plan, she warmed up.

They agreed that they would talk again before six that evening.

After she hung up, Karen returned to The Swallow Inn with food, soft drinks, fresh bandages, and a thermometer. Fifteen minutes later, she had Shirley Land's newspaper picture in her purse and her car keys in her hand and was ready to leave.

Malavida had given up trying to argue with her. She refused to listen to his logic. She brought some Gerber baby food and bottled water to the bed, where he was glaring at her, and put them on the bedside table.

"Till your intestines heal, this is what the nurse told me you were gonna get in the hospital. I hope you like creamed corn."

"I hate creamed corn and I want you to slow down and listen to me."

"I should be back by midnight. If not, I'll call and check in with you," she said. Then she picked up the thermometer, shook it down, and paused, waiting for him to open his mouth.

"Karen, you can't mind-fuck this guy. You heard Lockwood, there's a big difference between doing a paper profile and a field encounter, or whatever he called it."

"Who says I'm mind-fucking him?"

"I sorta got the hang of how you think. You're about six-tenths kamikaze."

"Look, Mal, I'm not going to do anything stupid or dangerous. I know how twisted Leonard Land is. Give me some credit, I'm smart enough not to wave a red cape at a psychopath,."

They locked gazes. She was still holding the thermometer. "Open, please. I have to find out if you have a fever before I leave."

"What if I don't cooperate?" he said.

"There's more than one place I can stick this, buddy," she said, waving it ominously, a smile on her lips, and he finally opened his mouth. His temperature was normal.

Her mind kept turning back to John Lockwood. Uneasiness about his condition hung in her thoughts like a dark mist. At least she knew he was alive. That gave reason to hope, but she had to keep moving. She was the last knight on the battlefield, the only person left who had a clear picture of what they were facing.

Ever since she had been a child, Karen Dawson would risk everything to win. Her playmates and siblings had learned early not to challenge her unless they were willing to deal with the consequences. She was now working all alone, and she had accepted that. She also knew that to make her plan work, she would need the cooperation of the police. She figured that by now, they probably suspected she was an accomplice in Malavida's disappearance. She had to find a way to overcome that.

Her plan hinged on her now-extensive criminal profile of Leonard Land, as well as her research into his mother's past. She thought she knew enough about his bizarre upbringing to manipulate him. The biggest influence in Leonard's life was Shirley Land. Shirley was responsible for what he had become. Karen had looked long and hard at the woman's picture in the old newspaper obit. Shirley was unremarkable, with a short, uncomplicated hairstyle and a narrow face. It was hard to think that this woman, long dead, was a torturer who had killed one foster son and turned the other into a monster. Karen studied Shirley's plain face. . . . The picture was black and white, but from the photo, she looked strawberry-blond. Karen thought she could pull off the physical part, but she knew the important thing would be what she said.

"Be good," she said to Mal, who glared at her from his bed as she set down the thermometer.

"Karen . . ."

"Yeah?"

"When I first laid eyes on you in the attorneys' room at Lompoc, I had you down as bait. I thought you were a patsy I could play for a sucker. I didn't care what happened to you or Lockwood. As a matter of fact, I was out to wreck Lockwood."

She was listening. Her remarkable brown eyes showed her brilliance.

"But that's changed," he went on. "I don't know how it happened so fast. Maybe it's like a wartime romance. . . . I don't know, but I've become attached to you. I don't want to see you get hurt."

She looked down at him and said nothing.

"It's Lockwood, isn't it?" Malavida said, hurt flooding his eyes.

"Lockwood doesn't know I'm alive, he's so tortured by Claire's death. That's all he's dealing with," she said, and reached down to take his hand. "Let's put all this behind us, then see what happens."

"You can't go after The Rat. He'll kill you. In a week, I'll be up. . . . I know it. We can keep going then. You need somebody watchin' your back."

"It's Saturday, Mal. We're in his killing zone. We wait a week, somebody else is going to get hacked up. We have to keep the pressure on. If I'm not back, or don't call by midnight, you're on your own," she said and kissed him lightly on the lips, then left the room.

Malavida could hear the van starting; he listened as it pulled away, the tires crunching on the shell drive outside. Then he leaned over and got the phone. His computer was still on the coffee table and his external 14.4 modem was on the dresser. He knew he was going to have to find a way to get his jukebox hooked back together. He was like The Rat: His best weapon was his computer. He struggled in pain to move his broken body to the edge of the bed. He tried to sit. His stomach muscles had been cut and resewn during the surgery, so he had to use his arms to get upright. He reached for the headboard and pulled himself to a sitting position. A searing bolt of pain shot through his intestines. "Shit," he groaned, hoping he hadn't ripped the whole stitched-up mess loose. Then he struggled to his feet.

"I wanna know where the hell Carlos Chacone is!" Fred T. Fred growled, the minute he heard her voice on the line.

"How would I know?" Karen lied. She was in a phone booth that faced a Cuban market. Heat lightning flashed on the horizon.

"Hey, listen, lady, that Mexican had more plumbing hangin' off him than I got in my entire bathroom. He didn't get up outta bed and walk away, draggin' all them tubes and plasma bottles. You helped him."

"I sure hope you can prove that, Captain," she said. There was a long, ugly silence on the line, as the rumbling sound of thunder finally reached her.

"I don't need to prove it to arrest you. And if I arrest you, I can also hold you for forty-eight hours, just to be pissy."

"I'm more worried about where Leonard Land is, which is one hell of a lot bigger problem. We know he's a weekend killer; it's Saturday, and unless we divert him, I think there's a good chance a woman could die tonight.''

''You don't know that for a fact.''

''All the profile points indicate it. We can argue about bullshit or we can get in business with each other,'' she said hotly. ''I'm coming to you for help. Chacone is pretty small stuff compared to this serial killer. Whatta ya say we try for big game? . . . The old eight-point hat rack.''

''You're pretty sure of yourself, aren't you?'' he growled. ''I've only been in law enforcement for forty years, so I don't need a lecture on criminal priorities from some Princeton Ph.D.''

''Then why are you talking to me about Chacone? You know I'm right. . . . I need help, so *help* me. I have a way to get this guy out in the open, but you gotta pitch in.''

''Let's hear it,'' he finally said, feeling sure he would come to regret it.

After he heard her plan, Captain Fredrickson's voice was full of amazement. ''Of course you're kidding,'' he said.

''I've done a very specific background check on Leonard Land. This started with his mother and her religious fanaticism. She passed her sickness on to Leonard. I think she killed her first foster son in Mississippi, in the early eighties. His name was Robbie Land, and he's never been seen again.''

''That case is twelve or fifteen years old. What you're talkin' about now is much different.''

''Everything is tied together. . . . You can't look at one piece without looking at them all. Captain, I want you to agree to meet with me. Hear me out. I think, once you see my whole profile, you'll agree that it's the only string we have. But if I'm right and we pull this off, he's going to react. I'm doing this with or without you. I just figured that you'd want to be in on it.''

\*    \*    \*

The Wind Minstrel sat in his underwear and stared at the walls of the barge in a rage. The Rat had betrayed him.

"The god of fuck and mutilation must be appeased," he screamed at the rusting walls. The Wind Minstrel's skin was on fire; the rash was all across his chest and under his arms. He shrieked with pain in The Rat's rusting, stinking garbage barge. He looked up at the picture of Shirley Land on the wall. He glowered at The Rat's neat lines across the picture, at his scribbled dates. "You have desecrated the timetable, you have shit on the resurrection of the Beast." His voice ricocheted in the cavernous metal room. "I am here but you give me nothing to possess," he screamed at The Rat's memory. He moved, in pain, to the large blowup picture of Shirley. He hated the bitch more than he hated his own existence. Her religious rantings were worthless hypocrisies—blatant, primal non sequiturs. He stood before the picture of his foster mother holding the cat he had strangled long ago. The cat was the first living thing he had destroyed, choking it till its tongue curled. His fire-ravaged skin glowed and looked almost purple from the low light thrown from the portable TV that flickered in the far corner of the barge. He slammed his head savagely into the crotch of the picture, which was taped to the metal bulkhead.

"Rat, you have betrayed me. We will be annihilated in the fire that follows my Second Coming."

Then he looked up at the picture. He saw a smear of his red blood on Shirley's crotch. "The bitch bleeds!" he screamed, as his own blood now dripped down his face and splashed between his toes.

Then he turned and saw something that shot a chill across his burning, ravaged skin. There, on the TV, was his long-dead mother. She was talking to some nigger bitch. He was staggered by the vision. He moved on quivering legs and knelt, as if in prayer, before the television set.

# 34

## LIVE REMOTE

Earlier, Captain Fred T. Fredrickson had pulled in four off-duty police officers to work the detail. They had been cooling their heels at the Ramada Inn parking lot, in two surveillance vans. All four of them were in black flak-vests, holding Ithaca shotguns, and watching Karen's room through their smoked-glass windshields.

Inside her motel room, Karen was in the bathroom with Trisha Rains and a redheaded make-up girl from WTAM-TV named Marlene. Marlene was looking at the picture of Shirley Land, which was taped to the mirror. They had already cut Karen's hair and dyed it with Lady Clairol's sunset blond. It had ended up coming out a mousey dishwater color that Karen hated.

"I don't know," Marlene said, looking at the picture. "It could be strawberry-blond, it could be mid-brown. Hard to tell from this black-and-white picture." She continued to work behind Karen with a hair dryer.

"It's okay. We'll just do the best we can," Karen said. "I couldn't find a color shot of her, so we've gotta guess."

Marlene began to re-style Karen's hair, looking at the picture. She turned it under as she blow-dried it, shaping it closer to her head. "Pretty frumpy do," she said off-handedly.

Marlene finished and Karen stood in front of the mirror in her slip, looking at her new short, light-brown hair. "I've gotta use makeup to do the rest," Marlene said. "I can add a little mole like she has on her cheek easy enough . . . and maybe, with shading, I can narrow your face slightly . . . arch the eyebrows."

They worked on her makeup, until they got it as close as time would allow. Then Karen put on a print dress with long sleeves and a lace collar that resembled the one in the obit photo. She had bought it that afternoon at a second-hand store. She finally walked out of the bedroom, where Captain Fred T. Fred was waiting. He got up as she entered and looked at her carefully.

"What a transformation. You look . . ." He stopped.

"Like the Church Lady?" She smiled. Then she sat with Trisha on the stained green sofa.

"I think this whole thing hinges on Revelation 13:13 to 15. If I'm wrong, I've screwed up a great haircut for nothing."

"Revelation 13:13 to 15? How do you know?"

"Under the brand on the dead women, it says, 'R. 13-15.' At first I thought it was some computer designation, or maybe it stood for 'revised' or Rat or something, but then on a hunch I looked up Revelation in the Gideon. Those sections are about building a beast."

"You think he's building a beast?" Trisha asked.

"It's probably more of a religious incarnation. I'm banking that he hasn't finished it yet."

Twenty minutes later they moved down into the parking lot and set up so that the TV camera could photograph the Ramada Inn sign and the building behind them. She was sure The Rat had been there before and would recognize the setting. He had to have followed Lockwood there, to phone in the anonymous tip that almost got them killed.

They stood in the parking lot in the warm Miami night, while the cameramen adjusted the lights and cleaned up the signal on the remote feed with the news director in Tampa.

At ten minutes past ten, the anchor, Hal Savage, threw the newscast to Miami. "Trisha Rains is standing by in Miami with an interesting update on 'The Rat,' South Florida's mutilation murderer."

"Thanks, Hal," Trisha said, looking into the camera. "We're here in the parking lot of the Ramada Inn in Miami, with noted criminal psychologist Dr. Karen Dawson. She's here to discuss a psychological criminal profile she's written on Leonard Land, the fugitive serial killer also known as 'The Rat.'" Trisha turned, and the shot widened to include Karen, who was sitting on a director's chair next to Trisha. "So, tell us about this guy. Why is he doing this? What makes somebody go out and repeatedly kill and mutilate?"

The shot was framed so that the lighted Ramada Inn sign was just over Karen's shoulder.

The Wind Minstrel was inches from the TV screen. He could tell, now that he was closer, that this was not Shirley. His heart rate slowed. For a moment, when he first saw her, he had panicked. If Shirley had been resurrected, then that would mean she had been chosen by God to come back and torture him. It would mean she had been given the power of the angels.

Then the woman spoke: "Leonard Land is a seven-foot-tall, twenty-seven-year-old, fat, bald man who is pitiful and cowardly," she began.

The words devastated him. Shirley had always screamed words like that at him.

"I will not be pitied," he screamed back at the bitch on TV.

"My profile shows him to be sexually inadequate. He believes he is the Anti-Christ or something approaching it . . . maybe even a disciple of the Devil."

As she spoke, The Wind Minstrel fought to hold down a rising tide of emotions.

"So, Dr. Dawson, you say he's fixated on his mother, who tortured him. What would she have done or said to him to produce this kind of horrible psychosis all these years later?'' Trisha asked, providing Karen with her transition.

''I can only approximate these thoughts, but she might have said . . .'' Karen turned to the camera and looked directly into the lens. She switched to the first person, using all she had learned about Leonard and his foster mother. She talked to him directly, as she hoped Shirley might have: ''Leonard, you are ugly! Pitiful, filthy, foul! You are the Anti-Christ! Fire is all that will cleanse you. You will burn in agony in God's Apocalypse.''

In the barge, the words hit The Wind Minstrel like a fist. He screamed in anguish, ''Bitch! You've come back!'' The Wind Minstrel was standing now. His long, fat legs rubbed together at the thighs as he began pacing. He no longer felt the pain on his nipples and skin. His mind was consumed with anger and distress. If this wasn't Shirley, then it was Shirley's ghost, or it was Shirley in the body of a whore cunt who looked and sounded just like her.

''God will strike you down!'' Karen continued angrily.

The Wind Minstrel shrieked again in anger as he threw himself into the rusting walls, slamming his head against the steel bulkhead to get the painful sound of her voice out of his ears.

''I am the god of fuck and mutilation. You cannot punish me. You cannot burn me with Trinity candles. You are *my* victim!'' he yelled. And then he paced in the small room, trying not to look at the Shirley person on the TV. He paced in a frenzy, trying to get his mind to focus on his plight.

''God rules the sunshine. But The Wind Minstrel rules the night,'' he whispered.

When the newscast was complete, Trisha packed up her equipment. They stood in the parking lot for a long moment.

''Thanks,'' Karen finally said.

''You're baiting this sicko. I wouldn't be you for nothing.''

Then, after Trisha got into her car and followed the remote truck out of the lot, Karen went up to the Ramada Inn. Two of the off-duty police were now positioned in adjoining rooms. The connecting doors to her room were unlocked, so they could get in fast. The other two policemen were outside in the stairwell. She turned out the light and, still dressed, stretched out on her bed and waited. At midnight, she called Malavida. He had seen the TV newscast.

"I thought you said you weren't going to do anything stupid," he said.

"Look, Mal, I'm covered. I have cops all around."

"This guy isn't going to hit you where you think, Karen."

"You're wrong. He's gonna come at me like he came at Claire . . . sloppy, no planning, no organization."

"You think that your profile lets you get inside his head. That's ego, Karen; ego can get you killed. You can't predict him."

"Did you take your temperature?"

"Don't change the subject," Mal answered.

By 4:30 in the morning, she had begun to lose some hope. It was now Sunday. She wondered what Sunday meant to The Rat. According to followers of the New Testament, Sunday was the day of rest. Seventh Day Adventists observed the Sabbath on Saturday . . . but Leslie Bowers had been killed on a Saturday . . . Sunday was the day The Rat talked to his friend in Oslo. What did that mean? Although Leonard Land killed Claire on a Sunday, Karen wondered if the "personality" that had dismembered Candice Wilcox would also kill on a Sunday. She was positive The Rat was nocturnal. Once the sun was up, he would be dormant. She wondered if she had misjudged him.

And then the phone rang.

# 35

## TASHAY

"**I**s this Ms. Dawson?" Her voice was tinny, she was whispering. In the background, Karen could hear her Death Metal music screaming.

"Yes," she answered. "Who's this?"

"It's Tashay . . . Roberts. You met me with Bob Shiff, only he don't like me to call him Bob anymore."

"Hi," Karen said. "How are you doing?"

"That Lockwood guy, he really got fucked up big in Washington. They say on the news he ain't never comin' back from the bird farm."

"But we can hope."

"First I was expecting him to call. I handed him a note that night with my number, but then I heard on the TV that he was in Washington and that he got . . . Wait a minute," and her hand was cupped over the receiver. Karen could hear a muffled man's voice and then Tashay was back on the phone. "Sorry, that fuckin' guy won't leave me alone. I'm backstage, we just finished a concert. Satan roared tonight. Cold-blooded shit . . . really out there."

"That's nice," Karen said, sitting up. "You had something you wanted to tell me . . . ?"

"I seen this guy you're lookin' for. He was here, backstage, tonight. He's been to see Baby Killer a buncha times. A big son of a bitch . . . no hair, really looks broke to the curb. Ugly fucker.''

"Is he there now?''

"He left. See, thing is, if I'm gonna help you, Satan's gonna be maximum pissed. He don't like cops. He told me not to call. . . . If I roll on him, it's like a major L-12.''

"L-12?'' Karen asked. Tashay sounded ripped.

"It's like loco times twelve.''

"What do you want?'' Karen asked.

"Two things. First, it's just gotta be you and me. We gotta meet someplace where the T. Bone won't see us. And you gotta bring a thousand dollars.''

"And what does that buy me?''

"It buys you this big, ugly prick's address. He gave Satan his address 'cause he wanted an autographed picture. Can you believe it? An autographed picture. We don't have band shots, but Satan took his address anyway . . . and I copied it down.''

"Where do you want to meet?''

"I don't care. I just don't want nobody to see us. And if there's any cops around, you can twist a braid, sugar, 'cause I ain't gonna say shit to the cops. . . . If Satan finds out I done that, my thing with him goes orbital.''

"How about we meet here, at the Ramada Inn?''

"You kiddin' . . . where you did the TV thing? Check that. How 'bout Satan's house tomorrow morning. He ain't gonna be awake. He sleeps till almost four in the afternoon.''

"Now *you're* kidding,'' Karen said. She searched her memory for a good place, some place public but where people wouldn't pay much attention. Then she remembered the park where they'd all gone after the Loomis Theater. "How about that park on Biscayne Bay,'' she said, "the one we went to.''

"Bayfront Park . . . okay. What time?''

"Nine A.M.,'' Karen said.

"Shit, honey, I don't get up till two. I'm in the music biz."

"Now you're in the information biz. I'll have cash. Be there at nine, if you want it."

Tashay sighed loudly; then she was talking to somebody else. ". . . the fuck you lookin' at, Martin?" Her hand went back over the receiver and Karen heard a loud muffled conversation. Then Tashay was back on the phone. "That asshole's been suckin' my flava all week."

"Nine A.M.," Karen said firmly.

"Okay, nine. But bring the grand in cash." And she hung up.

Karen decided not to tell Fred T. Fred yet. She had two reasons: First, she didn't think she could control Fred. He'd want to play it his way, and that might spook Tashay into clamming up. Second, Tashay wasn't very smart, but she was shrewd. She probably would be very careful before she gave up The Rat's new address. Karen was sure she could handle it.

She lay back on the bed and waited for the jolt of excitement to hit. It had always been risk that her life craved. But now, as she lay there, she felt nothing . . . no fire, no adrenaline, only a vague sense of distress and foreboding. She tried to pump up her engine. She told herself she would do it the way she always did: alone, with tools of her own invention.

Malavida had received the call from Karen at twelve midnight. After she hung up, he continued cracking into the computer at D.C. General Hospital in Washington. He finally managed to break through at about three A.M. In ten more minutes, he had John Lockwood's medical records up on the screen. He determined several things as he read them, including the fact that Lockwood was far from being comatose, as the TV had reported. He had come out of it and taken physical therapy. Malavida scrolled the doctor's notes:

JOHN LOCKWOOD'S CURRENT PROGNOSIS IS MIXED. HE HAS SUFFERED DAMAGE TO ALL FOUR REGIONS OF THE BRAIN DUE TO LOSS OF OXYGEN FOR A SUSTAINED PERIOD OF TIME (ESTIMATED FIVE MINUTES). THIS HAS RESULTED IN THE LOSS OF BRAIN CELLS AND HAS LEFT HIM WITH MULTI-DIMINISHED CAPACITY. THIS INCLUDES DIFFICULTIES IN MEMORY, SPEECH, AND COORDINATION, DUE TO BRAIN OXYGEN STARVATION IN THE ORBITAL GYRI OF BOTH FRONTAL LOBES, AS WELL AS THE CEREBRAL CHOROID PLEXUS. THE LACK OF OXYGEN CARRIED BY THE OCCIPITAL ARTERY, AS WELL AS THE PARIETAL BRANCH OF THE SUPERFICIAL TEMPORAL ARTERY AND THE DEEP TEMPORAL ARTERY, HAS CAUSED SOME DAMAGE IN THE INFRAORBITAL NERVE AFFECTING SPEECH, AS WELL AS THE SUPERORBITAL NERVE AND THE FACIAL NERVE. THE PATIENT'S PROGNOSIS OVER TIME IS GOOD; HOWEVER, HE WILL REQUIRE PHYSICAL AND MENTAL THERAPY TO REGAIN NORMAL FUNCTIONS.

It was signed Dr. Lawrence Sikes.

Malavida wanted to talk to Lockwood, but there was no phone in the Customs agent's room. It was then that Mal saw that his next scheduled therapy was at ten on Sunday morning. Malavida was determined to reach him.

The next morning, Fred T. Fred made things easier when he discontinued the surveillance of Karen, due to a light Sunday shift and a division commander who would not approve the overtime. The cops left after she promised not to move around and to call in periodically.

It was quarter to nine in the morning when Karen arrived at Bayfront Park. She was looking for the brown VW band bus that belonged to Baby Killer. She drove slowly past the park on Highway 41, scanning the area for any sight of it. From the highway, she could see Biscayne Bay. A brisk, gusting wind was pushing big sailboats across the angry water, driving their lee rails under, as they cut through the morning chop. As she drove on, she thought she saw the brown VW van parked next to one of the restrooms at the south end of the park. She pulled her rental van onto one of the access roads and drove toward it. As she got nearer, she could definitely tell that it was the same van that had been parked behind the Loomis. She drove toward it and stopped a few feet away.

The van appeared to be empty. She got out and looked inside. She could see nothing, so she knocked on the side door. "Tashay, it's Karen," she called out.

Nobody answered.

She looked at the restroom, which was a few feet to the right. After a moment's hesitation, she moved to the door, pushed it open, and called inside. "Tashay, it's Karen."

There was still no answer, so she carefully entered the ladies' room. Her heart was pounding in fear, not excitement, her own blood roaring in her ears.

The ladies' room stank. It was small and dirty. Wadded paper towels overflowed the metal basket like dead brown roses. There appeared to be nobody inside. "Tashay . . . ? It's Karen!" she called again.

And then she heard the faint sound of somebody moaning from inside one of the stalls. She moved to it and looked under the door. She could see a girl's bare feet.

"Tashay?" she called. She heard more soft, painful moaning. Then she reached out and touched the stall door. It was unlatched. She pushed the door open.

At first, she couldn't tell whom she was looking at. There was somebody in the stall . . . a woman. Her long hair was streaked with blood. Then the person looked up; her face was beaten and swollen. Several of her teeth were missing. It took Karen a moment to realize she was looking at Tashay Roberts. Karen's mind quickly started collecting facts: Tashay was seated on the closed toilet. Her arms were tied behind her back. She was barely conscious.

''Oh, my God,'' Karen said as the pitiful half-closed eyes of Tashay looked up at her.

Karen rushed into the stall to pull the girl off the toilet seat. Then she was staggered by a terrible blow from behind. It knocked her sideways. As she went down she saw a hideous man grinning. He had ugly black tattoos under his eyes and he was holding a baseball bat. He swung it again.

Just seconds before she lost consciousness, she realized that her assailant was Satan T. Bone.

# 36

## SHADOWLAND

Lockwood was struggling to stay on his feet. He had crossed half of the linoleum floor of the room on a walker. He was dizzy. His vision was so distorted that he had been fighting nausea for almost an hour. Ginger, his muscular PT nurse, kept shouting encouragement, but the words and the task reminded him more of the obstacle course in Marine boot camp than anything else.

The phone had been ringing for almost a minute before Ginger snatched it up. "PT, Ginger Cortland speaking."

"This is Dr. Chacone, I'm a cerebral control specialist," Malavida said with dignity. "The Lockwood case has been referred to me by Dr. Sikes. I understand the patient is with you. I'd like to speak with him, if he's available."

"Sure," she said and looked over at Lockwood. "If you can get your butt over to the phone, sweet cheeks, you can take this call and buy a rest."

Lockwood turned the walker around and put it out in front of him, shuffled forward, then repeated the motion. He could barely make his feet respond to mental commands. Once he was in the general vicinity of the phone, Ginger took pity and moved the rest of the way toward him, handing him the receiver.

"Yeah," he said weakly.

"This Lockwood?"

"Yep, Lockwood," he said, slurring his words and concentrating to keep them in the right order.

"How you doin', Zanzo?" Malavida said. "You sound limp as a plate of pasta."

"The fuck," Lockwood said, grinning.

"My thought exactly. You okay to talk?" Malavida asked. "You alone?"

"No. Ten feet standing Hitler me from is." He took a deep breath. "Fucked up my punch line," he said, depressed.

"Look, we gotta problem. It's Karen. Listen to me and tell me what you think—"

" 'Kay."

"She's down here taunting The Rat. She's been on TV, insulting him, trying to sound like his mother. I couldn't stop her."

"Got to stop her." He grimaced.

"I'm flat on my back, Zanzo. I can't go to the bathroom without calling in a committee. She snuck me out of the hospital, moved me to a motel on the Miami River called The Swallow Inn. Technically, I'm still a fugitive. I called the police department, pretending to be her brother. They told me they called off the stakeout this morning. She didn't come back here, so either this asshole got her or she's walking around without cover. Nobody knows where she is. She's way overdue."

"Shit," Lockwood said, the imminent danger helping to connect a few dots in his ravaged nervous system. He knew Karen was a daredevil. He prayed that she was safe.

"Look, Zanzo, I'm up for most anything, 'cept I can't get out of bed."

"Mal . . . I'm . . . my head works weird. I don't . . . can't remember stuff."

"Can you drive? Can you get on an airplane? I don't have anybody else. We call the cops, I'm back in Lompoc."

"I don't know. . . . I'm . . . I can't. Hold on." He put his hand over the mouthpiece and looked at Ginger.

"Could you water me?" He smiled, then looked embarrassed.

"Don't blush, I know what you mean, sugar." She pushed herself off the table and went to get him water. As soon as she was gone: "Mal . . . driver . . . need car . . ."

"I'll send you a limo. I've been stealing limo rides since I was sixteen."

"Fly . . . I can't get . . ."

"I know. I can handle that too. There's an Executive Terminal at National Airport. The limo will have your jet's tail number. John . . . can you focus on this? You know what I'm telling you?"

"Trying."

"Can you get to the main hospital entrance?"

"Think so."

"Be there at twelve noon today. I'll have a car waiting. I'll set the whole thing in motion and have you delivered to my room here, just like a basket of fruit . . . no disrespect intended."

For Lockwood, the hardest part of the trip was putting on his pants, then moving the twenty or so yards from his room to the main entrance of the hospital in Washington. He scraped the metal walker along the yellow linoleum floors and shuffled after it. He finally made the front door, where a black stretch limo was waiting. He was delivered to National Airport and a Malavida-supplied charter jet. Lockwood had to hand it to Malavida; the cracker was amazing.

At three o'clock Sunday afternoon, John Lockwood was delivered to The Swallow Inn on the Miami River. He struggled to get his walker out of the cab, unfolded it, and told the driver to go on. He made a slow, awkward trip to Bungalow 7, pushed the door open, and shuffled in. He found himself looking into the much thinner, but smiling face of Malavida Chacone.

"You look like the last reel of a Frankenstein movie," the Chicano said.

Lockwood shuffled across the room until he was looking down into Malavida's dark eyes. ''Least don't need a tube to piss,'' he replied.

Then, exhausted, Lockwood collapsed in a chair, and Malavida brought him the rest of the way up to date.

# 37

## TRIP

At first it sounded like something growling. It vibrated, shaking her whole body. She tried to ignore it, to push it down into her subconscious, but it would not go away. As her mind began to focus, she realized there was more. Drums and guitars, discordant and angry, and then something else . . . a low whimper that ended with a strangled high whine. She tried to move but couldn't. Her head throbbed horribly with the constant vibration and, as she came closer to the surface of consciousness, she began to realize she was badly hurt. Her jaw was in agony; her whole body ached. She didn't know where she was or what had happened. She had loose pebbles in her mouth. . . . She wondered why. Slowly she moved her tongue to touch them. In horror she realized they were pieces of her own broken teeth. She spit them out and slowly opened her eyes.

It took her a moment to focus. She was looking at something big and curved. She struggled to identify it. A tire well. She was on the floor in the back of a truck or van. She felt a change in direction and then the sudden vibration of wheels passing over lane dots. She knew then that the vehicle was in motion. She didn't know why she was there or why she hurt so badly. Her mind struggled to remember. She could see the back of a man's skinny right arm as he drove. She tried to ask him for help but she couldn't move her mouth. Where was she? What was that horrible music that was playing?

She fought to put more pieces in place and then she heard the moaning again. Her body wouldn't move; she tried to turn her head and finally managed. She was looking into a tangle of blood-soaked blond hair, not three feet from her. She tried to see through the mess but couldn't, and then the head moved and the hair fell away and she could see the face. It was bloodied and swollen. A girl, vaguely familiar. Karen thought she remembered her . . . and then a big piece fell back into place. The public toilet . . . the attack . . . the baseball bat swinging at her.

"Tashay," she finally whispered to the girl, "Tashay?" The girl opened her eyes and the two exchanged a long look. A silent message of desperation passed between them. Then Tashay Roberts closed her eyes without speaking, cutting off the unspoken communication. Karen tried to roll into a better position. She struggled to turn over. It was then that she discovered she had been lashed to speaker hooks that were screwed into the floor of the van.

The skinny driver heard her moving and turned to look at her. "Keep quiet. Make any noise, you're gonna be pissing backwards."

She could see him clearly now. He was milk-white, with long black hair. The intermittent sunlight through passing trees shot lines and shadows across his gruesome, skinny features. The ghoulish tattoos under his eyes gave his hollow face a skull-like intensity. Then Baby Killer started screaming a second verse through the speakers. Satan T. Bone's raspy voice filled the van:

> It ain't a nice place,
> So shit in her face.
> She's got no place to hide,
> So ya rip her inside.

Let the dogs eat her eyes. . . .
Yeah, dogs eat her eyes.

The horrible serenade continued. Tashay moaned.
Karen tried to gather her resources. She remembered
most of it now; the driver was Bob Shiff. He had hit her
with the bat. . . . She didn't know why. What she did
know was that she had somehow badly miscalculated,
and now was in a desperate fight for her life. She
could feel the van exit the highway and come to a halt. Then
they turned right and made a stop-and-go trip along a
street. She could see patterns of moving sunlight on the
walls and ceiling of the van. She could occasionally hear
cars pull up next to them. Finally they picked up speed
and Karen thought that they were on another highway of
some kind. A short time later they made a hard right then
pulled to a stop. She saw Shiff get out from behind the
driver's seat and heard him walk to the back. The rear
door opened and he leaned in. She could not turn her
head to see him, but she felt him above her.

"You two make trouble, and I be shootin' on yer ass."
He unhooked Tashay from the floor and dragged her out
of the van by her heels. She moaned. As he got her out
of the back, Karen heard her head hit the bumper. She
fell to the ground and let out a cry. "Shut the fuck up!"
he shouted at her.

Karen couldn't see where they were. Her head was
facing in the wrong direction and she couldn't lift it up
to turn around and look out the back of the van. She
could feel the hot morning air, and she filled her lungs,
trying to summon as much strength as she could. Somewhere far away she heard Sunday church bells ringing.
Moments later Shiff was back. He poked her.

"You awake?" he said.

She said nothing, tried not to move. He reached in and
over and untied her. She waited until he had unhooked
her hands and legs and had started to pull her out. Then
she focused all her energy, reared back, and kicked him
in the face as hard as she could. He fell backwards, yell-

ing in confusion and pain. She struggled to get to a sitting position, but she was dizzy and fell sideways. Shiff was immediately back on her, his skinny arms pushing her back into the van. Then he grabbed something. She didn't see what, but when he hit her, her head spun with the force of the blow. She felt no pain but saw a blinding light . . . and then nothing.

Malavida and Lockwood ordered a car from Hertz. They waited in Bungalow 7 of The Swallow Inn for the rental agent to deliver it. Lockwood had called the Miami police. He had tried to talk to Fred T. Fredrickson but couldn't get through. When he explained his concern about Karen's disappearance, he was transferred to Missing Persons. He was having trouble making himself understood, so he handed the phone to Malavida, who gave the information to a policewoman but refused to identify himself. Lockwood knew the case would be tossed on a pile with hundreds of runaways and would get little attention. After he hung up, Lockwood watched with distress while Malavida got out of bed and, using a chair for support, moved to the bathroom. Neither of them could get around at all. They moved like two old convalescents doing a Thorazine shuffle. Lockwood wasn't sure he could drive; he was still having trouble with depth perception. When Malavida returned, he sat on the edge of the bed. They surveyed each other optimistically. . . . Each thought the other looked like hell.

"How we gonna do this, Zanzo?" Malavida finally asked.

"Don't know," Lockwood replied. "Gotta find . . ."

"No shit."

Again they fell into silence. Then Malavida continued, "Before she went on TV yesterday, she showed me this picture of Shirley Land. It was an obit photo or something. She said she got it at the library along with some articles on how she died. I accessed the Miami library computer to see if I could pull anything up on Shirley, but this stuff must be too old. It's not in their information bank . . . probably on microfilm.''

"Microfilm," Lockwood repeated, as if he'd never heard the word before.

"Hey, get on board here, will ya? She could be in bad trouble. We probably don't have much time," Malavida said sharply.

"I'm, ah . . . not . . . I." Lockwood couldn't get his thought out. Periodically his vocabulary just seemed to disappear. He knew what he wanted to say but couldn't find the words. And then without warning, his grasp of language would come back. It was one of the most frustrating feelings he'd ever experienced.

Malavida watched him and knew it had been a time-wasting mistake to bring Lockwood down. He was worse than useless. "We're gonna get smoked," he said. "Neither of us can move and you need a brain transplant. The gimp squad to the rescue. All we need is Martin Short to drive the car."

Lockwood sat and looked at him, still waiting for the right words to form. "You shouldn'ta loved her," he said. "Wrong verb," he added.

"And you weren't trying?"

"Shouldn'ta done it. I told you. Said she was. She couldn't . . ." He stopped as the right words left him but his anger swelled. "Fuck!" he shouted.

"Hey, Lockwood, did it ever occur to you that I might be honest about my feelings toward her?"

"No."

They glowered at one another.

The rental agent showed up with the car ten minutes later. They had agreed to pay a fifty-dollar delivery charge, which, of course, would never get charged to them because Malavida had executed the whole thing by computer. All that needed to happen now was for Lockwood to take delivery of the car and sign the contract. Malavida was in a chair by the window when the agent knocked on the door. Lockwood used his hospital walker to get to the door. He folded it, placed it out of the way, opened the door, and stood teetering like the last drunk at a party. The agent took Lockwood's license and watched while he signed the contract. Before he left, the young man turned. "You guys okay?" he asked, concerned by their appearance.

"Sure are." Malavida smiled painfully.

"Upsy daisy," Lockwood chipped in, selecting the wrong cliché.

Malavida and Lockwood got into the rented gray Lincoln Town Car with some difficulty. They agreed that Malavida would drive because of Lockwood's impaired vision. Malavida got carefully behind the wheel and put his laptop on the seat. He watched the ex-Customs agent struggling to get into the passenger side.

"Get in there, cocksucker," Lockwood cursed at himself as he fumbled to get his legs into the car. Then he looked at Malavida for instructions.

"We got one choice," Malavida said. "We go to the library, see if we can get that material on Shirley Land. The picture Karen had was of the same woman we saw taped up inside that barge."

Lockwood knew there was a better move but he couldn't pin it down. He struggled to think what it was.

Malavida put the car in gear and started to pull out of The Swallow Inn.

"No," Lockwood said.

"Whatta you mean no? You got a better idea?"

"Yeah."

"Let's hear it."

Lockwood looked at him blankly. "Can't remember."

"You can't remember?" Malavida shook his head in disgust. "At least you're finally acting like a regular G-Man," he said, and accelerated out of the parking lot, heading back along the river toward the highway.

"Tashay Roberts," Lockwood finally said, "knows something."

"Who's Tashay Roberts?"

Lockwood remembered now that Malavida had been in the hospital when he and Karen had talked to Bob

Shiff and Tashay. He slowly formed the words, telling Malavida who they were and that Tashay had tried to contact them with information about Leonard Land. "Don't know address," he finally said.

Malavida pulled over, grabbed his cellphone out of his pocket, and called Tampa and Miami Information. There was no listing for either of them.

"These punk kids got unlisted numbers? Why?" Malavida complained.

"Owe money . . . junkies," Lockwood finally managed to say.

Malavida grabbed the computer off the seat beside him. He reached into the pocket of his jacket, took out a small leather cracking kit, then removed a fone-phreaking diskette. He hooked his cellphone to the computer's external modem and started to go to work on the phone company's computer. Lockwood was sweating in the late-afternoon heat. He put down the window but it was still unbearably hot in the gray sedan. It took Malavida twenty minutes to break through. There was no listing for Tashay Roberts, but Bob Shiff's number was there. The billing address was 1818 Coral Grove Road, Miami . . . less than ten minutes from where they were parked.

# 38

## ESCAPE

This time when Karen woke up she was surprisingly alert. She still felt horrible and her head and jaw ached. Her muscles screamed at her, but her senses were tingling. Even before she opened her eyes she could smell mildew and dust. She knew she was tied up, sitting on a cold floor. She could hear Tashay crying. Karen's hands were lashed behind a wood post. She opened her eyes and looked around; there were boxes and junk piled everywhere. She determined that she was in a garage, but there was no room for a car. The garage had been completely taken over as a junk room. She could hear Tashay but couldn't see her. Karen craned her neck and finally saw that Tashay was standing, slumped over, her hands tied to a chain under an old block-and-tackle that was hooked to the heavy center beam. Tashay was half hanging by her wrists, sagging with her knees bent, her head tilted down, her gaze on the floor between her legs.

Karen took a moment and pushed everything but her terrible dilemma out of her mind. Her mouth was a pulsating bright spot of agony. The broken teeth had exposed nerves that screamed in pain. Karen knew she had to blot it out in order to function. She knew from past experience that if she acknowledged the pain, it would control her. She had been through bouts of agony before.

She knew she had to put it on another level. Focus hard on something else. In the hospital, after the ALFA Wing fiasco, she'd had a lot of time to practice. She now focused her mind on her current dilemma and tried to dial the pain down. Her mind started to rapidly collect facts. She looked over at Tashay and saw that she had stopped bleeding. The blood that was on the floor between her feet was caked and dry. That told her they had been there for at least an hour. Satan T. Bone must be waiting for someone or something, she reasoned. Where were they? she wondered. From what she could see, the garage was a mess. Extremely disorganized. She didn't think the mess belonged to Leonard Land. She had profiled him as compulsive and obsessive. He would be a neat freak; this garage would drive him nuts. She now focused on Tashay, who had stopped crying.

"Tashay," she said, her voice low and whispery.

"Oh, God...oh, God...Why is he doing this? Why?" Tashay said and started to cry again, but she didn't look up.

"Tashay, you've gotta stop it. We've gotta get something going here." Karen tried to straighten up but her arms and shoulders screamed at her. She winced as she struggled to push herself up the wood post. She was still dizzy, so she stopped and sat back on the cold concrete.

"Oh, God...What'd I do? I was helpin' him, why is he doin' this? Why...why?" Tashay was becoming even more emotional, choking back huge, sobbing breaths.

"*Stop it!*" Karen commanded loudly. "He's going to kill us. You've gotta stop crying." And then finally Tashay brought her gaze up from the floor and looked at Karen. One of her eyes was completely swollen shut. The blood that had been flowing out of the cut in her head had stained her silk blouse. She was in short-shorts and had dried blood on her legs and thighs.

"I need to know what's going on," Karen said. She struggled to keep her voice calm. She could see Tashay was in panic, on the edge of hysteria. Karen surprised herself that she had such a firm grasp on her situation after having been knocked unconscious twice. "Why is Bob Shiff doing this?" Karen asked in a calm voice.

"I don't know. . . . I don't know." Her voice was slurred through swollen lips. "I swear. He's been actin' strange since you asked us about that guy . . . the big, ugly one . . ."

"Leonard Land?"

"Yeah. You were right, he came to all our concerts, but never to the house. Now, he's been here twice this morning. He's creepy. He calls Bob 'Robbie.' "

"Robbie?" Karen said . . . and then she knew who Bob Shiff was. He was the missing foster brother, Robbie Land. She and Lockwood had wrongly assumed he was killed in Mississippi in the early eighties. If Bob Shiff was Robbie Land, it answered a lot of questions. Her mind was reeling with this information, fitting it into the puzzle. She knew that serial killers are not born but made, usually by parental abuse. Of course, the right psychological pre-dispositions and stressors have to exist, but, if Shirley had raised Robbie the way she had raised Leonard, it was not at all inconceivable that they could come out with similar pathologies. It also explained the Death Metal lyrics and the worship of other serial killers like Gacy and Dahmer. She wondered if it was possible that Leonard and Bob worked as a team—like Kenneth Bianchi and his cousin Angelo Buono.

"Tashay, is Bob helping Leonard commit these murders?"

"What murders? Oh, God, why would he hurt me like he did?"

"Can you move your hands? Can you get loose at all?"

Tashay looked at Karen for a long moment, as if the idea hadn't even occurred to her.

"I hurt . . . I hurt so bad," she said.

"Tashay, see how close to me you can get."

Tashay Roberts moved slowly across the garage toward Karen. The block-and-tackle chain allowed her to get almost three feet nearer.

"Lemme see if I can get up," Karen said, and again she struggled to stand. She worked her legs under her and then started to rise up. This time, with careful effort, she controlled the dizziness. Her arms were lashed behind the post but she could slide them up slowly. The wood was rough and gouged her with splinters as she worked her way to a standing position. Then she rotated around until she could face Tashay.

"We ain't never gonna get loose. . . . We ain't never," Tashay moaned, and again she began to cry.

"Tashay, stop it. *Stop it right now!*" Karen knew that her only chance of getting away was to include Tashay. She had to get her focused on the idea of escape and away from feeling sorry for herself.

From this new position on her feet, Karen could see the rest of the garage. She looked up and saw that some gardening tools had been thrown up on the rafter beams overhead. The beams were only a few feet above where Tashay's hands were tied to the block-and-tackle.

"Okay, Tashay, you see above your head . . . the gardening tools up there?"

Tashay looked up but didn't answer.

'See if you can jump up and knock them down. See that hedge clipper? See if you can knock it off the rafters and over toward me."

Tashay looked at her again. "Bob and me was in the grip, y'know? We was rollin' deep. He says to me, 'Tash, we gonna get outta this bonk town, go to Europe.' He's alla time talkin' to me about the Riviera and goin' to see Satan Wolf in prison. So why's he goin' and shootin' on me like this? Why's he wanna go ruin it? Why?"

"Tashay, try and knock the gardening tools down. *Will you do it!*" she commanded, her voice taking on an edge as her frustration grew.

"Don't yell at me . . ." Tashay started to cry again.

"I'm sorry, okay? I'm sorry I yelled. Can you do it?"

"Why's he go an' do this to me? I don't understand. Why?"

"Jump up and knock that rake handle. See if it'll drop the hedge clipper down. Do it . . . jump . . . jump up and hit it, can you . . . ?"

Tashay looked up at the tools above her head, then back at Karen.

"I can't. My wrists hurt."

"You can. Just try . . ."

"Maybe if I do everything they want . . . maybe if we promise to be good . . . maybe then they'll—"

"Tash! Listen to me," she interrupted. "Leonard Land is a psychopathic serial killer. He's murdered three women I know about for sure. Bob Shiff is his foster brother. They aren't going to let you go. They're gonna kill you. They used you to get to me. They're going to kill us both. Our only chance, Tash, is to work together. You've got to help me. Can you do it? Will you try?"

After a long moment she looked up at the rake handle above her head, then back at Karen.

"You can do it. Try. Come on, honey, just once . . . try."

Tashay looked up, and then she made her first tentative jump in the air. Her wrists had been rubbed raw and she squealed in pain as she jumped up, pulling the short length of chain with her. She almost made it on the first try. "I can't do it," she whined.

"Almost," Karen said. "You almost had it. Just a little higher."

Tashay jumped again. This time she hit the tools. The hedge clipper, which was balanced diagonally across the rake, fell between the tools and clattered down onto the concrete floor between them. The noise seemed deafening. Karen prayed nobody heard the racket. She had to move fast; something told her they were almost out of time.

"Okay. Okay . . . good, Tash. Now you gotta get closer to it and kick it over to me."

Tashay moved as close as she could, then hooked her

bare foot under the long handle of the hedge clipper and flipped it over toward Karen. It landed right at the base of the post where Karen was tied. She lowered herself down the splintered wood and rotated around so that her hands were near the handle of the tool. She got a grip on it and started to carefully work her fingers down the handle, bringing the sharp edge of the shears toward her. Her fingers were numb from the ropes, but she finally got her hands on the cutting edge and positioned it so that she could start sawing the ropes that bound her. Then she heard a screen door slam outside and two men talking in low tones. She worked to cut the ropes off. She held on to the blade tightly, sawing frantically. And then she felt one give. She pulled hard and she was free. She stood and moved to Tashay, reached up, and untied her.

"Maybe if we tell Bob we didn't run when we could've, he'll let us go." Tashay was talking animatedly, her voice was too loud.

"Shhhh," Karen said, looking around. "Where's that door go?" she asked, pointing to a door at the rear of the garage.

"Nowhere, just out to the backyard. There's a big hill with trees, goes up to the park. But the door's padlocked. The key's over there," she said, pointing at a tool bench.

"Get it open. I'm gonna try to lock the front from the inside." Tashay retrieved the key and scuttled to the back door. Karen moved to the front of the garage and found some barbed wire. She grabbed it and started to wire the big garage door closed, wrapping it around several times. In her haste, the sharp barbs ripped open her palms and fingers. Then the wire accidentally banged against the light metal door, making a loud scratching sound.

"The fuck you doin' . . . ?" Bob's voice called from outside. Then she felt the garage door start to open. The wire popped free.

"Run, Tashay!" she yelled as she tried to hold the door closed. She managed for a second, and then Bob Shiff and Leonard Land pushed it up and grabbed for her. She dodged them and stumbled backwards, falling next to the hedge clipper. She snatched them up and swung them at Leonard Land, who was now moving toward her in his awkward lumbering gate. She cut him across the side of his face with the open shears. He roared in anger and grabbed her, picking her up high over his head. Then he threw her down on the concrete floor. She was rocked by the blow, almost losing consciousness. She grabbed his leg and tried to bring him down. It was then that Bob Shiff grabbed her and pinned her arms behind her. He looked around for Tashay, but Tashay was gone. She had escaped out the back door.

"It's her! It's the bitch Shirley!" the man named Leonard Land said. The blood from the cut ran freely down his cheek but he didn't seem to notice it.

And then they heard a car out front. All of them turned and looked out of the open garage into the setting sun, as a gray Lincoln Town Car pulled into the drive.

# 39

## TRAFFIC

**L**ockwood and Malavida were stunned when they pulled into the driveway at Bob Shiff's house and saw Karen on the floor inside the open garage. They saw Leonard Land lumbering toward her and skinny Bob Shiff looking out at them. Lockwood and Malavida struggled to get out of the car, as Land grabbed Karen up off the floor where he'd thrown her, then ran out the rear of the garage.

Lockwood had lost his .45 to the Miami Police Department when he'd been arrested five days before. They were both unarmed. Lockwood knew, even before he was out of the car, that he wasn't going to come close to making it in time. He watched in horror as the huge man moved in that same awkward run he had witnessed in back of Land's house near Tampa. He galloped across the lawn with Karen over his shoulder to the VW van, which was parked on the grass behind the house. Leonard threw Karen into the back and clambered in behind her while Bob Shiff, who was only a few steps back, jumped behind the wheel and started the engine.

Lockwood watched as Malavida stumbled after them. He also didn't have a chance to stop them, so Lockwood turned and hobbled on unsteady legs back to the Lincoln. He got behind the wheel and started it. Malavida had stopped his limping run and had sunk to one knee in the grass, holding his stomach in pain, while Bob Shiff popped the clutch, throwing huge pieces of dead turf out behind the van as it sped away.

Lockwood pulled the Lincoln up to where Malavida was kneeling. There was blood on his shirt where some of the stitches had pulled free, opening his incision. Lockwood reached over and threw open the passenger door. "In!" he croaked.

Malavida pulled himself up by the door handle and slung himself painfully into the passenger seat. Before he could get the door closed, Lockwood floored it and was in pursuit of the VW van, which turned right on Summer Cove Road.

They could see it moving fast, a few hundred yards ahead. Then it turned left onto Old Cutler Road and headed toward Miami.

"Whatta you gonna do?" Malavida asked through clenched teeth, one blood-covered hand still holding his ruptured incision.

"Run fucker off road."

"Karen's in there. . . ."

"Gotta stop 'em . . . ram 'em," Lockwood said, "or she's dead. Call the cops."

Malavida grabbed up his cellphone as Lockwood turned left onto Old Cutler Road, accelerating. The much faster Lincoln began gaining ground on the van. Lockwood figured he could almost catch them before they got to Miami, which was only a mile away.

Something about that didn't make sense. Lockwood knew Shiff could see him in the van's rearview mirror. *Why would they head back to Miami, where they would get caught in five o'clock traffic?* he wondered.

The Wind Minstrel sat quietly in the back of the speeding van with Leonard's computer on his lap. He knew all of The Rat's tricks and games. He knew he could change the world with the computer. Everything and everybody lived within the web of its influence. The

Wind Minstrel never went out in the daylight. He had
come out today only because his very survival was at
stake, and he cursed the cowardly Rat for leaving this
predicament for him to solve. His skin burned as he
hooked the computer to the cellphone. The Rat had already preprogrammed everything and it was only a matter of minutes until The Wind Minstrel would activate it.
He yelled at Robbie Land to go faster. The VW van
rattled at breakneck speed. The Wind Minstrel loved
Death Metal music but he abhorred Robbie Land. He was
just a pretender, a poser who called himself Satan, but
he was a fool with his worship of sick monsters—men
like Dahmer, who ate his victims, or John Wayne Gacy,
who killed to fulfill a sick fantasy. The Wind Minstrel
was holy. His murders were Grand Biblical Adventures.
He was the Anti-Christ, and walked on a higher plane of
ritual dedication. He was involved in a personal struggle
with the Almighty Himself to see which of them would
control the universe.

The Rat had cultivated Robbie, his one-time foster
brother, and had used him to catch the Shirley-like bitch.
The Wind Minstrel, working on the laptop, had established a cellphone hookup. He had just started his logon:

```
BITRAN LOGIN:
```

He logged in as root using a stolen password. He was
immediately accepted to the City of Miami's transpor-
tation computer control system:

```
WELCOME TO
"BI-TRAN"
ROOT
```

He typed in:

```
DTCS
```

In seconds the Distributed Traffic Control System appeared on the screen. It had been named SCOOT by the City of Miami.

In the back of the cramped van, Karen pushed herself as far away from the huge, sweating man as possible. The rear door of the van was locked and there was no escape. The pungent smell of him filled the small space. His odor was rank and reminded her of bad meat and sour dough. She could see the computer in his lap and wondered what he was doing.

And then the traffic light grid for the City of Miami came up on the screen.

"Street?" The Wind Minstrel yelled at Bob Shiff.

"They're back there. They're gaining on us. I can't go any faster," the skinny Death Rocker screamed. "We shoulda gone the other way. We're gonna hit traffic. They'll be on us!"

"What street?" The Wind Minstrel said, growling ominously.

"Old Cutler Road," Shiff called back.

The Wind Minstrel typed it into the computer, and up on the screen came an enlarged map section of Miami that featured Old Cutler Road.

"Cross streets?" The Wind Minstrel yelled at Bob Shiff.

They were approaching a street that Bob Shiff knew ran north, straight into Miami. "Twenty-seventh Avenue!" he yelled out.

"Turn left," The Wind Minstrel instructed.

"I'll hit a million cross streets," Bob Shiff pleaded. "We'll be trapped in traffic."

"You are in a holy presence," The Wind Minstrel growled. "This is my temple. It is written that the wicked risen in the Second Resurrection will go up on the breadth of the earth with Satan and follow his commandments. Now, turn fucking left, goddamn it!" he shouted; the veins on his rash-reddened neck bulged.

Bob Shiff cursed but turned left. Twenty-seventh Avenue was absolutely straight and filled with stoplights and five o'clock cross traffic. He was certain they would be blocked and quickly overtaken by the car behind them. Somewhere in the distance he heard a police siren. Then a strange thing happened. . . . Just as they got to the first stoplight, which was Coral Way, the red light turned green and they shot right through. Bob Shiff looked in his rearview mirror at the gray sedan following them. The light stayed green for only a second. Just before the Lincoln hit the same intersection, the light turned red, and the Lincoln slid sideways trying to avoid a red Volvo accelerating down Coral Way. . . . The Lincoln missed the Volvo by inches, then finally ran the red light and was again after them.

"Cross street!" The Wind Minstrel yelled.

"Eighth!" Shiff called back, and he heard the computer keys clicking. . . . Ahead of him, at the last second, the Eighth Street light turned green. They shot through it, and in the rearview mirror he watched as it immediately turned red again. It was then that Bob Shiff understood what The Wind Minstrel was doing. He had cracked into the traffic-light computer system and was controlling all the lights on Twenty-seventh Avenue.

In the Lincoln, Lockwood was too slow as he slammed on the brakes. The light on Eighth Street had turned red a second before they got to it. Lockwood was still fighting his bad depth perception and went squealing through the red light in a four-wheel skid, leaning on the horn as the flow of cross traffic swarmed into the intersection. He crashed into a yellow pickup truck, throwing Malavida into the dash. Fenders crunched and locked as the two vehicles skidded together toward the curb and came to a smoking, shuddering stop. Lockwood threw the car into reverse and floored it. The bumpers were hooked, and the Lincoln's tires smoked and screamed on the hot, sun-cooked pavement. Then, finally, he pulled loose, after dragging the pickup about ten feet into the intersection. People were yelling; horns were honking. Lockwood floored it, driving up onto the sidewalk and around the mess he had caused, then off again in pursuit of the VW van.

Lockwood looked over and saw that Malavida was curled up in pain from the collision. He was doubled over in his seat, holding his stomach. "Great move, Zanzo," he grunted through a clenched jaw.

"Something wrong with traffic lights," Lockwood said.

"He's into the system," Malavida whispered in pain. "He's controlling them."

Suddenly all of the lights ahead of them turned red. The next intersection they hit was the four-lane downtown junction for the Tamiami Trail. The cross-traffic was intense and Lockwood and Malavida sat in frustration at the red light, watching the heavy traffic flow past in front of them, completely blocking their pursuit. Finally, Lockwood slammed his hand down hard on the wheel.

"Now what?" Malavida said as they both scanned the street up ahead. The van was nowhere in sight.

# 40

## GROUND ZERO

They were huddled in the basement of the main branch of the Miami-Dade Public Library. The room was too cold and the stone, turn-of-the-century architecture didn't offer much warmth. Malavida was in bad shape, still bleeding from the opened incision. They couldn't get it to stop.

"Leaking like a Mexican fishing boat," he said through gritted teeth.

Lockwood attempted to put his hand on Mal's forehead to check his temperature but Malavida knocked it away. He looked flushed.

They had been plowing through microfilm for an hour, looking for the obit on Shirley Land. Finally, an article about her death came up on the screen. The date was July 10, 1984. There was a small picture with the article, which was the same one Karen had shown to Malavida. They both leaned in and read the story quickly. . . .

The article gave a brief description of the fire that had burned Shirley to death. There was very little about Shirley Land's personal history. The article said she was the only daughter of a Baptist minister, who also made a meager living by designing underground bomb shelters in the fifties. It noted that she was survived by a son, Leonard, who was fifteen years old. It went on to say that she had been active in church affairs and that she was being buried at the Old Manatee Cemetery in Bradenton, Florida.

"Dead end," Malavida said. He started shivering and now Lockwood was sure he had developed a fever.

"You gotta go to the hospital, man, before you shake apart and die from infection," Lockwood said, forming one of his first complex sentences since the halon attack.

"Shut up. I'm in this," Malavida said, determined to hang tough.

"Your funeral," Lockwood said, then added, "We're down to seeds and stems here."

He knew if he were working a regular investigation for Customs and had time, he would do a full search for Tashay Roberts. He would have choppers searching the Manatee wetlands for The Wind Minstrel's barge. And he would check all the old addresses where Leonard Land had lived, hoping to interview an acquaintance who could give them more information. But he had lost his power base. The cops would arrest both of them on sight and they were out of time. Karen might be dead already. Lockwood knew they had to get some traction and get it fast.

"Sometimes," he said, forcing the words into the right slots in the sentence, "sometimes delusional people will go someplace they feel safe, like home. . . ."

"He won't go back to that bomb site near Tampa," Malavida said. He was now shivering so badly he was having trouble staying on the chair. "We'll never find that barge again. There's a hundred square miles of swamp he could hide in. . . . We're fucked."

"Maybe here," Lockwood said, pointing to the article about Shirley's burned house in Bradenton, Florida.

"He burned that house down, and we don't have an address. It was twelve years ago. . . ."

"County records! Your computer?" Lockwood said.

"Okay," Malavida answered and then, without warning, he threw up on the stone floor.

\* \* \*

When she woke up, she was in a new place. A twenty-foot-square windowless concrete room. She had been unconscious when they brought her here. The last thing she remembered, Leonard Land had held her down on the floor of the van while Bob Shiff pried her mouth open and forced her to swallow two pills.

She was no longer tied. She slowly regained her senses, struggled to her feet, and went to the metal door at the far side of the room. . . . It wouldn't budge. She stood silently in the center of the room and listened. Her entire body was quivering. She then realized that it was absolutely quiet. The quiet was unrelenting. The room was frigid. There were no ventilation ducts except for two small tubes that came into the high ceiling five feet above her head. She put a hand out and touched the concrete, which was extremely cold. For the room to have such cold walls and be so deathly quiet, she suspected it was underground. She remembered her profile of brown rats, written six days and two lifetimes ago. Brown rats lived underground. Was this The Rat's hiding place? She fought back a powerful urge to just sit down and cry. She knew that she had very few tools left to use against him. The only thing she had was her profile on The Rat, gathered with guesswork over the last week. She thought she understood his sickness. She had to use her ability as a psychologist and apply her knowledge effectively. She needed to buy herself some time.

She looked at her watch. It was 10:30 Sunday night, or at least she thought it was . . . unless she had slept the night through and it was now Monday morning. She had no sunlight to tell her for certain. She had to assume the pills they had given her would last only four to six hours. They had forced them down her throat sometime around five, so she deduced it was probably Sunday night. In a pinch she might be able to use that. She tried desperately not to let her thoughts ramble or turn to self-pity. She tried not to think about the horrible pain in her mouth. With her tongue, she carefully touched her broken teeth, crying out and almost fainting as she struck the exposed nerves. Then she kneeled down on the floor and prayed to God.

"Dear Lord," she said in a whisper, "forgive my sins. Help me to withstand this pain. Help me to find a clear vision. Lead me out of this darkness. In the name of your Son, Jesus. Amen." And then she sat in the corner farthest from the door and composed her thoughts, steeling herself for whatever would come.

At eleven the door opened and Leonard Land was standing there. The harsh fluorescent lights turned his pale, rash-reddened skin an ugly purple. His grotesque body filled the opening, his ghastly bald features glowering. Then he reached behind him and turned a dimmer rheostat, bringing the lights low so that he was no longer clearly visible, only a huge outline in the doorway. His smell reached across the small room, gagging her.

"Don't stare at me, you bitch, turn your eyes away. You cannot conceive my glory, for you have told many lies." His voice was thin and high and his speech was singsongy.

She struggled to get to her feet, and, once standing, she pressed her back against the cold concrete wall. "I haven't lied to you. I've never met you before."

"You were sent by Shirley. In her likeness, and with her message." He smiled but the smile was leering. "I will use that against you after you become part of the Beast."

Karen listened carefully and finally she nodded. She had to get him to talk. Information was power. She thought he was constructing a woman in his mother's likeness but she needed to find out why to gain leverage. "Go on," she said.

"You told me there was one God, one personal glorified being . . . but you lied."

"I lied?" she said, watching closely.

"You spoke of the Devil, but never defined his glory. He is also Lord, the Anti-Christ. In the numerous chain of prophecies only the closing scenes are hidden . . . and you will tell me what they are and how to avoid the Journey of Redemption."

"I see," she said. Her legs were quivering with fear, but she tried to hide it from him.

"You told me that the doctrine of the world's conversion and the terminal millennium is a fable of these last days. But you lied about that too. It is written that this doctrine is calculated to lull men into a state of carnal security and causes them to be overtaken by the great day of the Lord as if by a thief in the night," he said.

He was reciting. She could tell by the monotonous phrasing that this was memorized doctrine . . . but from where? She didn't recognize it.

"You said the wheat and tares grow together," he continued in the same voice, "and that evil men and the seducers wax worse and worse. You said the inevitable day of cleansing is coming. You told me God had given you the message and told you how to avoid the Redemptive Journey. You must tell me the secret. I will not walk through the Hall of Sleeping Spiders or take a two-thousand-three-hundred-day Journey of Redemption through hell." He lumbered ominously toward her.

"Okay, I will give you the truth," she said quickly.

"It is not so easy," he said and took a syringe out of his pocket. "Before you speak I must place your head on the Beast. The Beast, it is written, will tell the truth. She cannot lie. The Beast will tell me how to avoid the fires of hell."

Karen knew he was completely delusional, lost in some apocalyptic religious struggle. She couldn't quite get a handle on why, but she was out of time. She had to make a move. He took another step toward her.

"Stop!" she commanded in a loud voice and he flinched, throwing a hand up to protect his face almost as if she had hit him. Then he straightened and glowered at her.

"You are not Shirley. I don't have to do what you say."

It sounded to Karen as if he didn't quite believe that.

She decided to take her one last shot. "On the Sabbath," she said firmly, "the Lord has commanded all to rest." Her legs were unsteady, her chest heaving, her teeth killing her.

"I don't give a fuck what He wants!" The Wind Minstrel shouted.

"Then you are a fool," she said. "The Lord will not countenance this crime on His special day. He will seek double vengeance against you. He *will* find you, and He *will* double the Journey of Redemption." She didn't know what the hell the Journey of Redemption was, but it sure had an effect on Leonard, because he took a step back and covered his ears.

"I will not listen to more of your lies. The Rat hides in daylight. God doesn't know where I am."

"God *has* seen you. You went to Robbie's in the daylight. God knows all about Robbie; Shirley told him. He's been watching Robbie, waiting. He has followed you here and he knows what you are doing. Do not make the mistake of desecrating the Sabbath. If you do, you will take his full redemptive wrath. The fires he will use on you will burn slowly. You will roast for a thousand years." She was trying to use the same meter; give the content of her words biblical proportion.

He rubbed his eyes and looked undecided. He was still holding the syringe in front of him. Then he moved toward her. She tried to get out of the way but the room was small; he grabbed her arm and threw her back into the wall, then pressed his corpulent body against hers, pinning her. His stench was overpowering. Her stomach leapt and she almost vomited. For a moment she thought he might try to rape her, but then he grabbed her arm, shoved the needle in, and depressed the plunger. She fought for several seconds, knocking the empty syringe out of his hand onto the floor . . . and then, for the third time that day, she was fast asleep.

# 41

## FINAL VICTIM

**S**arasota County Real Estate Tax Board records indicated that Shirley's property had been sold in 1989 to Joseph Allen. He had died two years ago and the Allen family had put the place up for sale. Because of the bad Sun Coast real-estate market, they had not received an offer, and the house was now boarded up and empty. The lot wasn't technically in Bradenton but lay across the city line in Sarasota, at the end of a lowland island known as Siesta Key. It was only thirty miles south of the mouth of the Little Manatee River where, a few days before, Lockwood, Malavida, and Karen had piloted the rented boat—all three of them still in relative good health. The week that followed had exacted a heavy toll.

Lockwood and Malavida drove the gray Lincoln back across the tip of Florida to the west. They turned north on Interstate 75 and began the two-hour drive up the Gulf Coast. Malavida had been getting progressively worse. Lockwood had to stop the car twice so Mal could lean out and throw up. When Lockwood had tried to convince him to go to a hospital, he flatly refused.

"Listen, Zanzo," he'd said through clenched, shivering jaws, "I'm doing this. Okay? You're just John Q. Dickhead now. You can't order me around. So shut up."

That was the last thing the two had said to each other

until they reached the outskirts of Sarasota. Lockwood had the map on his knees as he drove. He turned left on Clark Road and followed the humpbacked two-lane highway across the low wetlands; then he drove over the single-span Stickney Bridge onto Siesta Key.

The islet was low and sparsely populated. The road was dark with no streetlamps. They moved along looking for a shell road called Lower Key Road.

After driving for about two miles, Lockwood found it and made a right turn, heading west now toward the Gulf. The road narrowed and finally came to a stop at a crude cul-de-sac. The foliage was dense and reedy. Lockwood looked at his watch: It was 11:45 Sunday night. An almost full moon had climbed out of the eastern sky and hung there like a wedge of pale lime on the edge of dark black glass. Lockwood could see two driveways with mailboxes. He looked over at Malavida, who was slumped against the door of the car. His eyes were open but he was obviously out of the play.

Lockwood got out of the car and stumbled on unsteady legs to the mailboxes. He looked inside both and found nothing except ad brochures. The Allen house was supposed to be at 2464 Lower Key Road. He found an ad brochure "To Occupant" with that address and followed the driveway halfway down until he could see the house. It was a one-story stucco job with a slate roof. It looked like it had once been painted yellow but had faded to an off-white. The roof seemed to lean slightly. The yard was in a losing battle with the dense Florida undergrowth.

Lockwood slowly headed back up the drive to the car. He thought he was moving with slightly better coordination, but he still didn't trust himself to run or throw a punch. Maybe he could still swing a tire iron. He opened the trunk and pulled out the tool, hobbled up to the passenger side of the car, and looked in at Malavida, whose head was leaning against the half-open window.

"Stay here. Call the cops if I'm not back in five minutes."

"I'm coming . . ." Malavida said and opened the door,

but that was as far as he got. He couldn't get out of the car. He tried to put his legs on the ground, but gave up and just slumped back with his head on the seat.

"Like I said, call the cops if I'm not back in five minutes." Lockwood took the phone out of Malavida's pocket, flipped it open, and put it in his hand. Malavida barely held on to it. Lockwood then walked carefully on uncooperative legs toward the house. Before he got ten feet, he heard Malavida's voice.

"Hey, Zanzo . . ."

Lockwood turned.

"I got your back."

"I can see," Lockwood said, then moved up the drive toward the darkened house.

The house was foreboding. Lockwood searched around slowly, trying desperately not to make any noise. He had been pumping adrenaline for hours to keep going, and now, when he needed an edge, he felt dull and used up. He leaned on the railing of the stucco house for a minute. He could see dust on the front porch. It covered the wood deck like a sprinkle of fine brown sugar. He could see in the pale moonlight that nobody had been on that porch for a long time. He looked around for the VW. The yard was empty, the house unused. He realized this had been just a long, time-consuming dead end. Karen wasn't here. He had failed her.

He slumped down and sat on the wood steps of the porch and stared at the dense, overgrown foliage. They had come close but they had lost her. He didn't think Karen could still be alive after the chase down Twenty-seventh Avenue. Leonard Land and Satan T. Bone would have to kill her to silence her. He sat there, used up, in the warm night . . . and then, suddenly, he started to cry. He tried to rein in his emotions, but he couldn't. The tears ran down his cheeks and fell on the tangled grass at his feet.

Lockwood had not cried since he was a ten-year-old boy at the orphanage. He had been pounded silly for showing his tears back then. It was perceived as weakness. In the world he was raised in, the meek didn't inherit the earth—they got the shit kicked out of them. He had not cried when he'd been sentenced to St. Charles Academy five years later or when Claire had divorced him or even when she'd been murdered. Despite the anguish of that loss, he had held himself in strict control. But he could no longer hold back the tears; he was physically and emotionally spent, and they now spilled out in silence.

He struggled to regain control of himself. He knew he was crying for all of them . . . for Claire and Heather, for Karen, for Larry Heath and Alex Hixon, even for Malavida, who, despite Lockwood's earlier harsh appraisals, had now gained his total respect. What he couldn't, or wouldn't, admit to himself was that he was also crying for John Lockwood, for all he had missed and all he had refused to experience.

Sitting on that Florida porch step after thirty years, John Lockwood finally lowered his guard . . . and it almost cost him his life.

She didn't know where the table had come from, but it was now in the center of the concrete room. She was strapped on top of it, her arms and legs tied with ropes to each corner. She tried to rock her body but the table didn't move. It was either very heavy or affixed to the floor.

"Stop that, you cunt," a voice said.

She looked up into the harsh overhead light, and then into view came Bob Shiff. He looked down at her; his ghoulish black-tattooed eyes glistened with a mixture of fear and excitement.

"Help me," Karen said softly.

He shook his head. His expression was grim. "He'd kill me. I'd rather he killed you. That was pretty smart, telling him God would punish him for killing on the Sabbath. Made him all nutty, though. He says he has to punish you. He says he wants to see into your eyes when he cuts your throat. Then this will all be over. Once the

Beast is made, there is no more need. You're the final victim."

"You're wrong, Bob. This killing is a compulsion. He won't stop. He'll find another reason. This isn't over."

"Yes, it is."

"What about Tashay? She got away. She'll tell the cops," Karen said.

"I won't be here. I'm going to Europe. I'm going to see Satan Wolf before he's executed."

Then Karen heard what sounded like a metal ladder, and in a few seconds Leonard Land came into her limited field of vision. He never looked at her but started unpacking his coroner's tools. He had changed into a silk kimono and his pasty white skin radiated in the harsh light. He had rubbed Vaseline over his entire body; she smelled its medicinal odor. He was selecting his scalpels now and he slowly laid them out on the concrete floor. She couldn't see them being arranged, but she could hear the metal handles ring slightly as they were laid at his feet.

Then he raised his kimono and grabbed his penis and slowly started to rock in silence, attempting to masturbate over his tools. But he did not get an erection. He remained limp and grew angry, yanking at himself with uncontrolled rage.

"I need music! Get fucking music!" he yelled at Bob Shiff, who ran quickly from the room. Karen heard him climb the metal ladder.

The Wind Minstrel moved slowly and picked up the Stryker oscillating bone saw. He plugged it in and turned it on. He held it over Karen, bringing it within inches of her face. The sawtoothed lateral blade growled ominously as it oscillated back and forth, vibrating the flesh on The Wind Minstrel's corpulent forearm.

Bob Shiff saw something on the edge of the porch and for a moment, in the pale moonlight, couldn't make out what it was. As he silently crept closer, he saw it was a man. Then he recognized him. It was the same cop who had come to the Loomis Theater and showed him Leonard's picture, the one who had attacked them this afternoon at the garage in East Miami and chased them. When he crept closer, he thought he could hear the man crying, sobbing softly as he sat on the porch. Bob Shiff moved slowly and deliberately back to the VW van, which was hidden in the middle of the dense underbrush, away from the house. He opened the door silently and retrieved the same bat he had used on Karen Dawson in the Bayfront Park toilet. He then moved back toward the house and looked again at the crying man. He was afraid to tell Leonard, because Leonard was strange. Lately anything could send him into a homicidal rage. Shiff decided it wouldn't be hard to get around behind the man if he went to the back of the house and came up on the far side, so that the man's back was to him. The grass there would muffle the sound of his approach.

It took Shiff almost three minutes before he was standing behind Lockwood. The cop *was* crying, his head bowed, not paying attention. Shiff silently brought the bat back and, with all of his might, he swung it. . . .

Lockwood didn't know what warned him. Maybe it was his battle training in the Marines or an instinct from all the police work. Maybe it was moon shadows or a change in the sound of the keening insects. Maybe it was the ghost of Wyatt Earp—but he instinctively moved to his right seconds before he felt the stinging blow glance off his right shoulder. Bob Shiff saw him move and chased him with his swing. But it threw off his timing and he missed Lockwood's head by a fraction. Lockwood rolled on the ground to gain distance; he saw Shiff move toward him, bat raised high for a final strike. Lockwood was sprawled on the grass, his right leg under him, his right hand touching his left shoe. He was in a horrible position, unable to push off or gain leverage. He was two heartbeats from getting creamed.

Shiff moved in on him with the bat high over his head; then Lockwood snatched off his black loafer and, grabbing it with both hands in a two-handed shooting position, pointed it at Shiff. The moonlight glinted off the black patent leather and it froze Shiff momentarily.

"Drop it or you're dead, cocksucker!" Lockwood barked out an adrenaline-filled complete sentence and prayed this speedballing dust-bunny would go for the lame trick. In a bluff like this, attitude was everything. Then, miraculously, Shiff dropped the bat. "On stomach," Lockwood commanded. Shiff started to go to his knees but, from this position, he could see more clearly.

"It's a fucking shoe," he said in dismay and he lunged again for the bat.

Lockwood was now untangled and threw himself sideways, also grabbing for the wooden bat. The two of them struggled on the ground. In his weakened condition, Lockwood could not even control this tiny 120-pound heroin addict. He was slow and uncoordinated, and in seconds Shiff had the bat away from him. Lockwood lunged forward and awkwardly hit Shiff in the face with both hands. The blow rocked him back but didn't take him down. Lockwood now dove at him, trying to get his hands on Shiff's throat. The two men went down in the wet grass, and then Lockwood rolled over the tire iron he had brought with him but had completely forgotten. Shiff pulled free and jumped up with the bat in his hand. Then, grinning, he moved in on Lockwood, who struggled up on his knees, the tire iron in his right hand hidden behind his back. Shiff swung the bat at Lockwood's head but didn't see the tire iron coming from his left. Lockwood ducked under the Louisville Slugger and followed through with the tire iron, hitting Bob Shiff in the side of the head.

The noise was sickening and Shiff went down like chopped cotton. He lay in the grass motionless. Lockwood leaned over him and took his pulse; it felt thin and uneven, and then it just stopped.

"Fuck 'em," Lockwood said, exhausted. He grabbed the tire iron and stood up, looking around. Where the hell had Shiff come from? he wondered. There was nothing out here. And then he saw a small break in the tall grass at the edge of the yard. It looked like it might be a footpath.

The Wind Minstrel had waited until past midnight to avoid God's wrath. But now, it was Monday morning and he could wait no longer. Shirley had stopped his glorious erection. This messenger for Shirley, this look-alike, had destroyed his penile glory. He would kill her slowly to complete the Beast. He would take her head in a garbage bag back to his barge deep in the Manatee wetlands. He would assemble the Beast in the moonlight and pray to Satan for his miracle. Then he would wait for the Beast to speak and tell him how to avoid the Journey of Redemption. He looked at her, into her frightened eyes.

"Please don't. Please . . ." Karen said softly.

"Please don't. Please . . ." The Wind Minstrel mimicked. And then he put down the oscillating saw that he would eventually use to cut the spinal cord at the sixth cervical vertebra. He picked up the 10006 surgical scalpel and drew it once, seductively, across Karen's neck. Then he began his cut.

She screamed out in pain, as the scalpel sliced into her. . . .

Lockwood was moving down the footpath but he couldn't see anything. It was then that he heard Karen's scream. He looked around but couldn't tell where it was coming from. The screaming continued as he stumbled toward the direction of the sound, until finally he was kneeling over a small vent tube with a metal Chinese rain hat over it at the foot of the garden. The pipe was only two inches in diameter but he could hear Karen's strangled cry for help coming from deep below. It was terrifying and ripped through his soul.

*How the fuck I get down there?* He started thrashing around looking for a way. Then he remembered Shirley's obit. Her father had been a Baptist minister who designed bomb shelters. If this was a bomb shelter, there had to be a trapdoor somewhere right above the vents. He got to his feet and quickly tried to find it. He could now hear the terrible screams coming right up through the ground below. They seemed to be coming right up under his feet! He found a metal hatch that was hinged to a concrete lip, a short distance off the footpath. He threw it back and looked down. Fifteen feet below, he could see light. The screaming was louder. He turned around and started to climb down the metal rungs of the ladder, still clutching the tire iron.

The Wind Minstrel had laid open a flap on Karen's neck but had missed her jugular vein because she had bucked violently on the table. He had hit her, knocking her dizzy, but she continued to fight him. He was just trying to make his second cut when he heard Bob Shiff coming back down the metal ladder.

"Hold her," he instructed. Then he turned and saw Lockwood standing in the small bomb shelter clutching the tire iron. He screamed and lunged at Lockwood, who swung the tire iron and missed completely. The tool hit the wall and flew out of his hand. Lockwood threw two slow, awkward punches that barely connected and did no damage; his coordination was way off. Then Leonard Land, with the scalpel still in his hand, grabbed him, threw him down, then landed on top of him, pinning him under his 367-pound frame.

"Fuck you! Fuck you!" The Wind Minstrel shouted as he rose up and stabbed Lockwood with the scalpel.

Lockwood rolled desperately. The scalpel missed his chest and went up to the hilt in his right shoulder. The tip stuck deep in his scapula bone, and then Lockwood rolled further, pulling the scalpel out of The Wind Minstrel's hand. The blade was still embedded in Lockwood's shoulder when the huge killer grabbed for the fallen tire iron and swung it. Lockwood took that blow on the side of the head and it almost put him under.

Suddenly the lights in the bomb shelter went out. At first, Lockwood thought he had gone unconscious, but the pain never left. Then his eyes adjusted and he was looking over the huge man's shoulder, right up the round hatch fifteen feet above, into the moonlit sky. . . . Suddenly, something filled the opening. Then he saw Malavida's face in the center of the hatch.

Malavida threw himself down the opening, free-falling, headfirst . . . and landed on Leonard Land's massive back.

Malavida was momentarily dazed, but he managed to snake his arm around Leonard's neck and pulled back, trying to execute a choke hold. They struggled in silence for several seconds. Lockwood's head was not three inches from Malavida's. Their eyes locked, and somehow their stares gave strength to one another. Then, in the circle of moonlight coming from above, he could see Malavida's look of fierce determination turn to desperation. The Chicano had used up all his resources. Leonard started to rise.

"My shoulder," Lockwood hissed. "In my shoulder."

Malavida's eyes went down and saw the scalpel buried in Lockwood's shoulder. With his left hand he let go of Leonard's neck and grabbed for the scalpel handle, as Leonard rose and got to his feet. Malavida was riding his huge back, but the bloody scalpel had come out of Lockwood's shoulder and was now in Malavida's hand. Leonard spun around and slammed backwards into the wall, knocking Malavida into the concrete.

Malavida fell from the huge man's back and now, in the almost total blackness of the bomb shelter, Lockwood rolled to his feet and charged at the spot where he thought Leonard was. Miraculously, Lockwood caught him in the back with his shoulder and, with spent legs, drove him into the concrete wall as hard as he could. Then he heard Leonard scream out in agony. Leonard came away from the wall and stood in the center of the room, his eyes wide. In the dim moonlight coming down the hatch, Lockwood could not immediately tell what had happened. Then Leonard started grabbing weakly at his kimono. It was then that Lockwood saw the scalpel buried deep in Leonard's chest. Lockwood had driven him right into Malavida's blade. The huge man shuddered for a minute in the shaft of moonlight. ''Mother,'' he finally whispered, and then he fell forward on his face.

Lockwood crawled to Malavida, who was washed with his own blood from the ripped stomach incision. All of his stitches were now torn.

''Where's Karen?'' Malavida said softly.

Lockwood pulled himself up and moved to Karen, whom he could barely see, tied to the table. Her eyes were wide but she was alive. Lockwood looked at the gash on her neck and then, in the almost total darkness, he untied her and helped her off the table.

She knelt beside Malavida. Lockwood didn't think either of them could climb the ladder. Malavida was semi-delirious and bleeding profusely.

''Called cops,'' Malavida said, weakly.

''You okay?'' Lockwood whispered, completely spent.

The Chicano nodded. ''Hey, Zanzo.''

Lockwood looked over.

''Held your back.''

''You sure did,'' Lockwood admitted.

The three of them sat on the floor, Karen between them. ''Thank you,'' she said to them both. Neither Lockwood nor Malavida had the strength to answer her. Unexpectedly, relief filled Karen's eyes with tears. She took each of their hands and they sat there.

The three of them were still holding hands when the police arrived.

# 42

## A HOME WHERE HIPPOS CAN ROAM

All of them ended up at the hospital in Bradenton. Karen's throat and Lockwood's shoulder were stitched up, but Malavida was rushed into surgery. His fever had climbed to a life-threatening 105 degrees. He had developed peritonitis and they opened him up again, drained out his intestines, bombed him with antibiotics, and prayed. He was back on the critical list. Karen spent five hours getting her broken teeth temporarily capped. Tuesday night her teeth finally settled down enough so she could sleep. On Wednesday afternoon Malavida was upgraded to "serious."

The story unfolded on TV over the next two days, and it was obvious to the entire nation that the three of them had stopped a violent and seriously deranged serial killer. Lockwood had been on the phone to Bob Tilly in Washington. He was determined to keep Malavida from going back to Lompoc and was working with Tilly on an idea. The police had found The Wind Minstrel's barge buried under a tangle of vines in the wetlands. The barge's freezer delivered up a gruesome offering of body parts. It would take almost a month before tissue matches could identify all of them. Besides Candice Wilcox and Leslie Bowers, there were parts of three other women in the freezer. Tashay Roberts had not been heard from.

Lockwood and Karen ate most of their meals in the hospital cafeteria. Lockwood's speech was improving daily, but even so, they had fallen into long lapses of silence, consumed by their own thoughts. Lockwood called Minnesota every evening and talked to Heather. The sound of her voice warmed him like nothing else.

"Daddy, will we still go to a farm?" she asked him each time he called.

"It's a promise, Pumpkin," he answered.

Her voice communicated both hope and disbelief.

Malavida was sitting up by the fourth day. Tubes were hanging like tendrils off the pole by his bed, but his color was back. He looked up at Lockwood and Karen and smiled his beautiful smile.

"I guess I don't get my running start, do I, Zanzo?"

"No running for you at all for a while," Karen said.

"So I'm headed back to Lompoc?"

"I've been working on that," Lockwood said. "I think I got something arranged. But you'll be surrounded by cops."

"Great. What have you got me signed up for this time? Am I a target on the Customs Academy shooting range?"

"I got Bob Tilly, who's now Director of All Operations in D.C., to agree to take you on as a computer specialist. He's arranging for you to be transferred on an early release program from Lompoc. If Karen is crazy enough to want to get into the Pennet computer again, you can do it for her."

"And what about you?" Malavida asked.

"I'm gonna go look for a new home for Heather."

"Where?"

"A farm. I got a lead on a place in Northern California. It's on the coast at Drakes Bay. They need somebody to run the acreage . . . citrus, I think, buncha trees. I'll be like a caretaker or something. But Heather can have horses and we can settle down. You guys are welcome to come and help me watch fruit grow."

And then Lockwood put his hand on Malavida's shoulder. "I didn't think this would happen . . . but I've come to have great respect for you, Mal. I'd really like to be your friend," Lockwood said.

"You already are," Malavida answered. And they both knew it was true.

Through all this, Karen said nothing.

Later that night Lockwood and Karen decided to have their last dinner together. Lockwood had a plane ticket to Minnesota and was scheduled to pick Heather up the next day. They went to a little beach restaurant in Gulf City just north of Bradenton. In a touch of irony, from the window table they could see the mouth of the Little Manatee River. After they were seated, they sat in silence. Karen fidgeted with her napkin.

"I want you to take care of Malavida," Lockwood finally said. "I got real fond of him. Don't let him fall back in the drink."

"Okay," she said softly.

They ordered dinner, and then Karen reached out and took Lockwood's hand. "When I first saw you, I thought you were running on your own fumes . . . but I was wrong. You turned out to be special."

"Karen, this can't go anywhere. . . ."

"Why not?"

"I have to raise Heather."

"I'm good with children."

He sat quietly and didn't answer.

"You know about Mal and me, don't you?" she finally said.

He held her amber eyes with his before answering. "I can live with that," he said. "It's not that. . . ."

"John, I've gone through my adult life looking for things to excite me. I've been jumping off high places, strapped in strange-looking equipment, racing cars, crashing, anything to stay involved with my own life. It's self-destructive. I haven't made the right choices."

"Nobody does."

"Malavida is more than either of us thought when we picked him up at Lompoc. Aside from being handsome and smart, he's loyal and brave . . . but I don't love him."

"Karen—"

"Will you just shut up and let me do this? Okay?"

He fell quiet, waiting for her to finish. "I think I knew I was falling in love with you from the beginning. I told myself I wasn't. You aren't what my father would have picked. But I think it's time I started picking what I want. I didn't want to settle down. . . . I was programmed to be my father's little genius. Live his dream. But I've learned something through all this: The demon chasing me isn't boredom, it's the lack of true commitment. I know now I don't need thrills, I need substance. I was trying to hold on to my old routine because it was all I knew. I was afraid of my feelings. So I used Malavida to try and destroy any chance I had with you."

Lockwood thought she looked beautiful in the orange light of the setting sun. He would have liked to find out what they could've had together, but he needed to take care of Heather before worrying about himself. The only thing he knew for certain was that the timing was wrong.

"No go, huh?" she said softly.

"If I'm ever going to be what I want to be, I have to stop breaking promises to the people I love. . . ." It was all he could say. It was the only thing that still made sense to him.

The next day he flew to Minnesota. Rocky and Marge looked at him with distrust as he picked up his daughter and left on the next flight for Northern California.

They rented a white Ford pickup in San Francisco and drove along the coast to Drakes Bay. The road was wide and the day was bright, and they sat side by side on the front seat of the truck and sang: "Oh, give me a home where the hippos all roam, and Heather and the antelope play. . . ." Lockwood and Heather smiled broadly as they sang, but they were both missing Claire.

The farm where Lockwood was going to be the caretaker was large and rustic. He had been hired because of a recommendation given over the phone by Bob Tilly. From the hill where the caretaker's house was situated, they could see the blue-gray Pacific Ocean in the distance. There were fifty acres of pear trees, and Lockwood was instructed on how to handle all of the equipment by the grizzled old man who had run the farm but was retiring. Lockwood was told that during the canning season, contractors would come in with crews and pick the crop for him. All he had to do was test the soil, make sure there was enough water, and light the smoke pots during a freeze. He got Heather enrolled in the Drakes Bay Elementary School and they settled into a life that was peaceful and quiet. Several times he found himself thinking of Karen. He finally decided she had been the right woman at the wrong time, but he pushed those thoughts away. He had broken his promises to Claire over and over. He knew she was up there watching and he didn't want to disappoint her again. On weekends he and Heather shopped around for a horse. They ended up buying a four-year-old gaited mare with a quiet disposition. Heather named her "Miss Muffet."

Two months later, Claire released him.

When the dream started, he was walking in a desert. He was alternately too hot and too cold. . . . Then he came upon an oasis. Claire was waiting there. She was standing in front of a house and she led him inside. When he sat down, he could see that it was Rocky's living room. They sat on the faded print furniture. In the dream, Claire held his hand. She was even more beautiful than before. Her blond hair had grown long again, the way it had been when he met her.

"You can't be a good father if you're half a man," she told him. Her blue eyes looked at him with the same love that he had seen when they first married. "You tried to do the right things but I expected too much," she told him. "The things that shaped you, you couldn't control, and they drove us apart. But I will always love you, John. Always. I'm in a better place, darling. I can look down and see your pain. Whatever you do for yourself, you'll be doing for me. I know you won't ever again break your promises to Heather. Just don't break your promises to yourself.''

When he awoke, he lay still in bed. He could hear the wind blowing through the cypress trees outside the house. The dream had been so vivid that he was startled by it. Claire's voice had been so clear, exactly the way he remembered it. He listened to the wind and the sound of the leaves rustling.

He got out of bed but became angry at himself. The dream was his own subconscious attempting to free him. He had taken so much from Heather and Claire; now was his time to give back. But in his heart he was lonely.

He heard a noise coming from Heather's room and slowly moved down the hall. He looked in. The light was on and he could see her sitting at her desk, writing in her school binder. She turned and saw him. ''Oh, Daddy, just a minute, I want to put this all down. . . .'' she said, as she continued writing.

He entered the room. ''Pumpkin, you should be asleep.'' He went to her and sat on the edge of the bed. ''You have to get up early and feed Miss Muffet before school.''

''I know. . . . It's just . . . I had this incredible dream and I wanted to write it all down so I wouldn't forget,'' she said. Then she closed her binder and looked at him. ''It was Mommy. She came to see me,'' Heather said. ''She was just like before, Daddy. She was so beautiful. Her hair was long and, in the dream, she held my hand.''

''What did she say?'' Lockwood had a lump in his throat.

''She told me you were in pain. Is that true, Daddy?''

''Sometimes. Sometimes I am. But I'll get better. We both will.''

''She said that she loved us and that we had to let her move on. It was so clear, Daddy. So clear . . . like she was right in the room with me.''

''I know,'' Lockwood said softly.

He took Heather's hand and led her across the room to her bed. He tucked her in and then leaned down and kissed her. Heather held him for a long time.

"Daddy," she finally said, "she wants you to be happy."

Lockwood turned off the light, went downstairs, and called Karen.

# Acknowledgments

I would like to thank several people without whose help I would not have been able to write *Final Victim*. . . . Once again, WAYNE WILLIAMS has tirelessly helped me edit and sharpen with his insightful criticisms; STAN GREENE, whose computer knowledge gave this novel its accuracy; my editor at William Morrow, PAUL BRESNICK, who helped me in shaping the personal stories; GRACE CURCIO, my assistant, who got bombed with pages every weekend and always got them back to me by morning; CHRISTINE TREPCZYK and KRISTINA OSTER, assistants who never tired; JO SWERLING, JR., who read every draft and corrected my daffy punctuation; BILL GATELY, who gave me insight into his and John Lockwood's world; and, most of all, my wife, MARCIA, who put up with me through the year of writing.

If you've enjoyed *Final Victim*,
then sample the following
selection from **KING CON,**
Stephen J. Cannell's next
heart-pounding suspense thriller,
coming soon in hardcover from
William Morrow and Company.

**In the world of con men and sharpers**, it is the custom for the very best hustler in the game to be given a title of honor. In the thirties it was "Yellow Kid" Weil, in the forties "Titanic" Thompson, in the sixties, Victor "The Count" Lustig, but today the title is held by Beano X. Bates. **These four men were all known as . . .**

# KING CON

## 1

The poker game had been a card-hustler's dream; the players were strictly in the talented-amateur category and the stakes were unlimited. It was rumored that hundreds of thousands of dollars routinely changed hands in the invitation-only game that commenced promptly at seven-thirty every Tuesday night in the luxurious locker room of New Jersey's Greenborough Country Club. There was an investment banker from Cleveland who was a cautious bettor, and refused to step up even when he held sure winners. He'd also occasionally chase a bluff like a puppy after a pickup truck. There was a fat electronics-store owner who was constantly bathed in a sheen of his own sweat and was a shameless plunger. There were two brothers from Greenborough, who owned a Lexus dealership. They were trying to team play, but kept misreading each other. They talked trash, drank too much, and ended up losing five out of six hands.

Then there was Joseph Rina. He was only five-eight, but there was an aura about him. He radiated power and was movie-star handsome. He was reputed to be a New Jersey mob boss, although he had never been convicted of anything. His nickname on the street was Joe "Dancer." He sat at the green felt table, clothed in perfectly tailored Armani. He remained distant from the others, playing without comment, his magnificently handsome face giving away nothing. Joe Rina joined this game once a month. He would drive down from Atlantic City to the Greenborough Country Club and was generally the big winner.

Seated to his right was Beano Bates. He had been trying to get in this high-stakes game for a month. He was a well-known card sharp and con man, so he was playing incognito, under the name of Frank Lemay. Dark-haired and handsome, he had always traded on his looks and charm.

Although he was a world-class poker player, Beano never depended solely on his card-playing skill. He had two "shiners" working on the table: One was a money clip that he could lay on the table directly in front of him. It was shiny, but only reflected directly back. If you looked at the clip from any other angle, it appeared to be dull and non-reflective. Beano could deal cards over the clip, and the shiner would reflect the cards as they were flipped off the deck, giving him full knowledge of what was in play. The other was a "palm shiner," which he used when it wasn't his deal. It was a tiny, upside-down periscope. He could palm it, or hold it cupped in his hand on the green felt table, positioned so he could look down through the space between his fingers. The palm shiner was low enough on the table to read the cards being dealt off the deck across from him. These two shiner positions, plus his natural skill at cards, gave him an unbeatable edge.

By ten-thirty, Beano Bates, a.k.a. Frank Lemay, was eighty-six thousand dollars ahead. The poker chips were stacked in columns in front of him like colorful prisoners captured in battle.

At eleven o'clock they took the main break, and Beano found himself standing next to Joe "Dancer" Rina at the urinal in the overlit men's locker room of the ornate country club. White tile and chrome fixtures glittered under the bright ceiling lights, while the two men arched yellow streams into the shiny porcelain trough like two teenage boys pissing in a lake for distance.

"You been getting good cards," Joe Rina said without emotion, his movie-star face revealing no hint of danger.

"Sometimes the cards run that way," Beano replied as he watched his urine mix with Joe's and flow into a drain full of bar ice and black pepper.

"You call a lot of six-card optional," Joe said, referring to a dealer's choice game that Beano preferred because, after the fifth card was dealt, the players could exchange any one of their cards for a sixth card before betting commenced. Beano liked the game because it gave him more cards to scope with his money clip shiner.

"Yeah," Beano grinned, "that game's been working pretty good for me."

"You ever hear about Soapy Smith?" Joe said softly.

"Don't think I have," Beano replied, dreading the story, which he correctly assumed would be some kind of ghastly warning.

"They called him Soapy because he marked cards with soap. Kept a little sliver between his index and middle fingers, used it to stripe the cards. Soapy did real good in Atlantic City when I was growing up . . . drove a big, black Cadillac. All us kids wanted to be like him . . . lotsa women, great clothes. Always wore the Italian or French designers. Everything was great till Saturday, June eighteenth, 1978. . . . That was the day we all changed our minds about being like Soapy."

"Really?" Beano said, his smile pasted on his face, his puckering dick hanging forgotten in his hand. He put it away, zipped up, and moved to the washbasin, wishing he didn't have to hear the end of the tale.

In a minute, Joe Dancer's reflection joined his in the mirror. "Yeah. Poor Soapy got caught jammin' some players at the Purple Tiger, which was a little card club down on the wharf, by the pier. Those guys he was cheatin' were serious players, and they were real mad cause they trusted Soapy, so they held him down and jointed the poor guy while he was still alive."

"I beg your pardon?" Beano said.

"One guy, I think he'd been a medic in 'Nam, amputated

Soapy a section at a time, while the others held him down. They had a plumber clamping off veins and arteries so he wouldn't bleed out. Kept him alive for about fifteen or twenty minutes. By the time they took off his left arm, poor Soapy's heart stopped.''

Somebody flushed a toilet in the stall behind them.

''That's a damn good reason not to cheat,'' Beano managed, his insides now frozen like his smile.

''I always thought so,'' Joe said. And without any expression crossing his gorgeous aquiline face, he walked away from the sink.

The story made its point. Beano figured eighty-six grand was plenty. He decided to just hold even, maybe give some of it back, until the game time limit.

The game was called at exactly midnight, and Beano cashed in seventy-eight thousand in chips. Joe Rina left without saying another word. Beano stayed in the bar talking the losers down for about an hour, drinking and telling everybody it had been the best card night of his life.

At a few minutes past one, Beano walked out of the almost deserted country club and headed to his rental car.

What happened to Beano in the parking lot wasn't as bad as what had happened to Soapy Smith in Atlantic City, but it certainly made the same point.

He had just arrived at his car and was putting his briefcase into the trunk when he was staggered by a massive blow from behind. It hit him with such devastating force at the back of his skull that Beano instantly dropped to his knees, splitting open his forehead on the back bumper. He spun awkwardly around in time to see a nine-iron flying out of the darkness, right into his face. It was a chip shot from hell that broke all his front teeth and shattered his jaw, skewing it terribly. Beano fell to the pavement, then grunted in horrible, unendurable pain as four more horrendous blows from the golf club broke the third, fifth, and seventh ribs along his spinal column, also shattering his clavicle and sinus cavity.

Beano was barely conscious when Joe Rina stuck his handsome face down so close that Beano could smell his breath and his mint aftershave.

"You look pretty bad, Mr. Lemay," the mobster said. "You might be able to pull this stuff on that buncha buffaloes in there, but you should know better than to try and cheat Joseph Rina."

Beano couldn't talk. His jaw was locked by bone chips and a break that knocked it badly out of alignment.

"Now I'm gonna take my money back. But let me assure you this has been very helpful," Joe Dancer said with exaggerated politeness. "I've been having trouble with my short game. I think I wasn't keeping my head down and following through like my guy keeps telling me. Thanks for the practice." Joe stood up; then Beano felt pure agony as two more blows rained down onto his body for good measure. He started to cough up blood. Beano knew he was badly wounded, but more important, in that instant he felt something die inside him. It was as if the most critical piece of Beano Bates, his charming confidence, had left him like smoke out of an open window. It was his confidence and ego that allowed him to be the best. As he lost consciousness, he somehow knew that if he survived he would never be the same again.

He woke up in New Jersey, at the Mercer County Hospital. He was in ICU. The nurses told him he'd had ten hours of surgery, that three teams of orthopedists and neurosurgeons had spent the night putting his busted face and body back in place. His jaw was wired shut. There was a large pair of wire clippers next to his bed. When he was conscious enough to understand, the trauma nurse told him that if he felt like vomiting from the surgical anesthesia or antibiotics, he should get the clippers and cut his wired jaw open, so that he wouldn't vomit back into his trachea and lungs and choke to death. It was sobering advice.

He lay in agony for weeks, feeling every inch of his body throb. Even the impressive list of meds he was taking couldn't completely mask the pain.

The New Jersey State Police transcribed his statement from his hospital room. He talked to them through his wired mouth, forming the words like an amateur ventriloquist. Beano gave his statement under his assumed name, Frank Lemay, because there were three Federal warrants out on him for criminal fraud and various other sophisticated con games. He was also currently on the FBI's Ten Most Wanted List. It was better if the authorities thought it was Frank Lemay who had been beaten up by Joe Rina. He also didn't tell them that he had no intention of ever testifying against the handsome mob boss.

His old friend and fellow card sharper "Three Finger" Freddy Feinberg came to visit him in the hospital. The gray-haired card shark looked down in shock at Beano, who was still swollen and discolored like rotting fruit. "Jeez, man, you look like a fucking typhoid victim," he said. It had been Freddy who arranged for Beano to get in the game. "I told ya, Beano, I told ya, 'Be careful of that guy Joe Rina.' " And then Three Finger Freddy told him about a rumor that was buzzing around in the street. The word was that Joe Dancer was still pissed and had put out a contract on Frank Lemay, because he had not shown the grace and good sense to die in the country club parking lot like he was supposed to. Three Finger Freddy also told him about how the Rina brothers had taken care of disposal of bodies in the old days. It was another story Beano could have done without hearing.

The police told him that a New Jersey prosecutor named Victoria Hart was coming down to interview him prior to filing the assault-with-intent-to-commit-murder charges against Joseph Rina. Because Joe Rina was a popular tabloid star, the press was swarming to get a story. It was only a matter of time until Beano's alias would be penetrated, so he disconnected himself from the tangle of electrodes and I.V. bottles and limped out of the hospital. It was a move that saved his life, but he was now poised on the edge of a cliff, overlooking a landscape of revenge and violence that would change him forever.

**2**

The Florida midday sun cooked the half acre of used cars at Bob's Auto Ranch in Coral Gables. Shimmering heat waves danced along the tops of Beamers and Bent Eights, parked in shiny rows, dressed in cheap new fifty-dollar paint jobs. They begged customers shamelessly with BUY ME and TAKE ME HOME signs propped under the windshield wipers. Faded red and blue plastic triangular flags hung listlessly from guy wires in the stagnant heat like dead balloons after a birthday party. It had been a slow morning . . . mostly tire-kickers and be-backs.

Because he was sure Joe Rina was still trying to kill him, Beano Bates had dyed his hair blond and had added a mustache, which he needed to lighten constantly. He still wasn't completely recovered from the beating with a nine-iron that had happened six months ago. Remarkably, the brutal assault had not diminished his good looks. If anything, he appeared slightly more rugged. But Beano had been forced to hide, and not only from the Rina brothers. . . . Last week, he had made his second surprise appearance on *America's Most Wanted.*

Beano had been sitting in his fourteen-dollar-a-night motel apartment, feeding Roger-the-Dodger a Big Mac, when his segment had aired. The brown and black fox terrier looked up from his quarter-pounder and barked angrily, perking up his ears and snarling at the TV, as if he knew the whole story was bullshit. Beano looked lovingly at the dog. . . . You couldn't find that kind of fierce loyalty in criminal partners anymore.

On the TV, John Walsh droned on as a picture of Beano with his old dark hair color popped up on the blue screen behind him. "Beano X. Bates," Walsh said seriously, "is perhaps the most notorious and successful con-man operating in the United States today. A gifted actor, Bates can quickly separate you from your fortune. Among con men there is always an acknowledged king of the hustle, referred to in the game as 'King Con.' Beano Bates currently holds that infamous title. If you see this man, don't buy *anything* from him. Don't let him near your money or bank account, but call us here at *America's Most Wanted* or get in touch with your local police."

"Some con man," Beano muttered in disgust, as he wrapped the rest of Roger's half-eaten burger in a bag, saving it for later.

For the last two weeks, Beano had been selling dead-sleds and junkers to unsuspecting blue-hairs at Bob's Auto Ranch. He was on commission, not salary, trying to move the tired collection of stripped-down preacher cars and ominously noisy cement mixers that Bob was offering "on excellent terms." Despite the depressing inventory, Beano had done well at the Auto Ranch because he could convince anybody of just about anything. Bullshit was his greatest gift. He had made friends with the few attractive women who had wandered in, deciding he was more interesting than the rusting clunkers he was selling. He had dated one or two of them, but Beano was tired and was having trouble putting much energy into anything.

That particular afternoon, Beano was trying to sell a cancerous green Ford station wagon that Bob had taken in trade ten days ago. The car was basically lunched, but the service department had added some lipstick. They screwed beauty bolts onto the engine block and coaxed the tired, mashed-potato transmission back to life. They had sprayed and power-waxed the new green paint. The '86 Country Squire had ninety thousand miles on the odometer. In a final act of criminal camouflage, Bob's chief mechanic had rocked the clock back to fifty. It now sat dripping oil in the oppressive afternoon heat, a sagging road warrior dressed for its last inspection.

"A great high-occupancy vehicle. Ford sure knows how t'make 'em," Beano said with expansive awe to the mean-spirited old man who was teetering around, looking in the back, trying to put up the fold-down seat that was on broken hinges. " 'Course, all those minor defects will be addressed prior to ownership transfer." Beano smiled as the geezer tried to peel up the carpet and look at the floor to see if there was rust.

"Stinks back here," the old man said, looking at Beano and wrinkling his nose. "Carpets all got mildew."

Beano looked at him, not really caring if he sold the wagon. He fired a half-hearted line of bullshit over the dying transaction: "I'm not supposed to say this, 'cause Bob tries to protect all of our famous customers . . . but this car was originally owned by . . ." He stopped and looked at the old man carefully. "Y'know what? This isn't the right car for you. There's at least ten others we could look at."

"Owned by who?" the man said, his papery, thin skin reddening with faint interest as he looked at Beano with eyes yellowed by age and a bad diet.

"Well, I'm not supposed . . ." Beano paused and shook his head. "Can't say . . . sorry."

"Who? I can keep a secret."

Beano let a silent war of conscience play on his expressive actor's face, then caved in. "This car belonged to Vinnie Testaverde when he was still playing quarterback for the 'Canes. Reason it's got that kinda funky odor back there is, Vinnie told me he hadda park it at Morris Field behind the Athletic Department there at the University of Miami and people kept breaking in when he was at away games, hopin' to get like, whatta ya call it?"

"Souvenirs?" the old man contributed.

"Right, souvenirs." Beano nodded. "With the back window smashed, carpets kept getting all wet when it rained."

The deal hovered on the precipice of this new fact for a few heart-stopping moments as the old man contemplated driving Vinnie Testaverde's car.

" 'Course, you can't tell anyone, 'cause Bob doesn't give out the ownership pedigrees on these cars. I think it's nuts, but Bob, he's got a real thing about it." Beano was starting to get dizzy because he still hadn't fully recovered from the devastating beating and the midday sun was killing him. He wanted to go sit on his metal chair in the shade of the office, drink some iced tea out of his thermos, and curse John Walsh for making him live like a homeless fugitive.

Finally the old man looked up, a crafty defiance in his yellow geezer eyes. "You want fifteen hunnert dollars. . . . I'll go twelve," he said, beginning the familiar dance that used-car barkers call "the grind."

"Even if it wasn't Vinnie Testaverde's car, Bob won't let it go for twelve," Beano said, wishing he could get to the chair in the shade of the dealer's shed. Ever since the vicious beating, he'd been having intermittent double vision. The old man was beginning to split in two right before him, his whiskery cranial image moving slightly to the right so that he now looked like a double exposure. Despite this distraction, Beano knew the sale was his. Then he had a strange twinge of remorse for his cranky client because he knew the Ford wagon was tired iron. These bouts of conscience had never hit him before. . . . He had never stopped to consider the fate of a mark, but since the assault in the parking lot at the Greenborough Country Club, for some godforsaken reason, he'd started reflecting on the damage he had caused in other people's lives. He'd always told himself that marks were born to be fleeced, that he and Roger-the-Dodger had to eat, but lately these excuses seemed shallow. So he had taken the job at Bob's Auto Ranch, where he could use his charm and gift of gab in a semi-legitimate hustle. It was a temporary rest stop on his road to a new life.

By six o'clock the deal was closed at fourteen hundred dollars and the old man drove the listing wagon off the lot. Beano had promised to try to get him an autographed picture of Vinnie Testaverde, which was not going to be hard at all because he had ten of them left in his desk. He'd written the university and told them he was starting a booster club. He received the photos of the ex-Hurricane superstar in the mail from the Athletic Department ten days later. He'd also spent an extra one hundred dollars and ordered a Vinnie Testaverde autographed football from the Baltimore Ravens, where he was now playing. Beano was now good enough on the signature to fool the old Vinster himself. Beano would mail the picture to the geezer next week with an inscription from Testaverde saying how much Vinnie missed his old rusted-out beater, which had really been owned by an airport yellow cab company before Bob's paint shop had sprayed it green.

That night, Beano took Roger-the-Dodger out for a celebratory dinner of Chicken McNuggets and beer. The terrier sat on the front seat of Beano's newly acquired, low-profile '88 blue Escort and slopped the beer out of an oversized cup while he chewed breaded McNuggets. He was licking his lips, almost grinning. Beano had owned Roger for almost a year. He had been training him to be a shill: to shit on cue and to look expensive, which was often hard for ten-dollar pound-mutts, but Roger had natural talent. He knew how to project attitude. He could strut. Beano had perfected a variety of dog cons. He had a forged Kennel Club certificate that said Roger was a Baunchatrain Terrier and that his name was Sir Anthony of Aquitaine. Roger was also a great ice breaker. While a targeted mark smiled and scratched the terrier behind the ears, Beano would make his opening move. An added plus was that in a bust, Roger would hold his dirt. His pal Roger would never testify against him in court. The terrier was showing real signs of being a world-class sharper, but that was before Beano, using a dead man's I.D., got caught cheating Joe Rina at cards and got blasted onto the path of righteousness with a nine-iron.

"Don't slobber, Roge," he said, and the dog seemed to understand as he slowed down, lapping up his Coors Light with more restraint. "We gotta get us some traction. I know I promised I was gonna try and get Tom Jenner into a golf hustle, but he's an angry bastard when he loses, and with this double vision, I couldn't drop a putt in a wastebasket."

Roger-the-Dodger stopped drinking beer and looked up at Beano like a hold-up man who sensed his getaway driver might be losing his nerve. The dog definitely seemed worried.

Deep down, underneath all of the other stuff, the excuses about his vision and the bullshit about *America's Most Wanted*, there was a lurking realization. Beano knew that the beating by Joe Rina had introduced him to a cold, withering fear he had never known before. He had a numbing, paralyzing reaction every time he remembered the assault. Sweat would cover him like a fearful cocoon. Unreasonable panic wracked him. The most distressing note in this new mental orchestra was in the string section of his recently discovered conscience. He had started to remember the faces of his marks. He pushed his greed aside, and for the first time began to see them as people he had lied to and robbed. He tried to unburden his guilt by remembering the con man's excuse: *You can never cheat an honest man.* It didn't help. In quiet moments after work, when he was in the cheap one-bedroom motel apartment two blocks from the ocean, and while Roger was snoring at the foot of his bed, Beano started to wonder if he should get out of grifting. He had been overwhelmed lately by intense loneliness. His profession had isolated him. He had no friends, only people he knew. A con man couldn't afford to let himself become vulnerable. His problem was, if he went off the hustle, what would he do with himself? He'd been a sharper all of his life. He had no other worthwhile skills.

It had all started when he was six, working for his mom and dad, doing roofing scams. The Bates family was a huge, disjointed criminal enterprise. The National Crime Information Center and FBI guessed that there were more than three thousand Bates family members grifting all across the United States. Beano couldn't confirm or deny that fact, because he'd met only a hundred or so of his cousins, but every major town he'd ever been in had members of his family in the phone book, and his father told him they were all on the bubble. Con games were the family business. Members of his family all used X. as their middle initial, and by simply looking under Bates in any city's phone directory you could find his relatives. Most Bates family members played driveway and roofing hustles. They had elevated these two short cons to an art form.

Beano's parents had been nomads, constantly roaming, living in trailer parks and changing towns to stay ahead of the law. His mother and father would drive down streets in every new town they hit in their rusting Winnebago, looking for houses that had loose roof shingles. Then his father would park the motor home down the street from a prospective mark's house, get out sawhorses and hammers, and send adorable six-year-old Beano back to knock on the mark's front door.

"Sir," he would say in his sweet choirboy voice, "my daddy is down the street putting a new roof on your neighbor's house." It was a lie, but he would point his short, pudgy little arm at his father's Winnebago, now alive with manufactured activity down the block. The mark would smile and crane his or her neck to see. "Anyway," he would continue, always looking straight into the pigeon's eyes to communicate guileless sincerity, "Daddy noticed that your roof has lots of loose shingles. We have more shingles than we need for your neighbor's job. If you want, my daddy could make you a very good price on fixing your roof."

"Shouldn't you be in school, young man?" was a common question, and then little six-year-old Beano would drop the closer. . . . "My little sister has this real bad sickness and we gotta make enough money this summer for her to start her chem . . . chemo . . . something."

"Chemotherapy?" the mark would contribute, and Beano would nod sadly. This fact would hang over the opening pitch like the angel of death. He rarely failed to "steer" the mark.

His father, Jacob, would come down at lunchtime and look studiously at the roof. He would refuse donations for the non-existent sister's chemo, claiming family pride. "We ain't much for charity, but thanks and God bless you for your Christian concern," Jacob would say, often finding a tear in his eye and brushing its moisture visibly onto his cheek. Then he would climb up on the roof, rub his chin, and agree to do the whole roof for two thousand dollars, which by any estimate was a helluva deal. New roofs back then went for between five and ten thousand. Now, all thoughts of Beano's cancer-ridden sister were banished by the mark's greed: *These stupid hillbillies are gonna fix my roof for less than the material cost.* With that realization, the mark was hooked.

The next day the Bates family would arrive early. Beano would retrieve the sawhorse and ladder from the top of their motor home and carry it to the house. The homeowners would look out their windows and marvel at this tragic, industrious family, especially that cute, hard-working little boy. By nine A.M., Jacob would be up on the roof hammering loudly, making as much noise as possible to drive the family out. Once they were gone, Beano and his mother, Connie, would join Jacob up on the roof. They would hammer the loose shingles down and quickly paint the roof with heavy number-nine-weight motor oil. When the mark returned home, his "new" roof would be dark brown and glistening. Jacob X. Bates would take the cash from the grateful homeowner along with well-wishes for the dying sister, and Beano's family would get the hell out of Dodge. The next heavy rain might fill the mark's living room with motor oil, but by then they would be in the next state.

As a young man, Beano showed promise for much more.

He had learned to run big cons from his uncle, "Paper Collar" John Bates. He ran boiler rooms and bucket shops, Blue River real-estate scams and green goods hustles. He played the pigeon drop and did three big-store cons. He could dress up and be whatever he needed to be. He had a soft ear and could affect almost any accent or dialect. He was a master of disguises . . . a scratch golfer, a cardplayer without peer, and he would always find a way to shade the odds in his favor.

Now it seemed, at the age of thirty-four, after rising to the pinnacle of his chosen profession, after having John Walsh dub him "King Con" on national TV, he was about to flounder on the rocks of unreasonable panic. It was unbelievable and it shocked him, but Beano Bates had completely lost his nerve.

"Stop staring at me," he said sharply to the brown and black terrier, who continued to sit on the front seat of the Escort and look at him with canine concern. "At least if I quit, you won't ever have to shit on cue again. . . . You won't ever have to try and look like a five-thousand-dollar Baunchatrain Terrier," he said hotly.

Roger looked disappointed. He glanced out the window at the lighted golden arches. He sniffed at his beer without interest. Then he circled a place on the front seat three times before dropping anchor and putting his chin on his paws. He never took his gaze off Beano, watching him like a concerned parent.